PRAISE FOR MADDIE DAWSON

Praise for *The Survivor's Guide to Family Happiness*

"Maddie Dawson's novels should come with a warning label: May cause tears, laughter, or all of the above."
—Sarah Knight, bestselling author of *The Life-Changing Magic of Not Giving a F*ck*

"Like authors Liane Moriarty and Jojo Moyes, Maddie Dawson spins tales that tackle our most universal longings for love, connection, and family. I loved every witty sentence."
—Holly Robinson, author of *Chance Harbor* and *Beach Plum Island*

Praise for *The Opposite of Maybe*

"Dawson's charmingly eccentric cast of characters is at turns lovable and infuriating, ensuring a quick read helmed by a memorable, complex heroine."
—*Publishers Weekly*

"Delightfully witty . . . a messy, funny, surprising story of second chances."
—*Kirkus Reviews*

"At turns poignant and funny, this book is brimming with charm."
—Sarah Pekkanen, internationally bestselling author of *The Best of Us* and *The Opposite of Me*

"Dawson's lyrical, realistic portrayal of a modern-day relationship and all its complexities is rich with humor and insight."
　　　　　—Kristan Higgins, *New York Times* bestselling author of *The Perfect Match* and *Waiting on You*

"A quirky, warm, insightful, feel-good confection of a novel."
　　　　　—Jane Green, *New York Times* bestselling author of *The Beach House* and *Tempting Fate*

Praise for *The Stuff That Never Happened*

"This deceptively bouncing, ultimately wrenching novel will grab you at page one."
　　　　　—*People*

"Enjoyable prose and keen characterizations."
　　　　　—*Publishers Weekly*

"Surprising, illuminating, and always believable."
　　　　　—Susan Straight, author of *A Million Nightingales*

"A paean to family happiness as much as romance."
　　　　　—Stewart O'Nan, author of *Songs for the Missing*

Praise for *Kissing Games of the World*

"Engrossing, charming, and often funny exploration of love and relationships."
　　　　　—*Library Journal*, starred review

"Like Anne Tyler, [the author] seems to possess a nearly boundless capacity for empathy."

—*Connecticut Post*

"An absolute treat . . . filled with realistic twists, complex characters and a moving conclusion."

—*Publishers Weekly*

Praise for *A Piece of Normal*

"Delves into family relationships with humor and empathy, making this a pleasurable read."

—*Booklist*

"Richly textured, insightful novel."

—*Library Journal*

THE SURVIVOR'S GUIDE TO FAMILY HAPPINESS

ALSO BY MADDIE DAWSON

The Opposite of Maybe
The Stuff That Never Happened
Kissing Games of the World
A Piece of Normal

THE SURVIVOR'S GUIDE TO FAMILY HAPPINESS

A Novel

MADDIE DAWSON

LAKE UNION
PUBLISHING

Text copyright © 2016 by Maddie Dawson

Published by Lake Union Publishing, Seattle

www.apub.com

Amazon, the Amazon logo, and Lake Union Publishing are trademarks of Amazon.com, Inc., or its affiliates.

ISBN-13: 9781503939103
ISBN-10: 1503939103

Cover design by Janet Perr

Printed in the United States of America

For Jim

PROLOGUE
PHOEBE, TILTON, AND A.J.

1979

So he was really, really leaving, like his parents had told him he had to, and even though she already knew he wouldn't stand up to them, she had held out the tiniest bit of hope that *something* would happen and there would be a reprieve.

But no. Sometime between tomorrow morning and the end of the world, Tilton O'Malley would be taken by his father to attend the University of Snobs and Rich People, but right now, he was still theirs—hers and A.J.'s—and it was just another oppressively hot August night and they were running the streets. Only difference was that Tilton was wearing a wrinkled, button-down white shirt with his red-striped tie loosened—he'd been liberated from his parents' official preppy good-bye party for him, after all—but he was drunk and stoned and red faced and laughing way too much, like always. He kept bumping his hip into

Phoebe Mullen's as they walked down the middle of the street, trying to get her to smile at him.

She did even better than smile: she lifted her arms overhead and danced her flamenco moves, singing and flipping her long red hair and swinging her hips into his friend A.J.'s hip instead, looking right at Tilton, daring him to react.

Tilton flushed and turned away, but shit, he deserved it. He hadn't even insisted to his mom that they invite Phoebe to the party, for Christ's sake. That's how bad things had gotten. He had no guts. None, not one gut.

It was weird now to think that Phoebe had once thought he might take her with him. Tilton could get her a place near the college, her and the baby. Correction: ba*bies*; the other one would be born soon. She'd even worked out a budget for them: he'd have the campus meal plan his parents were paying for, and she could get by on beans and rice and Hamburger Helper. He'd live in the dorm, of course, but he could come and visit on weekends, maybe even do his studying at their kitchen table. And as for money, she was only seventeen, but she'd start a babysitting business in the apartment, a little day care, so she could be home with the kids.

Oh, she had been an idiot, as her sister had told her. And everyone knew it. She was the worst kind of idiot, making those plans. Holding on to all that hope.

She tucked her arm inside A.J.'s and smirked at Tilton.

"Come on, Pheebs, stop acting weird," Tilton said. "It's our last night! Can't we have fuuuuun?"

A. J. Barnes—skinny, appease-at-any-cost A.J.—agreed with him. He disengaged himself from Phoebe and passed Tilton the joint. "Let's go to the ball field and take care of that scoreboard. Once and for all, man."

It was a guy thing, this need to hit out the lights. Once they got to the ball field, Tilton jimmied the hinge to the supply shed, and the two of them threw themselves against the door, laughing as the plywood splintered into shards. Bats and balls crashed down around them. A.J. jumped back so fast that his cowboy hat came off, and he scurried to get it in the dirt.

For this she had sneaked out of the apartment, leaving her sleeping rosy-faced toddler with her sister. She'd had to—it was their last night, and she had to be here, to feel it all, because when she became a famous actress she would need to remember every single moment of the end of this relationship. And—she had to be resolved about this—this *was* the end. She, A.J., and Tilton had spent the past three years of high school sneaking out late at night, dodging headlights and cop cars, laughing and smoking joints, talking about stuff, reciting comedy, passing between them the Budweisers that A.J. filched from his stepfather's stash. And it had all been wonderful, the best thing she'd probably ever have in her whole life. Tilton was the first guy who listened to her, who thought she was smart and pretty, and made her feel like it didn't matter that she didn't have parents anymore and had to live with her sister in the most crowded, pathetic apartment ever. She—red-haired, freckled, artistically dorky—had somehow become cool, respected, acting with him in plays, singing in choruses, being his girlfriend.

And, well, there was the other thing, the *sex*. After they shooed A.J. away, she and Tilton would come back down here to the ball field and have sex under the bleachers. Baseball sex, he called it. They'd figured out how to do it just about anywhere—backstage at the high school, in the hallway of her apartment building—but his favorite place was in his mom's BMW *while it was parked in the family's garage* ("suicide sex," he'd called it, because he'd have to immolate himself if his mother caught him).

But not tonight. No, no, no. Tonight, sitting there on the bleachers watching him being so happy, she realized she was filled with hate. It was like a physical *thing* inside of her, a ball of hate that she could beam toward anything. She directed that hate toward his floppy blond hair as it caught the weak light from the street; then it went to the way he laughed and stuck his butt out, leaning into the strike zone. She turned her head and hated that the dirt was red, that the bleachers were blue and needed paint, and that she shouldn't be drinking because of the baby—not the sweet-smelling thirteen-month-old baby Kate who was asleep in her sister's apartment, but the new baby who would be born after Tilton was enrolled in his stupid college. The hate told her to stand up, and then she heard her own raspy voice screaming, "Come on, Tilty! Hit it like you mean it!"

He peered at her through the dark, and she imagined he could see the white stars she'd embroidered on her black cape, one star for every time they'd done it, except that then they were doing it so often she lost count.

A.J. had warned her this day would come. Way back in tenth grade.

"You know," he'd said, "they're going to make him go off to an Ivy League thing. You do know that, right? That we're not the kind of people they want him to end up with?"

"That's not true," she'd said. "His mom likes me."

"You poor idiot. *Like* is not the same thing as *end up with*," he said.

The ball rolled into the grass and stopped. Tilton yelled at A.J. to pitch him something that could be hit.

"I'll do it." She got up, heaving her belly, and went out onto the field. And then she threw the ball in a perfect, exquisite arc, which he hit back to her, laughing—laughing the way he did during sex sometimes, laughing in joy at the surprise of it all: the deep night, the white ball like a comet sailing over the plate, the fact that she knew him so well she could aim for the exact spot on the bat. The three of them watched as the ball crashed against the scoreboard, smashing the lightbulbs that made up the *o* in Home. A nearby police cruiser turned on its siren, and then they were all laughing and running down the path through the woods; she kept up, she with her seven-months-heavy belly wrapped up in the cape with the embroidered stars and flowers. She ran, as good as the boys, until they got to the oak tree, and then Tilton was at her elbow, his voice rough and urgent by her ear, saying "Please don't be mad," it wasn't *his* idea to go to that fucking college, his parents were *making him,* and she knew that, didn't she, and he loved her and he'd probably flunk out anyway without her there to write his papers for him, and when that happened, he'd just come back home. He'd be home by Christmas with a slate full of Fs.

"No, you won't," she said, and she didn't let him wrap her up in his arms when he tried to, because there was no way to explain to him yet again that it was even *worse* that he didn't want to go, that he was allowing himself to be pushed around.

A.J. said they should drive to the beach for old times' sake. Get stoned and chase the waves. Look to see if the sand had that bioluminescent stuff tonight. Tilton said they should take his mother's Beamer, but first they'd have to sneak it out of the garage.

They could watch the sun come up, he said.

A.J. slid his eyes over to Phoebe's. "You okay with this?"

She shrugged. The ball of hate said, *Hell, yes.*

She tried not to think about what would happen if Kate woke up, crying for her, and if her sister found out she'd sneaked out, which they had agreed she wouldn't do anymore. *No more throwing yourself at this guy, okay? Look at you, with the second one on the way now. For Chrissakes, what's going to become of you?*

"Here, this is for you," Tilton said, and he took a big hit off the joint and held the sides of her head and breathed the smoke into her mouth. He put his hands under her cape and stroked her big stomach. "Hello there, little baby, this is your daddy talking," he said. She closed her eyes, swimming against the current of him, almost drowning.

Last week he'd said to her, "We'll get married when I finish college. We'll have a lot of money, and we'll make more babies," and A.J., sitting beside them at the time, had snorted and given Phoebe that look again.

The guys pushed the car out of the O'Malleys' garage so the engine noise wouldn't wake Tilton's parents.

"You have to drive," Tilton whispered to her. "We'll push while you pop the clutch."

She stared at him, but he went in and out of focus.

"Can you do it, Pheebs?"

She got in carefully, ran her hands over the soft leather seats where they had made love so many times. It always smelled like money, this car.

"Do you hear me? Pop the clutch!"

The car was moving, and she slammed her foot on the pedal, and the engine roared to life, and in an instant the boys were piling into the car, sweating, laughing, slamming the doors, Tilton in her ear hissing, "Drive! Go! Go!"

She drove slowly, like she was maneuvering a parade float, but he was saying, "Go faster! Christ, there's a car coming! Floor it!"

She looked at him, stunned by a miraculous thought. What if they simply . . . left town? Tonight! They could leave tonight! She felt like this thought had been traveling to her from across the universe for so long and had only now arrived, in the nick of time. They could run away! Yes, the three of them—they'd head to the beach and then keep on going, up to Maine, maybe to Canada. She'd arrange for Kate to come; Phoebe's sister would gladly send her.

She said, "Tilty, listen," and his eyes were looking directly into hers so deeply he might have been able to see where the hate and the hope were fighting to the death.

He said, "Baby, can you drive faster?" and there was a loud crash and bright, spinning lights, and screaming—so much screaming—and then it was as though somebody had pulled some giant power cord to the world or something, because everything just turned . . . off.

ONE
NINA

Thirty-five years later

The morning after my mother's funeral, before I had changed the sheets on her bed, before I even knew if I was going to survive living without her, I went into the kitchen and took the fifteen unlabeled casserole dishes from the refrigerator and, one by one, scooped out their moldy contents and hurled all that food out the back door into the snow.

It was the happiest I'd felt in weeks. No, months.

Well-meaning people had brought these as an offering of kindness. People I loved who thought that not bringing food to the dying was maybe the worst thing you could ever do—and I had been grateful. But we couldn't keep up, my mother and I. The casserole dishes stacked up like accusations in the refrigerator. When I opened the door, they shouted their grievances.

I stood there watching as pieces of macaroni, ham, lima beans, squash, and unidentified red items went flying against the deep-blue

February sky, then landed on the snowbank, where they created an instant abstract painting. One spunky little yellow casserole dish escaped my hands and bounced off the railing of the porch and then crashed across the ice, and smashed into a million pieces near the garbage cans.

I gave that one a standing ovation, then got my phone and took a picture of the hillside canvas, now splattered with reds and beiges and greens.

I messaged it to Dan, my ex, with one sentence: *When someone dies, people bring horrifying food and I make art of it,* and he wrote back immediately: *You know Julie doesn't like it when you text me first thing in the a.m.*

Tough, I typed. *She shoulda thought of that when she started dating a married man.* He wrote: *WE ARE NOT MARRIED, NINA.* And then I wrote: *But we WERE* and clicked off the phone so I didn't have to hear from Julie about how I was being inappropriate and could I please respect the boundaries she and Dan were trying to set. Last week she actually wrote, *We are being patient because we know your mom is dying but please respect our space.*

I walked through the silent townhouse—silent, that is, except for the sounds of voices in the units on either side. Normal people all getting ready for their next normal day, not even thinking about how lucky they were to be alive.

It was seven twenty-two, the time of the day my mom and I used to have our first healthy shake of the day. We'd lie on her rented hospital bed next to the picture window and watch Kathie Lee and Hoda until some serious topic came up, which would then make my mother remember that we weren't laughing enough. She had decided to treat her stage-four liver cancer with laughter and green smoothies. The drowsy days had flowed into one another, one Mel Brooks movie after another, none distinguishable from the next. We were on Cancer Time now, she said.

Toward the end, she stopped being her regular self and started saying things she felt like talking about, even stuff I suspected she'd never wanted me to know. It was as though the filters had come off. For instance, she'd had sex before she got married. She told me it had happened in a man's car, on a hilltop, and it had been awkward as hell but the worst part had been that her underpants had somehow gotten lost under the front seat and it was dark so she'd had to go home without them, and the man returned them to her at work the next day in a brown paper bag—the kind you'd pack a school lunch in.

"Who would do such a thing?" she said. "Wouldn't a gentleman know to simply politely dispose of them and pretend he'd never seen them?"

"Wow," I said. "You're still carrying that?"

And she said, "Well, now it's become a funny story. I was waiting for that to happen."

Also, she told me, she'd always loved my father but, well, he'd been a bit of a stick sometimes, and there were two full years after the infertility treatments when she really thought she might have left him if they hadn't adopted me by then. And other things came up, too: she'd always meant to go to Austria and play the piano and wear stilettos. She hadn't ever been to the tropics. As a child, she wanted to raise chimpanzees. Silly dreams, she called them. She hoped I hadn't minded too much that I was the only child they'd had, that I hadn't been too lonely with just the two of them. I'd always known I was adopted, that they cherished me in a special way because they'd worked so hard to find me—"looked the whole world over," as my mother had put it when I was a child. But I had known enough not to ask too many questions; I knew, the way a child knows these things, that it would crush my mother if I asked where I had come from, who I really belonged to.

And then late one night came the big one: "If you want to know who you really are, if you want to find your real mother, there's a nun at the Connecticut Catholic Children's Agency who will help you," she said. "Sister Germaine, that's her name. In New Ashbury. That's where the orphanage is."

The world inside my head started spinning out, slowly. The orphanage was two towns over. I'd never known.

"Funny," she said softly, so softly I could barely hear her, "funny that you never asked. Your dad and I were a little surprised, frankly, at your lack of curiosity. He said it must be because you were happy with us. That you didn't need anyone else."

Later, after I thought she was long asleep, she said in a drowsy voice, "Oh, and there's a photograph somewhere. I can't remember where I put it, but you'll find it when you clean everything out, I suppose."

"A photograph? Of what?" I said. My heart sat upright in the bed.

"I don't know. Of you, I guess, and your birth mother. The adoption agency gave it to me the day they gave you to me." She made a clicking sound. "All that worry, all those years, about your real mother showing up. And for no reason. And now . . . well, we're safe."

Safe, I thought, was a funny word to use when every cell in your body has gone all malignant on you, and you're hours from death. But maybe safe is just a matter of perspective.

I, however, knew I was not safe. She died three days later with her faith intact and her conscience clear, knowing exactly where she was headed, but I needed a road map back to a life without her. Fueled by my stunning success with the casserole dishes, I sat on the kitchen floor and made a to-do list.

NINA POPKIN'S POST-APOCALYPTIC PLAN FOR REGULAR LIFE:

1. Return Mel Brooks movies to Netflix. Suggest they put a warning on them that they are useless—useless!—against cancer.

2.   Call the hospital bed rental place and tell them to get this stupid bed of death out of the living room!!!! Then move the couch and end tables and normal people furniture back in from the dining room.

3.   Take the portable commode, the shower chair, and the IV pole to the recycling place.

4.   Do the following in one very busy, probably very bad day: Call Mom's attorney, put medical bills in one pile, open insurance statements, clean out the attic, burn all your school papers she saved through the years (BUT BE CAREFUL not to burn the photo of you and your real mom, if it even exists), put condo on the market, sell all the furniture, move someplace fabulous.

5.   Take deep breaths. You did the best you could. You can't cure cancer.

6.   Stop texting Dan.

7.   Long-term: Go on a cruise to Barbados, take dancing lessons, buy a farm in Vermont, sign up for a space mission to Mars, open a bar, learn to make baked Alaska, take voice lessons, ice-skate at midnight, French braid your hair, fall in love with somebody wonderful.

8.   Stop crying.

A few hours later, I added:

9.   Find your real mom, find your real mom, find your real mom, find your real mom.

TWO

On my first day back at work, everyone who came into the Home Sweet Castle real estate office was surprised to see me there. They'd get all soft-eyed and sympathetic and then they'd say, "Ohh, Nina, how you doing, baby, you've been through a rough one, haven't you," and I'd just lose it. Over and over again.

Melanie, my best friend and owner of the agency, finally started telling people, "No, no, no, don't be nice to Nina, she can't take kindness right now," and that would make everybody laugh, even me. I'd sit there laughing and crying at the same time and dabbing at my eyes and my snotty nose, and Melanie would say, "That's right, baby, feel every single one of your feelings. Let them all just pour out, that's the way to healing."

When the place cleared out around lunchtime, she said, "And by the way, you know what else would really help you feel better again?"

When I didn't answer, she said, "Falling in love. It's the ultimate healer. Look at me."

Melanie has been my best friend since junior high, but she got married eight months ago to a guy she met online and she's already pregnant, and those two facts have made her maybe a little hard to take. She's gone from being a person who was always realistically cynical about everlasting love to being the kind of sentimental person who seems to think that love is out there on the World Wide Web for everybody if we'd only start working on our profiles.

This was majorly ironic. I'd always been the fearless one when it came to throwing myself at love, while Melanie dated probably two guys in her whole life before John Paul came along. She always said she hated the part of falling in love that's about losing control, while letting go of all sanity was my specialty. I loved it all: the breakups and makeups, the drama and trauma. And when, inevitably, my romances would end, I was even good at bouncing over to someone new. Mostly unscathed, usually even better for the experience.

But now I am thirty-five, and I still can't work out how you will yourself to keep things going. Even after I finally took the plunge and got married, Dan and I lasted just six months after the wedding, and then one night he took me out to dinner and told me he'd met Julie, and that she had the magic sauce he'd been looking for, so surely I could see that he had to leave, didn't I, because even though he really, really liked me, and maybe would always love me at some level, it wasn't the level that really counted with his shadow side and his mystical side and the side of him that wanted to turn vegan and loll about in hot tubs. He said all this as well as some other crap that you simply can't believe someone would actually say to you out loud, especially someone you love. Loved at some level.

So I'm back to square one. I do not pretend to understand how Melanie has gotten John Paul—a man from the Internet, yet!—to fall in love, marry her, and stick around for a pregnancy. And he's all right, I guess. He's an electrician and has a union job and nice teeth, and he loves church, motherhood, apple pie, peanut butter crackers, and puppies. Apparently Melanie loves him back and has no fears whatsoever about getting sick of him.

As for me? I personally couldn't ever have settled for a guy like that, someone utterly without irony and with no appreciation whatsoever of life's greatest catastrophic surprises. Even given what happened with us, I think I'd rather take a chance again with a guy like Dan who is so interesting that he can one day turn all vegan on you and talk about people's secret sauce like it's a thing.

So probably this means I'm doomed.

"Not for nothing," Melanie was saying now, "but I know that all this sadness isn't just about your mom dying. It's about Dan. And I think if you started dating, you could be happy again." She sat next to me at my desk and pushed aside the list I was making of the houses that our tiny agency has for sale, houses that might need me to stage them with furniture from Melanie's father's warehouse.

I looked over at her. Melanie has the sweetest heart-shaped face and soft brown hair that curls around her face, and it's no wonder that everybody she sells a house to wants to be her best friend forever. She always believes in happiness. Maybe because she has two living parents who adore her and gave her this great little real estate agency, and besides all that, she's got nice clothes and a baby growing inside her who will keep her family line going, and she knows exactly who she is and who her aunts and uncles and grandparents are and where they all came from and whether they prefer Coke or Pepsi, white meat or dark meat, and beach or mountains, and also what house they used to live in and all that.

"John Paul knows a guy who's really nice," she said, "and I'm not saying he'll be the love of your life or anything, but he might be fun to date. It'll get you out of this funk."

I reached over and took back the listings I'd been looking at. "This *funk* is called grieving," I said. "And also, if I do anything daring at all, it's not going to be looking for a guy. I'm considering two possibilities: either I'm going to sign up for the Mars space mission or I'm going to find my real mom."

"What?" she said. "How are you going to do that? Are you forgetting that we never found out her name?" She narrowed her eyes. "Oh God, tell me you're not going after Miss Gaines again."

I laughed. Back in sixth grade, Melanie and I embarked on a secret mission to discover my real mom. After spying on families and conducting secret sociological studies on everyone we knew, we decided that Miss Gaines, the gym teacher, had to be my mom, because her eyes were the same color and shape as mine, and she also had a little pooch of a belly, which Melanie said meant she'd had a baby.

For months I mooned over her as if I had a crush on her, and then one day I woke up with a blinding realization: No wonder Miss Gaines never showed even a flicker of interest in me, her natural flesh and blood. My real mom was actually Princess Di! Yes, I was an illegitimate child she gave birth to before she met Prince Charles, and then when he fell in love with her, she had to put me up for adoption, and that's when Josephine and Douglas Popkin got me.

I was far from being the only adopted kid in my circle. For reasons I've never understood, our quiet little Catholic neighborhood in Bernford had tons of them. Five on every block, at least. It was as though there'd been a Give Your Baby Away decade, and unplanned-for kids had been handed out randomly to strangers in town. And so after I told everybody how I was really Princess Di's kid and someday she might whisk me away to my true life in Buckingham Palace—well, suddenly lots of kids wanted some celebrity parents for themselves, too, so Melanie and I started a playground business called Who's Your Mama.

For two bucks, we would draw up a fantasy family history matching kids with rich, fabulous celebrities who, we announced, deeply regretted giving their children away and would someday come to claim them. Madonna was given a couple of kids, as was the mom from *Growing Pains*, and Julia Roberts and Meryl Streep as well as the whole family in *90210*. How we kept this secret from the eagle-eyed nuns I'll never know, but we did. Until one day a girl named Emily Scanlan waited for me after school and pulled my hair practically out of my scalp because she said she should get to be Princess Di's daughter, and her parents said she should tell the nuns what I was doing. They would probably expel me, and my mother would be destroyed. My saintly mother who had saved my life by adopting me.

So I stopped the business. By then, it was the end of the school year anyway, and my father had gotten in the car accident that had broken his neck and would soon break his spirit and eventually kill him, and suddenly it was clear this whole adoption fantasy thing had been ridiculous from the start. We were all just unwanted throwaway kids who should be grateful to have the mothers who stepped in to raise us.

"This time I'm going to the adoption agency and finding out for sure," I told Melanie. "My mom told me that there's a nun there who'll help me. She actually said the words 'your real mother' to me. Out loud."

"Get out! Josephine Popkin said that?"

"She did. And she even said that she was always surprised that I never asked her any questions about where I came from."

Melanie bit her lip, which she's been doing since seventh grade whenever things are not right. "Okay, so here's why I don't think this is the right time to do this kind of search," she said. "What if your real mother is dead?"

"What if she is?"

"Then you'll be doubly devastated."

"So I'll be doubly devastated. What of it? It's better to know than not, isn't it?"

Melanie sat there, chewing on that lip. "Stop doing that," I said. "You're going to make a hole in your face. Listen, I'm going to do this because I need something else to think about right now."

"I'm not saying you shouldn't ever—but right now? I mean, you don't know who she is. She might be awful, you know."

"Thank you. But I'm going to do this right now."

"Right now?"

"Yes. I think right this minute, in fact."

"But you're at work."

"Do you see any customers in here?" I said.

"Listen," she said. "If you must do this, at least come over to our place for dinner tonight. Don't be alone. You've had a very big loss, two big losses . . ."

I was pulling on my coat, and she came over and gave me a hug, and I noticed for the first time that her belly had a round little bump to it. Melanie was having a baby, and I had nothing.

"You're ridiculous," she said, "and I mean that in the best possible sense."

"You're ridiculouser," I told her, then blew my nose.

"When you come to dinner, would you please bring back my yellow bowl?"

"Oh," I said. "Gosh. I may have thrown it at the stone wall. It made an incredibly spectacular crash. I wish you could have seen it."

"God, you're awful."

I stuck out my tongue at her, which I'd been doing since seventh grade when she started calling me ridiculous every time we said goodbye. It was our ritual.

"I'll come to dinner," I said at the door, "but I swear I will leave in two seconds if you have a man there for me to meet. I am not in the mood for men just now."

And then I went outside and got into my Honda Civic that held the portable commode and the IV pole and the shower chair, all of which I'd spent an hour wrestling into the backseat before leaving the house, and I jerked the car into reverse, pressed on the accelerator—and immediately got my tires stuck in the pile of snow by the curb.

I did everything you're supposed to do—cursed, banged my hand on the steering wheel as hard as I could, and then, when that didn't work, I rocked the car back and forth, pressing on the gas, then turning the wheel—but it got progressively worse with every attempt. The tires kept burying themselves deeper and deeper in, and what had been snow under the tires was now turning to slick ice. There was a squealing noise, and after a while, the smell of something burning.

I mashed on the accelerator so hard that the car lurched forward, and the commode in the backseat took the opportunity to jump into the front seat and pin me down with its aluminum legs.

Sometimes when you're moving from the old to the new, the universe likes to remind you who's in charge by spinning your tires on ice and then throwing a toilet at your head.

At least that's the lesson I took away from it.

I turned off the engine and sat there with my head in my hands, waiting for spring.

THREE

A man was knocking at the window, smiling at me. I pressed the button and the window glided down, and a lump of snow landed on my lap.

"Yes?" I said.

Even in my demented state, I could see that he was handsome. He had curly dark hair with flecks of snow in it, cheeks that were ruddy from the cold, and the kindest, smilingest eyes. "Can I help you?" he said. Then he couldn't stop himself from laughing. "Excuse me, but is that a toilet on top of you?"

"I believe it is," I said coldly.

"Are you stuck?"

"I think I can beat this toilet at its own game," I said. "But thank you."

"No, no," he said and laughed again. "I meant your car. Can I help you get it unstuck? I think I have some rock salt in my trunk."

"Daaaad," said a voice somewhere behind him.

"Just a minute, honey," he said. "We're going to help this lady get unstuck."

"I'm huuungry," the kid said. "You said we were only going to be a *minute* . . ."

"It's fine," I said to him. "You really don't have to."

"No," he said. "You're really dug in here." He stood back and surveyed the rear wheel. "I think I even have a piece of plywood to give you some traction. You need some traction here. Hey, Kayla, do we still have that plywood left over from Tyler's science project? Kayla, honey?"

"*Indigo!*" she yelled. "God! When are you going to get it *right?*"

I figured I'd better at least make an effort to get out of the car so I turned and tried to wrestle the commode's legs back where they belonged, which caused the IV pole to lunge for me, inanimate objects being always willing to support each other. The man had ambled off, and once I got myself free and onto the street, I could see that he was rummaging through the back of a white Subaru Forester parked nearby, while a girl of about fifteen stood on the sidewalk, giving me murderous looks.

Her father was removing boxes from his car and placing them on the street, narrating his progress the whole time: "Now I'll just move these books over here, and surely the bag of rock salt will be behind *this*, no, no, maybe behind this other pile." I couldn't stop staring at the girl; she was dressed in combat boots, with a short, short skirt over torn leggings, and she had a purple stripe in her hair. She was now studying her fingernails, which were black, and I couldn't get over the jagged points of her bangs and the way she could hold that furious expression for so long. And—Indigo! What a name!

I wanted to go talk to her, but she seemed like she might be packing heat.

The man jogged back over to me at last with a plastic container of rock salt and started sprinkling it around my tires. "This oughta work if we give it a minute," he said. "It'll give us a little bit of traction." He straightened up and looked at me, smiling.

"Carter Sanborn," he said. It took me a minute to realize he was telling me his name. He was wearing a polo shirt and a blue windbreaker that was not nearly heavy enough for the weather, and his hair, true, did have some snow in it, but some of that snow was actually little glints of gray. And he definitely had some sort of winter tan going on.

"Nina Popkin," I said.

"For real? That's your name?"

"Is Carter Sanborn *your* name?" I said.

"God, I'm hungry," said Indigo, stamping her feet. "And it's freaking cold out here. Can we hurry up and go?"

"Really, you don't have to do this," I said. "It's so nice of you, but I'll call AAA."

"They'll take forever to get here. Just give me another minute, and I think the salt will start to work." He turned to his daughter. "Just another second, sweetheart. Then we'll go into the real estate office, and then after that we'll get us some dinner and you can cheer up your old dad." He looked over at me. "Adults always need cheering up in the winter, have you noticed? Especially when they have to move."

"You mean, moving around in general or you mean moving out of your house?" I said.

"Out of my house," he said in a low voice, glancing sideways over toward Indigo. "I'm looking for a condo."

"Oh," I said. "Well, I work right here at Home Sweet Castle. I bet we can find you a condo."

"That's what I was counting on," he said. "But you seem to be trying to leave."

"Yeah, but the owner, Melanie, is in there," I said. I turned to Indigo. "If you're cold, honey, you could go inside, and tell Melanie I sent you. She's usually got some cookies and tea."

"It's *fine*," she said and stamped her boots on the sidewalk.

Her father gave me an exasperated smile and rolled his eyes. "Tough times," he said. "Here. Why don't you get in and start the car and let's see if the salt worked?"

The tires kept spinning. Carter Sanborn, frowning, kept pouring more rock salt on the road, muttering something about traction but humming under his breath, showing what a supremely patient human he was.

"Seriously!" said Indigo. "This is taking, like, *forever,* and it's not even going to work! And it's freezing out here and I'm now literally *starving!*"

Her eyes met mine quite by accident, and I saw a little flash of something there, some awareness that she knew she was being impossible and relished it just the tiniest bit.

I glanced over at him to see if he was now going to lose his patience, but no, he was still smiling. "Plywood," he said, and he jogged back to his car. While he was gone, I exchanged a companionable glare with her just to show I understood what she was up against: a too-helpful dad being all too cheery.

"So these little cars—they're a mess in the snow, aren't they?" he said. He placed the plywood right behind the rear wheel, and said, "Now put it in reverse, and let the gas out a bit at a time. No rushing."

I got back in the car, and some magic of rock salt and plywood and the last vestiges of sunlight all conspired to help, and the car glided out of its spot, with only a tiny growl of protest. I waved my thanks, and in the rearview mirror, I saw father and daughter head into Home Sweet Castle, Carter still smiling with his arm around her, and Indigo clearly pulling away from him as hard as she could.

FOUR

I should confess something: I'm terrified of nuns. I don't know quite what happened in school that got me this way. Well, yes, I do. Maybe it was the way they would hiss at us. Or the rumors that they might hit us with rulers. Or maybe it's those scary black habits they wore back then—and the fact that we mostly couldn't see their hair. What were they hiding under there?

So the whole way over to the Connecticut Catholic Children's Agency, I had to keep saying to myself: Nuns are good, nuns are good. They married Jesus, which may sound like a crazy idea to my ears, but surely it has something to recommend it. Jesus was a nice guy, and at least you could be sure he wouldn't run off with anybody. All the other nuns were also his wives, so where was he going to go?

By the time I got there, I was shaking so bad that I had to lean against the car and take deep gulps of air.

I looked up at the red brick building with its fresco and columns and all those things I learned about in art history class, back when I was dating a guy named Ian—or was it Randall?—and we were having so much fun getting high and hanging out that I forgot to learn the names of the architectural details that I needed for the final exam.

Ohhh, I thought. *I know what this feeling is. I'm about to learn about the person who abandoned me. My first rejecter.* Dan was just an amateur compared to her. I was a part of her, flesh of her flesh, and yet she didn't want to get to know me, to see if I was going to turn out to be cute and funny and probably look like her and also that I might someday save her life if, say, our building was on fire but she was sleeping and didn't hear the smoke alarm.

She hadn't even been willing to *try* to see if we could have been good together.

And yet here I go, charging after her. So she can turn me away one more time.

It would almost be better if when I go inside they tell me that she had died, maybe in childbirth, and that's why she couldn't keep me. Maybe that's what they'll say: I'm sorry, but your real mother is dead. Don't feel bad about it for one second, but giving birth to you was the thing that did her in.

You were simply too much for her.

And I would just have to agree with them: yeah, I'm too much for most people.

I've got to say this for the Catholics—they make a science of how to say no kindly. They only toyed with me for a little while before admitting me into the inner sanctum to meet Sister Germaine. She turned out to be a pleasantly benign sort of nun, wearing a navy-blue pants suit instead of a habit, and she had straight short gray hair and glasses that glinted in the overhead light. We sat across from each other in a room that was paneled and carpeted and had shiny cherrywood furniture and pictures on the walls of Jesus with the little children. I had to squeeze my fingers to keep myself from hyperventilating as I explained how my adoptive mother had promised me that she, Sister Germaine herself, would help me find my biological mother.

She sat back in her chair and folded her hands, prayer-like, on her desk and looked so disappointed it was as though I'd come in to inform her that Jesus wanted a divorce. "Well," she said at last, "I'm afraid I can't tell you what you want to know."

"No, no, no. You don't understand. My adoptive mother said it's fine. She just died, and she wanted me to have this information."

She was shaking her head. "It doesn't have anything to do with your adoptive mother, dear. It's the law in Connecticut. We are not allowed to release any information about your adoption."

"But it's *me*," I said. "It's *my* adoption. And who I am. All I'm asking is for you to just tell me my mother's name. You don't even have to give me her address or information about my father. Just this one little fact."

"I can't."

"But why?"

"It's the law."

"Well, what *can* you tell me?"

"I can't tell you anything."

I had to hand it to myself—I made a couple more stabs at getting her to understand how unfair that was, and how mistaken she surely must be.

Still, she shook her head. "Believe me, if I had my way, I'd at least give you your original birth certificate, but the law requires that those be sealed, too."

"My . . . my original birth certificate? There's an original one?"

Why hadn't I ever thought of that before, that there might be another, real birth certificate—something besides the one I'd always operated under, that pretended that Josephine and Douglas Popkin were my actual parents? "Wait. So somewhere in this building you're saying that you have my original, actual birth certificate and that I had a different name and everything before I was adopted? I was somebody else, but I can't know anything about that?"

She closed her eyes. I'm sure she wanted to kick herself for bringing it up. "I'm sorry," she said. "It's a matter of privacy to the parents who gave you up for adoption."

"But what about me?" I said. "Don't I have any rights? Why do *they* get to say that I never can find out who I really am? Do you not see how massively, grotesquely unfair that is?"

"Fair or unfair, the law is the law. I'm sorry. Maybe the General Assembly will change the law sometime, but for now, this is what we've got." She shuffled some of the papers on her desk without meeting my eyes, clearly wishing I would get the hell out.

"Do you have any idea what it's like to be adopted?" I said in my steeliest voice. "To not know who you are or who you look like? Do you know that for my whole life I've looked into the faces of everyone I passed on the street, and wondered if they were my family?"

She was silent for a moment, and then she said with a sigh, "Why don't you leave me your contact information, and if your birth mother happens to come looking for you, I can connect you?"

"You know what else being adopted is like?" I said. I could feel my voice rising. "You don't know who you were supposed to be. What if my parents had decided to put me up for adoption three days before they did, and then somebody else might have adopted me? On my street alone there were, like, five kids who were adopted. I could just as easily have been Patti O'Brien, who got to have a pony and whose dad worked for an insurance company. Or maybe I would have been Jessica Reynolds, who had a little brother and whose mother sold Tupperware. Don't you see? I'm only me by the merest set of circumstances."

"Aren't we all just ourselves by the merest set of circumstances?" she said in a tired voice.

"No. No! That's just it. That's what I'm trying to say. I bet you know who your parents are. I bet you know if you have the same nose as your grandmother and if you laugh like your mom. Maybe the reason you're a nun is because of somebody in your family. You have a whole history that you know. People have told you the stories for years, and at Christmas you probably all tell them all over again. Don't you get it? I don't have that."

She sighed. "I'll let you know if your mother looks for you."

I gazed up at Jesus, but he wasn't going to be any help. He was too busy smiling down at the little children. *Help me,* I said to him silently. *I know I'm not a good Catholic, but you could do something.*

Finally there wasn't anything to do but to write down my phone number. Sister Germaine took it and walked me to the door.

"I think you may be having a reaction to your adoptive mother's death," she said. "You need to know that even if you do find your birth mother, she's not going to take the place of the woman who loved you. Try to remember that. The system worked for you. You went to a good home, to people who loved and raised you as their own. You need to let the rest of it go."

There are few things I hate as much as being told to let something go, but I turned my eyes to her benign, wan face, and I made myself take her offered hand, a warm, doughy hand with its short nails of kindness.

When I got to my car, I texted Dan. It wasn't early morning anymore, so he shouldn't mind.

Catholic Church says no way can locate real mom. Against the rules of religion. Jesus no help.

I waited to see if he'd text me back. He'd always been interested in the subject of my biological family; he often thought I looked like people we saw on the street. When he didn't answer in fifteen minutes, I drove to Melanie and John Paul's apartment.

The two of them welcomed me in, and I was relieved to see that there wasn't a man there whom I'd have to be nice to. John Paul kissed me politely on the cheek, and, still dressed in his electrician's uniform with his name stitched over the pocket, put on his coat and went to grill chicken on the balcony, standing in his boots in the snow. Melanie tossed a salad in the kitchen. They had Norah Jones on the stereo, and as usual, their house felt like an oasis of calm married life. Lavender walls and overstuffed couches, lamps that gave off a warm, buttery light. Honey this and sweetheart that.

"How would you feel about staging a break-in to the Connecticut Catholic Children's Agency and grabbing my birth certificate?" I said to Melanie.

"I totally would," she said, "but I'm pregnant and I don't want to have to give birth in jail. And what do you mean, your birth certificate? Don't you have a birth certificate?"

I told her the story of how adopted kids have two birth certificates, one with the truth and then another one with lies.

"Not lies," she said. "The new truth."

"Truth is truth," I said. "It's not old or new." I took a sip of wine and watched John Paul poking at the meat outside on the grill. He was a very stable, boring, grown-up man, and he was going to be a good dad, and he would make love to Melanie for the next fifty or so years and bring home a paycheck and get a pension, and those were all beautiful things that I would probably never have. They would have generations of family happiness, of Thanksgivings with family, of memories to draw on, things they would tell their children. Family stories.

Apparently I was going to spend my old age looking over the list of men I'd frantically loved and then dumped.

"It was a mistake to go looking for my mom," I said with a sigh. "I guess I should go back to being Princess Di's kid. Notify Buckingham Palace."

"Poor Nina," Melanie said. She gazed at me so sadly that I had to bat her away before I started to cry again. I actually had cried so much my eyelids were chapped. There ought to be a special cosmetic for that. Grief-Erase, they could call it.

Still, we managed to get through dinner without tears. And then at eight, after we'd finished dinner and I was delaying going home, my cell phone rang. I looked down at the unrecognizable number.

Melanie said, "I bet you anything that's going to be Carter Sanborn."

"Carter Sanborn?" I said. "Wait. You mean that guy in the street today?"

"Yeah, he said he unstuck your car. From what I gather, he's just been through a divorce and he's looking for a place for him and his kids. I gave him your card and told him you'd help him."

"No, no, no. We are not doing that. I think it's a very bad sign if he's calling me at this time of night. We don't want clients like that, do we?"

"You should answer it," said Melanie.

I pressed the button, and Sister Germaine's voice was suddenly in my ear.

"Miss Popkin?" she said. "This is Sister Germaine. I'm sorry to call you so late, but I have some news that might interest you, and I didn't want to wait."

For a moment I thought she might tell me that my mother had happened to come into the office just after I'd left, looking for me. This would be one of those life-changing coincidence stories she and I would be telling people for the rest of our lives. *After all these years apart, and then on the same day, we both went to the adoption agency knowing we had to find each other! Can you imagine?*

"I was here late, and so I decided to look in your records, and it turns out that you have a *sister*," she said.

I felt my heart do a somersault. "A . . . sister?"

"That's what the records show. A younger sister."

"Wait. Are you allowed to tell me that?"

"Yes. Siblings aren't protected under the law that protects birth parents. Apparently—and this is pretty unusual—your parents gave up two children for adoption. And it seems your sister is still in the area. Would you like me to see if she wants to meet you?"

My throat closed up, but I managed to say yes before I breathed in a bunch of air wrong and started choking so hard I had to hang up. The last thing I heard was Sister Germaine saying, "There are no guarantees, of course, but I'll call you if she agrees."

Melanie brought me a glass of water. "I have a sister," I said, dazed. "A sister. Oh my God. I have a sister. Like, somebody who is one-hundred-percent, honest-to-God related to me. My God, I think I'm in shock."

"Wow," said Melanie. "Are you kidding me? That's amazing!"

"But what kind of mother gives away two of her kids? What was she thinking? What in the world happened to her that made her do that?"

"Well, when you meet her, you can ask her about that. It can be your icebreaker."

"The agency is going to contact my sister and see if she wants to meet me." I shook my head, as if that would make all this feel more real. "A sister!"

Melanie was looking at me with concern on her face. "It's great news," she said slowly.

"And she's going to be wonderful. I can already tell. I have known about her existence for three minutes already and I am feeling absolutely no sibling rivalry toward her at all."

"That's how good you are," said Melanie.

"No, it's her. Even her vibe is wonderful. I bet we look alike! I've never known anybody with my same DNA, you know. Remember when we learned about that in school? And I'd go home and cry into my pillow. Because my DNA was on its own, stuck with me and not knowing where it came from."

Melanie was giving me that worried look again. "Be careful with your expectations, will you?" she said. Which possibly was the meanest thing she'd ever said to me, so I kissed her on both cheeks and danced off to my mother's sad little condo, where I cleaned out all the kitchen drawers and my mother's bedroom closet and searched for that photograph. It didn't turn up. Most likely it was somewhere in the attic. I stared at the attic door, but I couldn't bear to go up there. I wasn't anywhere near mentally healthy enough to tackle all that.

◆　◆　◆

So, Carter Sanborn was into boats. Boats, boats, boats. Even though it was winter, he wore boat shoes with no socks, and a thin, ocean-blue windbreaker, and I suspect the only reason he was in long pants was a concession to it being twenty-eight degrees outside.

He came into Home Sweet Castle right at opening time, bearing coffees and smiling and talking way too fast for early in the morning. It seemed that he and Melanie had worked out that I was to drive him around to look at neighborhoods. Apparently yesterday I had demonstrated to Melanie that I wasn't to be trusted yet with the rest of the home-buying public, not that there was much going on these winter days in our little office anyway. We were a small agency without much foot traffic, tucked away on a side street in Branhaven, a leafy suburb of New Ashbury. Most of our business wouldn't start heating up until the spring, when clients showed up, wanting information about the town's good schools, the marina, the town green, and its mix of housing—everything from colonials to bungalows to beach cottages and condos.

Carter told me he wanted to live near the marina, and he wanted a place that his children would gladly visit so it had to have some cool features, like recessed lighting and a Jenn-Air refrigerator.

I looked over at him, sitting in the passenger seat of my car. "Wait," I said. "Are you trying to tell me that children care about recessed lighting? *Indigo* cares about recessed lighting?"

He ran his hands through his hair, ruffling it up in quite a charming way. "Well, okay. Probably not. It's that recessed lighting only comes in modern places, and my kids said they don't want to live in some old dumpy kind of house, like they live in already with their mom. And . . . well, with me. I'm still there, too." He looked slightly sheepish.

"Huh," I said. "Interesting. How many children are there?"

"Two. Tyler is eighteen, and Kayla is fifteen."

"Indigo, you mean?"

He sighed. "Yes."

"And you all live together, even though you're divorced from their mom." I said it as a statement.

"That is correct."

"May I ask how long you've been doing this? Just out of curiosity."

"A year. Maybe a year and a half. I lose track." He took a sip of his coffee and I stared at him. He was gorgeous. Older than I liked in a guy, of course, but good-looking in a disheveled, flustered kind of way.

"Wow," I said. "When *I* got divorced—even before that, really—when my husband decided it wasn't working anymore, he moved out. Packed up and left that very day. He didn't even want to drive in our neighborhood anymore. No discussions, no lingering doubts, nothing. Just good-bye."

"See, that's just crazy impulsive," he said. "The man's obviously an idiot."

"Yeah, well, it turned out he'd fallen in love with his bank teller."

"You're kidding. How in the world—?"

"I *know*," I said. "I guess I should have been suspicious when he canceled direct deposit, shouldn't I?"

I always get a good laugh when I say that, but Carter was gazing at me with a concerned look on his face. I was startled to see that his eyes were so dark they seemed like they held bing cherries. *A divorced guy with kids. No, thank you.*

"That was a joke," I said. "I was making a joke."

"Oh. Sorry. I was thinking how horrible men can be."

"It's way too early in the morning for that discussion," I said. "Let's find you a place to live."

He smiled, activating dimples and showing even, white teeth. Strong nose, and that tanned skin—it was the kind of tan you get when you're outside all the time and think you're immune to the medical establishment's calls to wear sunscreen and so your tan never really goes away. Irresponsible, of course, but daring in its way. I kind of like a man who can stand up to the call for SPFs.

"So," I said. "Let's think of what you're looking for. The kids are going to be living with you full-time then?"

"Oh God, no. No, no, nooo. We're sharing custody. Their mother thinks they need their time with me, but she doesn't want to be around for it." He laughed. "Jane's kind of done with my view of family life."

"Huh. And yet it worked for a whole year to stay there living with her after you separated. That's kind of fascinating, don't you think? I mean, really."

"I'll grant you that it is a very complicated, unusual situation," he said. "And probably bizarre by most people's standards. But up until Sunday afternoon at, say, five o'clock, it worked pretty well. And then it didn't, and so I've been told to get the hell out."

"What happened on Sunday at five o'clock?"

"Jesus. Do all real estate agents go this deep into a person's psychological profile before they'll find him a house for sale?"

"Just the good ones."

"Well, it was brought to my attention that my ex would like to start seeing someone, and the gentleman in question thinks it's off-putting—I think that's the word he used—for me to see him come out of my wife's bedroom."

I started the engine. "Okayyyy then," I said. "Well. So, there are some apartments over by the water that have recently turned condo. Is that something you think you'd be interested in, as long as they have

Jenn-Air refrigerators and recessed lighting, of course? Or do you prefer to look at beach cottages?"

"Hmmm," he said. "I think I might need to take a look at everything. Would you mind?"

"No, no, that would be good," I said. "Melanie will probably be glad you've taken me off her hands. To tell you the truth, yesterday was my first day back at work after my mother died, and I didn't do so well at being with the regular humans."

"I know," he said quietly. "She told me. I'm sorry to hear about your mom."

"Also, I might burst into tears every now and then," I told him. "Don't take it personally."

"Perfectly all right," he said.

"But it would be great if you could try not to say again how sorry you are about my mother dying. Once is fine. And do not say that I'm in your thoughts and prayers. Okay?"

"Okay," he said.

And then we were quiet for a long time.

After a while he cleared his throat and said, "So, does it say anything in the Real Estate Rule Book about stopping to get ice cream every now and then? I always make decisions so much better if I have ice cream."

I glanced over in time to see his impish grin. "I can tell you're going to be a lot of trouble," I said. And I pulled into the Dairy Queen, where we both had large vanilla sundaes. With plenty of whipped cream. He was a man who liked his whipped cream.

So every morning for the next two weeks I drove over to Carter's suburban, tree-lined Oyster Cove neighborhood and waited for him outside his little yellow clapboard house with the wraparound porch crammed with bicycles locked to the railings and skis leaning against the siding. He would come out of the front door soon after I pulled up, and tramp across the packed-down snow to get to my car. Our first stop each day was Starbucks, where we both got a Venti French roast with half-and-half and a banana-nut muffin. He insisted on the muffins because, he said, we needed to keep our strength up so we could make it through the list of places I brought with me each day.

One morning he turned on the car radio. Paul McCartney was singing "Yesterday," and I sang along. Exuberantly. Flinging my arm out.

"Wow. You like the Beatles?" he said.

"All except for Yoko Ono."

"She wasn't a Beatle."

"Yes, she was. Wasn't she like the fifth Beatle or something?"

"Jesus, pull over. Pull this car over right now."

I kept driving and smiling.

"No, seriously," he said. "You did not just say that. The Beatles were all *men*. They didn't even have any female voices on their albums! What has *happened* to the younger generation—"

"Gotcha!" I said.

He stared at me. "Don't give me a heart attack like that."

After a while I said, "That Mick Jagger, though—you have to admit that he was the best Beatle of all."

He turned in his seat and stared at me until I was laughing so helplessly I almost couldn't see to drive.

What can I say? Over the next few weeks, it was almost like therapy, walking through homes with this smiling, happy man, smelling other people's cooking aromas, chatting with them about their lives, peeking into their closets and behind their shower curtains, then riding around eating ice cream and laughing in the car. Carter seemed to like just about every house we saw but made no move to buy anything we looked at. That was fine with me; I was too tired to do the paperwork. He made jokes and flirted with the older people who were heading off to Florida; he talked sailboats and teenagers and weather. In one hot, crowded apartment, a young mother had a new baby who wouldn't stop crying on her shoulder—and while I was talking with her, Carter gently reached over, took the baby away, and started singing the "Macarena." The kid went to sleep, possibly in self-defense, but still it was a win. The mom and I both just stared at him.

"The last time I checked, the 'Macarena' wasn't considered much of a lullaby," I said later in the car, and he shrugged.

"Babies are like the rest of us—they like to be surprised," he said.

One day we were driving near the marina, and I said, "So do you have a boat?"

"Nope."

"Seriously. You own a business supplying sailboats with everything, and you don't even have one yourself."

"That is correct. If you check your files, you may remember that I am a guy who just went through a divorce, and I have two kids who are going to need to go to college. So. No boat."

"Huh," I said. After a moment I added, "Well, I'm the same actually. I sell houses, but I don't have a house."

"Ah, Popkin," he said after a moment. "Life is going to bring us both so much!"

Day after day, we'd look at houses and condos, one after the other, until the midafternoon, when it was time for me to drop him off before his kids got home from school. One morning when he came outside, he was accompanied by Tyler, who turned out to be a young version of his father: a tall, handsome, long-haired guy in a plaid shirt (no jacket—apparently the Sanborn family didn't feel the need for winter clothing). He was carrying a guitar and a bookbag. Carter introduced us and asked if we could drop Tyler off at the town library.

"Of course," I said. "Hi, Tyler. I've met your sister, but so nice to meet you."

He jumped into the backseat, then leaned so far forward into the front that it was like he was spring-loaded or something. "Good to meet you, too," he said. "I hope you're gonna find my dad a good place to live."

"We're working on it," I said. "Do you have any special requests?"

"Really? Well, ah, sure. I'd like a music studio where I can record some songs, and I'd like a separate wing for my sister so I don't have to hear her talking on the phone, and maybe a great sound system in the living room for watching movies . . ."

"Absolutely," said Carter. "All that's on the list. Right, Nina?"

"Right after the Jenn-Air stove," I said.

"Anyway, I don't know why you need a vote," said Carter, "since you're not going to be here after this summer anyway."

"Yeah? Well, if you get a good enough place, maybe I won't bother going to college," said Tyler, ducking as Carter pretended to lunge for him.

"Oh, you are *so* going to college," Carter said, giving his son noogies. "I'm taking you there myself, and if I have to, I'll stay there all year and walk you to your classes. Every single one of them."

"Yeah, yeah, yeah," said Tyler. He turned to me. "Have you noticed yet that this guy has a pretty much one-track mind? It's like you press a button, and sit back and listen to the speech." He made his voice sound like a robot. "College is good, college is good, college is good."

I laughed. By then we'd gotten to the library, and I watched, fascinated, while they hugged good-bye outside the car. Carter leaned over and said something into Tyler's ear, and they both laughed. Then Tyler leaned in the window and thanked me, and off he went, loping into the library. When he got to the door, he turned around and waved.

"Wow, what a nice kid," I said.

Carter was watching the door. "My children are both the smartest and the dumbest people I know," he said. "It's a wonder they're still alive."

"It's a wonder any of us make it through adolescence," I said.

"Oh, but you have no idea," he said. Tyler, he told me, knew everything there was to know about geology and physics and getting Wi-Fi to work—but that week he had ruined his Toyota Scion because he somehow didn't know that cars need both gas *and* oil. Also, all he wanted to do with his life was to play the guitar. And Indigo was a straight-A student in the honor society—but her hair color came from indelible purple markers, and the cut was performed one night in the bathroom with pinking shears. Oh, and by the way, she thought she was named Kayla because of her mother's love for kale. She had even thought for a time that "kale" was spelled "kayl."

When I laughed, he said, "Trust me, Popkin. You can drive yourself crazy wondering how your children are going to make it in the world. It's a curse."

At some point, we started getting lunch together most days. The unspoken rule was: Starbucks, then three condos in the morning, then lunch and two condos, and maybe one house in the afternoon. Starbucks again on the way home. Occasionally Dairy Queen, just because.

One day I turned on the car radio, and the song "You and Me Against the World" came on. It's a sappy song, from a mother to her kid, and my mother had sung it to me once when I was about fifteen years old, looking at me with such neediness in her eyes that I'd had to pull away. And now here it was, randomly showing up on the radio. I wasn't exactly crying, but water sort of started leaking from my eyes as I drove. I stared at the road, which was getting blurrier, and I turned my head away from Carter and let the tears spill down my face, running into my mouth and off the end of my chin.

He reached over and wordlessly took one of the Starbucks napkins from the console and dabbed at my face.

"I think it might be raining in the car," he said. Then he added, "I know. It sucks."

After a few minutes, I said, "So, Helen Reddy—she dated one of the Beatles, right? George Harrisburg, maybe?"

"Don't make me grab this wheel and plunge us into a ditch," he said.

I was still smiling long after I drove him home that night.

He and Jane had been married for twenty years, and he would have stayed married for the whole duration if it was up to him, he told me, but she wanted a whole bunch of stuff out of life that he didn't see the point of. Like acquiring more college degrees, and also doing a little bit of world saving while she was at it. She was always wringing her hands over the rain forest and the melting ice caps and a bunch of capuchin monkeys that were having a tough time of it somewhere in Africa or Asia, as Carter explained it. In the mornings, he told me, she read him the most dire news stories she could find online, and then she gave him an accusatory look for not jumping up that moment to solve things.

"It's not that I don't care," he said, "but . . . oh, what the hell. I don't actually care all that much. Maybe there's something wrong with me." He ran his hands through his hair and smiled. Dimples again.

"So that's why she didn't want to stay married to you? Because you wouldn't save the capuchin monkeys?"

"Ahhh, no, I'm afraid I had other crimes, too, a whole list of them."

"Please. I must know," I said.

He sighed. "Really? Okay. I didn't listen, I talked too much about myself, I worked too many hours, I didn't notice haircuts, and I was usually late coming home for dinner. And, oh yes, I was defensive. Also—this is really bad—when she decided the whole family should be gluten-free, I brought home croissants and doughnuts and wooed the kids with them. I didn't take anything seriously. I know better now. If I had it to do over, I'd notice some haircuts and come home earlier. But by the time I figured out how to change, it was too late. We didn't love each other anymore."

"Did you cheat?"

"Cheat?" He turned and looked at me, and his eyes were serious. "You mean, go with other women? Oh my God, no. I would never cheat."

"My ex-husband said everybody cheats. It's just the way it is. No one can be faithful."

"Yeah, well, we've already dismissed that guy as an idiot. Not everybody cheats."

We were silent for a while and then I said, "So, what made you change?"

"Life changes you," he said.

I banged on the steering wheel like a maniac. "*What*, specifically? I need to know. How did you change? How do people change?"

He shrugged. "Maybe I just grew up, started paying attention to other people. I started hanging out with my kids more. Cut back at work. Got over myself and my own pettiness."

"So, when Jane decides she's sick of this new boyfriend, and wants to take you back for the sake of the children, you'll go back," I said in my breeziest voice. "All this condo searching is going to end up being for nothing, and maybe that's why you're not actually choosing one."

We were silent for a while, and then he said to me, "Maybe this isn't appropriate, but would you go out to dinner with me tonight?"

While I was waiting for him to come pick me up, I sat down on my mother's bed and made a list of the reasons not to fall in love with Carter Sanborn, as if that had even been on the table.

You know, just in case my heart was working on cooking up some drama, for lack of anything better to do.

1. Too old for me. WAY TOO OLD.

2. Divorced.

3. Yet, for some mysterious reason, still living with his ex-wife.

4. Not what I'm looking for AT ALL (polo shirts, windbreakers, boat shoes).

5. Terrifying teenage kids, one of whom has given herself the name of a COLOR.

6. Does not support gluten-free diets. (Then I crossed that one out.)

7. I am not looking for a relationship right now.

8. I am sad.

9. My mother died.

10. My ex-husband fell in love with his bank teller.

11. I can't seem to stop crying.

12. I am trying to find my birth family, and I need to focus on that.

13. Need to look into the possibility of that Mars mission job.

We went to his boat club, where there were nice people, although certainly not the kind of people I'd ever socialized with. For one thing, they were his age, which means they were old, and also they were people who know about sailboats and motorboats. They were planning their purchases and their trips for the spring. And drinking cocktails and laughing a lot. (My crowd tends to drink beer and wine, and their conversations about purchases are generally about which smartphone to get next.)

I decided that when I got home, I would add number fourteen to my list: Would have to learn what jibs and mainsails and tillers are.

But then, what the hell, I got into an interesting conversation with a woman who used to sell real estate in California, and somebody else who was telling a funny breakup story about a guy who'd tried to get her to learn Klingon. And I said that *I'd* had a boyfriend who wanted me to speak Klingon, too! She leaned over and whispered, "Boat-guy talk is every bit as intimidating, but at least you can get out in the sunshine sometimes."

To my surprise, Carter asked me to dance, and it turned out he knew how to jitterbug, which I'd learned a long time ago, and we had a wonderful time. The touch of his hand on the small of my back was deliciously tentative. I mean, this evening wasn't going to lead to anything, but it was good to know that life occasionally organized itself so that you could show somebody a whole lot of condominiums, listen to his stories about his kids and his ex-wife, and then go dancing with him—and it could be a good time and nothing else. I was so proud of myself, I wanted to call Melanie just to tell her I'd been smiling nonstop for a couple of hours.

When I got home, I mentally started another list while I was brushing my teeth. *Reasons to consider falling in love with Carter Sanborn:*

1. Dances well.
2. Knows a bunch of people who laugh a lot and don't talk about their PlayStations or debate the future of *Star Wars* characters.
3. Has a good handle on the Beatles and their relationships.
4. Looks into my eyes while he dances with me instead of pretending I'm not there.
5. Loves his kids so much that he stays in the house with his ex-wife just so he can see them every day.

6. Has beautiful hands with long, tapered fingers.
7. Also kind eyes.
8. Smells nice.
9. When I'm around him, my face hurts from smiling so much.

I looked at myself in the mirror, at my wild, crazy hair and bright eyes. And then I added one more:

10. Also, I might want to lick his face.

FIVE

Five days later, Carter and I were standing in the kitchen of a condo near the marina, admiring the view and the deck, when my phone buzzed, and it was Sister Germaine saying that my sister had agreed to meet me. I just lost my mind, laughing and crying at the same time. It had been so many days of not hearing, and with each passing day I was even more sure that my sister had thought it over and decided I wasn't worth the trouble.

"But here she is," I kept saying to Carter, kind of like an insane person who only knows one phrase. "Here she is! Here she is! My sister is going to meet me!" I paced around the room. "I can't believe this. I thought for sure she'd say no. Do you get this? I hadn't even let myself really hope before now."

I hadn't told him anything about my adoption. It had been enough that he knew I had a dead mother and had gotten left by a stupid guy who didn't have direct deposit at his bank. Why go into all the rest of my pathology?

But now there was snot. There were tears. Carter, looking mystified at first but then apparently realizing that he was going to have to administer some mental health services, sat down next to me on the floor and made me tell him everything: about the adoption, my mother dying, Princess Di, Miss Gaines, Sister Germaine, the missing photograph, the original birth certificate—everything. We sat there until it got dark while I explained how I could have been Patti O'Brien or Jessica Reynolds, and how awful it felt that I didn't look like anybody in my adopted family, and how no one had had my sense of humor or my spirals of curly red hair. I told him how I loved my adoptive parents so much, and that they were kind and attentive and thought that I was God's special gift to them, but that somehow I always felt I belonged elsewhere. It was as if they had borrowed me, and I'd always meant to get back to where I started from.

I said I was fed up. With gulping, heaving, horrible sobs, I told him that I'd had nothing but loss, loss, and more loss. My original family who gave me away, and then my father, my mother, my husband, the supply of boyfriends I'd entertained myself with, and now, if history was any indication, I would also lose Melanie to motherhood—and where did that leave me? With no one!

He sat and listened, every now and then reaching over to pat my arm.

"And the worst part is I don't even have any tissues!" I said at last. He looked startled and went into the bathroom and came back with some toilet paper that the tenants had left.

"I'm sorry. This is not the way I usually act as a real estate person. I am clearly very unwell."

"No, no. Of course," he said. "Don't think anything about it."

We put on our coats, and my scarf got caught in my sleeve, and he came over to help me, and all of a sudden he was two inches from my face, and I could smell the gingery sweetness of him, see the lines that cut deep around his mouth. I saw the tiny dots where his mustache would grow in, and the mole on his cheek. His face with those dark brown eyes swam in and out of focus. Then his lips were on mine, and it was the sweetest thing in the world, this soft, gentle pressure. Sensual, warm, questioning first kisses, tasting like sugar and ice cream and maybe a little bit of the sea outside. I let myself slide down the wall until I was sitting on the floor, and he slid down next to me, still holding on to me. In the dimness, his eyes looked wide and black. I could tell that he had taken up residence somewhere in my chest, right under the breastbone. Was I going to do my usual thing—jump in too fast? Fall too hard?

No, it's okay, my heart said. This is not the usual.

"I guess we should go to our homes," he said softly.

"Is that what you want?" I said. "Because if you would rather, you could come to my house. Maybe I could cook. You know, dinner."

His eyebrows went up just the slightest bit, and he cocked his head and looked at me like he couldn't figure me out. But then he smiled tentatively and said, "That sounds . . . wonderful. If you're sure."

And so I took him home, and we made spinach quesadillas together. I put some Miles Davis on the stereo, and before the quesadillas were even cooked, I turned off the burner, and led him into my bedroom, and he made love to me as though my crazy, sad heart might be actually breakable, and he was going to be its protector.

I was smitten. Again.

To be honest, being smitten with Carter Sanborn was not like any of my previous smitings. I was used to withholding guys who would sooner cut off their privates and fling them into the sea than commit to anything beyond that afternoon, but Carter seemed delighted with affection. Over the next few weeks, I saw how he brightened up when I came into a room. He held me when I was endlessly, *boringly* panicking that my sister wouldn't like me. He called me Popkin. He didn't freak out.

And unlike every other guy I'd dated over the years, including Dan, he seemed basically accepting of whatever was going on at the time. Also, he knew a bunch of funny words for sex that he would whisper to me: the ol' houghmagandy, the oompas-boompas, the horizontal dance. He had a way of smiling at me across a room that made my knees weak. He liked long kisses. Oh, and once he made guacamole just because I liked it, and then he scooped it up and put it on chips and fed them to me one by one, which is exactly the kind of support I have always been needing in life and never found.

One day we were driving somewhere, and I was talking about how relationships never work out, that love is always temporary, and the best you can hope for are some wonderful moments to remember.

He said, "How can you say that? How did you get so cynical? Look around you—there are people loving each other all over the place. You and I maybe didn't have good luck the last time around, but that doesn't mean we're stuck with that. We can get better at it, you know?"

"So you really like this guy," Melanie said to me one day.

"Yeah, he's good." I went back to typing an e-mail to a client.

She watched me closely. "So does he have *any* flaws besides being married before and the fact that he wears polo shirts and has an utter inability to choose a condominium?"

Actually, as it had ended up, Carter hadn't been able to settle on buying a condo at all. I'd finally figured out that he was better suited to living in a rental for a while, and I'd found him a furnished unit near the marina that could serve as temporary quarters. He'd moved in the week before.

"Just the polo shirts," I told her. "The married-before thing is fine. After all, *I've* now been married before."

"Yeah," she said. "I suppose that's true."

"Turns out I should have been dating divorced guys all along," I told her. "I feel like I've been serving as a training ground for unformed males so they can move on to the women they're going to marry."

"Okay, so my question remains. Any flaws?"

I thought for a long time. "Sometimes he doesn't rinse out his oatmeal bowl when he puts it in the sink."

"Huh," she said. And she stared at me for a long, long time. I could feel her eyes on me while I wrote up a listing.

Of course there were other things. He snored sometimes. He left his toothbrush on the sink. He left little balls of socks in the living room. But the main thing wrong was that he'd had so much—well, so much *life* before me. He'd watched his wife give birth twice, and he'd had new babies to hold and he'd helped toddlers learn to walk, and he'd had family dogs and cats, a couple of houses over the years, and plenty of cars, and besides all that, he'd owned a business for ten years.

And me? I was simply this aging kid who'd floundered around and who was still waiting for life to happen to me.

But I ached to be with him, as though he was the only one who could teach me how to live in the world and not be afraid. He knew how to be married, and how to fall down and get back up again, and how to sing along to the radio as though his heart had never been broken at all.

SIX

When the day came for me to go to the Connecticut Catholic Children's Agency and meet my sister, I got up at four in the morning and baked her a blueberry pie so she would love me. Because that's what you do when you're meeting a DNA relative for the first time—you make them a pie, right?

Carter got up, too, and sat there with me in my mom's kitchen, trying to calm me down. But I could tell that he was worried for me. He could probably picture the same possibilities ahead that I saw: things could go terribly, terribly wrong. We had no control.

"Maybe she isn't even going to show up," I said.

"She'll show up," he said. He came over and put his arms around me.

I stared into his eyes for as long as I could stand. "The pie," I said. "I can't remember how the lattices go."

"And by the way," he said, "you don't need a pie to make your sister love you. Everyone loves you. Even my smart-but-dumb teenagers love you."

I was terrified of his teenagers with their automatic coolness and all that power they strutted around with, but I didn't want to say that.

It was true I'd had some good conversations with them, and Indigo was finally beginning to look at me without seeming as though she would like to stab me—but each interaction was so exhausting that I practically needed to take to my bed afterward.

"That's all fine and good, but today's task is to woo my sister, and that's all I can think about."

"Yeah, but while you're wooing her," he said, "picture her as your friend. Picture her visiting us. Picture it all going well, why don't you?"

Then he did the thing that Dan would have killed himself before ever attempting: he helped me figure out what to wear. I tried on about four outfits, and he rated each one.

"What are you going for here?" he said. "I think you want to look approachable, friendly, beautiful—and yet not intimidating. Am I right?"

"I want—I want to wear something so great that she's going to want to borrow it," I said.

He picked out my deep-blue wool sweater with the cowl neckline and my black jeans. It was perfect.

"Hoop earrings?" I said. "Black boots? And should I wear a scarf?"

He threw up his hands, laughing.

"Listen, I love you more than words can say, but I'm not an accessories guy," he said. "If you ask me, the blueberry pie is all the accessory you need."

"Wait," I said. "You . . .*what?*"

But his cell phone was ringing in the living room, and he went to answer it, which was just as well, because I needed to get back to my worrying unencumbered by somebody else's optimism and love.

Yeah, so then I proceeded with the shenanigans I do when a lot is at stake: I waited too late to leave, rushed too much when I finally did leave, parked haphazardly in a snowbank, and ran with my pie held aloft, and then, predictably, slipped on the ice on the concrete steps of the adoption agency and fell on my ass. I sat there on the sad, frozen steps of the diocese offices, weaving back the lattices on my blueberry pie, weaving them in and out, and the pie gave off waves of despair. *Be calm for once in your life*, I hissed at myself. *You are closer than you've ever been to figuring out who you are. And you are loved by a very nice man, and he claims his teenagers love you, too, whether it's true or not.*

I wanted to stay on the steps and treat myself to a thorough meltdown, but my *sister* was waiting inside. Maybe she would be the kind of person who would cry with me, because honestly, I have never had a good crying partner, and it was time.

Sister Germaine was already talking to someone when I was ushered into her sanctuary. My heart was pounding so loudly I was sure everyone could hear it. Three things immediately became clear.

Number one, it was freaking ninety-seven thousand hundred degrees in that building, with the radiator triumphantly pulsing out even more great clouds of hot, dry, desert air. It was a wonder that people's flesh hadn't started melting.

Number two, the woman talking to Sister Germaine, this red-haired woman with her back to me—this woman who was possibly my sister—had on the most exquisite turquoise coat and brown leather boots . . .

And number three, when she turned and looked at me, I almost dropped the pie of despair on the floor. Either the Catholics had decided to be crazy tricksters, or my sister was Lindy Walsh from my old neighborhood.

"Nina? Oh my goodness. Nina Popkin?" she said, but my blood was beating in my ears so hard I couldn't really hear her, could only see her pink mouth moving as she held out her hand to shake mine. "Nina?"

You might think that knowing each other would make this all so much easier. We grew up three blocks from each other in a working-class neighborhood in New Ashbury. It was a Catholic neighborhood with the large and imposing St. Agnes Church on the corner, and everybody's family went there for Mass on Sunday, and just about every kid went to St. Agnes School, except for the few who went to public school. There were so many adopted kids—too many to count. Every street had its share. So why hadn't it ever occurred to me that one of them might be related to me?

Anyway, Lindy and I both went to St. Agnes School. Her family had a bunch of kids, as I remembered, some adopted and some not, and she was a grade behind me. One day she had cried at recess because she'd gotten a splinter on the swings and also she'd lost her sweater and her nose was running and she had snot all over her face, and I had to take her over to the nuns on playground duty so someone would give her permission to go inside. I am ashamed to say I didn't wait around; nope, I just turned her over to some sister or other and skipped back to my game of hopscotch. I had things to do.

Also, I remembered that she always wore her reddish, difficult, wiry hair in braids with choppy little bangs that were too short and always cut crooked, and the older kids teased her and the boys would steal her ribbons and run off with them, and her uniforms—well, they never fit quite the way they were supposed to, always a little saggy; and in fifth grade she belted out "God Bless America" at the school talent show, a little bit out of tune, and her slip showed. How can I remember those things? And she was my *sister* all that time? How was that even possible? I would have loved her, even in all her uncoolness, had I known.

And oh my God, now I remembered that once a kid in fifth grade said, "You look like that girl in fourth grade. That girl Lindy." And I socked him.

Now here she was, all grown up and poised and quite lovely. Creamy skin, auburn hair the same color as mine, but somehow richer and smoother without all the frizz I was prone to. Big hazel eyes that were looking at me curiously, as though she, too, was trying to sort and tabulate incidents from decades ago, before either of us knew their significance. I wished for a stop-action button so I could stare at her and drink her in, her gestures, her voice. *This is like me, this is not like me, like me, not like me.* We had the same dimple on our left cheek. Her gums showed when she smiled, like mine did. She was taller and thinner than I am—and judging from the leather boots and cashmere coat, probably richer as well. Also, there was something reserved and almost too polite about her, something that kept me from falling at her feet and blubbering about how long I'd waited for this moment and what a surprise it was to find it was *her.*

She said, "Nina Popkin?"

"Lindy Walsh?" We burst into shocked laughter.

When she hugged me, it was with the lightest possible touch. No drama, please. And no cooties of neediness. That's what her hug said.

Sister Germaine was fluttering around and clucking over the resemblance between us—saying things like, "You *knew* each other? Well, isn't that the most amazing coincidence, but sometimes this happens." Then she waved us toward the upholstered armchairs, where someone had set out a little silver tea service and a plate of cookies. So we smiled and sat down. Lindy was wearing a long tan sweater and black wool slacks and gold jewelry. Jesus smiled down from the wall, looking especially pleased with himself today, herding the little children under the tree with his outstretched arms.

"I'll give you a few minutes to get reacquainted while I go and get your files," said Sister Germaine, leaving the room. Lindy and I turned to each other and for the life of me, I could not think of one single thing to say.

She started picking some nonexistent lint off the knee of her slacks. Her face was hidden behind her hair, which shone in the lamplight. My throat had developed something of a lump.

"I made you a pie," I said, and then it was as though my tongue woke up and I couldn't stop myself from talking. "It's a blueberry pie. Of course I had to use frozen ones now, but in the summer I make this out of fresh berries, and my mom, my adopted mom, showed me how to make a lattice crust, and when I was bringing the pie inside, I slipped on the steps and the crust kind of got wrecked a bit and I had to sit there for a while and fix it. That's why I was late, in case you were wondering. Honestly I'm such a klutz sometimes, especially when, well, when things feel so . . . momentous. You know?"

"It's okay," she said. "It's a nice pie. Thank you so much for making it for me."

"So, we're sisters," I said. "My God, I can't believe I'm here looking at you. Can you believe this—that we knew each other? I can't get over it. That there we were, in each other's lives all that time . . ."

"Yes. Incredible, really."

"Do you still live in New Ashbury?" I said.

No, no, she didn't. She'd moved to Branhaven when she got married.

"Oh my goodness! I'm in Oyster Cove. We're so close!"

"Just a town away," she said. "And my salon is in Oyster Cove."

"It is? What's the name of it?"

"A Little Piece of Heaven."

"Oh!" I said. "I think I've passed that a million times." I smiled at her and reached over and touched her arm. "You know, I remember there was a day you were crying at school, and I took you over to the nuns. Sister, um, Sister Bernadette, I think. Remember her? On the playground. Do you remember? You probably don't even remember . . ."

"I think I was always crying about *something*," she said. She brushed some stray bangs out of her eyes. "Oh man, I hated school. I think the nuns were always mad at me for something."

"You'd gotten a splinter from the wooden swings, I think. But you were really so cute and sweet. Your uniform didn't fit you quite right."

"It was probably my older sister's. I always had to wear her hand-me-downs." She shifted in her chair and rolled her eyes.

Oh of course—now I remembered. She already *had* an older sister. I felt an uncalled-for proprietary twinge. I mean, she was *my* little sister first.

"Ellen Walsh?" she was saying. "Remember her? She was a grade ahead of you, I think. My parents adopted her first, then me, and after that apparently *somebody* told them about sex, because they had four of their own, all boys, one every year. Then, I guess, they finally figured out how to *stop* them from coming once they'd filled up the house. Well, more than filled up the house, actually."

I laughed, which was exactly what she was expecting. She'd even left a nice little pause for the laugh before she continued. So she was beautiful, funny—and ironic. I loved her.

"Ah yes," I said. "The Walsh boys. Who could forget them?"

"Hellions," she said, with unmistakable pride. "It's a wonder we all made it through without killing each other. We were always *that* family—the one with too many kids outside screaming at each other and playing baseball or keep-away in the dirt in front of the house, always with a houseful of yelling and trouble."

I tried to look sympathetic, but in fact I'd always envied the Walsh dynasty over there on High Meadow, where my mother wouldn't let me go play because she said Mrs. Walsh didn't need one more kid to look after. I'd only get hurt over there, my mother said. There had been rumors of baseballs hitting little neighbor girls, and maybe not so accidentally. I wondered if my mother had known that my biological sister lived there.

Lindy kept talking. "It was insane at my house. Like growing up in the circus."

"I remember your house," I said.

She looked at me for a long, thoughtful moment. "I have to say, I don't really remember you being around."

"Yeah, well, my mom was the overprotective type. I was an only child, and they were already old when they adopted me. Apparently they thought of adoption only after years of fertility treatments and stuff. Lots of failures. So by the time I came along, I think they were actually stunned to find a child in the house every single morning. We were very, very, very quiet people. I was afraid I'd frighten them if I acted like a regular kid."

"God, that sounds wonderful to me," she said. "Every single night I prayed for a room of my own, and for once to go to the bathroom without somebody coming and banging on the door. You probably had your own room and a pink bathroom to yourself and your own television set. And please, do not tell me you had a Princess telephone in your room, too. If you had one of those, please lie and say you didn't."

"No. I had my own room and bathroom, but I had to talk on the kitchen phone so they could monitor everything I said."

She looked at me with a tiny flash of interest. "Yes, that's what my mom said, too. She's one of those women who hyper-managed everything. Now that all of us are grown up, she still thinks she has to know everybody's business. Listen to me. I sound awful. She's really generous and wonderful. And I am so lucky and grateful that she watches my kids so I can work . . ."

"Oh! My goodness! You have kids! I meant to ask you."

"Yes. Three."

"Three? Wow! Please. I want to hear all about them," I said.

"Oh, they're a mess," she said, with that fond, exasperated look I'd seen on other young mothers' faces when they talk about their children.

That fake complaining. Usually I hate it, but she was my sister so I made allowances.

"Do you have pictures?" I leaned forward as she started scrolling through the photos on her phone and telling me everybody's names while I tried to memorize their faces as they flashed by. There was a hunky husband, Jeff—a construction guy with rippling muscles and nice eyes squinting in the sunlight—and three blond-haired, adorable kids. There were photos of her dancing cheek to cheek with Jeff; the kids riding a sled in the winter; the family decorating a Christmas tree in a massive living room that looked like something Martha Stewart might have coveted. Then photos of them on a patio, with a pool in the background, Lindy bringing out trays of food, hunky husband standing at the grill, children bobbing in the water. Lindy's children were so exquisite that my heart burned in my chest—Chloe, five, with a lot of yellow curly hair and a rosebud mouth, and the two-year-old twins, Davey and Razzie, plump and delicious-looking, with impish round faces. My niece and nephews. My relatives. I had relatives! And twins! Twins must run in my family! Who knew?

Then there were pictures of Lindy with her apparently millions of friends, all dressed up, holding wineglasses, holding those giant checks where people donate to causes. Smiling, beaming, all a part of important community things. You could tell everyone loved her. She snapped off the phone even though I wanted to keep scrolling back and back, as though I could see it all from the beginning: her children as babies, her wedding, Lindy as a kid again in high school and then in elementary school, weeping near the fence. I wanted to go back in time and have a do over, and this time I would absolutely hold her hand, tell her she was my sister, and not just turn her over to the nuns so I could get back to my playing. I wanted to see what she looked like in high school after I'd lost track of her, and hear about how she met her husband and what her pregnancies were like; I wanted to make a date to go shopping, even though I hate shopping. She would be good at it, and after we shopped for clothes, we could have glasses of wine somewhere, and we would sit on stools at those cute little high tables they have everywhere these days, and people would smile and say, "Look at those sisters. You can really tell those women are sisters."

Then she looked around the room, restless, and for a moment it was like the Road Runner cartoons when the coyote runs off the cliff but doesn't know he's falling yet so he spins in space. That's what I was doing, spinning.

"Where do you think that nun got to?" she said.

"She said she was getting our records, but I bet she's just giving us time to talk. Tell me about your work," I said quickly. "A Little Piece of Heaven, did you say?"

She gave me her card—she was now Lindy W. McIntyre—and she told me how she'd had to hire six new stylists and a manicurist for the salon, and she'd recently moved to a new, larger place over on McKinley Street that she'd decorated herself. It was a lot of work—a lot!—but it was making money now, and being there was like visiting an oasis, really. At least that's what she was aiming for—a place for women to come and be pampered.

"And how about you?" she said. "Tell me about your life. Husband? Kids? Work?" Her eyes flicked over me, sized me up, and I saw it all suddenly—that she was polite and friendly, but that we weren't going to be friends. It was the politeness of the woman who cuts your hair but who doesn't intend to have wine with you later or introduce you to her children. And why had I expected anything more? I didn't even have an interesting story to lure her with. She was successful and busy, and let's face it, I was kind of a misfit, still searching for stuff that I'd assumed would just land in my lap but somehow didn't.

So I told her the truth: ex-husband running off with his bank teller, divorce, mother's cancer and death. And it was all irredeemably grim, until I remembered the good news—that I was now in love with a *wonderful* man who had a sailboat business and two lovely teenaged children. I heard myself explain that he'd been married before for, like, twenty years, but he'd decided this was going to be the time he really *got it right*, and that, yes, the teenagers were a challenge for sure, with me not having been a mother before, but they were so *interesting* and Carter said they really loved me, and she said, "How long have you been seeing him?"

"Well," I said, and swallowed. "Four weeks, technically speaking."

Her eyes widened, and I wished I could somehow take that back and readjust the total, because let's face it: four is just not enough weeks. I showed her a picture of Carter, one I'd taken on my phone at the marina. But when she asked if I had pictures of his kids, of course I didn't. I scrolled uselessly through the phone, frowning. I had a bunch of pictures of houses I'd home-staged, and then some photos of my mother in her turban, smiling and waving at me, but nothing else. My mother's expression said I should stop trying too hard. I turned off my phone and smiled at Lindy, and then a brilliant idea bloomed inside my head.

"Can we talk about hair for a minute?" I said, leaning forward. "Because your hair is just beautiful! So smooth! How come you don't have these wacky, uncontrollable curls like I do?"

She studied me. "You need a keratin treatment," she said. "My hair is actually just like yours. You can't do it yourself; you have to go to a salon—it takes all that unruly stuff away. Twice a year."

"Oh! I haven't heard of that. Ker—?"

"Keratin. Best thing ever," she said. "It takes hours to do it right, but it's worth it."

"Thank you," I said, and we smiled at each other. "Wow, we just bonded over our hair, I think. Next you'll tell me where you bought those fabulous boots and your nail polish color and . . . well, who knows? We'll be BFFs."

She looked uncomfortable. "Listen," she said. "It has been really super nice to meet you, but now don't you think we can leave?"

I swallowed. "Well, but Sister Germaine said she's bringing back some information for us. She'll be hurt if we just walk out."

"What are you talking about? She's not going to be hurt. She doesn't care about us really." She narrowed her eyes. "Wait. Wait a minute. Is this like a whole orchestrated thing that you're in on? Is she going to pop back in here with our real mother or something?"

"No! Oh my God, no. I mean, I could only wish it was that easy to get to our mom. Sister Germaine has made it pretty clear that the law won't let her tell us who our mom is. Which is so sad because I've just always wanted to find out who I really am." I cleared my throat again. "Who I'm connected to. You know. You've probably always wondered, too, who your real mom is."

"Are you kidding me?" she said. "You're kidding, right?"

I shook my head.

"Listen, our mom is probably *not* somebody we'd want to know," she said. "Think about it. *She gave us away.* Most likely she's some drug addict who got herself pregnant and then couldn't handle taking care of us, and so she pushed us out of her life. Why do you want to open up a can of worms like that?"

She again picked imaginary lint off her slacks, and her face looked so closed down that I almost couldn't breathe.

"Really," she said, "I think I actually could hate her for what she did. Giving us up."

I drew back. "You hate her?"

"I do. Okay. Maybe that's too strong a word. Indifferent, then. I'm indifferent toward her. For a lot of my life I didn't think about her one bit. But then—"

"Not once? Never?"

"No. But then—when I was pregnant, I started thinking about how somebody gave birth to *me*. And how maybe she'd had all the same feelings I was having, like when I felt the baby kick. Maybe she was excited and a little scared because she didn't know how things were going to turn out. And then, I have to tell you . . . after twenty-four hours of labor when I did that final hard push and my brand-new sweet tiny baby came into the world—and I know you're going to think this sounds stupid and sentimental, and it probably is—but when I got to hold my own baby for the first time, it hit me then, what it means to love somebody. You know? Before that, I didn't get it. But that's when it slammed into me that I had been *rejected*. Not wanted *at all*. And, well, I started sobbing. Because I'm sorry, but that is *not* what a decent human being could ever do."

There was a buzzing noise in my head. I swallowed hard. "What? Wow, I thought you were going to say that when you had your own baby, you had *sympathy* for this woman who had given birth to you and then had to say good-bye to you. I mean, her circumstances may have been pretty dire, as you say . . ."

Her face looked tough in the light coming through the window, all that snowy, chilly light. "But *why* did she have to say good-bye? Come on. They would have had to rip my baby out of my arms and sedate me with a stun gun to get me to give up my child. *That*—what she did, I'm sorry, is the worst rejection a person could ever do. She carried me in her body for nine whole months, and then she gave birth to me and took a look at me, and gave me away? And you, too! She just said, 'Okay, kid, have a good life. I won't ever see you again'? Wow. And I need to invite *that* into my life? Give her another chance to turn me away again? No, thank you."

"But what if they made her do it?" I said.

Her perfectly arched eyebrows shot up. "They? Who's *they*? She could have stood up for herself. And now it turns out she did it *twice*? I'm sorry, but *that* is an awful person."

I wanted to say something, but I couldn't formulate exactly what it was—something about people, especially teenagers, not always being given choices—and then Sister Germaine was back, all beaming smiles, looking at us like we were the poster children for being reunited. I saw her smile fade as she took in Lindy perched on the edge of her chair, purse in her lap, her face an angry mask.

"Oh my goodness! You didn't have tea!" Sister Germaine said, as if the problem was that we'd let dehydration get the better of us. "Nina, will you pour us some cups of tea?"

"Of course," I said, and poured tea into the three sweet china cups with my shaking hands, hoping this would make Lindy stay put.

Sister Germaine put a folder on the desk and sat down. "I have a little bit of good news, ladies—some other information I'm authorized to give you." She leafed through the folder. "We already knew that you both were born to the same mother and the same father—kind of unusual for that day and age—and what I can *also* tell you is that they were very young teenagers. Very, very young and apparently quite in love. We don't want to romanticize them, of course, but it's very telling that they remained involved with each other for two pregnancies."

Lindy took a sip of tea and set her cup down hard.

"Ah, see?" I whispered to her. "They *were* forced to give us up. They didn't have the choice of keeping us." She mouthed to me, "Drug addicts," but Sister Germaine, flipping through the paperwork, didn't see. "Irresponsible," whispered Lindy.

"Yes, your mother lived with relatives—a sister, I believe, because her parents were deceased. You were born first, as you know, Nina, and your mother tried to raise you for a little over a year until she couldn't anymore. Being unmarried and in high school still—"

I felt my stomach go wobbly on me. "Wait. Are you sure? She didn't give me up as a newborn?"

Sister Germaine regarded me over her glasses and said softly, "No, dear. She tried to keep you. But being unmarried and in high school—it was such a hard life." She went back to reading my record. "Let's see, you were fifteen months old, it looks like. Yes. Fifteen months."

The room wobbled just the slightest bit. "Wow," I heard myself say. "So she *knew* me."

"Yes, she knew you," said Lindy. "Imagine that. Do you remember her? Think hard."

"No, I don't *think* so." I was feeling dazed. "Wait. Why didn't my adopted mother ever tell me that she adopted me as a toddler, not a new baby? I don't think this is correct . . ."

"It's correct," said Sister Germaine. "She was doing her best, the records said, but then once Poppet came along—I mean, *Lindy* came along—it was too much. Oh! I'm so sorry. I shouldn't have said that name."

I turned and looked at Lindy, amazed, but her face was angry.

"My name was Poppet? I did not want to know what my name had been. That was terrible of you to tell me that."

"It's a darling name," I said slowly, but then I couldn't pay a bit of attention to her. I was suddenly busy killing off all the images I'd entertained about my mother over the years. My mother was no longer a showgirl trapped in her love for an actor onstage, forced to give up her newborn daughter. She wasn't Princess Di either, or the mom from *Growing Pains*. She probably wasn't even a drug addict. She was just a scared, irresponsible kid who nobody ever gave a condom to, a kid with a ponytail and skinny legs poking out of a school uniform that she probably rolled up to be shorter than it was supposed to be; our father probably had acne and close-cropped hair and the bare beginnings of a mustache. God, it was like the worst cliché in the world. We were clichés that got dropped off at the orphanage. And she *knew* me. My God, she knew me.

All of a sudden I could feel Lindy and Sister Germaine both staring at me. Then Sister Germaine said, "I'm sorry if this is upsetting. But sometimes I think there can be a comfort in knowing the truth. I know you will come to that place, Nina, and that you will realize that you were given up for unselfish reasons that you may never know. We like to see adoption as an unselfish act—"

Lindy got to her feet. "All right, this is now officially ridiculous. You've obviously got our birth certificates right there, and you've already slipped up and told me my birth name. Why don't you just hand them over and give us our mother's name so we can get on with our lives?"

"Well, dear, I can't do that," said Sister Germaine. "It's—"

"Are they in that folder?"

"They are, but I—"

"Lindy," I said. "Please, no. I'm so sorry I put you through this—"

"This is not your fault," she said without looking at me. "You're the victim here."

Sister Germaine became preternaturally calm, as though she had wells of tranquility to draw on that ordinary humans could never imagine. She looked at me kindly and said that it was all right. "This room has seen a lot of anger and emotion. You're free, Lindy, to say what you feel. It's a frustrating situation."

To my horror, Lindy walked over to the desk and towered over Sister Germaine, who placed her hand on top of the folder protectively. For a moment I thought my sister was going to grab the folder and wrestle this old lady nun, one of Jesus's wives, to the ground. In the name of sisterhood, I would have to help.

Lindy planted both hands on the desk and, leaning toward Sister Germaine, said in a low voice, "Look, I couldn't care less who my birth mother was or why she gave us up, but this woman here—she cares so much! Do you have any idea how much she's hurting and how much she wants this?" She flung out her arm toward me. "It's all right there in her face. And you've got our birth certificates right there, and I'm seeing them, I'm *seeing them right here* on your desk, and yet you refuse to show them to us."

"I am not responsible for that law," said Sister Germaine quietly. "I'm as saddened by it as you are. And now I'm afraid I'm going to have to ask you to sit down, or else you will have to leave."

"Oh, don't you worry. I'm leaving. I can't believe this."

My sister walked back to her chair and got her coat and her purse, her face hard and impassive.

"It can be upsetting news," Sister Germaine said again.

"Before I go," Lindy said, "there's one more thing I want to know. Did our biological mother ever come looking for us?"

"No. But you mustn't—Listen, you can't base anything on that. The shame, the stigma . . ."

"Uh-huh," Lindy said and looked at me. "You see? She doesn't care what happened to us. And you know what? We don't need to take on this tragic story. It's not one bit who we really are."

"Tragedy is fine," I said, "we can work with tragedy." But Sister Germaine was standing up and making pronouncements about how lucky we were to have found the parents we did, blah blah blah, and a whole bunch of stuff about the Church and Jesus's will and the way things work out for the best.

Lindy was at the door now, looking furious. "Nina, it was very nice meeting you. I'm very sorry that your mom is dead and that you think this search is going to help you somehow. But here's what I want to tell you—two things, really. The first is, marry that guy. Marry him and have a baby with him, even if he's already got kids. You need one for *you*. And then, I guarantee, you'll know what love is and what family is, and you'll wonder how you ever even wasted one minute on our biological mother. And the second thing is—oh yes. The second thing. Your hair. You should go to somebody good and ask for a keratin treatment."

"Can I call you?" I said.

"No." She stopped, perhaps hearing how bad that sounded. "I'm sorry, but I can't. I just can't."

"I understand," I said, though I didn't.

"And listen. Give up on our mom, the birth certificate, everything. Make a good life without all this crap." And she shook her head and left, slamming the door behind her.

In the resounding silence that followed, Sister Germaine swallowed and said, "I think I should make sure that she gets out of here all right. Without any untoward bad reaction."

"No," I said miserably, standing up. "Let me go. I'll find her and tell her I'm sorry. She's not wrong. She's—"

"No!" said Sister Germaine sharply. "Listen to me, Nina, listen to what I'm saying." She dropped her voice and spoke very slowly and deliberately. "I am going to leave the folder on my desk. You will be alone in this room for ten minutes. Maybe fifteen. And then I will be back."

I'm scared of authority figures and kind of slow to pick up on cues, but even so it took me only seconds after she left to realize what she'd been telling me and to make my way to the desk, flip through the folder, and find the birth certificates. My eyes were greedy, scanning quickly over everything.

And then there it was: my name. Kate Louise Mullen. I was *Kate? Not even Katherine?* I traced my finger slowly along the typed name, around the embossed seal at the bottom. I was Kate! My teeth felt weird suddenly, like I'd been chewing on iron bars or something.

The words wobbled in front of me. I'd been born on July 12, 1978, to a fifteen-year-old named Phoebe Louise Mullen. Mother's occupation: high school student. Fifteen years old, just a month from turning sixteen. Father: blank. Place of residence of mother: Allenbury, Connecticut. Fifty miles from here.

I looked out the window, lost in thought. Allenbury was a small industrial city in the central part of the state, a town once known for textiles but suffering through a kind of depression now that the mills had moved out. Very Catholic, working-class community.

And I had once been a little girl named Kate and my mother was called Phoebe, and she had maybe loved me—at least loved me enough to give me her same middle name. I flipped to the next birth certificate. Lindy had been called Poppet Marie Mullen, born August 19, 1979, thirteen months after me. Father: blank.

Oh, this was going to be tougher to get over than I'd ever thought.

I ran my finger over my mother's name on both birth certificates. She was real, and I wanted to find her and look into her face. I wanted to know what happened after she gave us up. I wanted to know a hundred million things about her: what her smile looked like, if she had red hair like mine if her parents gave her birthday parties; I wanted so badly to hear the stories they always told on holidays, and if anybody ever said to her, "Oh, Phoebe, you're just like your mom, and you laugh just like your father, and . . . and . . ."

I wanted a context for my life.

My fingers were poised to go through the rest of the file—it was thick with papers and notes—but just then there was a soft knock on the door. I jumped back like I'd been about to touch a rattlesnake, and spun myself around to the window.

The door opened, and I turned my head. Another nun was standing there, frowning. "I didn't know you were still here. Where is Sister Germaine?"

"I—don't know," I said.

"Here, let me take this," she said briskly, coming over and picking up the file from the desk without looking at me, then closing the door behind her.

I looked around the room wildly. My pie was still sitting on the table by the door. The pie! I should take it downstairs, see if I could find Lindy. I could tell her that even if she didn't want people to know about me, maybe we could be secret friends and we'd never have to let anyone know we were sisters. Maybe I could meet her children from afar. I was their aunt, after all. Or I could be her client, somebody who came in to have my hair done once in a while. I would be anonymous to everybody else in the shop, but maybe I could work my way up to being her friend.

Then the truth hit me like a rock. Lindy wasn't interested in being friends with me. She'd shown up out of the most rudimentary politeness, but there was something cold and distant about her. She had a huge, quirky, loving family that she had the luxury to be exasperated by, and she'd made it quite clear that she didn't care what happened to me. Talk about rejection! She had said no in every way possible.

I picked up my purse and the pie of despair, and walked quickly down the hall, with my head down.

Oh, this place with its secrets, its ghosts of long-ago sighs, the tears and anger and sorrow so deeply ingrained that they were now part of the architecture. Problems could possibly be solved here, the walls and paneling said, but not the way you'd hope. Not ever the way you'd hope.

The receptionist glanced up from her computer screen as I left. "It's gotten lots colder out," she said. "Button yourself up."

SEVEN

"Melanie. I found out my mom's name."

I called her from the parking lot, right from the snowbank. I knew I was supposed to call Carter first, but somehow Melanie seemed to have the right to hear the news first, by virtue of being the oldest friend.

"What? You did *not*. Who is she? Is it Miss Gaines?"

"No. Miss Gaines is off the hook. My mom's name is Phoebe Louise Mullen, and I saw my birth certificate, and get this: she named me Kate. Just Kate. And she was only fifteen, so I'm wondering if nobody told her that most people named Kate have either Kathleen or Katherine as their real name."

I did not, *could not*, bring myself to say she gave me away when I was fifteen months old. That was a fact it was still too hard to digest.

"Your mother was fifteen?" she said. "Oh my God. Are you freaking kidding me? She was a baby herself. Phoebe what?"

"Phoebe Louise Mullen. And—oh, you're not going to believe this. *My sister is Lindy Walsh.* Lindy Walsh! Remember her?"

"Hold on. You're going way too fast for me."

"I know. It's incredible. My head is spinning. Our mom named her Poppet. Kate and Poppet. We sound like a sister act, don't we? But she's not interested in being sisters with me, I don't think. I don't know. I'll tell you all about it when I see you."

"Wait, I remember her!" Melanie said. And then there was a bit of a silence and then she said, "Oh my God."

"What?"

"All of this. Jesus, where are you? Get over here. I found your mom on Google."

"Melanie! No, no, no. I did not authorize you to go on Google. You creep! This is *my* mom. You look up your own mom on Google!"

"My mom's too boring for Google. But *your* mom!"

"Stop it! Melanie. Shut down your computer right now. Until I get there."

"Oh my God, oh my God. You're not going to believe—!" Then she lowered her voice. "There's something else you need to know before you get here. We have a . . . visitor."

"A visitor? Who?"

"Indigo. She's sitting at your desk."

"What? Why isn't she at school?"

"How should I know?" she whispered. "She's kind of . . . mysterious, don't you think? She came to the office looking for you—" Melanie's voice rose then. "Yes, I'm talking to her now, Indigo! She's on her way!" Voice lowered again. "So, get here, okay? I think you're going to be surprised about your mom. It's kind of incredible!"

"I think you may be surprised by how much I may hate you right now."

"You're ridiculous, and I mean that in the best possible . . ."

"Ridiculouser. And turn off your computer!"

Before I started the car, I punched in Carter's cell phone number. The call went directly to voice mail.

When I came flying into the office, Indigo was sitting on the floor as if at a protest, dressed in her black miniskirt and combat boots. Her eyes were smudged—she probably used black markers for eyeliner, I thought—and she was staring at her phone. Was she sad, or was this just typical teenage behavior? Who could tell? She made me feel the slightest bit guilty. Like I could have prevented some of her sadness, possibly if I stopped sleeping with her dad, just for instance.

Melanie gave me one of her side looks and rolled her eyes. Melanie was the person best in the world to know that I am unequipped to deal with a young person, particularly a young person who possibly has issues. We had been *the* most mainstream, obedient little teenagers you can imagine.

"Hi, Indie," I said, which is a nickname I happened to know she liked because she told me so. "Everything okay?" (That was code for "Why aren't you in school?" But she just said, "Iguessso," which even I know is code for "Nothing is okay.")

"Where's your dad?" I asked, and she shrugged and looked down.

"With my mom. They're plotting something," she said.

"Plotting something!" I said, and my voice sounded tinny to my own ears. "What in the heck are they plotting?"

"Nothing good," she said. "I don't know what they're talking about, but it's all hush-hush."

Huh. My mouth went dry. So! *This is the way it's going to end*, my heart said. My heart has seen a lot of action, and it prides itself on getting out ahead of any incipient heartbreak. *You've been seeing him for a month and now it turns out he's getting back together with his wife.* In fact, my heart turned out to know a whole lot of things I hadn't realized yet—like it remembered a phone call he took as I was running out the door, and my heart surmised that was from his ex, and that she probably had now seen that he was happy with someone else, and so of course she wanted him back. Most natural thing in the world.

Melanie said, "Come over here and look at this computer right now, because you are not going to believe what you see. Come on!"

She steered me over to her desk. "Ta-*dahh*! I present to you . . . Phoebe Louise Mullen! Look at her! Can you believe this?"

And sure enough, there was Google presenting me with a whole platter of Phoebe Louise Mullen images—images that, excuse me, I wanted to look at all by myself. Here was my mother, my real, genuine mother at last, and Melanie would not stop talking, and across the room was this girl who was giving me such needy, baleful looks, and was it true that Carter was really breaking up with me? Seriously? I could get over him, of course I could, but I didn't want to.

My curly-haired, redheaded mother, first as a silhouette and then as a young woman, laughing.

And then I saw what Melanie was trying to show me.

My mother had been the lead singer in an eighties girl band called Lulu and the Starbabies, a band I might have even heard of. Well, maybe I had heard of them. I couldn't right then remember for sure. They'd done a cover of "Will You Still Love Me Tomorrow?" and also some punk anthem about not taking it anymore, and something called "Is This the Way You Treat Your Baby?" which, as Melanie pointed out, had to be the most ironic title of all time.

Oh my God. In picture after picture, there was Lulu, aka my mom, and she had wild, red, teased hair and shoulder pads and tight purple leggings, and she was holding a microphone and a manicured hand up to the sky with her head thrown back. She looked like she was screaming. She looked like she could have had an eyeliner franchise. And a shoulder pad franchise.

I went through page after page of Google images.

Phoebe Louise Mullen was too fabulous for words. She didn't look like a woman who'd had two babies as a teenager and who had suffered.

Melanie kept scrolling through the pages, clicking on links, showing photos of concerts with their grainy, blurry light. And then studio close-ups of Lulu, which Melanie zoomed in on until every pore on my mother's face showed, every black track of eyeliner, every eyelash like a tarantula resting on my mother's eyelids, every red slash of a mouth. She seemed to have a scar along one cheek. My head swam. Had my mother somehow given birth to Lindy and me as a teen and then given us up simply so she could . . . be famous? This wasn't so far from the Who's Your Mama fantasy stories, come to think of it.

I could just hear what Lindy would say, that this proved our mother was a selfish bitch, abandoning us without a backward thought and going off to seek her fame and fortune, taking drugs, screaming into microphones, stomping around in her thigh-high boots.

True, I would have to agree. But at least we can see her. At least we know who she is now. Isn't that worth something?

At some point, I realized that Indigo had gotten up off the floor and eased herself between Melanie and me. She was watching us intently but we couldn't stop scrolling. Melanie kept saying, "Look at her here! Oh my God, that hair! Those shoulder pads!"

"She looks like you! She has your eyes! And if you frizzed up your hair, you would totally look just like her!" That was Indigo. I turned to her, and she stared at me. "So for reals, you've never seen your own mom before?" she said.

Then Melanie and I took turns telling her my whole story, giddy with the new challenge before us. My mom existed!

"And this woman is so findable," said Melanie at last. "You are going to have *no* problem at all tracking her down."

"You should order her music from iTunes," said Indigo. She pressed some buttons, but nothing came up. She shrugged. "We may have to do more hunting," she said. "Not all music is on iTunes. We'll find her."

"You think so? These were all such a long time ago. She might even be dead now for all I know."

"She's probably not dead," said Melanie. "She had you at fifteen, so she's fifty now. That's not very old."

"That's my dad's age," said Indigo. And we were silent out of respect for that stunning realization. And then Indigo said, "We'll do a Whitepages search. And LinkedIn, Facebook, Twitter, People Finder. Don't worry. I'll find her by the time we leave here today." Her bitten black fingernails were flying over the keys.

Melanie and I exchanged glances over her head.

Three minutes later, she said, "Here she is! She lives in New York, right in Brooklyn! On Washington Avenue. That's a cool place to live. My friend Maya goes there sometimes."

The little bell tinkled over the door, and Carter was standing there, with the very strangest, most regretful expression on his face. He tilted his head and tried hard to smile, but I knew. Oh, I knew. I had to make myself remember not to run over to him, grab his hand, and dance him around the room while I shouted out my news. For once in my life, I was going to hang back if a man was about to break up with me.

I looked back down at the computer, now on a new link, and gazed at the address of Phoebe Louise Mullen. *I am coming to see you*, I promised her. *And I will save your life if you ever need me to. My kidney is your kidney.*

"Dad! We found Nina's mom," said Indigo. "And guess what. She's your age."

Carter's face was a sheet of glass. "What? That's wonderful, Nina." He didn't look right. "Indigo, can we talk for a few minutes?"

And to my surprise, Indigo burst into tears. I couldn't breathe for trying to work it all out. He went over and took her in his arms, and she buried her head in his shirt, smearing it with about a pound of black makeup. But he didn't seem to mind.

"I knew she was going," she was blubbering. "I knew it, I knew it!"

"It's going to be okay," he said to her and rubbed her back.

Then he looked at me—me, who was having seven different kinds of heart failure just watching the two of them—and he mouthed, "Jane. She's moving to Virginia."

"She has to take me with her! I can't stay here! Please make her take me!" said Indigo.

"It's okay, baby," he said. "You'll live with me only until the end of the summer, and then you can go and join her. It's going to be okay."

"Complicated," he mouthed to me. And then to illustrate just *how* complicated, he did an elaborate little pantomime, spinning his hands around in midair and crossing his eyes, while the whole time his daughter leaned against him, staring at me with her big, blackened, streaming eyes.

But here's the thing: even right away I could see there was some lightness about Carter that I hadn't seen before.

I suddenly knew why he hadn't been able to pick out a condominium to buy in all those weeks of looking: he couldn't bear leaving his kids.

Later, much later, Carter and I went out to dinner alone, and over glasses of wine and plates of spaghetti, I told him all about meeting my sister, how I knew her before, how the nun had left me with the birth certificates, and how I was now officially the daughter of somebody who used to wear glitter and tights and sing for large crowds.

"I was right, though, about Lindy," I said. "I don't think she's looking to be friends."

"Maybe she just needs some time to get used to the idea," he said.

"No, it's not that. She already has a huge family. She doesn't need a new sister. She said as much." I folded my hands. "I'm the only one who cares about our mother or what happened to us, and she thinks it's because I don't have more people to think about."

"Well," he said. He was drumming his hand on the table. If I looked closely at his left hand, I always thought I could make out the little indent where once a wedding ring had gone. Twenty years leaves a mark.

He looked tired. "Nina, you're a wonderful person, and she'd be lucky to have you as her sister. Give her some time. She's probably in shock."

"It seems like both of us have had a lot of family complications today," I said.

"Yeah, I hadn't seen this coming," he said and ran his hands through his hair. He was at his most charmingly disheveled tonight. Jane, he told me, had been offered a job managing some kind of start-up of a sustainable farm corporation in Virginia, and she needed to go right away to start hiring and planning. She couldn't take the kids because she needed every ounce of energy for her work. So for the next seven months, he'd be a full-time dad. Then who knew what would happen? Tyler would certainly go to college, and Indigo would go join her mom.

He laid his hands flat on the tablecloth and looked at me. He was frowning, but I could still see that lightness about him I'd noticed earlier: deep down, he was pleased that he didn't have to give them up.

"So what do you want to do?" he said.

"What do *you* want to do?"

"Well, I understand if you don't want to, you know, keep on going with me. This isn't what you bargained for. Tyler will most likely be fine, but I'm going to have a pretty unhappy teenage girl. I don't think I can inflict her on you." He smiled, a sad, crinkly-eyed smile that made him seem every minute of his age. "Part of me thinks I should at least try again to talk Jane into taking her along now, except that I can't stand the idea of losing her. She's unhappy here in school, but she'd probably be unhappy down there, too, in a new environment. So the way I see it, she might as well be unhappy here, where I can be on hand to cheer her up."

He picked up the dessert menu and then put it down again. "I don't know what to tell you," he said. "I might be in hell."

"Are you breaking up with me?" I said when I couldn't stand it anymore.

"What? No. No! I'm giving you an out," he said. He reached across the table and took my hand in his. "Maybe, as a person with good sense, you don't want to take on teenagers and me and this crazy life I'm about to have."

"I want to continue seeing you," I said shyly. "I'm not really afraid of your kids. Well, okay, so I am a little. But if it doesn't work, it doesn't work. We'll shake hands and say good-bye."

"Totally," he said. "As the kids would say."

"And, um, you don't have to sign something that means you're going to live the life of a monk or anything, do you?"

He gave me a wide smile. "As of yet, there has been no mention of my having to take vows of celibacy or any other kind."

"Well, I hope you'll refuse when they pull the papers out and force you to sign."

He looked at me for a long moment. "What are you doing right now?"

Crazily enough, it turned out I wasn't doing anything. We pretty much skipped out of the restaurant and headed to my apartment, where we sat up late listening to music and baking chocolate chip cookies and drinking more wine, and then we went to bed, where Carter looked into my eyes while he made love to me and told me again and again that he loved me and he couldn't live without me.

And I said the same, even though it was way too early to be saying those things.

EIGHT

LINDY

Before Lindy McIntyre got out of bed the next day—before she'd even fully opened her eyes—she had outlined her four basic goals for the morning, because when you had a crazy-busy life like Lindy's, her life coach had said, it was important to make goals. Without goal setting, deep breathing, and occasional affirmations, according to Shoshana, Lindy might as well have had a sign painted on her forehead that read: I Am a Wreck of a Human Being. Please Kick Me.

She counted her goals on her fingers. Number one: Get Chloe to wear her adorable purple knit tunic with the striped leggings to school because it was kindergarten picture day, and *of course* Chloe was going to put up a fight. She was going to want to wear the cheap, shiny Elsa costume that Lindy's mother had bought at the dollar store because, like every other five-year-old girl in the country, she'd somehow been turned overnight into a Disney princess. And really—how was it going to look if the entire kindergarten population of girls showed up dressed like Elsa on picture day? It would be a statement that the parents had simply given up, that's what. And Lindy had not given up.

Okay, goal number two: Be nice to her mother this morning when she arrived to watch the twins. No going into the other room and biting her knuckles when her mother criticized her hairstyle or her spotlessly clean kitchen (which was evidence, apparently, that Lindy wasn't paying proper attention to her children if she cared so much about how clean the stove was—go figure). Also, no tapping or counting while her mother was around. Instead, she was going to dig deep inside herself and find the gratitude because really, she was really lucky—so very, very lucky—that she didn't have to leave the twins with strangers while she worked. And after all, Lindy's mom had raised six kids practically without breaking a sweat, and Lindy should not mind that her mom felt this gave her lifetime expert status on *everything* even though the world had freaking changed and her mother had no clue about so many, many things that Lindy knew were wrong, wrong, wrong. Like the doughnuts Mrs. Walsh brought for the children every morning, and the fact that she set the kids in front of the television whenever she felt like it, and how she didn't give them naps if it wasn't convenient.

Lindy paused for a deep breath. *I am grateful for my mother. I am grateful for my mother. She is only trying to help. I wrap her in compassion.*

Next. Where was she? Oh. Goal number three: To put the vegetables she'd cut up last night into the slow cooker with the quinoa before her mother arrived and pointed out again (and again) that feeding kids vegetarian food doesn't give them enough protein. "And don't talk to me about tofu. Or kale," as her mother had said. "Kale is nothing more than a *decoration for the side of the plate.* If God had wanted us to eat kale, he wouldn't have made it out of wood. Period."

Next to her, Jeff snorted in his sleep. Lindy looked over at her husband. Goal number three should be to wake him up and start making love to him. Oh, wait. That would be goal number four. She had lost track. How long had it been since she'd had sex with him, anyway?

Ages. He used to be a morning sex guy; just turning over in bed in the morning could get him all jazzed up and hungry for her. But lately both of them had been working too hard—he at his construction business, managing eight employees and driving around like a madman all day to check on their progress, and she with her salon, which every month seemed to have more customers and more paperwork. So, go figure— both of them were doing great by the world's standards, but somehow they'd lost their minds. Also, Jeff played racquetball in the evenings after dinner; once the kids were in bed, at least three nights a week he'd head to the gym, saying he needed it to relax. And stay in shape. She wanted him to be in shape, didn't she? That's what he had said to her: "I do this for you, baby."

Of course she did. But she shouldn't have to remind him that sex used to be his favorite way to relax. Or that marriage meant they were supposed to talk to each other, share their lives. He hadn't even asked her how meeting her sister yesterday had gone. He'd forgotten all about it.

Jesus, her sister.

Deeeep breaths. Where was she? Oh yes, goal number four, or was it five? This one was all encompassing. She wanted to spend some indi-vidual quality time with each child before she left the house, *and* she wanted to feed them a healthy breakfast before her mother showed up with the Dunkin' Donuts bag; and oh yes, put away all pieces of paper that her mother might find interesting. Last month she'd come home to find her mother waving around Lindy's invoice for a Coach bag, totally aghast that she'd spend so much on a *purse.* And yes, it *had* cost three hundred thirty-seven dollars and fifty-nine cents, which was ridiculous if you thought Walmart purses were just fine. But as Lindy had tried to explain, she was a spa owner now, and she needed to have a name-brand purse because in her business, people judged her on the kind of purse she carried. She was trying—and succeeding, lately at least—to attract the moms from Chloe's school as clients, the ones who drove Teslas and put Cole Haan shoes on their toddlers, and who wanted to have perfect shiny highlights that made them look as though they'd spent the last four months romping in the sunshine and never giving the slightest thought to their hair. But of course Peggy Walsh didn't want to hear about that. She'd made no secret of the fact that she already thought Lindy and Jeff had a lifestyle that was one Ugg boot away from being pretentious (her worst insult)—and now the Coach bag, with its incriminating little Cs and its bust-out retail price, had pushed them so far into The Land of Uppity-ness that they might never be able to recover in her eyes. As though this neighborhood, this style of living, was all pretend somehow, simply because neither she nor Jeff had come from money.

But what was so wrong about their lives, really? True, Jeff was in the trades, and she was only a hairdresser, but they belonged here. They *worked* to belong here. He and his buddies had built them this beautiful five-bedroom house with an inground swimming pool, and Lindy had learned to entertain and to speak up at PTA meetings, and work harder than everyone else while making things look easy. That was the trick: to make it all look easy.

They were brilliant at looking like they belonged.

From down the hall, she heard Chloe loudly telling the twins that she was the snow princess and they were the snowmen who couldn't talk because their mouths were pieces of coal, and then the bedroom door crashed open and all three kids came tumbling in, talking and singing and cannonballing their way into the center of the bed—and Lindy was laughing, scooping them up in her arms, covering their fat pink cheeks with kisses.

Jeff said, "Oh God," and buried his head under his arms so that he wouldn't have his eyes poked out. But the twins got on top of him and pulled his arms away, and then he laughed and became Papa Winter Bear and growled at them and put them in the special churning washing machine that he claimed to keep under his pillow, flinging them back and forth while they shouted and giggled and kept saying, "Again, again!"

Lindy eased herself off the bed. *Everything's perfect*, she thought, gazing at the chaos of them, looking like a family magazine shoot, a portrait of love, all together in the king-size bed: the milky light coming through the sheer curtains, the happy tumble of her blond-haired children, the twins in their matching Spider-Man pajamas, Chloe wearing a nightgown from *Frozen*, the tangle of limbs everywhere, and, of course, the handsome, dark-haired father gathering them up in his bare, muscular arms.

She forgot the list of goals.

Because if you squinted your eyes, you might think this was absolutely, wonderfully, unbelievably perfect, she thought. You wouldn't notice that the mother had worry lines on her face or that she was tapping out something on her thigh, or that the handsome, dark-haired, nicely muscled father hadn't looked at her even once, and that the children were actually screeching and competing for attention, and that it was going to take a miracle to get them ready for the day without tears.

And just like that, the moment was gone.

"Jeff," she said. "*Jeff.*"

She tapped her arm where a wristwatch would be. There were only forty-two minutes until her mother arrived. "Shower," she mouthed to him, and he nodded. She slipped off to the bathroom and stood for a moment in front of the full-length mirror, took eleven deep yoga breaths, did eleven Kegels, touched her toes, and stretched her arms overhead. Eleven was the best number, because it was an odd number, like the number of tiles in the shower, which she counted while she let the shampoo lather soak through her hair as she scrubbed at her teeth—not hard, the dentist had warned; it takes the enamel off. And don't forget to floss! She rinsed her mouth and her hair at the same time, putting on conditioner and shaving her legs with the excess, then dried herself quickly. There! Three minutes twenty-one seconds.

Thirty-seven minutes until her mother arrived. Odd numbers were best. Her hair fell in wet little auburn ringlets around her face, and she got out the blow dryer to tame it then stopped in her tracks, remembering.

Her sister. Nina. Her sister had gotten so intense about her hair yesterday. What a needy person she'd turned out to be! That whole thing had been a nightmare, in fact. Those eyes that kept searching her own, no place to hide from all that need, all that hunger for a family connection that didn't exist.

Lindy had been right to walk out of that crazy meeting. She didn't need another mother, or another sister, for that matter. Her life was just fine without them. And honestly she didn't even think about the fact that she was adopted anymore. It didn't matter at all, not in the least. She tapped on the mirror five times and looked at her fingerprint.

And then, God help her, she was just standing there in front of the bathroom mirror trying to comb out her hair, and tears were running down her face.

Poppet. She'd been called Poppet.

What the hell kind of a name was *that*? Such whimsy! And why would you give someone a name knowing it would never be used, would never actually *be* that person's name, because that small, helpless person was about to be sent away forever, with nothing of yours to take along?

It was 7:05 by the time she got back to the bedroom, and holy hell if Jeff wasn't still in bed, checking his phone messages and scowling like he had all the time in the world. Chloe was doing ballet in front of the full-length mirror, and Razzie and Davey were quietly doing something to the remote, which would no doubt mean that it would never work again.

"Can you believe this?" Jeff said, looking up at her, and she wanted to tell him, No, that whatever it was, she couldn't, didn't want to believe it. "Regina Clarke actually texted me at 3:08 a.m. to say she changed her mind again about the tiles. This is the *fifth* time we've gone back and forth." He shook his head. "Who thinks about backsplashes at three in the morning?"

"Wow," said Lindy. She remembered three in the morning. Davey had awakened with a nightmare, and she'd sat on the floor next to his crib, one hand on his back through the bars so he'd fall back to sleep. She opened her top bureau drawer and picked out a black pair of panties and a black lace bra, straightening the piles again before she closed the drawer.

"Yep, so the day begins," he said. He got out of bed and stretched and groaned, flexing his arms. He was inordinately proud of his arms, earned through construction work, and she was always amused at how much he appreciated the ripple of his own muscles. They *were* pretty spectacular, along with his flat stomach and slim hips. "Now," he was grumbling, "I gotta go to the tile store before picking up Moe. Or maybe I'll call and get Henry to do it." He was talking to himself more than to her. "So, workout, shower, call Regina Clarke, tile store, Moe, check on other job on Fulmar Street, Regina's bathroom to get the guys started, estimate on the kitchen project over on Liberty Street . . ." His voice trailed off.

"Listen," she said. "I don't suppose you could get the kids' breakfast ready while I wrangle them into their clothes, could you?" Let's see, if she wore the black cashmere turtleneck with her new black leggings, she wouldn't have to go down to the dryer to get the beige sweater she'd planned to wear; she could put on her lavender knit topper and . . . and . . .

He sighed one of his famous put-upon sighs. "Did you not hear all the things I have to do?"

"Just do the breakfast," she said. "Please." Did she really have to explain to him that her mother was going to be here in thirty-two short minutes (an even number, unlucky), and that she wanted to get the downstairs cleaned up and the twins fed their healthy breakfast before the junk food arrived? And of course there was Chloe to reason with on the Elsa question. No easy task. Back to her lavender topper: she had a perm to do first thing, so it might get stained—but she could wear a smock. Did the cleaning service deliver the smocks last Thursday? She couldn't remember. She'd meant to check.

"Oh, shit. It's the end of the month. I have to do my invoices, too." He cracked his knuckles.

"I thought you were going to hire somebody for your invoices," she said.

"Yeah, well, *you* try hiring when you're spending every minute running to the tile store and dealing with morons," he said in a louder-than-necessary voice. "I'm not sitting in a nice salon all day like some people, you know. I'm on the road."

"Well," she said, "it just so happens I know somebody who's looking for freelance accounting work. One of my clients. She's excellent. I'll call her later if you want."

He started to say something negative—she could see the look, knew it all too well, that shield that came up whenever they talked about their respective businesses, especially since hers ran more smoothly because she did her paperwork on time and he hated to do his—but then he forced himself to smile and shrugged. "Okay, then. Wonder Woman rides to the rescue again, huh?" and he headed for the bathroom.

"Jeff?" she called after him. "Don't shower *now*, okay, honey? Could you do the breakfasts? Please?"

Long silence, and then he said to the kids without looking at her, "Okay, guys! Daddy Dragon Eggs in five in the kitchen!" and left. She heard him thumping angrily down the stairs.

She scooped up the children and herded them to the twins' bedroom, clapping her hands eleven times and singing her Get Dressed song: "We're getting dressed . . . dressed . . . dressed . . . we're looking good . . . good . . . good . . ."

"I'm wearing my Elsa dress for the picture! I'm wearing Elsa for the picture!" called Chloe, stripping off her Elsa nightgown and Elsa slippers and jumping on the bed. Lindy didn't answer, just tackled the twins, taking off their pajama pants and wet diapers in one fluid motion, then stuffed them into the Pull-Ups they'd recently started wearing, in the hopes that someday they'd be toilet trained. Her mother said it was time.

Davey put his head on her shoulder, and she took in the deep, sweet, little-boy smell of him. The life coach said these were moments she should treasure. *Now I'm cuddling my son . . . now I'm reasoning with my daughter . . . now I'm seeing a sunbeam dance across the beautiful oak floor . . .*

She sighed. Of course it was great having this lifestyle—the house, the pool, the friends, the parties—but sometimes, getting ready for work, checking items off a checklist, she thought how great it'd be to simply sit on the floor with Razzie and Davey while they were fresh from sleep, loving the feel of their pudgy little fingers, looking at the curve of their ears, listening to their lisping voices. A whole day would go like this, in her fantasy. Outside there were still piles of snow from three days ago, but in here, the heater softly hummed, and the house that Jeff and his buddies had designed for their family had a solid, secure, almost quilted feel to it. Nothing could harm her here. It was where she belonged.

But of course she'd get tired of hanging out here every day. Running her own business—now that was actually fun, spending every day with her six employees/friends, designing events, like "Fun with Your Blow-Dryer" and "Manicures and Margaritas." Write-ups and even an award for Best Salon in the local paper. Sure, there was paperwork, and there were hassles and challenges, but she thrived there, rather like a tightrope walker who's discovered just the right pace to make it across to the other side, and knows better than to look down.

Out of the corner of her eye, she watched as Chloe searched for her Elsa dress, and when the time was right—as she was putting on the boys' overalls and snapping up the crotches—she said casually, "Oh, Chloe, honey, the Elsa dress had a big stain on it so I sent it out to the dry cleaners."

That was not even remotely true; the truth was that at three in the morning, when Lindy came in to comfort Davey, she'd seen it on the floor and had whisked it away to the top of the closet, so that Chloe wouldn't put it on this morning.

"You sent it to the *fry cleaners*?" Chloe said. Her eyes were wild.

There were sixty-three floorboards between here and the wall. And sixty-three was divisible by three, which was good.

"Dry. Dry cleaners," she said. "So they can get the stain out. It looked like grease."

"Why couldn't you just wash it?"

"Because it looked like grease. They need their special chemicals for that."

"It didn't have grease!" Chloe spun around and landed on the bed. "It didn't have grease!"

"All little children who want Daddy Dragon Eggs better get down here!" bellowed Jeff from downstairs.

"Go, boys. Daddy has your eggs." It was seventeen minutes until her mother came. Odd—good. Lindy shuffled the boys over to the stairs and they worked their way down, holding onto the railing and shouting as they went. She walked into Chloe's room—all decorated in pink and lavender—where Chloe was now lying on the floor in a heap, sniffling about how the boys had each other but she had no one to play with. Why couldn't she have a twin sister? It wasn't fair.

"If I had a twin sister, I could wear *her* Elsa dress," she said, and Lindy laughed at the crazy logic of that, and then Chloe said, "You can't laugh at me! You *have* a sister, so you can't laugh at people who don't have sisters! It's not nice."

Little do you know, thought Lindy. *This morning I seem to have a surplus of sisters.* And once again Nina's face showed up in front of her. Was this the way it was going to be, Nina popping up in her thoughts all the damn time? Those embarrassingly yearning eyes, and the way she'd tried to seem so brave when anybody could see she was about to dissolve into tears! *You were adopted, get over it.*

She shivered. "Listen, let's think of something else you can wear for your picture, since the Elsa dress isn't happening."

"If I can't be Elsa," said Chloe, bouncing on the bed, "then I'm not getting my picture taken at all."

"Well," said Lindy, "I think you are definitely going to want to have your picture taken, because when you grow up, this is going to be the official picture of how you looked in kindergarten, and you're going to want to look back and see yourself. Also there will be one of your whole class standing together, and trust me, it's going to be so much fun to look at it when you're older and see how everybody turned out."

"No, thank you." Chloe bounced up and down. "I don't care how they turned out. Not if I can't be Elsa."

"Chloe."

"No, Mommy. Me and Juniper and Jasmine and Malarkey *said* we were all going to be Elsa on picture day, so I have to."

Thirteen minutes until Peggy Walsh time.

"Listen," said Lindy. "I *might* have a solution. Let's do your hair like Elsa—and then you'll look more like her than anyone else. You're the only one who has long blonde hair like the real Elsa, and I can put it in a long braid, and you can wear it over your shoulder."

Chloe was briefly silent as she weighed her options. "Okay, but I'm not going to wear some other dress. Because that would look like I just *thought* I looked like what Elsa would wear but I didn't really know."

God, it was like negotiating in the Middle East.

"Fine," said Lindy. "No dress then. I get that. Let's think of what Elsa would like if she didn't have to wear all those dresses."

"CHLOE!" called Jeff. "YOUR EGGS ARE GETTING COLD!"

"A FEW MORE MINUTES!" Lindy called. Then to Chloe: "We need to hurry."

"I think Elsa would like purple if somebody asked her."

"Yes," said Lindy. "I think she would." She held her breath. "Do you know what I think Elsa would think was really, really special? Your purple tunic with the yellow-and-purple-striped leggings."

There was a long silence while Chloe stared into the closet. Then she said, "I agree that she would *like* leggings, but only if she could wear the purple Ugg boots with them. Then she would *love* it. And the tiara. And the long braid."

Lindy felt anxiety drain from her as though some benevolent force had reached down and uncorked her head.

Then it was crazytime. She got Chloe dressed and her hair braided, and then she ran downstairs and put the vegetables into the slow cooker with Sunday's homemade broth. Jeff had somehow managed to jump in the downstairs shower while the twins ate, and was now standing around in his bathrobe, making a pot of coffee for her mother before she got here. His coffee was a private joke between him and her mother; she called it his "fancy-schmancy gourmet-snob coffee," as opposed to what he called her "rot-gut high-octane stuff," that he claimed was going to kill her.

Lindy was on her game, ready for the big finish, as she made Chloe's lunch. "Do you want spinach on your turkey sandwich?" she asked her daughter.

"Can't I have peanut butter and honey?"

"Oh, sweetie, there isn't any honey. Could you have spinach and turkey just for today?"

"Okayyy, but just turkey. *No* spinach."

Razzie stood up in his high chair and tried to climb out over the tray, and Lindy put down the knife and swooped in to grab him, all the while saying to Chloe, "You need a vegetable," without missing a beat. She put Razzie on her hip. "How about carrot sticks on the side?"

"Ohhhh . . . kay. If I have to." Pouting.

"And today you need to eat your apple, too. Okay? Razzie, I'm putting you back in your chair."

"I done, I done," he said.

"Okay, then why don't you wipe your mouth on your napkin—no, not on your sleeve, please. Go and play until Davey is finished, too."

He opened the drawer with the Tupperware and started unpacking it and stacking it on the floor. At first she was going to stop him—it actually pained her to see what a mess he was making—but she reminded herself it was easier just to clean it up later than to enrage him, and she went back to making the sandwich.

Over the pounding of the blood in her head, she saw her mother's car pull into the gravel driveway and stop just past the snowdrifts, and she cast a desperate look around the kitchen to see if everything was indeed done. "Here. Would you put the sandwich in the lunch box?" she said, in a sudden panic. She'd remembered that she'd left the bill for her new turquoise coat on the dining room table. Her mother would be relentless about that one.

"But I'm late!" Jeff said. "And maybe you've noticed I'm not exactly dressed for work."

"We're all late," she said. She ran through the dining room and swooped down on the invoice just as, from the kitchen, she could hear her mother greeting the children, who were going appropriately ape-shit wild over her.

"Chocolate doughnuts!" she heard Chloe yell.

And her mother's voice: "I see she's got *you* doing all the work this morning while she dolls herself up."

And Jeff, damn him, laughing indulgently. "Emeritus, wait 'til you try *today's* coffee."

"I'm not drinking that yuppie pretentious stuff!"

"You don't know what you're missing."

Lindy went into the kitchen just as her mother discovered that Chloe had Ugg boots on. More pretention alarms were going off.

"Well, look at those feet, young lady!" her mother was saying. She shook her head at Lindy. "I cannot believe what I'm seeing."

"Hi, Mama. You look beautiful today," Lindy said as she reached over to get Chloe's lunch box and backpack, and nudged her daughter toward the door.

"Well," said her mother. "I'm not so sure of *that*. You know me. I don't much care how I look, as long as my children and grandchildren know me. That's what's important."

"I agree," said Lindy, and she kissed Jeff on the cheek and bent down to hug the twins and grabbed her evil Coach bag and gave her mother an extra-big hug. "You're the tops, Mom. Aces."

NINE

NINA

Dear Phoebe Mullen,
Hello. My name is Nina Popkin, This letter is the hardest letter I have ever written in my life. My heart, as it happens, is in my throat as I'm typing these words to you. I am your daughter . . .

Dear Phoebe,
Hi! Guess what! I am your long-lost daughter. The one you named Kate and gave away when I was fifteen months old, and while I don't have any hard feelings about that, I just would like very much to meet you and

Dear Lulu aka Phoebe aka Mom,

I saw you on YouTube, and heard you sing. You sing like an angel, and I seem to remember that once you sang to me. I don't want to frighten you or anything, and maybe you should sit down before you read any more of this letter, because I am your daughter Kate. Kate whom you put up for adoption. I am thirty-five now, as I hope you are aware.

Would you be open to meeting me? I know that my birth and adoption must have been a very painful time, and that you were just a young girl when it happened, and I don't want to make you feel uncomfortable because, believe me, I don't want ANYTHING from you. I just want to see you and maybe hear your voice and find out why you needed to give me away. I promise that if you agree to see me, I will be very grateful and will not make you sad in any way. Because everything turned out GREAT for me! Really great. I was raised by a good family, I promise you! But I've always wondered who you are, and who I really belong to. You know? My adopted mother says she has a picture of you and me together, with a guy who's probably my father, and she (my mother) just died and I haven't found the picture yet, but that's because she saved every single piece of paper she ever touched in her life and I am still going through all of them but I just so much want to believe that you really wanted me and that

Also, I found my sister. The one you named Poppet. Her name is Lindy now. She is also fine. If you agree to see me, maybe she would come, but she might not. I hope this doesn't hurt your feelings. I recently met her, and we are not exactly friends. Not yet, at least. LOL.

Oh, and another thing. I know about Lulu and the Starbabies. Wow! You were beautiful.

Please call me. Please, please, just a phone call would mean so much.

And if you don't call, I won't bother you. I promise.

With love,

Your little baby Kate

Nina Popkin

I put down my pen and cracked my knuckles. It was Saturday, and I was curled up on Carter's couch in his temporary rental condo, which was furnished in a style that could only be described as "1970s' Bachelor." Plastic leatherish couch, protozoan-shaped coffee table in fake walnut, gold shag carpet, and, yes, a lava lamp. An honest-to-god lava lamp.

Tyler, covered in an old brown Army blanket that looked so scratchy it was almost like a punishment, was hunched over some iThing, and Indigo was sprawled out on the floor, scrolling through her phone, wrapped in a black fleece throw with pictures of skulls on it, and sniffling every now and then. Outside the sliding door we could see the snow coming down in big fat flakes in the dying light of late afternoon, but inside there was nothing but misery.

Carter was in the bedroom with the door closed, but we could all hear snippets of his quiet, serious conversation with his ex. "For Christ's sake, Jane, this has been at the speed of light. Of course they're going to be upset, what did you expect?"

"*I'm* not upset," said Indigo from the rug. "She should just get the hell out of here if that's what she wants to fucking do with her life, and we'll raise ourselves. It's fine. Don't give it another thought."

Tyler said, "Oh, right. You're not upset one little bit."

"Shut up," she said.

"No, you shut up."

"No, you shut up."

I sighed loudly, without meaning to, and when they looked at me, I said, "Oh sorry. I'm just writing to my mom. Hoping to say *something* that will make her want to see me." I laughed a little. "This whole mom system, right? Leaves a lot to be desired."

Indigo told Tyler, "She got adopted as a baby, and now she's trying to find her real mom." He nodded.

"Yeah, I found out she was this famous singer in the eighties—" I said.

"Oh. Who?" he said. He looked interested and not just out of politeness.

"Nobody you ever heard of, dude. She was Lulu and the Starbabies," Indigo said.

"Was she famous?" he wanted to know.

"Yeah, at the time," I said. "But her real name is Phoebe. Phoebe Louise Mullen."

"She just learned her mom's name yesterday," Indigo said. "And get this: a nun let her look at her birth certificate, which she shouldn't have done because it's illegal, but which she did anyway because she felt so sorry for Nina. And get *this*: her mother had Nina when she was fifteen years old. No offense, but I think that's kind of gross."

I was startled. I hadn't realized she had taken all that in while Melanie and I were talking and scrolling through the pictures the day before.

They stared back down at their screens. From the bedroom we could hear Carter's raised voice saying, "No, no, we all know how you've waited for this opportunity, Jane. But you can't blame Kayla for being hurt. They're not raised yet, you know. You and I made a *deal*. Shared custody, living in the same town."

"Anybody else feel like a walk?" I said.

"Anybody else feel like a bottle of arsenic?" said Tyler, and I couldn't help it—I laughed. And he looked at me and laughed a little bit, too. Then I helped Indigo up off the rug and the three of us wandered into the kitchen nook and I handed out forks, and we stood at the counter eating the rest of the blueberry pie right out of the pan. Tyler put on some rap music, which did a great job of covering up whatever pain and heartache was going on in the next room. They scraped their forks along the metal pan in a way that made my teeth hurt.

"C'mon, Ty. Seriously? How's Dad gonna take care of us?" said Indigo. "His food is lousy, he can't do laundry; I don't think he even knows he has to get us places."

"Why are you always so hard on him?" Tyler said. "He's like the best, most caring dad ever, and he's going to be awesome to live with. It's going to be fine."

"This just sucks. Why didn't she ask me to go with her to the farm? I'd move to a farm in a heartbeat."

I put the pie plate in the sink and stared out the window.

He laughed. "You'd go to a farm? Really, *you* would go to a farm. You'd hate it, you know that? Some small-town bullshit, kids who've lived there forever. What? You want to start being a 4-H kid? Think they're going to like those combat boots and that purple hair? You'd be a pariah."

"I'm a pariah now, dumbass. Nobody likes me."

To my surprise, he looked pained. "That's not true. Nobody in high school ever thinks anybody likes them. And anyway, you have Maya. One best friend is all you need."

"I have it in *writing* they don't like me. Look at my Facebook some-time, huh? And Maya only likes me because she's new, and she's not in with the other kids yet. Once she realizes she doesn't have to hang with me, she's gone. Believe me, they hate me there. Nobody ever even *likes* my Instagram. I post all kinds of stuff, and nobody responds. Nobody! Do you know what that feels like?"

"So what? God. You take all this shit way too hard," Tyler said. "High school sucks, but you think moving to a farm in Virginia is the answer? The answer is *you*. You've just gotta give people a break sometimes."

"I give everybody a break. But nobody gives me one."

"You could start by giving Dad a break. He drops everything whenever you need him. Look at that. He adores you."

"Easy for you to say. You're the golden child. Plus, you're off to college next year, and you've got your own car. Know how many times Dad forgot to take me to therapy? Three times! Three, Tyler."

I rested my head against the window glass. There had been therapy. That was probably a good thing. There was so much I was going to have to learn. If I stuck this out, that is. I couldn't quite wrap my head around the fact that sometimes Indigo sounded like a thirty-year-old and then seconds later could be a petulant child.

"*I'll* pick you up and take you there, all right?" he said. "Just stop, will you?"

After a moment, I turned away from the window. "Hey, I think we should go get some ice cream or something."

Nobody even looked in my direction.

"It was like a joke with my therapist," Indigo said. "Oh, it must be Dad's day again! Clocks aren't really his thing, huh? Ha ha ha."

"Dad is Dad," said Tyler. "I think Mom didn't tell him when the schedule changed, is what happened."

"Okay, so what if that's right? Then why didn't he ask?"

"Listen to yourself! He didn't know it got changed, so how could he know to ask? Be reasonable, Indigo. It's all going to be fine. I'll come if he can't."

"You have rehearsals. For your play. Or don't you remember?"

I cleared my throat. "Maybe I could pick you up," I heard myself say. "I'm not always busy at work these days, so I bet . . . maybe . . ."

"Fine," said Indigo, folding her arms and throwing herself down on the couch. "But I'm thinking maybe I'll just quit therapy anyway. It's too much of a hassle. It's not helping. Obvi! Just *look* at me!"

We all watched the snow coming down hard now, which was what had made me think of ice cream in the first place, the way it clumped in hills and mounds, covering everything. I had a sick feeling in the pit of my stomach, like all this was way beyond anything I could ever fix or know what to say about. If this was modern-day family life, I probably wasn't going to be up to it. I staggered over to the couch and plopped down next to Indigo, and to my surprise, she scooted over and put her head on my shoulder. I gazed down into the strands of her dark purple hair.

We were still sitting like that when Carter came out of the bedroom. He looked tired but determined to be cheerful, to put the best possible spin on everything. I actually felt a little bit sorry for him, coming out to find his children in such a heap.

"Oh my, my, my," he said. "It's going to be okay. Don't worry! Oh my goodness, it's so gloomy in here. Let's turn on the lights, shall we, and figure out what to do about dinner."

I confess that what I wanted more than anything in the world right then was to get in my car and drive fast down the road, get back to my mother's halfway-dismantled apartment, and turn off the phone and stay there until Carter and his children forgot my name.

I'd learn some Lulu and the Starbabies songs and go find Phoebe Louise Mullen and be her family, and oh, it would be so great, my *real family*—we'd sit around the supper table and sing fun songs to each other in the calm weekend twilight, and she'd say, "Oh Kate, baby, I'm so glad you found me."

Carter was going into the kitchen and assessing the bleak contents of the refrigerator. He said he was going to go buy some stuff for dinner. Maybe they should get a cheesecake. Would people like the plain kind or the kind with the cherries on the top?

He cracked his knuckles and looked at me and the kids, all sitting on the couch wrapped in their blankets, and he sighed.

"Okay, I know you're upset," he said. "Here's what's happening. Your mom is leaving at the end of next week, and I'm going to move back home. I know this sucks for you, and it probably comes as a big shock, but we'll make it work. Okay? We can do it."

"Sure," said Tyler.

"Kayla?" he said. "I know you wanted to go with her, and I'm sorry that won't work out. But maybe you can go for visits, and Mom'll come home a few times, I'm sure. And I told her we'd have a weekly Skype date. Okay?"

"What's gonna happen when the boat season gets super busy, and you can't be home?" Indigo said. "What about that?" She looked up at me. "Are you going to help? Are *you* going to move in with us?" she said.

"I . . . don't know," I said.

Carter looked pained. "Kayla, please. Don't put Nina on the spot."

She was still looking at me, with those big, blank, mascara-less eyes. She looked like a giant, smooth-faced, purple-haired baby, and she was pulling me in. I could feel the tug of her. She mouthed, "Please help, pleeeeease."

"Listen, this is for seven months," Carter was saying. "We all just have to try. Okay? Can we do it? We'll make it an adventure."

I'm ninety-percent sure he just meant the three of them, but they were all staring at me, with these pathetic pound-puppy expressions on their faces. And I admit, I could feel the same crazy what-the-hell impulse working on me again, that little pulsing that makes me get involved with guys too soon, way before I've thought everything through.

Only now it wasn't just a man. It was also two kids, and it was as if I were already being carried off down the current of them.

With an immense struggle, I got to my feet, pushed aside the blanket with the skulls. My throat felt clotted up, like I'd swallowed a whole wad of sorrow or something.

"You know, I've really got to go," I said. "I have . . . a thing. I forgot. I'm supposed to do some work tonight." I found my boots over by the door and pushed my feet into them. Gathered up my purse, which was lying on the floor next to the chair.

"Sure," said Carter.

"We'll talk later," I said. He came over to kiss me on the cheek, and I gave him a quick peck and fled. Out into what was surely going to be the last snow of the season, already coating my windshield and my car with ice.

◆　◆　◆

I drove back to my mom's condo, and walked through it, turning on all the lights as I went. I could hear televisions blaring through the walls from the neighboring units, and somewhere a dog barked. But basically there was a delicious, sweet silence filling the place. I could take a long hot bath, then order Chinese takeout, and stream a Netflix movie to watch in bed. I could sleep all night without having to talk to anybody. I could cry if I wanted to. Or write in my journal. Talk to my friends on the phone.

Heaven.

I kicked off my boots and picked up all the mail on the floor in the front hallway. There were bills, bills, bills, and underneath everything, a card from my mother's hairdresser. "How I miss your sweet, smiling mother!" she wrote. "Every three months that sweet little perm and once a week the wash and set. She always told me stories about you. So proud! A mother is a tough person to lose. Hope you're doing okay."

And I was stabbed with grief again.

The darkness pressed against the kitchen window, and even when I closed the blinds, it still managed to seep between the slats, coming for me. Usually I could feel my mom here, could sense her presence among the pots and pans and the tea cozy and the candy dishes in the living room. But now she had gone and this was simply a condo in need of a coat of paint and some spiffing up. The shell of her life and illness. The place where everything had come to an end. It seemed like years instead of six weeks since the morning I'd thrown out all the casserole food.

I took a hot bath, but the water wasn't quite hot enough, then the phone started ringing so I got out. It was only a telemarketer wanting me to consider giving myself a chance to win a cruise. I hung up without responding, and stood there shivering in my mom's bedroom, wondering what to do next.

Cry, cook some dinner, call Melanie? I didn't know what to do with myself. I went into the kitchen and sat down on the cold kitchen floor, still wrapped in the towel. My mother might be found in the kitchen after all, if I concentrated.

Josephine . . . Mom, I said. *I'm so lost. And I'm lonely.*

Please help, pleeeease.

That was what Indigo had said.

Oh yes. There's an Indigo now, I said to my mom. *You wouldn't believe her. So precocious and so feisty and yet so young and sweet-spirited and troubled, too. And she has a brother named Tyler who seems to want to skate through the world playing music. And their father . . . he might love me. I love him, I think.*

But I don't know how to help them. They are all so bereft.

We are all so bereft. You have to choose happiness. Happiness is a matter of making up your mind.

That last one may have been my mother's voice. It was hard to tell.

I sat there waiting to see if she had anything more to add. And then I stood up, got dressed, and threw some more clothes in a bag, and I turned off all the lights and turned the heat down, and I got in my car and I drove to Carter's stupid little apartment.

And there they all were: laughing and arguing and eating cheesecake, trying to figure out if real cheesecake was better when it was the dry kind or the soft, mushy kind. Tyler was looking up cheesecake on Wikipedia, and Indigo was sketching something on a pizza box. They all stared at me in surprise, and Indigo smiled. What kind of cheesecake did I like? And was I one of the pathetic people who insisted it have fruit on it? That was from Tyler.

I stood up for fruit; I did. And got ridiculed for it, until Indigo came over and linked her arm in mine and said there were worse things than fruit on cheesecake and that I could probably be taught to appreciate the finer things, like mushy soft cheese.

"Which Beatle was the drummer?" Carter asked me, laughing. "You can't have cake until you answer that correctly. His initials are RS."

"Rick Springfield!" I said, and laughing, he kissed me, right in front of his kids.

Later, they shuffled off to stare at their screens some more. They fought over what music should play on the stereo; Carter was for soft jazz, which he implored them to listen to and like, but Tyler wanted folk songs, and Indigo wanted rap. They bickered and squabbled. The heater made too much noise. Carter said Tyler should scrape the car windshields now that the snow had stopped. Tyler said he was too tired.

I had to breathe deeply. My little suitcase was still near the door, looking like it was going to stay here for good.

And then I made myself think of one beautiful moment. When I had arrived there that night, when I had returned, Carter, wearing an apron, had let me in, and his eyes had widened at the sight of me there, like a child who sees that he wasn't abandoned after all. It sledgehammered my stony little heart, that look. And before he told the kids I was there—for just a moment—we stood in the hallway, out of sight of the kids, and he had gathered me up and kissed me, tangling his fingers in my coils of curly hair.

"Are you really back?" he whispered. His crinkly eyes smiling, looking right into mine.

"I am," I said. "I want to move in." I had heard a buzzing in my ears. Part of me was saying, *Stop, stop!* But there was something else, saying, *This could be love, this could be family, this is what you need to take a chance on.*

So this was love. I had decided. Sometimes you just have to make up your mind to let it in.

TEN

LINDY

"I know you said I shouldn't come, but I'm going crazy with my hair."

Lindy, who'd been straightening a display of hair conditioners, looked up from the counter to see Nina standing in the shop like she was a real customer, someone with an actual appointment. Nina, with a nervous—perhaps even hysterical—smile on her face, Lindy thought, removed a navy-blue watch cap that was doing her no favors, hair-wise, and shook her head at Lindy. "Look at this frizz. I think it's dry from the heater being on all the time. That's a thing, isn't it? Heater hair?"

Lindy could feel that her lips had gone into a straight line. She'd been in the back doing next week's schedule, and then for some stupid reason, unfathomable to her now, she'd come out to the front desk to check something on the computer and then gotten involved with the bottles of conditioner. Their labels needed to face the same way. She couldn't imagine why she was here. Her brain had gone blank.

She did not want everyone in the salon to know about this adoption/long-lost-sister-drama thing. That's all she needed, to have some unsavory personal story becoming the subject of gossip and speculation. It had been two weeks since she'd met Nina, and she still hadn't decided how she felt about the whole thing.

She was, frankly, already a little rattled today. Jeff had texted her that he was going to grab some beers with a client after work. Just like that: not a question, a statement. She'd typed back, *Sure. Why not? Why ever would I mind doing all the cooking and child care and cleaning? Have a ball!* And he hadn't answered. So *fine.* She might have to explain the finer points of sarcasm to him once he got home.

Now she shifted gears. She looked around to see if anyone was watching her. No one was paying a bit of attention. The salon had its afternoon buzz—jazz playing softly, women's voices and laughter in the background. The comforting smell of hair products and perfume. She leaned across the counter and said, "Nina, I'm sorry, but I thought we decided . . ."

Nina looked as though she might cry. "I know, I'm sorry, we did. Listen," she said, in a low voice. "I really hesitated before coming here, but it's just that so much has happened since I met you, and I wanted you to know some news."

"I thought we agreed that I don't *want* any news," said Lindy. "I'm not interested in finding out anything else. I can't—" She tapped quickly on the countertop—five, seven, nine times. She'd go to twenty-five if necessary, but she didn't want to go that far. "Really. I'm sure you're very nice and all, and I don't want to hurt your feelings, but I can't. I don't want to know. I'm not like you."

Megan, the receptionist, came up to the front then and turned a charming smile to Nina and said, "Did you have an appointment?"

"No, but I'd like to make one," said Nina quickly. "I think I need . . . what is it again? A ker—"

"Keratin treatment," said Lindy, through her teeth.

"Fine," said Megan, who started scrolling on the computer screen. "Do you want it with Lindy, then?"

"No," said Lindy as Nina said yes. Megan laughed and looked flustered.

"Wait. Could we have a moment?" said Nina. "Lindy? Please?"

Lindy hesitated. "All right, come into the back." She gave a huge sigh so it would be clear that this was a one-time thing only, then led the way through the shop. She was going to have to be firmer about this in the future, or she'd be caught up in all kinds of drama that she didn't need and didn't have time for. Lindy could feel Nina taking in the purple walls with the exposed brick, and the individual stations with their black onyx countertops, and all the friendly, shiny-haired employees working on clients' hair and chatting.

She ushered Nina into her office and closed the door, tapping three times on the door frame. Her desk, she was pleased to see, was at its best: organized, with things stacked in their proper places, the chair pushed in just so, the Tiffany-style lamp dust free and giving off a warm glow . . .

"Wow," said Nina. "This place you have here is wonderful. Look at that lamp! That's the real deal, isn't it? I kind of know about furnishings because of my job, so I really can appreciate how well you've decorated this place. It's got good feng shui. I'm always trying to bring some feng shui to my clients, and you've got it in spades."

"Thank you," said Lindy. She sat at her desk and folded her hands so she wouldn't tap.

"Oh, and I brought you something," Nina said. She dug around in her bag, and Lindy could see that her purse was filled with haphazard pieces of paper, a CD, a wallet bulging with coins, a hairbrush, two pots of lip gloss, and a mascara wand, most of which tumbled out onto the carpet. To Lindy's surprise, Nina used the toe of her boot—her boot, that had just been walking on the sidewalk!—to nudge the items over so she could easily scoop them up. Lindy felt her hairline tingle at the sight of this. She had to squeeze her fingers and close her eyes for a moment.

"It's one of those energy bars—and a bottle of vitamin water," Nina said, and finally produced them. Lindy hesitated before she took them. "I figured you were probably really busy here and didn't have much time to eat most days."

"Yes. Thank you. Did you have something you wanted to tell me?"

"I found out our mother's name."

Lindy felt her color rise. Now this—here was the exact problem. This had been something she'd been trying not to think about. What if her birth mother also turned out to be someone she knew? What if the whole horrible situation that had led to her being given up for adoption was now going to take up residence in her life and her thoughts, ruining everything? "Listen, I—"

"I know, I know. And I'm really sorry for bothering you."

Lindy squeezed her eyes closed.

"Could I just tell you this? Please?"

"All right," Lindy said through clenched teeth. "One thing."

"After you left Sister Germaine's office the other day—now promise you won't tell anybody this—but she actually left me there with our records. She told me I'd be alone with the files for ten minutes. And she gave me a really long look, full of eyebrows, like, *Do you get what I'm talking about?* And so, as soon as she left, I went and looked at the files. And there were our birth certificates! The real ones. I had enough time to read them both. We already knew you were Poppet, but guess what! I was called Kate. Can you believe that? Not even Katherine. Just Kate."

"Huh," said Lindy.

"Our mother was Phoebe Louise Mullen. Neither birth certificate listed a father's name for us."

"Good. I don't care who he was."

"Of course you don't. But I googled our mother and found out that she lives in Brooklyn. And guess what? She was actually sort of famous for a while. She was in an eighties girl band called Lulu and the Starbabies. Did you ever hear of them?"

Lindy started putting the papers on her desk at right angles, without looking at Nina. "No. I haven't ever heard of . . . Lucy and the Whaty-whats."

Nina laughed. "Lulu and the Starbabies. No, I hadn't heard of them either until now. It's the weirdest thing to think about, isn't it—that she exists out there in the world somewhere, and that she had this big life after she gave us up, and that with modern-day technology we can actually *see* her. She's on YouTube." She shoved her long legs out in front of her. Her skinny jeans had a well-placed little frayed spot right on the thigh. She smiled at Lindy with her bright hazel eyes. "She kind of looks like us."

"I don't think I'm going to see it. I told you, I don't—"

"Oh, but it's so interesting. Really, you don't want to see your famous mom dancing around on a stage and singing songs?" She got out her phone and pushed some buttons and tinny music curled out of it as she placed it on the desk.

"I—can't," said Lindy. Her head was starting to hurt. "Listen, this doesn't make me want to know her. This makes it worse, that she was famous. She isn't somebody who cared about us."

Nina turned off the phone. "Okay. Fair enough. Well. I thought maybe seeing her would make you *less* mad at her, but maybe not."

"You don't understand. I'm not one bit mad at her. I'm indifferent to her. I don't want to know anything about her."

"Okay," Nina said. She looked around the office. "Wow, this place is simply extraordinary! I can't get over it. How long have you been here?"

Lindy let a long beat of silence go by and then said, "Four years."

Nina smiled at her. "So your little Chloe was just a baby when you started it? It really is very nice."

"Thank you," said Lindy.

"Oh, another thing," said Nina. "It turns out that I've—well, I'm working on getting myself a family, too. Like you told me to. Sorry!

I'm not implying that I'm doing it because you told me to or anything, but—well, I moved in with that guy."

"That guy?"

"Yeah, remember? The one I told you I was seeing? The one you told me to marry, which was probably very, very good advice, and I'm thinking hard about it. His ex-wife has taken off to save the world apparently, one leaf of kale at a time, and he's got custody of the kids so I moved in with him to help him."

"Wait. You *moved in* with him to help him? As I recall, you'd only been seeing him for a few weeks. Why didn't you just offer to take meals over sometimes? Wouldn't that have been better?"

People lead such messy lives, Lindy thought. *The life coach would have a field day with this one.*

To her surprise, Nina laughed. "Well. No. I mean, I guess I moved there not *just* to help him—that does sound kind of lame, doesn't it? I moved in with him because I love him, and we're seeing if, you know, things work out. If we can be a family. You know."

Lindy shook her head. This woman was making her so tired. "Listen, don't take this the wrong way, but do you think you possibly have an impulse disorder?"

Nina laughed again in what sounded suspiciously like delight. "I might. I'm always jumping into things and then trying to figure them out later. If you knew how many boyfriends I'd had, you'd probably want nothing to do with me."

Lindy managed to keep herself from pointing out that she already didn't want to have anything to do with her. Instead she said, "How many?"

"Oh, hell, I don't know. Probably around thirty-seven. Does that seem like too many?"

"Do you know how many I've had? One, and I married him. Two if you count a guy from tenth grade who took me to the school dance and then tried to feel me up, so I threw my cup of Coke at him."

"As you should have. Maybe that's what I'll tell Indigo to do. That's Carter's daughter; she's fifteen and a handful."

Lindy shuffled things on her desk. Her hand was shaking just a little. Chaos did that to her.

"You did tell me to get married to Carter, though, and have babies so I wouldn't think about our mom so much."

"Did I say that?"

"You did. I probably wouldn't have moved in with him so soon—I mean, I do have *some* sense, most of the time at least—but then his ex left, and he has these two kids, and they're kind of sad, really. And I like them, although I don't really know a lot about kids. Still, I have a lot of good will, and maybe that will see us through, you know? Also, it's only until the end of the summer. Then the boy is going to college, and the girl is going to live with her mom."

"I have to get back," Lindy said, standing up. "You know, I have—"

Nina took a deep breath and stood up, too. "So, the other *big* thing I wanted to tell you is that I wrote our mom a letter. And if she answers, maybe we'll get some more answers."

"Look, I really hate to be rude, but I have a ton of things to do." It was after four, and tonight was the school open house, and she had to make a speech about how the PTA was going to finance computers for the first grade. And she was on a fitness regimen and she was determined to walk ten thousand steps every day, and she had to pick up the sitter on her way home.

"I'm sorry. I really would never want to make you feel bad. I just keep thinking how it is that we're sisters, and if things had been different, the way they should have been, we would have grown up in the same house. We'd be Kate and Poppet, hanging out. We would've loved each other. After all, I'm your first relative. Really."

She smiled then, such a sad, longing smile that Lindy had to close her eyes to keep it from piercing her.

After that, Lindy had an unmistakable headache. What was she *doing*, letting this woman into her life? She finished paying the bills, then walked through the salon and tried to smile and nod at the customers. It always helped to be out on the floor, seeing how smoothly it all ran. She told Marietta Beasley that her new haircut made her look twenty years younger, and she fetched hair glaze for Susannah's station, and did a rinse-out for Kimba, who was overwhelmed with two customers needing attention at once.

She had to clear her head and get her bearings again, get Nina out of her system. It was so weird to think that she might have been somebody else—that if she'd been Poppet, she would be an altogether different sort of person.

It was time to think about tonight. She'd have to get up in front of the whole assembly of parents and make a speech. Why had she said she'd do this? She knew exactly why: because Heather Quinlan, the PTA president, had said publicly at last month's meeting that Lindy was a superhero, and announced that the PTA couldn't have possibly put together either the Halloween carnival *or* the Holiday Teacher Appreciation Breakfast without Lindy organizing them. And then, even more important, Heather had also come into the salon with her adorable daughter, Jenesis, and they'd gotten matching haircuts and then raved about the place. And after that, Heather had told at least five other moms how great A Little Bit of Heaven was, so Lindy had run a mother-daughter special that caught on like wildfire.

Which meant that now she had to put on her superhero demeanor. Which called for caffeine. Restless, she went out for a Skinny Soy Latte, aware too late that she was only getting it because it was the drink Heather Quinlan had brought her the day of the haircut, presenting it to her like it was the only possible drink anyone would ever order. She hadn't even liked it particularly, so why had she ordered it?

To fit in, said the voice in her head. *Because you're always trying to fit in. Because you think you don't belong. Which might also be why Nina drives you so crazy, all that naked need in her face.* She shivered.

Walking back to the salon, she called Jeff on his cell and suggested that since they already had a babysitter lined up for the evening, maybe they could go out to dinner after the open house. To her surprise, he agreed.

"We haven't eaten out without the kids in so long," she said. "It's like a date. We can discuss adult subjects."

"What *adult* subjects did you have in mind—things along the lines of world peace and climate change, or more like sex toys and porn flicks?" he said, and he laughed in that low, sly way he used to, and she felt somehow cheered up. It was snowing outside the salon window, and the sight of the fat white flakes didn't have their usual effect of making her feel tired and sick of winter; instead, she felt buoyant and hopeful. The nice blanket of a late March snow would cover the gray landscape, and Lindy and Jeff's marriage would be healed by an evening out, a couple of drinks and candlelight, and good conversation. She would finally have his attention long enough to tell him about Nina, how exasperating and tenacious she was, how there seemed to be a yearning in Nina that was almost scary at times, but that also was . . . well, fascinating. Maybe she'd trail her hand along his thigh under the tablecloth, like she'd done once when they were dating and maybe they'd repeat what they did on that long-ago night: rush out of the restaurant, leaving their dinner half-eaten, and make love in their parked car.

The school looked beautiful, all lit up against the snow. The classrooms were colorful and inviting, and parents stood and sipped apple cider and ate sugar cookies in the cafeteria/auditorium while from the stage Heather Quinlan talked to them about how *important* and *terrific* and *awesome* it was that they supported their children's education by coming out to see the teachers midyear this way. She actually used those words, putting each one in italics as she spoke.

"Good lord, she missed a career on the stage," whispered Carly McDonald to Lindy, and Lindy smiled. "Does she *always* have to *overact?*"

"I think she's nice," Lindy said. "And oh, Carly, this is my husband, Jeff."

Jeff, always presentable at these kinds of things, leaned over and shook Carly's hand, smiling, and then Carly told him what a wonderful wife he had, and he grinned and nodded as if he thought so, too. Just then a group of kindergarten teachers came over and started complimenting Lindy's outfit, telling her they were coming in for haircuts now that spring was practically here. Someone thanked her for the teacher breakfast and then they all cooed about how that breakfast had been the best ever, in all their years of teaching. Brilliant, just brilliant, to have that young guy play the guitar for them. And the little gift bags of hair products—so lovely!

Then it was time for her to go onstage and give her report—and even though she was nervous walking up onto the stage, she counted out the seven steps (lucky!) and then she was perfectly relaxed looking out at the smiling faces of the crowd—all of them her friends. She belonged at last.

Afterward, Jeff stood beaming at her side as person after person talked to her. She could feel him there, the supportive husband, and he was maybe even blown away to see how many people *liked* her. She, who'd always been so shy, so afraid of being looked at, was now the center of attention. She felt herself loosening up, her smile becoming more genuine. When they talked to Chloe's teacher, Jeff was positively glowing in a way she hadn't seen for such a long time. He was so handsome compared to the other fathers, and really quite adorable as he tucked himself in at the tiny little kindergarten table. When he started admiring Chloe's drawings on the bulletin board, Lindy nearly melted. There it was again: that feeling as if she were floating above, squinting as she observed them—the handsome father, his hand lightly touching the wife's elbow, both of them leaning together as they admired their daughter's artwork, so blessed to have created this amazing child. And yes, the teacher was also mesmerized by him, by his easy-going smile, his divinely deep chuckle.

Later, on the way to the restaurant, she said, "So was this worth giving up a night of racquetball for?"

"To be out among the Lindy McIntyre Fan Club?" he teased. "Are you kidding? What could be better than that?" He steered the car through the snowy streets in silence and parked right in front of Il Forno, where they had gone on their last anniversary. She picked her way across the snow, and he took her arm.

Inside, it was dim and quiet, a Tuesday night crowd—or lack of one. There were a few people seated at the huge curved mahogany bar, talking in low voices, and at a couple of tables near the fireplace, which had a blaze that looked as though it was on its last hour. The hour *was* late for dinner on a weeknight, and for a moment Lindy was worried the staff would be annoyed at them. But it *was* their favorite—with the white tablecloths and the comfortable armchairs and the wall sconces and the deep paneling and the waiters who spoke almost in a whisper. They'd had so many good celebratory moments here: anniversaries, yes, but also the dinner when she told him she was pregnant with Chloe, and the summer night he told her they'd gotten the okay for the financing on the house. Now, she guessed, they were simply celebrating that they were still together, despite it all—or maybe, *maybe,* they were celebrating that she was up-and-coming in the world of the PTA and that they had finally arrived! They could live in this area without feeling like outsiders. Maybe that's what they could toast to.

The hostess led them to a table in the back, and Lindy couldn't help herself. She blurted out, "Oh, could we sit in the front by the window instead?" and then winced. Jeff always hated it when she asked for anything extra from service people, but now he smiled at her and said, "Yes, indeed, the window. We need to see and be seen tonight. Because that is *who we are.*"

Lindy grimaced. He couldn't help being slightly snarky, even on a night as great as this one. Once they were seated and the waiter had brought their glasses of wine and taken their dinner order, though, she reached over and grasped her husband's hand. "I'm so glad we're here! It's been so long! This really is like a date."

"That it is," he said. He crossed his legs and leaned back in his chair. His eyes were like little beads shining in the candlelight.

So she made small talk about safe subjects—Razzie's cold was getting better; Davey had put on Jeff's shoes and tried to walk downstairs wearing them; Chloe had found the Elsa dress at the top of the closet and gotten furious with Lindy for hiding it. On and on, smiling. No talk of work or schedules or, worse, racquetball nights.

"Oh!" she said, as though she'd only that moment thought of it, which wasn't true. She had hoped he would ask on his own. "I don't think I ever got to really tell you about Nina."

"Nina?" he said.

"My sister. No, not the usual sister." She waved her hand in the air. "The one who has the same birth parents as me. I told you I was going to the orphanage to meet her—remember when that nun called?"

"Yes. Oh yes!" he said. "Sorry. I remember now. And you met her, and I believe you said she was kind of . . . screwed up."

She frowned. Had she said that, really? "Yeah, well, she is, but there's more to her than that. It's mostly that she's kind of obsessed with this whole being-adopted thing. She told me she's spent her entire life wondering who she really is, wanting to go up to people in the street and ask them if they might be related. Can you imagine?"

Jeff took a sip of wine and glanced out the window.

She found herself tapping on her knee. One, two, three, four, five . . .

"So," she went on, "I feel sorry for her, of course, but I don't really get it. I never felt all that angst about adoption, as you know—and then today she showed up at the salon. Out of the blue. I took her back to my office, because frankly I don't want the whole salon to hear all this crap about me being adopted. She had somehow managed to look at our birth certificates and find out our real names, and our mother's name, and now there's no stopping her. Apparently."

She waited for him to answer. She had raised all kinds of issues that might lead to questions if she'd been talking to a normal person, she thought. His phone beeped in his pocket, and she telegraphed him, *Don't answer it, don't answer it.* He glanced at it surreptitiously but then looked back at her.

"So she's coming into your salon, and you don't want her there?"

"Well, I don't *know* if I want her there or not," Lindy said with a sigh. "It's a dilemma I'm having. I mean, she's kind of needy, and she wants me to care about finding our real mother, by which I mean our *birth mother,* and she's managed to find out who that woman is. So now she's going to come into the shop from time to time because she says I'm the only family she really has. I said I'd give her a keratin treatment."

He frowned. "Well? Do you want her there or not? Why are you giving her hair treatments if you don't want her?"

"No, that's not the point," she said. She'd forgotten how she had to spell out exactly how she was feeling so he'd know how to reply. He wasn't into wandering through the confusing range of feelings she might be having and helping her sort them out. "It's not whether I want her there or not. I don't *know* if I want her there. I don't mind seeing her. She's funny, in this weird sort of way. And there's also a way in which . . . I don't know . . . I can't explain it."

"Well, is she creepy? Is she stalking you?"

"No, no, no. She's not like that at all. She's . . . it's like she has a missing piece or something. She wants family so badly. So she's kind of sad even while she's funny. She's divorced, but she's seeing a guy who's a lot older and has teenagers, but she doesn't feel like she belongs." She was about to say, "I don't know why I'm telling you this," but he was already slouched down in his chair, cracking his knuckles, his attention drifting to another part of the restaurant.

"It's okay," she said. "It's fine. We don't have to talk about Nina on our date night."

He nodded. She wished he'd ask her questions, but maybe that would be wishing for a whole different Jeff. He was a good father and a good builder and he was charming and sexy, but he was a fixer of problems, not a wallower in emotions. What was that saying—if you are a hammer, then every problem looked like a nail? He might be a hammer. But her eyes stung; she was thinking about Poppet again. Knowing the name had made it so real. Now it seemed there was a part of herself that *was* Poppet—an unwanted, abandoned part of her that she didn't know had been there all along—and she couldn't bring herself to tell Jeff her name. And what did *that* say about them?

She honestly didn't know.

The waiter came and put their plates down in front of them. Lindy had ordered salmon with risotto and root vegetables, and she looked down at the plate feeling overwhelmed, while Jeff was attacking his rib eye like he hadn't eaten in weeks.

She tried again. "Nina and I have the same hair and eyes," she said softly. "But she's much taller than I am and she's got this—I don't know—inner confidence. It's like she goes through the world knowing her powers, but she's also vulnerable and sweet. And I know I have my family, but Nina's point . . . Nina's point is that we, she and I, have the same DNA. I don't share DNA with anyone except her and the children. And *also,*" she said more loudly, because he was holding up his hand now like he needed her to stop. "*Also,* Jeff, someone who was supposed to love me gave me away to strangers one day! Gave me away! And why? They gave us both away, and she was fifteen months old and I was just born, a few weeks old at the most. Who would do such a horrible thing? It's getting to me! I'm sorry, but it's getting to me."

She did not tell him her birth name. She tapped fifty-five times on the bottom of the table to keep herself from saying it. *I am Poppet. Poppet.*

"Well, if you want to know my take," he said, chewing a piece of steak, "that's all the more reason that you don't need any of this. Look at what it's done to you. You don't need this. You've got your family, and also, baby, you've got enough on your plate with running the entire school and making sure all the food labels in the cabinets face the same way, don't you?"

He saw her face and said, "I'm *kidding*! But seriously, get yourself out of this. You've got all these people who love you and are counting on you because you're wonderful, and you don't need to go breaking your heart finding these people who gave you up. Your mom—I hate to say it—but she's probably some kind of lowlife. You don't want to know her, trust me."

"I want—I want us to be happy," she said, and her voice sounded far away in her own ears, and what she said didn't really make any sense anyhow. She'd almost said, *I want you to love me like you used to,* but luckily she caught herself. He always got exasperated when people needed too much reassurance over what should be obvious.

Also, he might not have noticed yet that he'd fallen out of love with her. Husbands fell out of love so easily, it seemed. That had been a whole topic at the last Manicures and Margaritas night, actually: how tough it was to keep a man interested once there were kids and household chores. Leilani had sat there and ticked off on two hands the number of marriages she'd recently heard of that were breaking up over petty stuff. It was an epidemic, somebody said.

Anyway, the wine had made her head buzzy; that's all this was. When she stood up, he had to take her arm before she slipped. She put her face next to his, and that's when it happened—when she went to brush his cheek with her lips, he quickly slid his face away from hers, and turned away. She froze. What did that mean? Did he not even want to kiss her anymore?

She felt a cold fear spreading through her chest. He was done with her. Oh God, he was going to leave—she hadn't been able to hold on to him. She was a fraud; even her business was some stupid place where shallow people came to make themselves feel better about their stupid artificial lives. She didn't do any *real* good in the world—and besides that, she was a bad mother, and she spent too much money and cared about all the wrong things; she had no values and no smarts. Her mother was right about her. She looked out the window of the car, and swiped furiously at her eyes.

"Lindy," he said. "What's going on? You're not crying, are you?"

"No," she said. "No, I'm fine. Just fine." Because one thing, the main thing she remembered from the school yard, was that you never, ever, *ever* wanted to let somebody know how scared and tiny you felt. Even your husband.

Especially your husband.

ELEVEN

NINA

Can you fall in love with a whole family? This was my first time, so I wasn't really sure. I knew I was still grieving for my mom, and in no state to make final assessments on pretty much anything, but suddenly I found myself—well, happy. Markedly, noticeably happy.

True, Indigo had a new piercing, and Tyler had a bedroom that reeked of something herbal and scary, but I couldn't have been happier. I was in an exhilarating new element, fearlessly living a Big Life, and all my nerve endings were on hyper-alert in a way they hadn't been before.

I got up every morning like a demented sitcom mom, fearless and ready to face a slate of challenges that mostly did not get me down by bedtime. I was loved. I was thriving. I was cooking dinners for a family of four. I was having conversations about girlfriends and homework and whose turn it was to take the garbage out. I was driving in the carpool—an honest-to-god *carpool*—and not only that, I was going off to work every day, staging houses and answering phones, being all needed and competent and everything. I actually went out and bought a color-coded calendar and hung it in the kitchen with everybody's schedules on it, in different-colored inks, and really, who doesn't long for that kind of purpose and organization? And when I was standing in line to purchase it, I may have even tossed my hair and sighed and said something along the lines of, "I just *have* to get that brood of mine organized!"

Well, nobody in the store knew me, so it was okay.

And so what if Indigo rolled her eyes whenever I'd act stepmotherly with her? She saw right through me, I could tell.

But not since the early days of trying to kick cancer's ass with my mom—the days before we gave up and turned ourselves over to Mel Brooks movies—had I been so needed, so important to someone else's story.

Sure, I was living in what was clearly another woman's discarded house, which, from a professional standpoint, was something of a home-staging nightmare. Jane had bohemian, peculiar, eclectic taste— fringed lampshades in the living room, an armoire in the bedroom that was probably haunted and needed to be kicked and fought with every day before it would allow me to take any clothes out of it. Jane's style baffled me: she tended toward bamboo matchstick shades on the windows, paired with chintz curtains. Really—bamboo *and* chintz? A worn flowered rug in the living room that looked as though it dated back to the 1930s, and overstuffed couches and chairs upholstered in brocades, couches that went *oof* when you sat down on them, as though they were issuing an opinion on your weight. But the kitchen had marvelous copper pans hanging above a kitchen island, and I had always, always wanted a kitchen island. It was almost the first thing I pointed out to prospective homebuyers when I showed a house: "And it even has an island in the kitchen!" Like I meant the Bahamas or something.

The only rough day was Thursday, when Jane would Skype with the kids. Carter, too. It wasn't that I minded. But there'd I'd be, all necessary and everything, helping Tyler learn his lines for the senior play (he was playing a rather convincing Nicely Nicely in *Guys and Dolls*) or maybe I'd be quizzing Indigo on the periodic table of the elements, and then—despite my wickedest, hardest wishing that maybe this week the call would be skipped—there would come the little Skype tone from the computer on the desk in the corner of the living room, and off everyone would go.

Mom was home!

There'd be nothing for me to do but try to stay out of camera range, to pretend not to mind, perhaps to dish up slabs of blueberry pie for them after they finished talking—but God, it was so *pathetic*. I was so *peripheral*, you know; they'd had years of togetherness, of being a family, and even their bad times were things they had in common. They may have been fractured as a family, with anger and tears and way too much kale, but there was this hour once a week when I was just an outsider and they came together, reconfiguring themselves into something of a real family. Like bones knitting or something. It wasn't always friendly; it often wasn't intimate or close. Jane's face often looked drawn, and Indigo bit her fingernails while she sat slumped near the computer, and Tyler was huddled somewhere off to the side, his normally handsome face looking inert.

Whenever I'd talk about all this with Melanie at work, she would say that for her, the worst thing would be the ickiness of sleeping in another woman's bed with her ex-husband, and maybe it should have been, but I didn't even really mind that. Jane had thrown away so much; it was as though she'd just put her whole life at the curb for anyone to haul away, and I was there to scoop up the detritus of her life, husband and all.

But who could look at Carter and think of him as detritus?

Of course there was the possibility—I had to admit this, even as I was awash in falling in love—that I would never really belong here and that I would give up on it. (I had watched myself walk away from things I loved before, after all.) Maybe in the end, all I would ever be was a well-appreciated houseguest. The kids mostly treated me like some older friend, saving their worst for their father or for Jane on her weekly calls, and I knew that was because they didn't really trust me yet. And sure, I liked them—most of the time—but they weren't mine. They weren't anywhere near being mine.

One day I told Melanie that I wasn't sure all this was going to last. Maybe Carter would blindside me with the news that it wasn't working out. Maybe Indigo and Tyler would want their father to themselves. Maybe I would realize that I could no longer exist as a helpful sidekick, pantomiming a family life, and like all the other times I've broken up with guys, I'd leave once again. "You never know," I said. "People leave."

"It's not going to happen again," she said. "You're different now. You seem totally committed this time. It's like this is what you've been waiting for."

"But what if his ex-wife wants him back?" I said, and Melanie laughed.

"Honey, they've been divorced for over a year, and she's moved away! They're not getting back together. What is *wrong* with you any-way? This is it. This is happiness. Accept it. Let it wash over you."

"You are ridiculous," I said to her.

"You. Ridiculouser," she said without even looking up.

I knew things that Jane didn't know. Carter either.

I knew that Tyler, for instance—mysterious, guitar-playing Tyler, with his 4.0 grade point average and his huge brown eyes and shaggy hair—sometimes didn't go to school when he left in the morning. I also knew that he had a girlfriend named Lolly and at least twice when it might be presumed that the house would be empty, they came back home and shut themselves up in his room. And sometimes I'd glimpse him around town in the middle of the day when he should have been in school, loping along, or sitting in a coffee shop, or playing music with a bunch of guys. He never saw me, and I didn't want to approach him.

And I also knew that it took all of Indigo's bravery to try to discover her place in the weird world of high school, and that in her room was a folded-up, highly decorated piece of paper that she'd titled, "Indigo's Fuck-It List: How to Be Cool, by Indigo Sanborn." And that it had a whole list of things she was planning to accomplish to prove that she wasn't merely another geeky honor student but had some badass qualities to her. She'd already checked off dyeing her hair purple, cutting class on an exam day, and saying a swear word to a school administrator.

Still to go—and these items were decorated with paisleys and dragons—smoking weed, getting really drunk at a party, stealing a piece of school property, getting taken to the police station because of bad behavior, being an activist *doing something really important,* writing obscene graffiti on a brick wall somewhere, making a public scene, and—this one stopped my heart—finding a guy to have sex with who wouldn't end up "being a drag by wanting a relationship." (This last one was decorated with hearts with slashes through it.)

Just reading it made my neck go out for the rest of the day.

But really, what the heck did *I* know? Maybe this was what modern families were like—this cohort I was in, composed of dangerous, interesting, adorable little outlaws. Maybe all parents spent their time simply trying to keep their kids alive until adulthood, and maybe I wasn't here to be the probation officer for these two. I was happy to drive them around, to remind them to do their homework, to make their breakfasts every morning, to remember that Ty liked banana-nut muffins with cream cheese, and that Indigo wanted three pieces of bacon and a runny egg on an English muffin, and that she liked to lick her fingers as the yellow yolk ran down her hand.

And at night, I lay next to their irresistible father who made love to me like I was the only woman on earth but who then said things like *Kids will be kids,* and *It's all good,* and *Everything works out for the best,* and *Please don't let's spoil the moment talking about the kids' antics.*

Forget tattling on Tyler. But I knew I should at least tell Carter about the Fuck-It List, especially Indigo's plan to have sex. Fifteen is an absurd age for sex. A father had a right to know—and surely he would have a way to stop her. I'd meant to mention it to him before, but how did you bring something like that up, particularly when you'd been snooping when you found it, and when the man at your side was saying, "Let's not talk about the kids, let's just talk about us"? I kept going back and forth on this. I should tell him; no I *shouldn't.* If I did, Indigo would never tell me anything again. I decided I should put on my Wonder Woman suit and solve the problem on my own.

Right.

Sometimes he and I would slip outside after the kids had gone to bed, and we'd walk down to the park and look up at the bright, frozen stars. Those times, it was like his heartbeat and breathing were my own. I don't even remember what we talked about, or even *if* we talked. On one of those nights, he got out Tyler's guitar, and we sat out on the deck, wrapped in our fleece jackets, and he sang "I Will Remember You" to me in the most raw, soulful voice I'd ever heard.

These were the times I was always going to remember. Also when he'd be shaving in the morning and he'd say to me, "Tell me again. Which Beatle played the drums?" and I'd pretend to look confused and say, "The Beatles had drums? Was it that guy with the funny glasses? Elton John Lennon?"

But—and this is all on me—it's just that sometimes, lying next to him after he'd gone to sleep, I would think that maybe my whole point in life was going to turn out to be a caregiver for people I didn't really, really, really belong to.

Looking out the window at the tree branches that scraped against the house, I'd wonder if my mother had gotten my letter, and if she was going to call me.

Funny, how you can have a million happy moments staring you in the face, and still you haven't budged from the original problem that had plagued you since you were five.

Where is my real family, and why did they give me away?

One Tuesday morning, I decided that I had to find that photograph, and I ditched work and went to my mom's condo. I hadn't spent nights there since I'd moved in with Carter—I'd not seemed to need the solitude I thought I might crave.

I forced myself to go up to the attic, trying to shake off the chill and the claustrophobia of that small, cramped space that held every little thing from the past. There were all my years of school papers, every handmade greeting card I'd ever drawn for my parents, ballet costumes, yearbooks, field hockey uniforms, scrapbooks. There was, creepily enough, even a little box that contained my baby teeth.

My mother had loved me so very much. Had recorded and preserved every moment of my childhood that she could reach. I wondered what she would make of my new life—me with a calendar and a carpool run! She probably would've loved it for me, especially the idea of me trying to be a stepmother to a teenage girl. But she would have told me to be careful. She was always telling me to be careful. She would say I should move slowly, make sure, not give my whole self to something that might not result in a happy marriage. She would say, *Why did you move in with him so fast?* It was odd, how I missed her even more than I ever had, now that I was searching for my birth mother. It was Josephine I wanted to talk to, Josephine's face that came up in my mind as I saw myself as a mother.

I plowed through box after box, not letting myself stop even when I was tired, even when my eyes were burning with tears or dust or whatever it was. All this *feeling* pulling me forward.

And I finally found it. It was at the bottom of a box that had my parents' marriage certificate and photo books of them in their younger years, pre-me, stuck in an unmarked manila envelope.

The photograph.

I knew it instantly. It was as though it radiated a strange, unearthly heat in my hand. I scrambled over to the window so I could truly study it.

It was a faded color photo with a crinkled edge, the kind where the colors had all turned pinkish, and in it were a guy and a girl, standing in front of a VW bus. She was wearing a long skirt and had wild, curly, reddish hair cascading over her shoulders and partially hiding her eyes. The guy had long hair and was wearing a cowboy hat, and neither of them was smiling. She was holding a tiny baby in a blanket in her bare arms, and standing in front of her was a little girl, just a baby really—and this is what killed me: it had to be *me*. I was looking up at her seriously, like I knew I was about to hear that all future birthday parties and Christmases would be canceled. No, that's not true; I was too little to understand either of those things. I was a baby, and my red hair stuck out in little curlicues, and I was wearing a blue flowered dress that was slightly too long and sturdy white baby shoes, and I was holding on to a teddy bear. I might be about to cry.

My parents could not be trusted to keep me, and maybe even then I knew it. Or maybe I just needed a nap.

I studied the guy. He had to be my dad. *My teenage father, the guy who couldn't seem to make it to the drugstore to get condoms when he needed them most.* He had his hand on my shoulder. I wondered what he'd said when she told him she was giving their babies away. Or maybe it was his idea.

Probably it was his idea. Maybe he was the one who thought she should go be a rock star.

I had to lie down on the attic floor. There was a small patch of sun on the wooden floor, and I lay there and watched the dust motes falling and thought about my sad baby self, and my mother with her red, curly hair, standing so inert next to me. My heart pounded.

And then after a while, I got tired of the dust and the grief and the cold, and I pulled myself up and went to get Indigo at school to take her to her therapy appointment.

As usual, the pickup lane at the high school was crowded with SUVs and honking cars, kids spilling out the main door, milling around checking their phones, absentmindedly walking into traffic. You had to be on your toes to do the afternoon pickup and not kill any pedestrians. Indigo materialized from the ambling crowd and threw herself into my car like the force of nature that she is. I handed her an apple, and she told me all the injustices wrought by high school that day: the homework that didn't get collected even though she did it all, every single problem perfectly. The lunchroom scene, which she said was worse and worse—it'd been bad enough that nobody knew where they were allowed to *sit* without getting glared at, but now also the school had banned *bagels*, of all things, because of an obesity epidemic. "It's as bad as my mom," she told me, and I tried not to laugh. "It's okay," she said. "You can laugh. We have to laugh. Who else wants cows around instead of people? Instead of, *hello*, their *daughter*? Only my mother, that's who! What the fuck?"

When we stopped for a red light, I stared out the window. What had my birth mother preferred instead of me? Simply every other thing in the world. I'd probably been the worst thing that had ever happened to her. Until she had Lindy, that is—then we both were.

I handed Indigo the photograph, which I'd tucked in my jacket pocket.

"This teenager there—see her? That's my real mom," I said. "And I'm the worried little baby standing in front. That's my sister in the blanket. For all I know, they're about to get into that VW bus and take us to give us away."

"Wow. And that guy with the cool hair and cowboy hat—that must be your dad. He's sorta cute, right? Oh, wait. I can't trust your taste, because you think *my* dad is cute, and he's a mess."

"About that," I said.

"No," she said. "Please don't even."

"Hear me out. One question. Does it, you know, bother you at all that I'm living at your house, where your mother and father lived? I mean, that's weird, right?"

She was eyeing me. "Eww, don't even tell me we're about to have a talk about how you and my dad are doing it. Okay? Because that would be so *totally* inappropriate on so many levels."

"Of course. Sorry."

"Just kidding!" She socked me in the arm. Hard. "Don't be ridonculous. I know what goes on. You will find that I've been raised to be a very liberal, open-minded person, and actually I think you are very brave to have anything to do with him."

"Brave? I happen to love him."

"But he's such a pain. I mean, he's a fun pain and all that, but jeez. He's kind of clueless, don't you think? *And* he's got you doing all the work. I guess you probably noticed that."

"The work? I like—"

"Oh, I know, I know what you're going to say. But look at you. You're doing this pickup because he can never seem to remember to do it. And you cook the meals and, for all I know, you're probably washing his underwear, too. And his socks."

"I—"

"I know, I know. You don't have to apologize for yourself. I'm taking a women's studies class, and we talk about stuff like this. We all know it's super gross what women do for men, but it's how we were socialized. We do it for security." She took a bite of her apple and looked at me. "And you don't even have the security of a marriage license, not that you should, but still. That's what women have to get them some legitimacy."

I stared at her. "What century are you from? It's not really like that," I said. "I can't explain . . ."

"And also—well, the way you dress. I mean, you do it clearly just to please *him*. My mom didn't do that kind of thing, so it's super interesting really, for me to see what a younger woman feels like she has to do to keep a man."

"The way I *dress?*" I said. I looked down at my pink sweater and skinny jeans. "These are the clothes I've always worn!"

"No, no. It's totally okay," she said. We were at the therapist's office by then, and she jumped out of the car, then leaned in the window. "I shouldn't tell you this, but I'm actually ready to get me some sex, too. I decided I should do it before I fall in love with some guy, because I want to learn about it, not have it be all-important and messed up with love. My friend Maya and I decided that last week."

"Wait! We have to talk about this," I said, but she'd flounced away, and all I could do was stare after her and wonder if we were all going to survive whatever was coming.

I probably had the same look on my face that I had in the photograph, when I was fifteen months old.

I drove to A Little Piece of Heaven, without meaning to. I was driving around, honest, and suddenly I was just there. Yes, I had houses to stage, and yes, I had to be back soon to pick up Indigo from her therapy appointment, but right now I needed my sister.

Lindy actually sighed when she saw me come in. Then, probably because there were other people around, she smiled at me.

"This isn't your appointment day, is it?" she said.

"No, no. That's next week. By the way, you look fabulous today," I added, before she could say anything along the lines of *What the hell are you doing here then?* She did look wonderful, except for that scared expression she seemed to always have in her eyes. I was beginning to notice that she looked like she was always uncomfortable, waiting for something awful to happen.

"Thank you," she said. Her eyes darted around the studio like she was worried that people were going to be suspicious. *Me again, no appointment, and now handing out compliments.*

"Could we—? Could I tell you something?"

"All right," she said after a moment. "Come on back. I only have a minute though."

I followed her through the salon, basking in the music that curled out of the speakers. Some of the hair stylists smiled at me. Two visits. I might be becoming a regular.

"So," she said, closing the door. "What? I'm guessing you must have heard from our mother?"

"No. But I did find the photograph that my adoptive mother told me about. Look at this. It's us!"

I was surprised that she took it. She was so freaking timid about everything, like she had to guard against getting hurt.

She held it in both hands and stared at it a long time.

"Oh my God," she said at last.

"I know," I said. "Look how sad this all is. Look at the way I'm looking up at our mom. And that guy is our dad."

"Our *alleged* dad."

"Okay. Some guy with long hair. The guy who managed to keep his name off the birth certificate."

I expected her to say that we couldn't be sure any of those people had anything to do with us. It might be a random photograph of complete strangers for all we knew. But she said, "Phoebe and the sperm donor. That's how we'll refer to him."

"So do you think they were about to leave to go drop us off? I look like I'm about fifteen months, don't I?"

"Ugh," she said, and handed me the picture back. "It's horrible to think about."

"I know. Look how cute we are. How could they give us away?"

"To be fair, we can't see my face. I'm all wrapped up in that blanket. I might not have been cute. Maybe I was screaming with colic all the time, and they couldn't take it anymore. You were just collateral damage."

"No, no. I'm sure I was a whiny brat. Maybe they were afraid you'd turn out like me, and that sealed the deal."

She actually laughed. I realized with a start that I had never heard her laugh. I didn't know she had that setting.

"Hey, if you have another minute, I need some parenting advice," I said to her, suddenly emboldened.

She glanced at her watch. "I have about five minutes."

"Okay, here's my dilemma. Indigo—that's Carter's daughter, who happens to be fifteen but is very advanced in terms of how many tattoos and piercings she has—today told me that she's decided to have sex to see what it's like, before she falls in love with somebody and sex starts to mean too much."

She moved some objects around on her desk, restacked a pile of papers, squaring their edges. "That's an interesting choice."

"Yes. And my question is: Do I tell her father, or can I handle this myself?"

"Jesus. How should I know?"

"You're a mom. Would *you* want to know?"

"My daughter is *five*."

Then she sighed and said, "What if you just talk to her about how you feel about sex—love, excitement, how it's beautiful when you love the person and how yucky it can feel when you don't, et cetera, et cetera. *That* speech."

"Hmm. I think my mom might have neglected to give me that speech. She just gave me the 'Do not under any circumstances kiss boys because they are all only out for one thing' speech."

"That's the only one that Peggy Walsh knew, too. You might have to fly blind on this one. But really, isn't this is her father's problem, not yours?"

"I know, I know. But maybe I need to give her a woman's perspective. Also, I don't want to rat her out."

She gave me a long look. "I bet you'll be happy when those kids are packed off to their mother, won't you? Then none of this will be your problem at all."

Would I? I suddenly couldn't think.

I checked my watch. "Actually I've got to go pick up the culprit right now."

"Hey," she said, and her voice was strangely shy and young. "I can't believe I'm saying this, but could I—could you maybe make a copy of that photograph sometime?"

"Sure, I'll bring it by," I said. "When I come for my keratin-treatment thing."

"That would be lovely," she said.

"I think I'll make a copy for our mom, too, for when she calls and we get to go meet her."

She got that funny look on her face again, the one of exasperated worldly wisdom. "Nina, honey, you do understand that our mom isn't going to call us, don't you? She's not interested in getting to know us."

"I *don't* know that, as a matter of actual fact."

"Don't you think that if she were going to call, she would have by now? It's been—what? Six weeks since you wrote her? She does not want us in her life, which is why she gave us up in the first place. You think she wants to revisit all that pain?"

"Why are you doing this?"

"Doing what?"

"Saying all this stuff."

"Because I think the sooner you get used to the idea, the happier your life is going to be."

"Oh, so you're saying these things for my own good? To protect me?"

"Well, yes. I don't even really know you, but I hate to see you disappointed by our lowlife, druggy mom and our cowboy-hat-wearing father. Two people who were probably too stoned to use protection. I mean, how clueless do you have to be to not go get yourself a condom at the drugstore? *Twice.*"

"Lindy, listen to yourself," I said. "Think about this: if they had used protection, we wouldn't *be here.* For one little tiny second, be glad of that, why don't you?"

She blinked, like she'd never considered that. Then she said, "She's not going to call, that's all I know. I know that for a fact."

"Oh, and you control the universe?" I said.

"Just the Northeast," she said.

So the next Tuesday, proving that Lindy does *not* control the universe, my mother called me.

It was almost time to leave work and pick up Indigo from school and take her to therapy—and I was alone in Melanie's father's furniture warehouse, picking out paintings and throw rugs for a home I was staging—when my phone rang with an unfamiliar number.

There was a silence after I said hello.

"Hello?" I said again, and I just *knew.* I felt the breath leave my body. I stared out a window at the robin's-egg blue of the sky, waiting. The concrete floor of the warehouse was cold under the soles of my boots. The silence was huge, as big as the sky.

"Is this—?" I said softly. My voice disappeared in the vastness of the warehouse.

There was a throaty laugh in my ear. "Nina? Are you Nina?"

"I am," I said. "Are you . . . my mother?"

She laughed again, a laugh full of cigarettes. "Well, I guess I am. I got your letter, and it's been sitting here for a while now, and then today I thought I should see what you wanted to say to me."

"I just wanted to say hello," I said. I swallowed hard.

"I have to tell you in advance that I don't have it in me for a sentimental sobfest kind of thing," she said.

"No. No sobfests. I only wanted to talk. To know that you exist."

"You're not going to try to make me feel guilty, are you? Because I honestly don't think I have it in me. You know what I'm saying? So if that's why you wanted me to call you, I figured I'd better tell you that up front. Just say you hate me, and we'll hang up and go back to our lives, and that will be it. No hard feelings."

"No, no, of course," I said. "I don't hate you. I just wanted to hear your voice."

"So . . . now you've heard my voice. You can probably tell I've smoked for years, right? Do you smoke?"

"No, I don't."

"Did you ever? Even as a teenager?"

"No. Well, I smoked one cigarette once. Half a cigarette. But I couldn't figure out how to breathe in the smoke. So I put it out and didn't pick it up again."

"Good for you," she said. There was a silence and then she said, "I have to be honest with you. I'm not maternal or anything."

"No, no," I said. "That's not why—"

"I'm simply somebody who made a lot of mistakes and had some bad things happen, and sometimes life has been horrible and sometimes it's been wonderful, and I wake up every morning and thank God I'm still standing. You know that song, 'I'm Still Standing'? That's me."

"Oh yes, I know that song." I sank down in an armchair and leaned on my elbow and wondered if she'd had to get drunk to make this call.

But at least she did call. I would always have these few minutes, whatever else happened. There was a long silence, and it occurred to me I should've made a list of things to talk to her about.

"I wanted you to know that I've always . . . I've always wanted to meet you, and I've always thought about you, wondered where you are and if you're okay," I said. "When I was little, I actually used to think that maybe sometime we'd meet up and I could save your life or something."

"Oh," she said. "Well. I could have used that a time or two, I guess."

I squeezed my eyes tight, trying to remember all the questions I'd thought about asking her over the years, back when I'd be lying awake in my little twin bed as a child—back then I'd known exactly what I wanted to say to her. How was it that now I had nothing?

"For years, I carried around my report card with all A's to show you just in case I ran into you somewhere. I used to think everybody I met might be you."

She cleared her throat.

"Did you know where I was? I mean, where I lived and what family I got adopted by? Did they tell you?"

There was a long silence and then she said, "They didn't say much, just said it was a couple who couldn't have their own child. An older couple. I think they figured I didn't deserve to know." She laughed again, roughly, and that started a coughing fit, a fit that grew a bit distant, as though she'd put the phone down. I could hear water running and the sound of a cabinet opening. Was she getting a drink of water? From afar she said, "Hang on a sec," through her coughing. Then she came back to the phone. "I'm not sick. So don't start with how I should go to the doctor, because this is just allergies. Okay? You nonsmokers don't understand."

"No. Sure, I understand," I said.

Now she was all business. "Look, whether you admit it or not, you probably hate me for what I did, so if you want to tell me that, why don't you just say it, and then we can hang up. Go on. I can take it."

"No, no, I don't hate you. Of course I don't hate you. I just always wanted to know what happened. Where I came from and all. Who my people are. I feel like I don't really belong anywhere, you know?"

"But don't you know the truth by now?" she said. "Nobody ever feels like they belong anywhere. The whole world. Imposters, every one of us."

"Yeah, but some people, they have family members that they *know*. They know whether their grandfathers had mustaches . . . and oh, I don't know, whether they worked with their hands or if they were artistic, and did they like the beach better or the mountains."

"Mustaches, huh? That's what this is about? Let me think a minute. No. Can't say that either of your grandfathers wore a mustache."

"No," I said. "You know what I mean. Our story. *My* story! I've always wanted to know our family's story. Where we began, how—well, you know. How things worked in our family."

Her voice was quieter when she answered. "Maybe sometimes it's better not to know those stories. People have such sad lives. And you have to make your own life. Every day you get to start over anyway, work on your own story."

I was silent.

I heard her take a long drag on her cigarette. Then she said in a different, lower voice, "You see? This is why it took me so long to call you after I got your letter. Because I don't know what to say to you."

"I found out . . . well, I know about my sister. There were two of us."

"Yes," she said so quietly I almost couldn't hear her. "Two of you. Two little girls."

I swallowed, scared that any moment she would hang up. "Tell me something about your life. Your old life."

"I . . . can't," she said.

"It's okay, I know you had to give me away. Us. You had to give *us* away. That something must have happened. Was it . . . so hard? Did you ever love me? Did you cry when they took me away from you?" Why didn't I write a list of questions for this? Why, why, why?

There was a long silence, so long that I thought maybe she had hung up. Then she sighed. "I don't think I can explain it to you," she said. "In fact, I know I can't. It was a terrible time for me. That's all I can say. Listen, I need to hang up now. I've got something boiling over on the stove."

"No! Wait. Can I just tell you something? I have a photograph. My mother gave it to me."

After a moment she said, "Did you have a good mother? Just tell me that much."

"Yes. Oh yes. They were both very kind. My mother *and* my father. I was their only child. They were quiet. Schoolteachers."

"An only child! Imagine that."

"Did you ever want to know what happened to me?"

"Yes," she said so quietly I almost couldn't hear her. "But I couldn't. The records were sealed. I don't even know how you found *me*. It was all supposed to stay a secret."

"Well, I got around it."

"Maybe you shouldn't have. I told you, I'm not what you think. And I don't have anything to give you. I'm not going to be your mom, because it's too late for all that mother-daughter crap. Your mother was the person who adopted you and raised you."

I took a deep breath. "I have this picture . . ."

I could hear her suck in her breath. "Oh, so you got that, did you?"

"Is the guy my father?"

"No. He's not."

"Oh! He's not? You're sure?"

"Quite sure. I sent that picture along with you. It was—well, it was the only thing I had to give you." She cleared her throat. "Listen, honey, this sucks. I did what I had to do. I was *fifteen* when I had you. Okay? It ripped my heart out that I couldn't keep you, but I knew you'd be better off without me. No back and forth. Clean break. Best for everybody. I have to get off the phone now and go pound my head on the cement wall or something. This is just as weird as I thought it was going to be."

"But wait. Tell me. Did you have a happy life? Was it the right thing after all, what you did?" I squeezed my eyes closed, knowing I had gone too far.

There was a long silence, so long it stretched a couple of years. Seasons changed. I may have celebrated a few birthdays. Then she said, in a thick voice, "You had this little stuffed dog. Socks was his name, and you would try to say it. You'd get this frown on your face and try to say *sssss*. And you used to chew on the sides of your crib. I'd wake up in the morning to the sound of you gnawing on your crib, like it was your breakfast or something. I never saw anything like it. I said to my sister, 'Maybe she's missing something in her diet,' and my sister said, 'Yeah, wood! We're not feeding her enough wood.'"

"Ah yes, Sister Germaine mentioned an aunt." I was gripping the phone so tightly my hand started to cramp. "Was—is she older than you?"

"Yeah. You and I lived with her. Our parents were dead, so we all lived together. She had a baby, too. Older than you, and you always tried to do everything Kevin did. One day the two of you took all the toilet paper rolls and put them in the toilet. Every one of them. So proud of yourselves! And we hardly had the money to buy more. But you looked so cute standing there dripping wet, holding a soggy toilet paper roll that must have weighed about five pounds. I couldn't be mad at you. Oh, and one day, I had decided you shouldn't have a bottle anymore because I thought you were too big, and I knew—well, I knew already that I couldn't keep you—I tried to get you to drink out of a cup just so you'd know how, but you hated it. You were such a stubborn little one! You went on strike and refused to drink anything and you threw the cup on the floor every time I gave it to you. My sister said—my sister said—"

She went quiet.

"Tell me. What did she say?"

Her breath was ragged. "She said you'd get used to it, that you would get used to anything. I think I cried more about not giving you that bottle . . . after, I mean. It's crazy what you remember."

I squeezed my eyes shut. After a long moment, I said, "I was Kate."

"Yes, you were. Kate. Kiss me, Kate, that's what we used to say to you. From the play. I was Kate in the show in high school."

"Oh, that's why I wasn't Katherine."

"Kate," she said firmly. "That's what I wanted."

"And you named my sister Poppet."

"Yes. God. Silly little name, isn't it?"

"It's cute. You don't run into many Poppets. Did she look like a poppet or something?"

"I-I don't know. It was a name I thought of. At the moment."

"She's Lindy now."

"Yes. You said that in your letter."

We were silent, both breathing into the phone. I swallowed. "I've seen the videos of you as Lulu."

"Now how did you know about *that*?"

"Google."

"Good God."

"Your hair in the videos is so amazing. We have kind of the same hair, except yours was—I don't know—awesomely huge."

"The eighties. The Greed Decade, complete with hair gel."

I laughed. "Lindy has amazing hair, too. She actually runs a salon and spa. I'm going in next week and she's going to do some kind of treatment to my hair. Get the frizz out. I just met her, and it's so weird, how we bonded over hair."

"Women can always talk about hair."

"Is yours still big and gorgeous?"

"If by big and gorgeous you mean frizzed out and completely and utterly insane, the answer is yes."

I happened to look down at my watch. It was five minutes until pickup time for Indigo. But how could I leave? My mother started talking more about her hair and about the other two women in the group—presumably the Starbabies—and how they got booked on *Saturday Night Live* but then the booking got canceled because of their manager who'd taken all their money, but it was a funny story really, the way she told it. Her agent fought with Chrissie Hynde's agent.

"Did you ever get married again?" I said.

"Well, I wasn't married to your father, you know. We were too young. But later—well. How *many* times did I get married, is the question. Three, almost four. A couple of starter marriages and then a keeper for five years. I get bored. I'm probably not the easiest person to live with."

"I had a starter marriage myself. Lasted six months. Then he met somebody else."

"Six months would be respectable in my list of marriages. I had one that was six weeks. We got married in Vegas, and I was performing—and before the gig was up, we had gotten divorced in Vegas, too. Yessir. I am nothing if not efficient. Of course he was an actor, so there you go. I say they should let priests marry and forbid actors from marrying."

I heard her puff on her cigarette as she waited for my laughter.

"I live with a man now," I said. "He's about your age, which is weird. He has—"

"He's *my* age? What's up with that? Jesus. Do you have a father complex or something?"

"A . . . father complex? I don't think so. For your information, neither one of you is so very old. I believe you had me when you were—"

"Yeah, yeah. I know when I had you."

I wondered if she was thinking how that had been the worst day of her life. Had it really been so awful? I cleared my throat and said,

"Listen to us. We're talking like friends. Do you think we could see each other?"

"Why would we do that? I've told you—"

"But what if we met for coffee or something? One meeting. I'll show you the photo if you want. No blame, no guilt. We'll just look at each other—human to human. No mother-daughter crap. Just us. It would be enough."

"It would hurt," she said.

"So what's a little pain? And maybe it would help more than it hurts. You know, for years I thought everybody I passed on the street might be you—store clerks, bus drivers—"

"Stop," she said, but I didn't stop.

"In middle school, I decided the gym teacher must be my mom because—well, I can't remember why. I think I just wanted to see you so bad. And now I can't believe I'm talking to you!"

"Listen to me. You don't really want to know me. I'm not who you think I am. I'm not a mother."

"It's okay. I already said no mother-daughter stuff. Just us."

"But you don't know. It could get bad."

"How would it get bad?" I said. "We won't let it get bad. We'll be friends."

"There are things I can't talk about. That I can't ever talk about."

"That's okay. You don't have to talk about anything you don't want to. The only thing I really want to know is that you're okay. That you survived it all, you know. Giving up two babies."

"Yes. Two of you," she said roughly. "Some track record."

I ran my hand over and over the smoothness of the coffee table in front of me. All this furniture, all these stacks of leftover couches and chairs and end tables. Reupholstered, rehabbed, and now going off to their new task of making a place look untouched and beautiful so a piece of real estate could sell. A cover-up, really. My whole life was about paving over people's lives so they looked presentable from the outside. I closed my eyes. I wanted to see my mother more than anything in the world, even though that might be a sort of paving over, too.

After a moment she spoke again, and her voice was thick, like maybe she was about to cry. "Well, it would have to be for drinks. I don't do coffee. And God knows I'll need alcohol for this. Are you even old enough to drink?" She laughed.

"I'm thirty-five," I said.

"I know. I was joking. To me, you're still fifteen months and one week and two days."

"That was the day—?"

"That was the day."

"And you remember."

"I remember everything. I have whole roomfuls in my brain that are dedicated to the past, and to you, and about what was supposed to happen and didn't. But mostly I keep the door to those rooms locked. Makes it possible to live without drinking arsenic for breakfast. Most days, at least."

I took a deep breath. "Can I bring Lindy?"

She hesitated. "Maybe it should just be the two of us." Then she exhaled loudly and said, "Oh, what the hell. Go for broke! Bring her! We'll do this thing. One and done."

"One and done?"

"Sweetheart, I am *not* signing on for a lifetime here. We're not going to be a Hallmark movie about reunited families. This is our human-to-human, no guilt, no blame, one night of drinks and a viewing. And that's all it is. No questions will be answered, do you hear me? I have a whole bunch of shit from the past that legally I can't talk about, even if I wanted to, which I don't."

"Fine," I said, although I had a momentary chill.

She and I made arrangements. Lindy and I would come to Brooklyn two weeks from the following Saturday, but not to her house. No, no, no. She picked out a bar where she said it was loud and noisy and nobody could hear anything, but that was perfect because that would keep the questions down to a minimum, ha ha. And there were hot *young* guys there, she told me pointedly. Maybe I'd meet somebody more age appropriate. There was so much we hadn't talked about, I realized.

It would take time, but I knew that we were going to be family, in spite of what she said.

◆　◆　◆

My hands were shaking and my eyes filled with tears as I drove to the high school.

I was twenty-five minutes late, and my heart was tumbling around my chest like a tennis shoe in the dryer as I punched in Indigo's phone number at the first red light. She didn't pick up. *Crap.* Nor was she in our usual pickup spot when I finally got to school. Called her again. Nothing. She wasn't one of the kids milling around in the student parking lot, or hanging out on the front steps. I parked and went looking for her. Usually her bright blue hair served as a handy beacon for finding her.

But not today.

I went into the main hallway and asked a tall guy with a serious nose piercing, "Do you know where I might find Indigo?" He had no idea who I was talking about. Of course he didn't. This was a high school with over a thousand kids in it, and Indigo was a sophomore. Also, she might not even go by that name at school.

But also, is this so terrible of me? I wasn't really worried one bit about Indigo. *My mother is going to meet me! My mother is going to meet me!* That was all I could think about.

She was my mother, my real mother, and I knew that as soon as I saw her, it wouldn't matter if she wasn't what I expected, if she wasn't all that nice, if she was a smoker and a drinker, or if her life had been hard. I would look at her and we would know we belonged together, that if she ever needed a kidney transplant, my kidney would probably fit nicely.

The sky was suddenly a brilliant blue, and all the teenagers walking in front of the school were handsome and lovely, and Indigo was of course fine somewhere; she'd be mad but so what? We'd figure it out. The important thing was that I now had me some people. And I didn't buy that bit for one minute about how this was going to be a one-time thing. My mother would meet Lindy and me, and it would lead to everything. There were going to be cousins and at least one aunt and probably some uncles and grandparents I could get to know—people I'd even visit in the nursing home with my blueberry pies and all my good will and best wishes. And sure, at first it might be awkward and I'd be the stranger who grew up outside their midst, but then they'd see that I was one of them, and I'd be accepted.

They'd tell me all the stories I needed to know, and we'd lie around, basking in one another's company, and I'd call each of them by their title *and* their name: Grandpa Horatio, or Aunt Flo, or whatever. Cousin Deuteronomy.

Whatever. They would be mine. Mine and Lindy's.

I sat on the wall in front of the school and texted Lindy: *OMG. SHE CALLED ME. SHE CALLED! SHE WANTS TO MEET US.*

My phone dinged right after that, and I was sure it was going to be Lindy telling me this was never going to work out, and who needed a mom anyway, blah blah blah. But it wasn't.

It was Carter texting me. "You've got Kayla, right?"

TWELVE
PHOEBE

Shit.

Now she'd done it.

She'd talked to Kate. And for what? Damn it to hell, she had told herself that this was the *one thing she would never do under any circumstances*: look for her daughters, or talk to them, or insert herself and her sad story into their lives in any way. And now she'd jumped right into it, almost without her own permission. For God's sake, what the hell was wrong with her?

Why hadn't she thrown that letter away? Why had she even opened it?

Because it was a handwritten letter, that's why, and she'd thought maybe it was from her sister in Oklahoma, or her aunt in California. No, that wasn't true. She'd seen it was postmarked Connecticut. But maybe it was somebody asking about piano lessons or voice lessons. Or telling her they admired her, because that still sometimes happened—people discovering her on YouTube and tracking her down, to say the Starbabies had been so great. Oh, it didn't matter. The point was: she'd opened it.

She'd felt an instant mixture of sickness and excitement.

"What kind of a joke—?" she'd said aloud, there in her own clean, white, spotless kitchen. The letters had just clattered to the floor outside the door, and she'd stooped down to pick them up. The boy waiting for his mother after the piano lesson looked startled, thinking she was talking to him, no doubt. She'd leaned against the coolness of the wall, out of his line of sight, and read and reread the pages, gobbled them down like they were pieces of candy. Toxic candy.

So. Kate was Nina Popkin now. All grown up. She didn't enclose a picture. Phoebe shook out the envelope just to be sure. Nothing.

If you were going to turn your mother's world upside down, wouldn't you at least include a photograph? So she could see you? But no. Of course, Nina Popkin didn't owe her anything.

A headache was blooming just behind her right eye.

You named me Kate, and I have always wanted to know you. I have looked for you.

Shit.

"You wouldn't like it, Kate," Phoebe whispered. "Go live your life, and forget about me."

She should have thrown the letter in the trash can right then, is what she should have done. But then Pauley's mother had banged her way up the back stairs, calling out, "Yoohooo!" and Phoebe had walked the letter over to the junk drawer and stuck it inside.

Later that night the letter wanted her to read it again, and so she took it out and read it two or three more times. Kate did little loops on her uppercase *I*'s and *P*'s, the way they used to teach handwriting before everything got spare looking and plain.

I have looked for you. Please call me. Let's talk.

Even then, she didn't throw it away.

She thought she'd just keep it around a few more days, in case she wanted to read it again. She wasn't going to call the number or anything. Of course she wasn't going to do that. But she might need to read it once more before she got rid of it altogether.

The next day, she'd put some pot holders on top of the letter, along with the duct tape. Then she put a carton of cigarettes on top of all of that. The letter was completely hidden. For good measure, she put the kitchen scissors and the screwdriver on top of everything and closed the drawer.

Her headache didn't go away.

Might as well have been a snake in that drawer. Just waiting.

Lying there nights, she would think she should throw the damn thing away, rip it into pieces, run water over it in the sink, flush it down the toilet. Because what was the point of it all? How long had she suffered over that whole horrible chapter of her life, how many years had it taken for her to fall asleep at night without seeing Kate's huge eyes welling up with tears—and how long until she had stopped hearing Kate crying, "Mama, noooo!"

Jesus, what it had taken to barricade that last day in a place in her mind where she could bear it! The day she'd actually had to hand Kate over. So thick with grief, it was like she was already dead instead of just wishing she was. Hardly able to stand up, but holding on to that baby like a mama tiger, as her sister Mary said later. "I didn't recognize your eyes," Mary said. "I never saw anybody look like that."

Mary saying that like she didn't know what it cost, the huge price. And Phoebe about to leave soon, getting out of town, moving to California. *Go to Aunt Jessie and get a fresh start, that's what you need,* Mary had said. *Don't think about what happened anymore, all the mistakes, the babies will be fine, the other one already in a good home and now this one will find a good home, too, she'll be so happy; don't be sad, you're giving her the greatest gift of all, a steady home life, people who will care for her.*

The social worker from the agency had been large and squatty, in her bright blue dress, and she'd held out her arms and said, "Okay, it's time, give her to me," and when Phoebe didn't immediately hand Kate over, but had kissed her about forty more times—forty heading to forty thousand—the woman had reached out, kindly but no nonsense, and had taken her. Maybe she had to do that because Phoebe couldn't have ever handed her over. But she'd *taken* her, that screaming child holding out her arms trying to get back to Phoebe. And Phoebe had had to walk away quickly, so hollowed out the wind was blowing through her; except for Mary holding her up she wouldn't have made it. Even inside the house, with the windows closed, they could still hear the shrieks as the social worker put Kate in her car, placing her in the car seat. Phoebe knew that Kate was probably arching her back, the way she did when she didn't want to go. *Oh God. Be gentle with her. Take good care of her. Please, please love her. Please. She's known so much love. Please.*

Stop thinking of all this again. Just stop it. You lived through it once, and you don't have to live through it again. So stop it.

But she couldn't stop.

Thank God Poppet had already been signed away; that had been hard enough, only two weeks old and already Phoebe couldn't even care for her, couldn't get out of bed, everything was darkness and her mind was filled with blood and milk and shit and her hands shook and she couldn't sleep but couldn't stay awake either—somewhere in that middle world of bad dreams. The baby had come too early, the night of the accident, and Mary and her husband were screaming at each other in the next room, their marriage falling apart because of Phoebe. And Mary's son, Kevin, and Kate crying crying crying and the new baby a pink, screaming thing, raw and primal wide mouth, batting fists, and *there was no way*, Mary said, *no way they could get through this, Phoebe can you even hear me, let's take care of this now, give the baby at least a forever home.*

Forever home. She hated those words.

A forever home first for Poppet, and then a month later, the letter coming from her aunt Jessie: *Come to California for high school, we'll help you start again. You'll have other babies later, darling, let's be practical now, you need to save your own life and think of your babies, too. They deserve good homes with a mother and a father who can take care of them.*

And Mary: *It's your only hope. It's unselfish, it's for the children, just sign the papers and go, go, go. Have a life.*

And Phoebe: *Good-bye Kate Poppet Kevin Mary life in the back bedroom laughing hope choice.*

Whole continents of hate had moved inside her. Volcanoes erupted. Earthquakes and seismic shifts. People acted like she would put it all behind her and start again, like that was even possible, and it would be okay, like adoption was the Best Idea. Tragic, yes, they said, but everybody would get over it.

And yet: Even in California, living with her aunt in a subdivision with bright sunlight and air so bleached out it was hard to see without squinting most days with the swimming pools and guitars and beach boys. Still, there were babies everywhere. In grocery stores trying to climb out of carts, running down the sidewalks to their mothers, playing at parks, gurgling in strollers, resting their peach-like heads on their mother's shoulder. And Phoebe saw each one of them. Every air current burned her beyond recognition.

She taught herself to look away, to go numb. Numb, numb, numb. Don't cry. Don't scream.

You could stay numb for a very long time. Forever, if you had to.

One day she yanked open the kitchen drawer and took the letter out. She was ready to light it on fire with her cigarette lighter and drop its pieces into the sink, watch them burn and wash it all down the drain. Get back to her meditation ritual and her cleansing ritual and her piano music and the soft, satisfying comfort of tidying up her house. The little things she'd learned she could control.

But first . . . she'd dial the number. She'd listen to Kate's voice. Maybe she'd get voice mail, and she could simply hear her daughter's inflections, the way she said her words, hear a smile in her voice that meant she was okay after all. Maybe that was what she needed.

But Kate had answered. The real Kate.

Fuck, fuck, fuck.

I just wanted to hear your voice. That's all.

I just wanted to rip your heart out once more and put you through the worst time of your life, because I can.

I saw the videos of you when you were Lulu.

Will you come and meet me? I just want to see you. I just want to know my story. I'll bring Lindy, too, okay?

She called her sister. Mary had left Connecticut twenty years ago after she married Shelby, her second husband, and he had family in Oklahoma, including a mom in a nursing home, and Mary had nobody here, really, she'd said. Phoebe was nobody, apparently, not worth staying in Connecticut for. Yet for so long, before the babies, Mary and Phoebe had been a family of two. Two survivors. Mary had practically raised her after their parents had died—both of them dead in one year, her mother of cancer and then him, of despair.

Oh shit. She was *not* going to tell Kate any of these stories! How could she tell this without making herself sound pathetic.

And . . . well, if she told these stories to a new friend over a glass of wine, she'd say, "And *then* the bad parts started!" And they'd laugh—that gallows humor, because what else *could* you do? She told it in a way to elicit laughter, was the truth. Because she had recovered, and she was stronger for it. That's what she said anyway.

"I talked to Kate," she said to Mary now. She'd practiced saying it, had circled the apartment, straightening things up, waiting for her music students, repeating the sentence. "I talked to Kate, I talked to Kate, I talked to Kate."

Like it was an everyday occurrence.

"Oh God," said Mary. "What do you mean, you talked to Kate?"

"I called her."

"Because of the letter? I thought you weren't going to do that."

"I know. But I did."

The clock was ticking in the kitchen, so very loud. She should recommend her kitchen clock for a part at the high school if they ever staged "The Tell-Tale Heart."

"How did she sound?"

"Good. Young."

"Well. Of course."

"She wants to meet me."

"Naturally she wants to meet you! Why wouldn't she? You're not going to, are you?"

"I don't know."

"What did you tell her?"

"I told her I would."

"But why? It can only hurt you."

"The other one will be there, too."

"Jesus, Phoebe. What are you doing to yourself? You're opening up a can of worms is what."

Phoebe squeezed her eyes shut. "I told Kate that I wasn't going to feel guilty about anything. And that I wouldn't answer any questions."

"You said you wouldn't answer any questions?" Mary laughed. "Now how are you going to do *that,* you nut? What about when she wants to know who her father is, and her grandparents?"

"I'll tell her there's only one marvelous aunt."

Mary laughed again. And then they changed the subject. Mary's son was working at a law firm in Texas, and his wife was pregnant. Mary was going to be a grandmother!

More family!

After Phoebe had hung up the phone, she made a vegan dinner for herself and ate it in her neat little kitchen, on the IKEA table. People thought it was odd how a vegan could insist on smoking, and maybe that *was* odd, but it made sense to her. She led a quiet life, with her teaching and her tidying, and collecting vegan cookbooks. She still sang at clubs sometimes, and there was a Brooklyn College teacher who liked for her to work with the acting students on improving their voices and their accents. She'd ride the subway and spend a day with the students, looking into their fresh faces and feeling the timbre of their voices resonating through her bones, carrying her home on the subway with her eyes closed. She was done with men now, with the ups and downs of love and not-love, and men disappearing on her—ghosting, the kids called it. Of course there had been plenty of times when she'd been the one to float away, like a ghost herself.

She was calm now. She knew she looked older than fifty, and that was okay with her. She had a skinny body and a lined face, with lots of wrinkles around her deep-set eyes and two long lines etched on either side of her mouth. Her red hair was graying and had a big white streak in the front. It was such a relief that she didn't care what she wore anymore——a relief to give up the hair dye and the men and the short skirts, all of it. Now she wore sweatshirts and leggings, a lucky necklace of rocks on a black string, and comfortable shoes.

She sat in the dark, meditating on a picture of the Buddha. She wasn't Buddhist, but she liked the picture and had bought it at the Tibetan market on Seventh Avenue.

The hate was all gone now. Where did such things go? Maybe the Buddha had sucked it up out of her, along with the fear and regret. She was okay. She was going to be fine, whether she saw Kate and Poppet or not.

That was the truth of it.

THIRTEEN
LINDY

Lindy was having what she was starting to think of as a Poppet kind of day. Those were the days—and she was having more of them lately—when she couldn't seem to shake the feeling that she had been meant to be someone else. Which was maybe why when the text came in from Nina, she didn't say no.

Poppet wanted to meet her mother, even if Lindy didn't.

Really, she thought, *I have to stop.* That helpless, unwanted baby couldn't be running things. Lindy had to regain control.

So she drove home after work only to find that her mother, against Lindy's explicit requests, had planted the kids in front of the television, and they were now slack-jawed, dead-eyed zombies, eating sugary cereal out of the box while sitting on beanbags in the family room.

"Hi, my sweet patooties," she said to them. Nobody looked at her, but Razzie stuck his thumb in his mouth and rolled off the beanbag pillow and onto the carpet, without taking his eyes from the shrill-talking Muppet chirping something about feelings.

Feelings. God.

She picked up the cereal box, which had fallen over, and ruffled the hair of all three of them, then went into the kitchen, where her mother was drinking a cup of Dunkin' Donuts coffee and doing a Sudoku puzzle. The lunch dishes were lined up in the drainer, not put in the dishwasher as Lindy would have liked. Her mom didn't trust dishwashers for some insane reason; she always washed them herself, then insisted on air-drying them because dish towels apparently harbored germs. So the kitchen always looked chaotic.

But that wasn't what had Lindy clenching her teeth. Nor that her mother was ignoring the children. Her mother deserved a break during the day—of course she did!—but Lindy and Jeff were very careful about how much TV they let their kids watch, and screen time for the twins always ended badly, with them whining and being impossible, overstimulated and underexercised. And really? Honey Nut Cheerios as a snack food? Not even any milk? But were you allowed to be upset when somebody was doing you such a huge favor by keeping your children? That was the problem right there.

But it wasn't even that today.

"Hi," she said to her mom, and put her purse down on the counter perhaps a little harder than necessary.

Her mother looked up at her and tightened her lips. "Well, *you're* in a mood, I see. What's going on with you?"

Peggy Walsh was wearing a powder-blue sweater with a little white collar poking out above, and she had on her usual baggy jeans (her babysitting pants, she called them). Her gray hair was cut short, even mannishly short, and could have looked so much better if she'd just let Lindy put a rinse on it, to bring out the shine. But of course she wouldn't. It was almost a point of pride with her, how little she cared about her appearance. Like she had so many other, better things to think about.

"Nothing, really." Lindy leafed through the stack of mail: bills, bills, a catalog for kids' spring clothing, blah blah blah. Her head was buzzing unpleasantly.

"Well, good, then." Her mother started gathering her things—her blue plastic pocketbook stashed in the corner, her coat thrown across the stool. "Things were fine here. Kids seemed extra tired, so I let 'em have some *Dora the Explorer* therapy. Razzie had a poop about three o'clock. Not in the potty, of course. Phone messages are on the counter."

"Mom," said Lindy.

"What?"

"When you adopted me, was there another child, too? Did I have a sister?"

Honestly she hadn't known she was going to say that—it just came out. Her mother looked stunned for about four seconds, and then she started laughing one of her deep, bitter, life-is-hard, what-fresh-hell-is-this non-laughs. "Now why in the world would you be asking *that*? That's all ancient history now."

So that was a yes.

"I just want to know," Lindy said. "There was a sister, wasn't there? Fourteen or fifteen months older than me?"

Her mother closed her eyes and rubbed her temples. "I don't remember."

"Really? Because I met a woman who says she's my sister—and she looks like me, and she got adopted by another family in our neighborhood actually, and I—"

"Lindy, for heaven's sake, where are you going with this? I don't know who you met or why anybody would tell you this stuff at this late date. Do we honestly have to rehash the past?"

Lindy was silent for a moment. Then she said, "No, I just wanted to know. Did they offer you both of us? When you adopted me. Did they want you to take my sister, too?"

"Oh, for God's sake, this is all ancient history now. I had my hands full with the family I did have; I don't remember what went on back then about a family I didn't have."

"Fine. Okay. Case closed. Doesn't matter one bit." Lindy slammed the cabinet door as she got out a water glass.

When she turned around, her mother was staring at her. "I don't see how this is important to your life. Unless it's something you're saying to make me feel bad. Ohh, I get it! You're mad that the children are watching television, aren't you, and that's what this is about."

"I'm not—"

"Yes. Yes, you are. I know that look on your face. You always get huffy when you come home and they're watching TV. You have this idea that children have to be engaged in something educational every single minute, that they can't have any downtime."

"I just don't like them watching so much TV, because then they're wrecks later. You should see how I have to practically scoop them up—"

"Fine! You *should* be scooping them up! That's life, Lindy! That's what motherhood is! Kids are trouble!"

"Okay," said Lindy. "Forget it. I'm sorry."

"*Okay?* It's not okay. You know what's going on here? You don't have the slightest idea what it's really like to be a hands-on mother. You think coming home and giving them a bath and putting them to bed is all that's required of you! Your kids won't be little forever, you know, and you're missing out on some pretty important days."

"Please," said Lindy. "I know what I'm missing out on. I just asked if you'd been given the choice of adopting my sister, and suddenly you're attacking me."

"I actually feel sorry for you, do you know that? Every day I leave here, and I feel sorry for you. Having to maintain all this—this pretend world—"

"This is not a pretend world. It's a world in which the furniture matches. Also, I don't know why you can't be proud of me. For all this.

For how hard I work. Can't you even once think, 'Wow, Lindy is doing her best! It may not be what I would have chosen, but I can see that she's working really, really hard.' Can't you do that?"

"You're being childish," her mother said—her go-to insult when her children disappointed her—and then walked over to the back door, still with that half smile on her face that Lindy wanted to obliterate. "You're the only one of my children who needs a cheering section. You know that? That's supposed to come from within. Having the biggest salon in town, pampering all those rich women who don't give a damn about you, isn't ultimately what's going to bring you lasting happiness. Your true happiness is going to come from your *family*. Oh, but perish the thought! That's so—so old-fashioned. My values are completely out-of-date, I know."

Lindy felt that old familiar clutch of fear she'd always had whenever her mother's eyes went cold. It was like when she was a child and her mother would send her to bed without supper, banished from the rest of the household, away from the laughter and the uproarious family life into the dark, where she had to stay in bed, alone and quiet, and think about how bad she was, how unworthy and ungrateful. Mrs. Walsh had the support of the priests and the neighbors and the ladies' auxiliary and the teachers and the nuns to prove it. Whatever *children* thought didn't matter. And never let it be forgotten that Lindy was just a kid she'd taken in, a good deed she'd done.

Even now, all grown up, she still depended upon her mother. How could she and Jeff afford all that child care if her mother quit coming each day? They couldn't. Plus, Jeff didn't believe kids should be left in just *anyone's* care.

"Mom," said Lindy. "Stop." Her heart was racing, and she thought for a minute she was going to throw up. "Mama, please . . ."

But her mother had already turned the doorknob. Before she stepped outside, she said in an icy voice that sliced at Poppet's heart, even while Lindy stood there taking it all in, "And yes, if it's any of your business, I do remember now. There *were* two of you. After we took you, they contacted us and asked if we'd take another child. Your sister. We said no."

"Oh," said Lindy.

Her mother looked furious. "I couldn't do it. I'd already adopted Ellen, and the thought of three kids under three years old was too much for me. Something I would think that *you* of all people could understand! But why would you, come to think of it?"

"I didn't—"

"And you know what else? Your saintly *father* of course thought we should have taken the other girl, too, but what do men know about what goes on in a house? Nothing. You women today have husbands who help with baths and dinner, but we didn't have that. Your father didn't lift a finger, and I knew it was all on me! I didn't *have* a mother who would show up at my house every morning and help out! It was just me! So I said to him, 'Someone else will adopt the other one, don't worry.' Satisfied? Does this make you happy now?"

"No," said Lindy. She tapped hard, squeezing her fingers together. Sometimes if you squeezed while you tapped, things worked better. "Listen," she said in a low voice, and she couldn't believe she was saying this, and maybe she wasn't really saying it out loud, "listen, I think I might get to know my birth mother. She called my sister today."

Her mother's face went pale. So she *had* said it out loud. Some part of her floated up to the ceiling and sat there watching. Lindy was quaking, but Poppet stood her ground.

"Oh, well, that's just wonderful!" said her mother. "Why do you want to do that? Opening a big fat can of worms is what you're doing—and it's a slap in the face to me, too. How do you think that makes me feel, Lindy, when *I'm* the one helping you out, day after day, and being in your life? And now you're going to run to—to that woman who gave you away? This is the thanks I get?"

"It's not about that," Lindy said quietly. "I just may need to know more about who I am."

"Who you *are*? You think somebody who gave you away right after you were born is going to have any information about *who you are*? That woman didn't even *know* you!"

Lindy was aware that the children had come into the kitchen and were standing in the doorway. Davey was holding his wet diaper in his hand as well as the TV remote, and Chloe, wearing an Elsa crown, was staring with wide, frightened eyes. Only Razzie ran over and grabbed Lindy around the knees, smearing Cheerios into her black leggings. She reached down and hugged him, then the other two came over, and she kissed the tops of their heads over and over again.

And then her mother just left, gathering up her things without saying good-bye. Lindy heard the car door slam and the car speed out of the driveway, spewing gravel so hard it was like the very driveway had joined in on her mother's side and was firing at Lindy, too.

"Grandma is mad," said Chloe.

"It'll be fine," said Lindy. Poppet had gone quiet.

FOURTEEN
NINA

After I got off the phone with my mother, I couldn't find Indigo.

I drove to her therapist's office and waited in the reception area to see if maybe she'd somehow gotten a ride there and needed me to drive her home, but after forty-five minutes, when the patient and therapist came out, blinking in surprise, Indigo wasn't the patient.

"Was Indigo here today?" I asked the therapist, a worn-out-looking woman. Her glasses hung from a beaded chain around her neck, and she put them on and peered at me. I must have looked disheveled, perhaps even insane, because she drew back and said she wasn't permitted to answer any questions.

"Indigo," I said. "Actually Kayla Sanborn. I was supposed to drive her here, and I wasn't . . . available because something came up. Did she ever come?"

"I'm sorry, but you are not her mother, and I cannot answer questions about any of my patients," said the therapist. I turned away.

I should have talked to my mother in the car on the way to meet Indigo. I should have put her on the speakerphone, or said I'd call her back. I could even have put her on hold for a moment and called Indigo to say I'd be late. But I didn't do any of those things because the truth was I hadn't wanted to risk having my mother stop talking.

I drove to Carter's house but nobody was there, so I called him on his cell. I told him I'd lost Indigo, and he said not to worry, that children never stay lost for long. They always seem to come back no matter where a person misplaces them.

"But I was supposed to take her to her therapy appointment, and—"

"Therapy schmerapy," said Carter. "So she misses one. What's the worst that could happen?"

"But I'm home now, and she's not here!"

"It's okay, Popkin. Don't worry so much. I think she went to a friend's house. That's why I texted you, to see if she'd told you not to come pick her up. I couldn't remember. I can't keep track of all this stuff. She'll be back for dinner," he said. "Listen, sweet one, you've got to relax. I think you're going to have a much harder time in parenting adventures if you don't learn that things generally work out."

Generally work out? Did he not know what was going on?

Maybe that would have been the point to mention the Fuck-It List—and the very real possibility that she was out performing mischief to keep herself from being considered a good kid. I really was going to have to talk to her about that. If things continued. Which they might not if the Sanborns decided that my services as a stepmother-to-be were not needed anymore, and I moved on to my real family, which I could feel forming out in the world. Even as I was talking to him on the phone. Maybe Phoebe was on the phone right now, calling her relatives, letting them know the good news: my babies are back in my life!

Maybe, in fact, I should just leave. Pack up my two garbage bags full of stuff and go back to Josephine's apartment for good. Declare that this wasn't working out.

Then Indigo arrived, marching into the house, glaring at me, kicking at the entryway table that was always stacked high with mail. A lamp briefly considered falling to the ground. She threw herself on the couch and pulled her mangy old My Little Pony blanket over herself, something she'd retrieved from the attic a week or so ago. It was a definite step back into the womb of childhood, Carter had said, amused by it.

"Listen, Indigo, I'm so very sorry that I didn't pick you up on time."

Silence.

"I was planning to come; I was about to leave, in fact, but kind of an amazing thing happened to me."

"It's fine. Forget it. Maya's brother gave me a ride," she said.

"You went to therapy with Maya's brother?"

"Nope. I am fucking not going to therapy anymore."

"What do you mean, you're not going to therapy anymore?"

"I'm not going. I can't get there; I don't have anything to say to Dr. Liz, she's not helping me; I want to kill myself most of the time anyway, so why go see her?"

"Whoa, whoa, whoa. You want to kill yourself?"

"Oh, don't try to pretend you care *now*."

So that's how it was going to be. I protested that I cared, that I in fact cared very much, and if she was serious about thinking about killing herself, then we had better go to the hospital because that was *not okay*. A person couldn't just throw that around like it was nothing.

"I don't mean kill myself like really *kill myself*," she said. "Duuhhh. I wouldn't do that!"

I threw up my hands and pretended to be figuring out what that sentence meant, drawing it out in the air and frowning. Which made her laugh. Which then made her mad, because she was too mad to laugh.

"STOP IT!" she screamed, and I jumped in real alarm. And then she really did laugh, and I went to sit next to her and took hold of the satiny border of the My Little Pony blanket. "I had one of these once," I said. "My Little Pony has been around, like, forever."

"Don't try to make friends with me over My Little Pony. Have some respect for yourself."

I don't know why that made me laugh, but it did, and then she pushed me, but she was trying not to laugh, too. I grabbed her and hugged her, not sure if she was going to slug me. But she didn't. She may have even exerted the slightest bit of pressure back. Infinitesimal, but still.

"I talked to my mother today," I said after a long time of us silently sitting next to each other on the couch.

"Your mother that died?"

"No. I don't know if you are aware of this or not, but it's very hard to talk to dead people. Mostly they don't answer."

"Oh, then I guess you've never heard of séances."

"Oh, then I guess you think that's a real thing."

"Oh, then I guess you don't know that my friend Sylvia talks to her dead father all the time at this woman's place over on Stanley Street. And they light candles."

"Well, I stand corrected then. But I talked to my living mother."

"What? How?"

"She called me. She got my letter and she apparently thought about it for about ninety-seven thousand days, and then today she suddenly decided to pick up the phone and call me. It was the first time I'd gotten to hear her voice."

"Nooooo, that's not true . . . she's Lulu, and even *I* have heard her voice."

"Jeez, you're a stickler for details. Okay, it was the first time I'd heard my mother speaking to me in her regular talking voice, not singing to the public in the nineteen-eighties."

"What did she sound like?"

"She sounded like she might have smoked about a hundred cigarettes since this morning."

"So that's why you couldn't come get me? You were talking on the
phone."

"Yep, your honor, that's why," I said cheerfully. "I was yakking away
with this woman who gave birth to me. I hope this will be pardoned
in your eyes."

"I guess so."

"Thank you, your honor. And guess what. I'm going to get to meet
her. We made a date to see each other."

"What are you going to wear?"

"I don't know! But that is such an excellent question, and you are
exactly the right person to ask it."

"Because you don't want to look like you're trying too hard. No
offense, but you sometimes look a little bit like somebody who is trying
just a little bit too hard."

"Really."

"Sometimes. And you laugh too much at other people's jokes even
if they're lame."

"I do?"

"So, when you meet your mom—this is all I'm saying—maybe you
should just wear, you know, something super cool that says *I don't care*.
I think you should wear leggings or your jeans with rips in them—"
Then she stopped and made a face. "No offense, but I take it back about
your jeans with the rips, because—well, you're actually kind of too old
for those, you know? I think it looks seriously sucky when old people
try to look like kids. But don't worry, I'll help you. I'm going to have to
think of what you should wear and how your makeup should be. But
the main thing is do not laugh at anything she says unless you really,
really like it. Make your face look neutral. Like this."

And she set her face into such a mask of nonfeeling that I almost burst out laughing again, except that there was a tiny part of me that had started to worry about how phony I might look in my ripped jeans.

"Do it, too," she commanded me.

So I did. We both sat there, not moving our facial muscles and staring straight ahead, and that's how we looked when Tyler and Carter burst in the door with the news that Tyler had been accepted at three of his desired schools. Three!

And that night, to commemorate the two good things—my mother's call and Tyler's acceptances—Carter, looking as happy as I'd seen him, insisted that we celebrate by boiling lobsters for dinner. It was a hysterical time—one lobster got out of the bag and scuttled across the kitchen floor, and the kids and I laughed as we watched Carter chasing it with a paper bag and the salad tongs into the dining room, where he finally cornered it behind the breakfront and marched it back to the pot of boiling water before doing a victory lap around the kitchen.

Later, Tyler played a new composition he'd written on his guitar, while Carter spun Indigo and me around the kitchen and taught us how to make his special recipe of coleslaw with horseradish. After dinner, he put on all his old Beatles albums—just in case anyone might be in need of further education, he said—and stretched out on the kitchen floor with a beer, while I taught Indigo how to make a blueberry pie.

I thought about my own upbringing, with my quiet bookworm parents and how we three would tiptoe around one another. An evening of celebration—like the one when I got accepted to college—consisted of calm conversation and planning for the future.

Why wasn't anybody talking about which school Tyler should go to? Why weren't they Skyping with Jane, or doing their homework? But no. In the Carter Sanborn world, everything had to be a celebration. I looked across the room at the way his eyes were shining and they looked too bright, too glittery, and when he came by and swooped me into a hug and kiss, I felt myself pulling away.

Around eleven, long after Indigo had taken herself off to bed, she called me into her room and said, "Don't tell my dad I'm not going to therapy anymore, okay?"

"Okaaaaay," I said. "You want to tell him yourself?"

"I'll tell him eventually. But I don't want to talk to him about it yet."

"Well . . . but shouldn't he know? I mean, he pays the bill, right?"

"God, Nina. Everything doesn't have to be about money," she said sternly, and I had that feeling again that I was the dumbest person in the world and that Indigo was considering whether to take me on as a rehab project. My application was still being processed, evidently.

"I won't tell him tonight, but I really do think he should know. Also," I said, "there's this other little tiny thing I want to bring up, and maybe now isn't the time but—"

"What? Just say it!"

"Okay." I stepped farther into her room and closed the door. "I don't recommend that you have sex with someone you don't care about just because you want to get it over with. Sex is kind of a cool thing and worth waiting for with the right person. Also, you're way too young to have sex now. It could really mess you up. And last but not least, any guy who had sex with you now could be arrested. It's not even legally allowed. Okay? Do you get what I'm saying?"

There was only silence in the darkness. Then she said, "You know, this isn't really about you. You're literally not even family."

I had to stagger my way to the front room after that, hand over my poor, stupid, faintly beating heart.

Early the next morning, I put a pot roast into the slow cooker, heroically cutting up beef and potatoes and onions and carrots before I'd so much as had a cup of coffee. Then I made both breakfast and lunch for all four of us. Clearly I'd become the poster child for Trying Too Hard, but we needed meals, didn't we? And nobody else was going to make them.

Carter had just left—something about inventory now that the orders were flying in for the summer boat season—and I had just poured myself a cup of coffee when Indigo asked me to sign a permission slip for her to leave school early with her friend Maya.

"Who will pick you up?" I said.

"Oh. Her brother. He picks us up sometimes."

"Ah, yes. I remember you saying he was the one who picked you up yesterday when I didn't come."

"God!" she said, rolling her eyes. "Why are you making such a big hairy deal about this?" Then she started fiddling with her backpack, not looking at me, which I knew meant that something was up.

"But does your dad know that Maya's brother picks you up? How old is this guy anyway?"

"Nina! What the hell? He's *twenty*, okay? He's been driving, like, forever. And he's my friend's *brother. God.*"

"But where are you going after school? Why do you need to leave early?"

"What is this, the Inquisition? Are you the police or something? My dad lets me do this. Call him if you don't believe me." She let out a huge, outraged sigh and said, "I am an honor student, in case you forgot, *and,* if you need to know, we are going to be working on a project together for our social studies class, which is about as innocent as you can get."

Innocent? I wanted to say. You're the one with that list in your bedroom. I don't think anything you do is innocent!

But I didn't. After all, I'd been snooping when I found that list, and so, according to the Laws of Parenting, I couldn't use any information from it. Even I knew that. Instead I said, "All right, I'll sign," and she said huffily, "*Thank* you! God!"

And then—ta-dah!—I went to my hair appointment with Lindy.

When you're a customer at A Little Piece of Heaven, they first bring you a glass of sparkling water with your choice of a strawberry, a lime, or a cucumber floating in it, whether or not you have ever in your life wanted fruits and vegetables in your water glass. You realize this is a magnificent idea. And they give you these extra-silky black smocks to wear—and they fuss over you like you're some kind of celebrity. I already knew the music was divine, but I had no idea how comfortable the chairs were, or how sweet it would be to have my sister washing my hair, not looking so exasperated for once.

After the shampoo and the scalp massage, we went to her station, and she lifted sections of my hair and studied them. "It has its own ideas about curling and cowlicks," I said apologetically. It was on its worst behavior that day.

"The keratin will cure that."

"So . . . how are you?" I said.

She sighed. She wasn't great. Chloe was home with the throw-ups, and her mother was calling her every fifteen minutes with updates.

"Oh, I'm so sorry," I said. "Must be so tough when the kids are sick. I bet they all get it when one does."

Her mouth was set in a straight line. All business. "Before we do the keratin, I want to cut some of this dead stuff off," she said. "Do you mind?"

"Cut away."

"Are you comfortable with a much shorter cut?"

"By much shorter, are we talking crew cut?"

"No."

"Then whatever. You're the expert. I just want to look like—you know, a reasonably put-together human female when you're done. If you have any latent sibling rivalry, I'd prefer this didn't show up on the top of my head." I laughed to show how much of a joke that was, but she didn't join in.

She started snipping away in sections. I closed my eyes. She was so close to me, I could smell her minty breath, the floral aroma of the shampoo she'd used, and something else, maybe the essence of her. Her body was warm so close to mine—my sister, flesh related to my flesh. A real person.

We'd had the same parents. But then something had happened.

Amazing to think this. Do other brothers and sisters go around realizing this fact over and over again—that they came from the same people? Do they look at each other and marvel at the amazing coincidence of it all? I've never heard anybody mention it.

Finally I cleared my throat and said, "So I have a little bit of news."

She didn't say anything.

"Our mom called me."

Her hands stopped moving with the scissors. "For real?" she said in a low voice.

"For real. And I talked to her for a really long time."

Silence.

"She's great. She's careful, you know? Doesn't want to talk about a lot of things so the conversation started out weird, but then it got better. I feel like—I feel like this is going to lead to good things. Family-wise, you know."

I twisted my hands in my lap underneath the smock.

She sighed and looked around, then whispered, "Nina, *she gave us away.* We're not part of that family anymore."

This again. "But there were circumstances. You know there were circumstances."

"Yeah? What were they? What?"

"I don't know. She said she couldn't talk about it. Legally."

"*Legally?* Oh my God, that *is* incredible. Legally, you say. Listen to yourself. She's making all that up to justify what she did."

"Listen. She's funny and kind of . . . guarded. She seemed worried that I was calling to make her feel guilty or something. She kept saying she wasn't a very nice person. She's very up-front about all her flaws. Down-to-earth."

"Uh-huh. See? I knew she wasn't very nice. People tell you who they really are, if you listen and pay attention. If she says she's not nice, then she knows."

"Well, I took that to mean the opposite. Don't you think that people who claim they're not very nice are usually the nicest people but they're holding themselves at fault for minor indiscretions?"

"Giving away two children doesn't feel like a minor indiscretion to me."

Her phone rang in her pocket. "Great, the fifteen-minute update is here. Hi, Mom. How's it going now?" She made a face at me. "Razzie just threw up," she whispered to me. "We're in for it now. Yeah, I'm doing a treatment, but I'll come when I'm done . . . No, no, I'm still fine, you? Okay. See you later."

She put her phone back into her pocket. "My life," she said. "Some days it's just unbelievable."

"What else is going on?" I asked her. "Tell me."

Oh, she said, not only were the kids sick, but her brother Danny and his wife left their basset hound with her and Jeff while they went on vacation, and also her sister in Albuquerque was asking if she could send her three kids here for part of the summer because they wanted to know their grandmother better. In addition to all that, Lindy was president of the Mothers of Twins and there was some dissent on the board. On and on. It was all busy and problem-y and then there was the PTA stuff, which I didn't really want to hear about, but I listened anyway because it was simply nice to be in Lindy's presence, even if she didn't want to know our mother.

"That sounds like a lot," I said.

"A lot of too much to do," she said. Then she was back to looking at my hair like it was a science project gone awry, something that would need every bit of her concentration. She turned on the blow dryer, then she got some kind of smelly solution junk that she smeared on sections of my hair, a little at a time.

She said, "Come on, let's get you some magazines while this stuff sets."

There was a private room in the back of the salon with couches and soft lighting, and I settled down among the pillows and magazines. She tucked a shawl around my shoulders.

I said in a low voice, "Just so you know, our mom wants to meet us."

She blinked. "See? That's exactly what I was afraid of. And that is *not* a good idea."

"Come on. I think we should do it. Go into New York and have a glass of wine with her. She said it would be a one-time deal. A one-off. Meet, greet, shake hands, get a good look at her, give her a good look at us, and that will be it."

"But why?"

"I don't know. For curiosity. For love? So we can say we did it? For whatever."

Lindy didn't say anything, just pursed her lips. Maybe this wasn't the best day to talk about this, with the kids sick and all, I thought.

"Just think about it," I said. "I told her we'd come. It's this Saturday, at a bar in Brooklyn, and all you have to do is sit there and have a glass of wine with your birth mom, a person you won't ever have to see again. Then years from now when your kids find out you were adopted, you can tell them that at least you met your birth mom, and here's what she was like."

"Will I? You think I'll want to explain that I was given life by a woman who's probably a drug addict and also in the Mafia? And who couldn't manage to operate a condom?"

"Sure, and you can also tell them she shot a guy in Memphis just to watch him die. You can use her as a threat anytime you need to."

"Just so you know, it's Reno. That's where people shoot someone just to watch them die, according to Johnny Cash," she said.

"Noted. Come on, Lindy. I think we *have* to do it."

"Tell me this," Lindy said. "Does she *want* to get together with us? Is she the one making this happen?"

"Well, no. Actually not. She's another one who doesn't know how great this is going to be. But she's agreed to come."

Lindy burst out laughing. "Are you kidding me? For God's sake, Nina, are you bullying *all of us* into being a family?"

"Yep. Whether you want to or not. Because it's going to be great."

"It's going to be awful. I bet you anything she doesn't show up. And then . . . when that happens—well, could we stop with this whole pretense?"

"Okay," I said, but I was stung. Did she mean the pretense that she and I are family? I think that's exactly what she meant. Was I supposed to give her up after this? "So we'll go together," I said. "And look at it this way: at least you won't have anyone throwing up on you that night."

"I don't know."

"Listen to me. I'm your big sister. Your *real* big sister. Not that other one who left and moved to Albuquerque after spending your childhood making you wear her hand-me-downs and probably used to tattle on you and got to do everything first and wouldn't let you play with her stuff."

"It's like you were there," said Lindy.

"See? That's why you have to do what I say," I told her. "I'm the new and improved version of a big sister."

Hours later—after being flat ironed and rinsed, then coated with a special mask for a half hour, then blown dry again and styled within an inch of its life—well, my hair turned out gorgeous: chin-length, layered and smooth, but not curly, just curlyish. It was chastened and apologetic, this hair, willing to lie where Lindy told it to, and behaving like it *wanted* someone to show it who was boss. When I went to pay, Lindy waved my money away.

"This is my down payment on you agreeing not to keep pretending," she said. I went to hug her, and she held me at arm's length staring right at me with her startlingly clear hazel eyes, which frankly looked a little shiny. Was she having an emotion?

"Listen," she said in a whisper. "I do get it. I know what you feel. My mother—my mother at the very least should have taken both of us. We belonged together. But your family isn't the people you share some DNA with, okay? Your family is going to be other people, and your job is to go and find them and make them love you."

"But how do you do it?" I said. "How do you make people love you—really love you, when you don't belong to them?"

Then, of course, her phone rang because she was the busiest person in the world. Maybe her mother wanting to report that yet *another* child was throwing up, or the PTA wanting her to chair some new committee. And Lindy sighed in that mock-exasperated way she does so well, and reached into her pocket, turning away.

Outside, my phone rang, too, and it was Carter.

"Want to have a romantic evening out, just the two of us?" he said. "We could go to the club. It's been a long time."

"What about the kids?"

"Those animals?" He chuckled. "They can fend for themselves. Kayla is at somebody's house."

"Maya's house. I wanted to talk to you about that. I wrote her a permission slip to leave school early."

"You did? Awesome. Remind me who Maya is again."

"*Carter!* Please tell me you're kidding. Maya is Indigo's best friend. And she's new here, but anytime now she's going to be discovered by the cool kids and she won't be Indigo's friend anymore. She's got it all, from the fifteen-year-old standpoint: looks, smarts, and moxie."

"Indigo told you all that?"

"Duhhh. Where have *you* been?"

He said mournfully, "I know. That's all car talk, when she spills her guts. Now that you're doing the car runs, I'm not getting my share of the intel. Shit. Well, would you still consider going out with me? On a date? Even though I'm woefully behind on all things."

"What's Tyler doing tonight?"

"Tyler is eighteen. He doesn't have to say what he's going to do."

"But it's a school night. Are you sure?"

"I'm sure," he said, sighing. "They're fine. Popkin, despite what you may think, I am a good father. I love and adore my children. I lived in the house for one solid year with their mother from whom I was divorced, just so I could see their grumpy faces every morning and know what they were up to."

"Okay," I said quickly. "But one other thing: I made us a pot roast this morning and put it in the slow cooker. And it might be delicious enough to make us want to stay home . . . just saying."

"Nope. We need fun. Tyler can eat that if he's home."

Funny that *I* was the one who was the proponent of family dinners, table conversation, and doing the dishes together when nobody else cared that much. Maybe they'd had enough of that kind of life already.

"All right," I said with a sigh. "Let's do it."

That afternoon at work, Melanie turned to me. "You know, we said that in the spring we were going to list your mom's condo for sale. Are you ready?"

I was sitting at my desk, staring at a Facebook post from Dan.

There was a picture of him, sweaty, beaming, holding a little bundle in a blanket. For a moment, the blood was beating in my ears so hard I couldn't hear anything else.

Eliza is here! he wrote.

> The best thing I ever did! This is the happiest day of my life! I am so overwhelmed and blessed and deliriously happy with my beautiful wife who somehow knew all along that what I needed was a child, and so what if my ex-wife had begged me to have a baby with her, ha ha. I told her I wasn't ready, but boy you can sure get ready when you marry your bank teller like I did! #soblessed #Idon'tmissyouNina #bestdayever.

Okay, so he didn't write all that. But he and Julie did have a baby.

I hadn't texted him in so long, but now I wanted to write to him: *But you said . . .*

Instead I said, "Oh no no no no no no no."

Which Melanie thought was the answer to her question—and guess what? It kinda worked for that, too. My head started to hurt.

"No," I said. "Don't list the condo."

Going to the boat club again was great—twinkling white lights over the fireplace, the surf pounding far below the floor-to-ceiling windows, the sea foam glinting in the moonlight, and a little band playing soft, mellow jazz, off to one side.

Carter and I sat at a table overlooking the water, away from his rowdy, laughing friends and their boat talk, and he reached over and took my hand across the tablecloth. "How are you?" he said. "You look absolutely beautiful. Your hair, by the way, is exquisite."

"Come on. Next you're going to start telling me my shoes are wonderful, and I'm going to have to crawl across the table and start making out with you," I said.

"Really?" he said. "Is that all it would take? Let me be the first to mention this then. Your shoes are *amazing*."

He was staring into my eyes. I could feel myself sliding off somewhere, my second glass of wine lighting me up from within, or maybe the heat was just from his gaze. I took in his stubbly, sexy beard, his capable, large, warm hand on mine. His look was like something I could reach over and scoop up with both hands. Golden.

He smiled slowly, showing those divine even white teeth of his. His lips were slightly chapped, and his tanned face glowing, and he took my other hand in his, and said, "Come with me," and then we were out on the dance floor and his hand was pressed against the small of my back as we glided around, probably too close. He smelled salty and gingery, and I put my head against his shoulder and felt his heartbeat mingling with mine. I wanted him so badly right then that I would have gladly ducked into the back room with him and made out with him until people forced us back to the dance floor.

"Wow," he whispered into my ear. "You really needed a night out."

I put my mouth on his ear in reply, and he pulled me in tighter. And then we were kissing.

Someone—a couple he knew—danced up near us and the man said, "Look at you two. You know, we have cots in the back room for these kinds of emergencies."

Carter did his polite social laugh, and danced me away to a farther end of the room. "You make me so happy," he said. "This is good, isn't it? We have a good life."

"We do," I said.

"Hectic, crazy, but so much fun."

I put my mouth on his.

His pocket started to vibrate.

"Is that your phone, or are you happy to see me?" I said.

"A little of both." He pulled away slightly and wrestled his phone out of his pocket and looked down at it. His forehead creased.

"Oh boy. Gotta take this." He let go of my hand and walked away. There was a person-size chunk of cold air next to me suddenly, and I shivered. He ducked out through the sliding doors onto the deck; I watched him through the window as he paced. When he came back in, he said, "The evening has taken an interesting turn."

"Interesting bad or interesting good?" I said.

"It's parentally interesting. Seems I have to go fetch Kayla from the police station. She was picked up doing, ah, some public artwork."

"Public artwork?"

"Graffiti. Sounds like they're not going to charge her with anything, though. They just want me to get her. Sometimes my children have the worst possible timing when they're out discovering their own limits."

We said good-bye to everyone and put up with a round of good-natured ribbing about not being able to keep our hands off each other, and then held hands as we ran to the parking lot. The April night was one of those teasers of a New England almost-spring: the slight promise of warmth in the air—not velvety warm yet, and certainly no crickets chirping, but wispy clouds lit by the lights of the city, floating high over everything.

"I'll make this up to you," he said as we drove in the darkness.

"No worries," I said. "This comes first. I know that."

Two big items got crossed off the Fuck-It List that night.

Graffiti *and* a trip to the police station. If there'd been a Fuck-It List item about nearly losing your life dangling from a rope on the side of a hill *while* you painted the graffiti, that would have gotten crossed off, too. Only Indigo hadn't come up with that. That idea was all the fabulous Maya's, whom we met at the police station, along with her fabulous mother and stepfather, who seemed to have come to the police station wearing their coats over their pajamas.

Children were sorted out, and warned. *Graffiti is a crime, dangling from ropes is a crime, being out past curfew is a crime.* Maya's family, heavy-lidded, silent, hardly comprehending, it seemed to me—or maybe this was merely the latest in a long list—shuffled out to their car, with Maya tucked between them, turning back to give us fluttery good-bye waves and dazzling smiles.

Carter looked every bit the part of the stern, concerned, law-abiding parent as he signed the papers and talked to the cops. His hand rested lightly on Indigo's shoulders, in just the right protective sort of way.

But when we got to the car, he enveloped her in a hug and said, "Oh my goodness, Kayla, you have to tell me everything about what happened tonight! What the heck? Climbing a hillside at night? Baby, baby, baby! Were you so scared?"

Was she *scared*? I guessed that she wasn't, not until things started to go badly awry. I watched my breath fogging up the passenger-side window while I waited for her response. I pictured my father—my sweet, meek, schoolteacher, follow-all-rules father—and what he would have said to me in similar circumstances. Anyway, I hoped she'd say she had been scared shitless and that she didn't want to have a Fuck-It List anymore, that simply being an honor student was enough of a challenge. (Well, sorry, but that *was* my first choice.) Or maybe she'd say that she would no longer channel her longing for her mother into such socially unacceptable acts. Or that Maya couldn't be trusted. Or that she was grateful for life now that she hadn't died on the hill.

Any of those answers would have been acceptable.

Instead what she said was, "I don't want to talk about it."

"Well, I can understand that," said Carter, "but, honey, I think we have to talk about it, a little bit at least."

"I wish Nina was my real mom, because she *gets me*," she said at last.

"*I* get you, sweetheart," he said, and she was silent.

I wanted to tell her that yes, I *did* "get her," and if she were *my* daughter, there would be no more Fuck-It List—she would be back in therapy in a heartbeat, I'd be making sure she got her homework done, she would be grounded for a good long time until she could prove herself trustworthy and kind, *and* she would be sentenced to telling me every single thought that came into her head. Or something. Whatever. I'd figure it out as I went along. I'd love her and talk to her and make sure she did the right thing. I'd stand guard at her bedroom door if necessary, like Granny Clampett, until she straightened herself out.

But Carter had that gloomy look on his face again that I remembered from when I first met him. I couldn't think who he reminded me of, and then it came to me: he was Eeyore. Long-suffering, agonizing. I couldn't believe it.

We got home, and instead of grounding her and scolding her, he kept telling her how much he loved her and Tyler, and how it was okay to miss their mom—and how she needed to know that he was always one hundred percent on her side for everything, and he always would be. We all stayed up way too late, and Carter put on David Bowie because "it's time you're introduced to one of the great risk takers of all time," he said. Then Tyler came in at midnight, red-eyed and startled to see us still up, and that was okay, too. We were a ragtag group that I was quite sure their mother wouldn't have recognized as her family, and then—well, then it got to be one thirty in the morning, and we went to bed. After hugs all around.

The trouble was, I couldn't sleep. I lay there, looking at Carter's lined face smashed up against the pillow, and I listened to him snore and I got madder and madder at him.

"Carter." I shook him awake. "Carter, you have to talk to me."

His eyes fluttered open, unfocused, and came to rest on my face. My angry face.

"What's the matter?" he said. "Is something wrong?"

And I let him have it. I told him that getting taken to the freaking police station for dangling from a rope in the nighttime is nothing that a parent should simply shrug off.

"First of all, remember that she wasn't, in fact, dangling from a rope," he said. "She didn't get on the rope."

"But she *wanted* to. That's what she was about to do when the police came and stopped her."

"But she *didn't*," he said.

"And then you even rewarded her," I said. "You made it seem like we were having a big party to celebrate that she'd done this dangerous, highly illegal act."

That's when I told him about the Fuck-It List, which I should have probably done before this, and I also said that she'd told me she planned to have sex soon so she could get it over with before it mattered, before she really fell in love with somebody.

"Sex!" I said. "And she's fifteen years old."

I guess I was half afraid that he'd get so furious with her that he would pull her out of bed and we'd have a huge, scary scene; she'd say that I'd betrayed her and I'd have to leave; and then Carter and I would break up because we'd all be so hysterical watching everything implode around us. You know, like you see in the movies.

Instead, he blinked at me. "Okay, two things," he said slowly and sadly. "Just calm down, will you, because I know this kid, and I bet you money that she is not going to have sex. Teenagers say a whole bunch of stuff, trying on identities. You can't take everything they say seriously."

My God, you'd go insane if you tried. Also, she misses her mother. She didn't want to stay with me. She's mourning. And also—I know you meant well, and God knows I understand the impulse—but snooping is *wrong*."

"Yeah, I get that," I said. "But I wasn't snooping about the sex thing. She *told* me that. And while we're on the topic, Tyler and his girlfriend sometimes come here and spend the day in his room when they should be in school."

His face changed just a bit, but he recovered. "Tyler's sex life is none of my business. He's gotten into three good schools, he's being responsible, and all kids experiment. You want them to experiment, Jane!"

I stared at him. "Nina," I said. "You're talking to Nina."

"Sorry. I'm just tired. Please. Forget about it."

"Did Jane feel the same way I feel? Because honestly, Carter, snooping may be wrong, but maybe it's helpful to know what they're doing, because they don't know all the dangers out there. Why can't Indigo express her feelings about her mother in some socially acceptable way, like crying or writing bad poetry? Why does she have to dangle by ropes and then tell you that she wants me to be her mother?"

"I thought you'd *like* that," he said. "She cares for you."

"Carter!" I practically started banging on his head. "Carter, she doesn't mean that! She's just saying it, trying to get a reaction from you. She loves her mother. She's pissed as hell at her right now for moving away. She wants attention, she wants to make you stop her from doing bad things—and you won't do it! You just paddle along downstream, smiling and turning up the music and making everything a celebration. How bad is this going to get before you do something?"

I had been sitting up in bed, gesticulating and gesturing all over the place. I was so wound up that I was practically hyperventilating. Now I flopped on my back.

If I'd ever wanted to see Carter mad, this was my chance.

"Listen to me," he said, and his voice was like a low growl. "These. Are. My. Children. And whether you think you know them and me or not, let me tell you one thing right now. I know what I'm doing! I have a parenting philosophy, and it may be different from yours, and hell, it's probably different from eighty-seven percent of the parenting population out there, but I believe, for your information, that children learn by taking risks and yes, sometimes by getting hurt. They try out identities and different names and hairstyles, and they try so hard to break free of the bonds that hold them to their parents, and we have to let them. Do you hear me? We have to let them, because that is how we, as a species, are designed. The whole push-pull thing. The running into danger and then back to safety again. This is what kids do!"

"But it's not," I said. "She needs your protection. She's a *child.*"

I saw the vein in his temple start to throb. Thank God. I didn't even know he *had* an emotional setting that would cause his veins to throb. But then he calmed down. He actually smiled wistfully.

"Look at you," he said. "Caring and all."

"Somebody has to take charge. She could get into real trouble here. You've got to ground her. It's a kindness to take charge here. It's for her. She's begging you to do *something.*"

He ran his finger along my jawline. He spoke in a low, fervent voice. "If I start punishing them, they're going to shut down, and I'll never know what they're up to. That's what I believe. They will stop . . ."

"Loving you?" I said. "They won't stop loving you."

"Popkin, it's the middle of the night. I don't know what else I can say. I'm on top of this, okay? My kids are going to turn out to be the same as everybody else: flawed, lovable, impossible, and at times the most exasperating people on earth. They're going to make mistakes, but I can't protect them by grounding them."

"She needs better friends. She needs to be proud of herself for being an honor student, not to be ashamed of it. She needs—"

He held his hand up. "Listen, if I could, I'd go to that school and I'd force every wonderful, appropriate teenage girl to be her best friend, but I can't do that. The friend we've got is the super-cool Maya, and we just have to wait until good sense kicks in."

"But do you think it will?"

He leaned over and kissed me on the nose, a kiss of finality. "Hope so. Now let's try to get some shut-eye. Can we sleep? Please?"

I couldn't. Because I knew this was the beginning of the end between Carter and me, and if I was going to be honest about it, it was a little bit of relief to know finally what was going to wreck the relationship.

He was nice, I'd say, *and he was sexy as hell, but he was the most screwed-up father in the whole world!* I'd analyze him to my friends, I'd diagnose him with divorce guilt, a need to be loved, a pathological desire to be his children's friend. After a while I'd forget the part about how I'd been happy there, and how he'd made me feel so loved and cherished. I'd excise those parts, as I was so skilled at doing.

He turned over in his sleep, and faced away from me. Just the way it was going to be in real, awake life.

FIFTEEN

LINDY

Back when they were building the house, she and Jeff had made love in every single room—to christen each of them, he'd said. They'd come to the house after work and lie on the plywood floors, careful to avoid splinters and nails. Chloe, in fact, had gotten started in the kitchen on a hot August night when they'd picnicked there, with a bottle of wine and some cheese. Jeff always said that's what made Chloe so fun and feisty: she was formed from alcohol and fermented dairy products on a bed of nails.

These days it seemed impossible to think of having that much spontaneous sex. He didn't even look at her that way anymore. Unless it was totally inconvenient—like when they were leaving the house in the morning he'd sometimes leer at her and raise his eyebrows suggestively. Which proved that he probably didn't even want sex. He just wanted to be on the record as somebody who remembered that it existed.

She got it, of course. All the other moms said it was the same at their houses; nobody was getting any. That was just the way life was in these child-raising, working years. And when you threw in a racquetball habit at least three nights a week—well, it was hopeless.

But that night, damn it, she decided to plan for sex. During dinner she smiled at him and said she was looking forward to a little *downtime*. Wink, wink. He smiled and winked back, which meant he'd read her signals.

She gave the children an early bath, and the whole time she was scrubbing their fingernails and behind their ears all she could think was that cuddling up with Jeff would save her.

As soon as she had everybody in bed—had sung the songs and read the stories and fetched two glasses of water and refilled Davey's bottle because he wasn't ready to give it up yet, and who was she to fight him when she had no fight left in her—she changed into her black lace underwear under her sky-blue kimono, even putting on the hated thong. She strategically dabbed perfume and combed out her hair and made her way downstairs. Jeff, bless him, had loaded the dishwasher and was washing the pans.

She felt an immediate sweep of gratitude, so sharp it almost made tears come to her eyes. She touched his back. "God, I need a glass of wine," she said.

"Tired?" he said.

"Oh, you wouldn't believe it. Nina came into the salon today, and I did her hair, which turned out great, if I do say so myself. And you won't believe this, but not only has she found our mother but she's actually talked to her—and then I came home and got in a big fight with Mom. The second one this week. The whole day has been terrible. Until this minute." She curved herself into the crook of his arm, at the precise moment he moved it away, which surely was a coincidence.

"Here, I'll pour you one," he said and smiled at her. His eyes were just the slightest bit vacant, not really looking at her. "It's going to be all right. You know, you don't have to invite Nina into your life if you don't want to. You did her hair, and now you don't ever have to see her again. And you certainly don't need to talk to your birth mom. As for your *actual* mom—you and she always work stuff out."

There. Problems all solved. Proud of himself, he handed her a glass of pinot noir and carefully folded the dish towel, smoothing out its wrinkles. To please her. She knew he didn't give a crap about how the dish towels looked.

"Won't you have a glass of wine, too? I was hoping . . ." she said carefully, and that's when he made a sad face and said he'd promised to play racquetball with Joe from work.

"What?" She made herself smile. "Really? Racquetball tonight? Didn't you just play last night?" Which of course was the wrong way to say it.

He might have been irritated, but he smiled at her indulgently. "I'm sorry, but I made a promise to Joe," he said. "But—behold, madame, the magnificence of your kitchen, your sparkling pots and pans, your clean countertops! You, my sweet, can be a lady of leisure, while I will go and pursue the ridiculous goal of beating Joe at a game that makes no sense and causes great pain and sweat!"

Stop talking like that, she wanted to snap at him. *Look at me!*

But she didn't.

"And," he said, with a flourish, "there's something else. I even put in a load of laundry!" He beamed at her. "I *noticed* it needed doing, and I know how you love when I notice things."

She turned away. Yes, of course, noticing was something she always talked about. But couldn't he notice how much she needed him? And by the way, why didn't he want to spend time with her when it was time to unwind? *Why* did racquetball rate higher, anyway?

Maybe she should go over and start undressing him right here in the kitchen. Unbuttoning his shirt, undoing the belt. Smiling into his eyes. But what if she tried to seduce him, and he didn't go for it? Where did you go from *there*?

"Fine," she said. "Okay."

She got out the vacuum cleaner and started furiously working on the baseboards in the dining room while he dashed upstairs and changed his clothes. She really was going to have to get a Q-tip and clean that little ridge in the baseboards, especially where the corners met and dust collected. It was disgusting. When he came downstairs, he kissed her on the cheek.

"You'll be awake when I get back?" he said.

"Maybe. I don't know." She let her gaze linger on how handsome he was, the shadow of a beard, his bright eyes, like he was a mischievous imp getting away with something.

"Well." He stood by the door, looking at her, cocking his head, almost like he wanted to say something. But then he left. He'd probably been about to explain again how he'd earned his time away. Lately it seemed that he only did stuff around the house or with her so that he could get away from her with a clear conscience.

Unwanted. How long had she been unwanted? Turned out forever, pretty much.

But that was ridiculous! He'd married her, hadn't he, and he had built her this house; he went to functions with her; he brought home his paycheck . . . *stop it! Just stop it!*

She went upstairs to take a hot bath. She would read in bed, fall asleep early, try to stop thinking.

I'm your first relative. Wasn't that what Nina had said?

Lindy tried to take the deep cleansing breaths that the life coach said would chase all bad thoughts away. *Leave the overwhelm, go back to the familiar pattern of breath following breath.*

She climbed into bed, concentrating on the smooth silkiness of the sheets—600-count Egyptian cotton, the kind she loved—and the firmness of her favorite pillow, squeezing her eyes shut and listening to her breath. *Gain control again. Control through breath.*

But that was boring. She opened her eyes. *Breathing.* Who didn't know how to breathe? Besides, she was too restless to sit in her bed concentrating on something that automatic.

She got her laptop and brought it back to bed, scrolled through her e-mails, read a gossipy piece on Miley Cyrus. And then, almost without permission, her fingers typed into the search engine: *Lulu and the Starbabies.*

It was stupid, but her heart was pounding. *This doesn't mean anything. All you have to do is look at her, and you can turn it off if you don't like it. Why are you so scared? WHY. ARE. YOU. SO. SCARED?*

And then there she was: Lulu.

Lulu singing, strutting across the stage, flinging out her arms. There was a heart-stopping moment when she looked right into the camera, as if looking through the years into her daughter's eyes, so much pain and darkness in those eyes. Lindy swallowed hard and closed her own eyes. Her voice, soaring, screaming into the microphone. All that feeling, all that anger and pain.

How could Nina have watched this and not mentioned the pain?

She watched all the videos she could find, and then she sat in the middle of the bed, waiting for Jeff to come home, needing him to be beside her. *I'm Poppet,* she would tell him. *I am Poppet, and look at this woman who birthed me. Look where I came from.*

The heater came on, like a sigh. Where was her husband, anyway? It was nearly ten thirty.

All of a sudden, panic rose up in the back of her throat. He wasn't playing racquetball. *Nobody* played racquetball this much! Why hadn't she realized this before? It was insane, thinking he went to racquetball every single night. She got out of bed and changed into sweatpants and a sweatshirt, her hands shaking. Then, not even letting herself stop to think, she went into the children's rooms and eased them out of their beds, bundled them up against the cold, and put them one by one in the car. The twins stayed asleep; they were still at the age when you could have storm troopers landing on the roof and they wouldn't wake up, but Chloe stirred in her sleep and rubbed her eyes and mumbled, "Where are we going?"

"For a little ride," murmured Lindy, as she turned on the engine and cranked up the heat. She could barely breathe. It hadn't been easy, carrying everybody down the stairs. In the rearview mirror, she could see Razzie sucking his thumb and Chloe's eyelids closing again. She backed out of the garage and carefully navigated down the street to the clubhouse. She didn't let herself even think. She just drove straight. Headlights swept her eyes. Maybe one of the oncoming cars would turn out to be Jeff's, in which case she'd have some explaining to do.

Maybe she'd fall into his arms and say, "I just thought . . . you're so passionate about racquetball every night . . . I thought that maybe you were seeing someone else . . ." And then he would kiss her all over her and say, "Oh, you are so crazy! How could I even look at another woman, when I have you? I'm playing racquetball to stay in shape for *you,* so I can deserve a woman as awesome as you . . ."

Ha! As if!

She turned left into the clubhouse parking lot, and steeled herself. But sure enough, there was his Lexus. There were a few other cars in the lot, too—his racquetball buddies, no doubt. The gym windows were still lit. Games were going on.

He was there.

She exhaled, a long, slow breath. Relief. He was where he said he was. Thank God, thank God, thank God.

She was turning the car around when a prickle started around her earlobes and traveled down her neck. What if—well, what if he really *was* there, but he was with some woman, some racquetball queen? Or what if he'd left in somebody else's car?

There wasn't anything she could do about that. She wasn't going to leave the children in the car while she ran inside to check on him, ferret him out. And she certainly wasn't going to drag everybody in there, face the humiliation of being *that woman,* the suspicious wife.

She turned the car around and headed home, feeling more tired than she'd ever been before. The relief she'd felt just a minute before was already gone.

SIXTEEN

NINA

I spent the next few nights at Josephine's condo. I told Carter that I had a lot of work to catch up on before I went to Brooklyn to meet Phoebe. He said, "Ahh, I am so happy for you that at last you get to meet your mom. Listen, let's don't have our little fight get the better of us. Maybe we just need to catch up on our sleep. Don't you think that would solve everything?" Then he said, "Good night, Popkin. I do love you, you know."

I didn't say "I love you" back. I wasn't sure I really did love him right then, was the truth of it. He had so much wrong with him. In theory, his parenting plan of supporting everything his kids did and not hassling them and not grounding them sounded good, but somebody needed to tell him it wasn't the way real life worked.

It actually seemed heartless, when I really thought about it. Like not teaching them to read or something.

One day when I was showing a house, I took the woman of the couple aside—a fortyish mom type—and I said, "Do you and your husband agree how to raise the kids?" And the woman lifted her eyebrows in surprise and she laughed and said, "God, no. Kids, money, sex—those are the big fights in any marriage. But mostly kids."

So there it was. You sign on for fights when you have kids.

Maybe, I thought, *I should simply square my shoulders and keep saying what I want to say.* But the only thing was, I had no standing in this particular fight. I wasn't a parent; they weren't my kids.

And, oh yeah. I didn't *want* to fight. What good is a relationship that consists of fights all the time? Better to just leave.

On Saturday morning Indigo came to Home Sweet Castle to find out what I'd decided to wear. "I thought we were going to pick out something for you together," she said in an injured tone. "Please don't tell me you're wearing *that.*"

I was wearing a very nice turtleneck, a black cardigan, and some khaki pants.

"Indie, I can't go wearing my torn jeans or leggings. This is New York. And this is my mother! Also, I have to look at least as nice as my sister."

"No—no turtlenecks!" she said. "How could you even think that was going to work?" She left and came back an hour later with black jeans and a filmy snakeskin shirt and a short black cardigan. "Here, wear these."

"Wait, where did you get these?"

"We're borrowing them from Maya's mom, who's about your size."

"I can't wear her clothes! Does she even know you took them?"

"Don't worry about it. She's also adopted so she gets it."

I looked at Melanie, who shrugged and said, "I think the new clothes would be better, too," so I tried them on, and sure enough they fit, and I looked way more like somebody who belonged in Brooklyn in them.

"You look awesome," said Indigo. "Now don't try too hard. You know how you do."

"Thanks. You give me a lot of confidence."

"You're the person I tell the truth to," she said. She straightened the cardigan's hem, which was riding up apparently. Then she glared at me. "Also, when are you coming back? To live at our house again?"

"I-I don't know," I said.

"No, no. Don't say that. Just come back to us from Brooklyn, okay? Will you promise? My dad's going nuts. He misses you like crazy."

Lindy and I had agreed to meet in front of the Cranky Snail in Brooklyn and wait for our mother to arrive. Lindy said she wanted to go alone in her own car, and I didn't argue with her. It had been a while since my club days in New York, back when I was dating a stockbroker guy named Jared, so I was happy to relive my youth by taking the Metro-North train and two subways to get to Brooklyn, just to prove I still had my street cred.

By the time I made my way from the subway stop to the bar, I was in such a wonderful New York frame of mind that I could barely contain my excitement.

Lindy was already there, trying to maneuver her car into a minuscule parking space between two station wagons. It took her about eighteen tries, and I was there to applaud each one. "Okay, more to the right . . . now turn the wheel sharply to the left . . . pull out a little bit . . . you got this!"

When she got out of the car, she was completely rattled. "How do people *do* this every day?" she said. "Why do people *live* here?"

I laughed out loud. "Look at you!" I said happily. "I've never seen you all natural and flustered like this! Welcome to Brooklyn!"

"Is it my hair? It's my hair, isn't it? I've got to find a comb."

"No. No, you're fine. You look beautiful. Come on, let's go inside and get a table." I reached over and squeezed her arm. "I'm so excited for this! Are you excited?"

"I don't know," she said. "I kind of think this was a sketchy idea, to tell you the truth. I almost turned back about five times on the way here."

I laughed and linked my arm in hers. "Obviously we need to get you a drink."

"Maybe that will help," she said, but she looked doubtful.

The Cranky Snail was a dark, moody sort of place, something you'd picture being filled with flappers and gangsters back in the 1920s; there was a long mahogany bar on one side of the room, with overstuffed couches and armchairs on the other side, beaded curtains leading to the bathrooms, black fans hanging from the white tin ceilings.

I steered her over to two pink couches near the bar, where I could keep my eye on the door. We'd arrived thirty minutes early so we wouldn't miss Phoebe's entrance, but I still scanned the room to make sure she wasn't already here, sitting at the bar perhaps. On the phone she'd sounded like the sort who might be slamming back some serious drinks.

But it was early; there was hardly anybody in the place, just a few hipsters in watch caps and jackets sitting in the back. A waiter named Gus came by and took our order; I got a gin and tonic, and Lindy ordered a daiquiri that came in a tall glass with little umbrellas and a bunch of fruit on a toothpick. When Gus brought over our drinks, I said to him, "Do you happen to know a woman named Phoebe? Around fifty or so? Does she ever come in here?"

He thought for a moment. "I don't think so. What does she look like?"

"Red hair maybe? But we're really not sure," I said. "She's actually our *birth mother,* and we're supposed to meet her for the first time tonight. We've never seen her before."

He said, "Is that right? Wow!" and so I told him how I'd always dreamed of meeting her, and then by accident I found out I had a sister—I pointed to Lindy, who looked pained—and Gus said, "Are you kidding me?" like he wanted to know the whole story. But Lindy, tapping on her knee, seemed like she was hoping a trapdoor would materialize out of nowhere and whisk her out of sight, so I said to him, "If you see somebody looking for her daughters, that would probably be us."

"That's awesome. If I see anybody who looks like you two, I'll be sure and send her over," he said and glided away.

I took a sip of my drink and watched as Lindy smoothed her napkin and set it at a right angle to the table edge. She had coral manicured nails, so perfect and shiny that they almost broke my heart for how hard they were trying.

We looked at each other. I smiled. She didn't.

"I hope you're not going to tell everybody in here about us," she said.

"Sorry," I said. "I just thought she might be a regular here. You know."

"I think—I think this is a private matter," she said and sipped her drink. "Let me see your hair. How do you like it?"

"I love it! There's just one little rebellious section here in the back that sticks up sometimes—like it's resisting being told to lie down by hair products. It thinks it can prevail over keratin."

She frowned. "Hair doesn't have a mind of its own," she said. "You need to use a hair clip and spray it until it's where you want it." She rummaged through her purse then handed a clip to me. "Here, put this in for a few minutes, and I think it'll lie right down. If not, I have some spray you can use. In the restroom, of course."

"Of course," I said. Had she really thought I'd simply start spraying my hair right there in the bar? "Thank you. You come prepared."

"It's what I do." She sipped her cocktail, then set the glass down in the center of the napkin, and unfurled the edges. "So how are we going to recognize her?"

"Oh!" I said. "I almost forgot. I brought the picture of when we were little. I'll just prop it up here on the table, and then maybe she'll see it and know it's us."

"That's crazy," she said. "She's never going to see that."

"Well, I'm studying every face as people come in. I think I'll know her when I see her. By the way, I hope you have lots of pictures on your phone of your kids. She's going to want to see her grandchildren."

She gave me a pained smile. "*If* she comes."

She took a long drink of her daiquiri. I sipped my gin and tonic and wished this could be a little more fun. Three more people came in; somebody was yelling in the back about a basketball game. If Carter were here, he'd be making jokes and picking out possible mothers for us, thinking up conversation starters—anything. Lindy had her arms crossed and was looking into the distance with a frown on her face.

"How's your family?" I said at last.

"They're fine."

"Everybody well now?"

"Nina. This is ridiculous. I have to say this one more time: this is wrongheaded and stupid, and we shouldn't have come. I think I'm going home. This woman isn't our mom. I think this might even be disrespectful to our mothers. Don't you get that?"

"Just wait, okay? I *know* that from your point of view technically she's simply our egg carrier. But she did push us out of her tender little teenaged cervix, so I think we have to give her that much. Also, her body nourished us for nine whole months. I'll bet she even had to give up smoking crack and drinking and sleeping with her drug dealers for at least that long."

"Maybe you could try not to be sarcastic. How would that be? I'm going to the restroom and then I think I might just leave." She emptied her glass and stood up with her purse, just as Gus was back, handing her another. "From that gentleman over there," he said, gesturing behind me.

"What?" She grimaced at me. "Should I take it?"

I shrugged. "Totally up to you. You've come all the way from Connecticut. You might as well have a few drinks and enjoy yourself as long as you're here."

She sat back down. "I've never done anything like this. What's the etiquette?"

"The etiquette is to say thank you, then drink the thing. If you want it."

She took the glass from the waiter and smiled at him. "All right. I might as well. I got married young, you see. I didn't have much of a bar life."

"Yeah. Well, you didn't miss all that much," I said, and Gus laughed and said, "Good luck."

Lindy was looking over my head, smiling at the man at the bar. Fluttering her fingers in a wave.

"However," I said, "what you *don't* want is to—"

"Oh, God, Nina. He's coming this way."

"See? A simple thank-you would have been fine. You didn't need to issue an invitation."

"How was that an invitation?" she said. "All I did was smile and wave."

"You did a flutter wave."

"What does that mean? I didn't do anything!"

"A flutter wave means flirting. How do you not know that?"

By then the guy, an oily type in his forties, all tight pants and gelled hair, had sauntered over, smiling and holding a glass of whiskey or something. Turning to Lindy, he clicked his glass against hers, then sat down next to her and grinned.

I rolled my eyes. *Don't waste your time,* I wanted to tell him. *My sister is an introvert of the highest order, and besides, she doesn't want anything to do with you.*

But there she was, politely sipping her drink and twirling the little umbrella and letting him tell her about his job as a club owner and how he once met Mick Jagger and how he was only here tonight because he was stuck in Brooklyn while he waited for word about a sitcom he'd written. Blah, blah, blah. Blowhard, all lies. I rolled my eyes again and scanned the crowd. At least this guy could maybe keep Lindy from leaving until Phoebe got there.

I kept hearing him yammering on and on, a low hum of bragging and complimenting, with drinks coming every now and then, and Lindy saying, "Oh!" like this was some kind of mysterious process, not cause and effect. Like she was so out of her element that she didn't even see what was happening until it was too late. I kept checking my phone for messages, but at some point I noticed that the light had gone out of Lindy's eyes, and that she'd started picking invisible lint off her pants and her sweater and even the couch she was sitting on. There was a little pile of three paper umbrellas on the table. When I tried to get her to look at me, she wouldn't. Her jaw was set in a hard line, it was officially nighttime, the bar was filling up, and Phoebe was not coming.

Our mother was not coming.

The blowhard must have decided to make his move, because suddenly he leaned over to set his glass down and he stuck his face up so close to Lindy's that I could see her recoil like he was blasting bad breath right at her.

I heard him say "dinner" and "too loud" and "go somewhere."

"Okay!" I said loudly. "I think we're done here."

The guy looked up at me. "That's just what I was saying to Lindy. She and I are thinking of splitting. Would you like to join us?"

"Actually no, that wouldn't be possible," I said.

"Then I guess it's just you and me, Lindy girl. I'm staying right up the street. We can get some dinner and then go to my place. You'll like—"

"She said no," I told him.

He didn't take his eyes off her. "No, she didn't. Come on, what do you say?"

"Oh God, Lindy," I said. "I guess you didn't tell him about the bedbugs, did you?"

Her eyes met mine, and she hesitated only a moment before playing along. "No. I'm so tired of having to explain our bedbugs to everyone we meet."

"I know," I said. "But it's the only fair thing to do." I looked at him and scratched my shoulder. "We've been *infested*. Our apartment gets fumigated tomorrow—but we've both got bites, and Lindy, I think I saw a dot of something on your arm. Is that one now?"

"Ouch!" she said and put down her glass so she could slap at her right arm. "They're *horrible*."

The man stood up. "Okay, okay," he said, backing away. "I get it. This is fucked up."

"It is," I said.

When he'd moved back into the crowd, she smiled. "How did you know to do that?"

"I have my own sad little areas of expertise," I said. "You do hair, I do dating dilemmas and bar scenes."

"Well, thank you."

"You're welcome."

I looked at the door. *This would be such an excellent time,* I thought, *for Phoebe Louise Mullen to come sailing in.*

We would happily talk about this story for decades if that would only happen.

Which it didn't.

Phoebe didn't show up.

Not then.

Not later.

Not ever.

I put the photograph back in my purse.

We left the Cranky Snail soon after, and went looking for a place to eat. Thank goodness I hadn't had much to drink, or I would have started to feel sad. Lindy was swaying the slightest bit. The street was bustling with people, and every restaurant we peeked into was jammed. Finally we decided on a Mexican place that had a mariachi band playing in the back and cacti in containers at every table. Lindy sat down and scrolled through her phone, sighing.

"What is it? Trouble?"

"No, just that Jeff is with the kids, and he wants me to know how hard it is for him." She put the phone down and rested her head on the palm of her hand. Her eyes were tired. "What the hell? Like I don't have them nearly every night while he plays racquetball—and do I complain? But oh, if *he's* the one at home alone, he has to text me to tell me that . . . lessee . . . yeah, Razzie spilled milk on his pajamas and the PTA president called during dinner and, oh yes, the garbage disposal got clogged." She put down her phone and folded her hands on the table. "Sorry. Just stupid married-people stuff."

"Men," I said. "Can't live with 'em, can't shoot 'em."

She laughed so unexpectedly hard that I had a stab of fear. She was drunk.

The waitress came over and we ordered guacamole and taco salads because Lindy said we really needed to eat some vegetables and then she suggested maybe we should also get some margaritas—*is that the drink with the salt?*—and I said sure to the drinks, but we should maybe also get some water, so we ordered that, too. She tapped her fingers on the table when the waitress moved away.

"How disappointed are you? That she didn't come," she said, her words only slightly slurred.

"Let's see. On a scale of one to ten, ten being the time I heard there was no Santa Claus, I am a six point two."

"Six point two? Noooo. I think you're way more, *way more* . . . disa . . . disap . . . than that."

"Am I? Well, maybe tomorrow, when I accept that there's no way forward, I'll get up to a nine or so. But right now I'm kind of happy to be here with you. I mean, this *is* nice, right? Now that I got you away from that creepy guy. Sorry. I should have intervened much sooner with him."

"You wanna know something? He was nutty, but also kinda funny, you know? I never, never have a night out without my family or with some—some PTA person." She leaned forward and her eyes were just the slightest bit unfocused. "Nina, I have to tell you that this feels weird. Really, really weird."

"What? Me? Am I weird?"

"No, you're just . . . you're just . . . so different from me. You—you *throw* yourself at things. I don't know what I'm doing here with you, or how you got yourself into my life. I mean, I was so clear that I didn't want anything to do with finding our mom, and then . . . here we are. In Brooklyn, and I was getting hit on by a strange man, and now I'm drinking . . ."

"It's okay," I said.

"But seriously, do you think you're maybe a little bit—well, don't you have any—forgive me, but any *sense*? I don't think I would have done any of this."

"No, I suppose you wouldn't have. But it's not bad, is it?"

"It might be bad."

"But how?"

Her face suddenly crumpled. "Because it's . . . um, I hate to tell you this, but I was happier before I knew all this, this"—she waved her arm in the air and brought it down too hard on the table—"this mom stuff. Before I knew I was Poppet. Now I think I'm Poppet sometimes and I know that my mother didn't adopt you, too, when she took me. And now . . . it hurts."

"Aw, Lindy. I didn't want to hurt you," I said.

She was wiping her eyes on her napkin.

I reached over and touched her arm. "I'm sorry this has hurt you, but maybe the hurt is a little bit worth it because of what we'll get."

"What?" She leaned forward, wobbly. "What do you get for the hurt, because I would really like to know."

"You get self-knowledge, and you understand why you are the way you are, why some things scare you, why you worry about being rejected . . . and we get each other, and that's real. Maybe something really good."

That was the moment she turned green.

"I think—oh my God, I'm going to be sick!" she whispered and jumped up, her hand over her mouth. I leapt out of the booth, too, and we ran to the ladies' room, and I held her hair back from her face while she threw up. She kept trying to push me away, but I stayed with her and said, "It's okay, it's okay. You're going to be fine. Just let it all go."

When she was all finished she wiped her mouth and slumped against the wall and said, "I hate that you saw that."

"It's fine," I said, flushing the toilet. "Glad to help. We're sisters. Also, I have some toothpaste in my bag. You want to freshen up?"

"God, yes. Ugh, I haven't done that since—well, I don't even remember when. I don't think I ever did." She started laughing and crying at the same time. Snot and mascara were all over her face. Clearly we had moved into what one of my old nerdy boyfriends would have called some kind of DEFCON 1 situation, and I had to be on high alert. Gently I walked her to the sink where I wet a paper towel and handed it to her.

When she saw herself in the mirror she looked like she might cry. "Ohhh nooo! I'm disgusting, aren't I? Look, I've got vomit on my shirt."

"Easy. Here, it's okay, we can scrub it off. It's fine."

I dabbed at the spot near her neckline. She closed her eyes and leaned against the sink while I scrubbed.

"It's okay. We're good. It all came out. And here's the toothpaste. Sorry I don't have a toothbrush."

"Thank you," she said. "I hate myself."

I wasn't drunk in the slightest. My gin and tonics had been watered down to the point of ridiculousness, and after Lindy got sick, I didn't drink my margarita. So it made sense that I take her car and drive her home.

She was quiet for most of the way. I got her a cup of coffee at McDonald's off the highway, and she wrapped her hands around it while staring out the window, glassy-eyed. Her car was fancy, a Lexus SUV, equipped with three kid car seats, lined up and perfectly clean. They looked like children had never ridden in them.

"This will all be a funny story someday," I told her.

"You might make it funny, but I won't."

"Sure you will," I said. "Just the part about the drink man alone will be hilarious. Try telling it at the PTA meeting and see if it doesn't get some laughs."

"Nina," she said. "Shut up."

"Nice talk to the sister who had toothpaste handy when you needed it," I said. She closed her eyes, smiling.

A long time later, she said softly, "Just so you know, I wish she had come. I was rooting for us."

"Yeah," I said.

"Now we don't know what to do," she mumbled.

"We'll think of something," I said.

"We had her phone number. We could have called her. Or gone to her place and knocked on the door."

"I thought of that," I said, although it had only occurred to me briefly and then I'd dismissed the idea. "But we don't want to force her, do we? And we don't want to make her feel like we're stalking her."

"Good," she said from somewhere near sleep. "You're a good person, Nina."

◆　◆　◆

Of course, once I got her safely to her house, I needed a way to get home, too, so I called Carter to come get me. It was one in the morning, so even though Lindy invited me to come and wait in her house, I told her I'd wait outside for Carter. She was in no shape to argue.

She lived in an almost fairy-tale subdivision with lots of huge two-story houses set back from the street, manicured lawns, landscaping, and streetlights that looked like they'd come from Merry Old England. All quiet and gigantic and safe. So perfect for Lindy.

I sat on the curb, tireder and wireder than I'd ever been. When Carter arrived, I stood up and he got out of the car and came over and kissed me soundly, his eyes searching my face, and when I told him my mother hadn't shown up, he looked genuinely sad.

"I know how much you wanted this," he said. "Maybe there was a mix-up."

"No. There was no mix-up. I think she didn't want to come because she's probably scared of all the feelings she'd have to have. So we sat and waited for her, and then Lindy got sick and couldn't drive herself home, so that's why I'm here."

He looked like he was trying to decide how I felt. "Was it at least a good sisterly evening?"

"No. Yes. I don't know. I think I'm too much for her somehow. She doesn't want to be friends. She's so scared of everything. My mother and my sister both seem so scared of life, you know?"

"And you are my sweet, brave Nina," he said. He took my hand and held it. "Will you come home with me, or do you want to go back to Josephine's?"

"Your house, I guess," I said.

"See? That's how brave you are." He kissed me several more times and then he said the thing I hate the most when people say it after something bad has happened: "You know, though, things do tend to work out for the best."

"Please. Next you're going to be telling me I'm in your thoughts and prayers. What did you and the kids do tonight?"

"Well," he said. "We Skyped with Jane, then we played poker for a while, then Tyler went to his girlfriend's house and I had to go to work. I don't know what Indigo did; she said she was going to watch a horror movie on Netflix."

I felt tears backing up behind my eyes because I was so tired and also I was out of ideas about my mom, and I knew it wasn't enough, being the only brave one out of three family members. Also, I wanted to tell him that things *don't* always turn out for the best, and that maybe Indigo shouldn't be alone so much. Instead I let him kiss me under the streetlight and I let him lead me into his house and upstairs to his bed.

The bad part about being the first one to know a relationship is over is that you have to wait for the other person to catch on. I remembered that now. As bad as it is to get dumped, it's also bad to be the one doing the dumping.

I'd have to tell him tomorrow, once all the kissing had stopped.

The next day was Sunday, and Carter had to get up early and go in to work. A bunch of orders for boat parts had finally come in, and he had people showing up at all hours to get their equipment. This, now, he'd told me as he got dressed, was going to be the bad part of the year, when he had to work overtime just to stay on top of things.

I hung around the house with Indigo and Tyler, and listened as Indigo got in a big fight with Maya over whether or not she cared seriously enough when bad things happened in the world, or something like that. I could hear Indigo yelling into the phone, *I am too an activist—and you're going to see that you don't know what you're talking about! I do so care about animals!*, and Tyler slammed his coffee cup down on the table and said he couldn't stay in this house anymore because he had to learn his Nicely Nicely lines or else he was going to get dropped from the play, and who could do anything in this madhouse that was run by Indigo's moods? And then they were off and fighting about who had it the worst. She shouted at him that at least he had friends he could count on, and at least he was getting out of this stupid-ass high school where people didn't care about anybody else, and he told her she needed to lighten up or get a life or grow a pair or something like that—and I, the person who grew up without siblings and so doesn't know beans about how much fighting might be normal, tried to intervene and get them to stop but it was no use; they were both too mad.

"Really," I said. "Neither of you means this stuff. Indigo, everybody will believe you're an activist when you do activist things. You don't have to insist on it so much. And, Tyler, I'll help you with your lines if you want me to. We can go sit in the den and work on them."

Indigo looked at me with narrowed eyes. "No one takes me seriously! And you—you're not even in our family, so I don't know why you're always butting in."

That again. I turned away so she wouldn't see how that slammed me. That day I took one of the garbage bags of clothing back to my mom's condo without telling anyone.

I texted Lindy late in the day: *So did you live?*

And to my surprise, she wrote back: *I did. Thank you for life lesson on men bearing daiquiris.*

So much more to tell, I wrote, smiling as I typed it. *Dinner soon perhaps? Guacamole?*

And she wrote: *Sorry.*

Sorry. That was it.

SEVENTEEN
PHOEBE

Here's the part nobody ever told her: being alone wasn't so bad when you got used to it.

The students came in the afternoons, of course, so she wasn't completely alone. Some took piano, some took voice lessons—the voice students were the hardest, because of all the eye contact, the feeling. Of course there was feeling with the piano students, too, but it was easier somehow to concentrate on hands and feet on the pedals and not make it about emotional connection. Although that's all music was, really—emotional connection.

And if she got lonely, there was all of Brooklyn right out the front door—hipsters and old people and screaming, whooping children—so many that you wondered if perhaps the stores weren't manufacturing them in the back and handing them out to customers.

"You, madam, are making a very wise choice with that whole-grain bread and that Greek yogurt with the chia seeds. You are now qualified to receive a child. We have a strapping boy of two right here, and he comes with his own Bugaboo stroller."

Yeah, she'd fucked up. Lost her own family.

Shit. She'd *meant* to go meet them. She'd gotten herself dressed, but then the phone rang, and it was Mary calling to talk about the ceremony for Kevin that was taking place in May, and could Phoebe possibly come? She'd be *family*. And *family* was important.

Family, family, family. Why the hell was everybody so obsessed with family? Half the people in America weren't even fond of their family members; the papers were full of families breaking up, turning violent, inflicting pain on their members. Yet wherever you looked, any television show you turned on, any comment thread on the Internet— everybody was extolling the virtues of family like it was the be-all and end-all of human existence.

The truth was, she'd gotten so disgusted by that talk with Mary— when Mary had been the one who'd broken the All-Important God-Almighty Family Bond and moved away after Phoebe had come back from California—but oh, Mary didn't seem to remember that. She'd moved, in fact, because of family. Just not her own family, no sir; Shelby's family. And now she wanted the pretty picture of the whole family for the photographs—Kevin getting his diploma or award or whatever it was, his aunt standing next to him. Big deal.

She'd gotten off the phone and gotten into a hot bath and put on a little Bach and then some Amy Winehouse and she'd drunk a glass of wine and tried not to think about family. Enough!

She'd had a family, thank you very much—a few families, actually, over the years—and none of them had been all that great. Her mother and father had been all right, at least from a child's perspective. She barely remembered them at all now, to tell the truth. Her mother was from Ireland, and had lots of siblings back in the old country, and she'd gotten herself married to Edward Mullen at sixteen, and they'd moved to New York with his family, where he became a big, seemingly brusque firefighter, except he was really like a big marshmallow instead. Always weeping but in a sentimental way—tears just leaking from his eyes like all his feelings touched him so deeply, he loved everything so much, so much. Everything was okay. Loved his two little girls more than anything! Taught them dancing and singing in the living room of their flat. Phoebe was always lining up the pillows and blankets to be her audience while she put on plays and presented musical extravaganzas. Paraded around the house in costumes made from whatever material she could find.

She knew, the way children know these things, that her father was among the best of the dads. He played with his kids, and he brought home his paycheck every week, unlike a lot of the other fathers who drank—brought it home to Maeve, stocky and bosomy and smiling, waiting to turn it into beef stew and potato soup and little doilies that she liked to crochet and donate to the Ladies Auxiliary and the orphans' fund and all that. Never thinking that her own two children were going to end up orphans.

And then she got sick.

In those days they didn't tell you what was wrong—and Phoebe's mum kept saying she was getting better, that the medicine was helping—*see how today I could talk without coughing, so please honey get my cigarettes for me, will you, and clean the kitchen before your father gets home then tell him I did it?*

So the day Maeve died, the shock waves crashed over them and wouldn't stop. Every day, she remembered it all over again. Her mum was dead. Dead, dead, and not coming back. Phoebe was still in junior high school, a nice Catholic school, and when the news came, she felt like she'd been hit in the stomach with a bowling ball, hardly able to breathe, and she was called to the nun's office, and oh, all the nuns and the priests coming to talk to her, taking her hand in their doughy, sweaty palms, pressing her. *Can we say a prayer together, for your mother's eternal soul?*

Yeah. Like that would help.

Back then, people didn't put everything out there like they do now. What you mostly got were platitudes wrapped up like Christmas presents: *God doesn't give us more than we can handle. It's always darkest before the dawn. Whatever doesn't kill you makes you stronger.*

We are so sorry. Join us in prayer. Let's pray for your mother's eternal soul.

Let's not. Let's scream bloody murder and hurl ourselves into traffic.

The truth, the truth that she could feel in her bones and in every cell in her body? Everybody acted so sorry for her, but nobody had ever really liked her anyway. Kids were either indifferent to her or gave her a hard time because she had freckles and her name was weird. Phoebe. They called her Feeble. Ha ha ha. The adults didn't like her much either because she was always questioning things. *Can't you just accept?* they said, until she hated that word *accept*. They might as well have been telling her, *Can't you just give up? Do what we say.*

No more questions, the priest said. Like she was just supposed to get over it and move on. *Be strong. Worship God, because God wanted your mother to come and live in Heaven with Him, and He knows best.* And her wanting to ask the one big question that was on her mind: "Don't any of you think God is kinda . . . mean?"

But she soldiered on, coping, not letting anybody know how furious at God she was, praying every night just like she always had.

Then—Daddy. Apparently God wanted Daddy, too.

Six months later, he stepped in front of a train. Left a note: *I couldn't go on. Maeve was my lifeblood. I am so, so sorry. I love you girls more than anything, but you will be better off without me. I am no good to you now. I'll just be a burden, with all my pain. Learn to be happy.*

Learn to be happy! What the hell?! In what class did they teach *that* particular skill?

Flurry of life stuff all of a sudden. Mary, eighteen, had to sell the house, and luckily she managed to attract a husband right away, a boy she'd been dating in high school who had a future in his father's auto parts store. She and Phoebe discussed it like it was a family business deal they were contemplating. Should she marry him? Would he help them keep from starving?

"Do it," Phoebe had said. She wasn't wild about Derek, but she liked him well enough. And he said he didn't mind a younger sister living with them. It would only be for a few years.

They got married in a quick ceremony in the city, and then Derek was asked to open a satellite auto parts store in Connecticut, and so they moved to Allenbury. Phoebe, too. No money for parochial school anymore, thank God, so now she should go to a regular high school. A fresh start. Maybe, she and Mary decided, this would be the lucky break they'd been waiting for.

And it was. Mary got a job in the auto parts store, doing the invoices, and Phoebe went off to high school. She was weird, but it was okay. She wore outlandish clothes that she sewed herself—there was even a velvet cape she'd made from scraps with little mementos on it. She'd walk down the halls of the school, flipping it around, and kids loved it. By then, the late seventies, the curly hair she'd been fighting with her whole life was coming into style, thanks to Barbra Streisand. And who knew, but the quirks that made her weird when she'd been little—all that acting out and pretending and make-believe—well, it turned out to mean that she was artistic and dramatic and musical. Her mother had given her piano lessons long ago, and she used to sing with her father. Somehow, by some miracle she almost couldn't comprehend, she fit in. There was glee club. And the art room became where she was known to be talented and magnificent. Her questioning of authority was seen as brilliant and brave. Teachers liked her—well, the avant-garde, cool ones—but those were the ones you wanted in your corner anyway.

And then *Kiss Me Kate*. She got the lead. And somehow she got Tilton. She became Tilton O'Malley's girlfriend, and for a while it seemed they ran the school.

The school's golden boy. And his all-that-jazz, fearless girlfriend.

No more now. Her hand was beginning to shake. No more thinking.

This was why it was good to be alone. You could push away any thoughts you didn't have a use for. Turn on the meditation tapes, put your headphones in your ear, and shut away the whole world. No one to say—as so many had—*Now, Phoebe, you need to face your fears. Get out there again and get trying.*

Kate and Poppet, you don't want to know all this stuff. You were the stuff of dreams; don't you know that by now? Don't make me tell you all the bad parts.

Do yourselves a favor, and go away.

That's what dreams are supposed to do—they float away.

EIGHTEEN
NINA

To my surprise, Indigo was shocked, appalled, and infuriated at the fact that my mother didn't show up—and her anger seemed to grow through the next week until one day when I was driving her to a consignment shop, she blew up.

She sat sideways in the passenger seat so her huge, black-fringed eyes bored into the side of my head while I attempted to concentrate on the road.

"This is unbelievable! If she didn't want to see you, then she should have told you that in the first place. Not made you sit there like a super dork waiting and waiting, your eyes on the door, thinking any minute she was going to walk in. It's, like, totally despicable! She *knew* how much it meant to you!"

"I *know.*" I put on my left turn signal. This was a new consignment shop we were going to, one that specialized in more edgy, previously used, combat-ready clothing, someone had told her. There was going to be a school dance, and she needed a new flak jacket.

"Wait," I said, changing the subject. "Why are we getting the same old kind of flak jacket thing? Why don't we look for something kind of out of the ordinary—like a nice outfit, if you're going to a dance?"

Then her eyes narrowed. "Waaait just a sec. What if she *was* there, but you didn't recognize her? Because I bet she's changed a lot from 1980."

"I thought of that," I told her, "but I looked into every single face. And I put that photograph on the table in front of us so she'd see that, at least, and know it was us. Now what if we get you a dress?"

"Are you freaking kidding me? Who's going to see a photograph . . . in a *bar*? Come on!"

"I know, but it was all I could think of to do."

"You could have stood up and made an announcement," she said.

I looked at her over the top of my sunglasses for a long moment, then she said, "No, okay, I suppose you couldn't have." Then she was quiet for a few minutes before saying, "Do you mean an ironic dress?"

"Ironic or non-ironic, either one. Something that looks kind of . . . different. Special occasion, you know."

She looked out the window. "My mother hates dresses. She never wears them."

"Well, I like them."

"I'll think about it. You really think I could pull that off, a dress look?"

"I do."

She was looking at herself in the rearview mirror. "I was also thinking I should do something with my hair. Something more chill. Do you think your sister would dye it for me?"

"What? The Magic Markers aren't working for you anymore?"

"Shut up." She laughed. "It's just that I think I could get a richer color with regular dye. Maya told me that, and since your sister does hair, maybe she'd do it."

"Maybe."

She was watching my face. "And then I could, you know, meet her."

"Possibly."

"So what's next for you and your sister and the search?"

"I don't know. I can't think."

She snorted. "What do you mean, you can't think? I say double down now, and *really* go find her."

"But—but—think about this. Do I really want to let her reject me again?"

"What? *What?* Who *are* you, anyway?" She practically jumped up and down in the seat. "Aren't *you* the woman who spent her whole life trying to locate your *mom*, and now, excuse me, but you actually *know* what her name is and where she lives—and *this* is the time you decide to wimp out and say, *Oooh, nooo, what if she rejects me? What would I dooo?*" She made her voice sound like a high-pitched cartoon character and ground her fists into her eyes like she was crying fake tears.

"All right," I said with a sigh. "You're absolutely right."

"*Yeah,* I'm right. Don't be crazy. I can see you need my help."

"Okay." I tried to stifle a smile. "I can see that I do. And I'm flattered to have your services. What do you think we should do?"

She looked out the window. "Where were you born? What town?"

"Well, the birth certificate said I was born in the hospital in New Ashbury. But my mom lived in Allenbury. Do you know where that is?"

"I've heard of it. Is that where you grew up?"

"No. I got adopted by people who lived in Branhaven."

"Huh," she said. She yawned. "Well, maybe we should go to Allenbury and see if maybe somebody knows your mom there. You know, go to the school and look around."

My heart leapt in my chest. "Wow, Indigo, that's such a good idea," I said slowly. "I wonder why I didn't think of it."

"Because you're kinda off your game. I haven't wanted to mention it, but you're not really as sharp as you were when I first met you. No offense, but you just aren't."

She was giving me her narrowed-eyes, head-tilted, judgmental, teenage-girl appraising look, which I knew in my heart of hearts meant that she liked me, that it was good she was safe enough to say the things to me that she couldn't say to others, blah blah blah. I should have been flattered, but I was wounded.

"Really," I said. "What do you think has caused this lapse in my sharpness? Any ideas?"

"I was talking to Maya about it, and we decided—now don't go getting super mad or anything—but we think it's the man-woman thing. Love, I guess you'd say. It's not your fault, of course—it's just what women *do*. That's why I'm never going to get married or anything."

I wanted nothing more than to reach over and start pummeling her right there and then. Yes, while I was driving. After *that* wave passed, I then wanted to slam on the brakes and push her onto the side of the road and drive away, cackling.

Alas, though, she was a little bit right. I hadn't even let myself think of the obvious. The town where I was born was only about fifty miles away, not even a terribly long journey, and surely there were people who might remember my parents. Maybe people who even remembered *me*. It was a little bit of a daunting thought. A put-your-money-where-your-mouth-is thought.

I swallowed hard. I should do it. I *had* to do it.

"So! What costume do you want to wear?" she said when we were in the consignment shop. "Let's look for something really dope for you to wear."

"Dope?" I said.

"Yeah, dope. Awesome, cool."

"Why can't you speak regular English? Never mind. I get it."

She smiled. "Some costume that's black and hard-assed—"

"Why do I need a costume? I think I'm just going to go as me."

"Huh," she said. "Interesting. Well, okay. I guess that's one way."

Later, on the way home, after we'd purchased a very scary-looking flak jacket, the second in her collection, and a pair of overused boots and a retro, empire-waisted royal-blue dress with polka dots, she said,

"Maybe I'll be an adoption activist. Get the laws changed so people like you can find their real parents easily."

"That sounds like a good plan," I said.

"Nah, probably I won't do that. I'm actually thinking more along the lines of an animal activist. You can't be totally effective at both adoption *and* animals, right? Not and keep your sense of integrity out in the world."

"Maybe you'll be an activist activist. Activize and activate everything!"

"Yes! And instead of being Indigo, maybe I'll change my name to something else. Cricket, maybe. Although that's so slight of a name. Something hardier. Crow. No, too spooky. Dove! I'll be Dove. Kayla Dove. Because I'm also an advocate for peace. I could get a dove tattoo."

"Please," I said.

"What?"

"Nothing." I shook my head. Because there was utterly no way to explain to her that I was feeling such a tightness right then in my chest, and that it came from an almost crushing love for her and her wacky view of life—so precocious, so young, so . . . crazy. How could I ever consider splitting up with her father when it would mean leaving her behind?

I had four homes to stage in the next two days, which didn't leave me much time to think about heading up to my mother's old high school. Plus, I wasn't completely sure I wanted to do it. And if I did do it, I wanted Lindy to go, too. But there'd been no contact between us since that last text: *Sorry.* And I was tired of always being the one to try to talk Lindy into things. Me, the person she said had an impulse disorder and didn't have good sense. Several times I'd thought of contacting her again, or going into the salon to see her, but what was the point? Really, how much more clear did she have to be that she had no use for me?

Anyway, life was busy. One Thursday, I was dropping off a plate of cut-up vegetables and some onion dip to the theater arts room after school. It was Hell Week, which meant that the school play was going to debut in seven days and the actors and crew had to be at mandatory rehearsals every single night. Parents—by which they loosely meant me—were assigned to bring in food to keep everybody alive.

At the back of the school, another harried-looking mom was unloading aluminum foil pans of pasta from the back of her Subaru Outback. "That smells amazing," I said, helping her carry them inside, and she said, "Ah yes, pesto. Nothing like it, is there?" We could hear the rehearsal going on from the stage—Adelaide was singing about the grippe, one of my all-time favorite numbers. I looked around, but I didn't see Nicely Nicely, only a bevy of swan-like dancing girls, Adelaide's dance troupe.

"So you're Tyler's . . . person?" the other mom said, and we both laughed. "Sorry," she said. "I didn't mean that to sound so weird. It's just that it's hard to know what to call people these days."

She had nice twinkly eyes and fluffy brown mom hair. I stuck out my hand, and she shook it.

"Of course. I'm Nina Popkin."

"I'm Kathy Culpepper. Glad to meet you. I've noticed you around since—you know, since Jane left. We all think it's so brave how you've jumped in and taken over all these parenting things. Carter's a lucky man."

"Well," I said, stammering. "I'm lucky, too. You know."

"We've all been watching to see what would happen after Jane left. Hmm, I shouldn't put it that way. Not to make you paranoid or any-thing—like we're *watching you*, ha ha! But Carter is such a nice person, and we felt bad for him, the way things happened. But of course you never know, do you? Any of us could have the same fate. It's life."

She looked at me, like it was now my turn.

"Yes," I said. "It's life, pretty much."

"Good to get to finally talk to you," she said. "Tyler's doing great in his part. Have you seen any of the rehearsals yet? He's really got talent."

Then we did a lot of congratulating—her daughter, it turned out, was Lolly, Tyler's girlfriend, and she was playing the part of Adelaide.

"Oh," I said, and had to look away. Kathy Culpepper probably had no idea that Lolly spent some days in Tyler's room instead of at school. I wanted to ask her. Really—were parents everywhere completely clueless? I supposed my own parents were, too, but it was hard to believe I'd ever have gotten away with as much as these kids did.

"I'm going to slip into the auditorium and watch the dance number," Kathy said. I was about to say I'd go watch, too, but then I got a frantic text from Indigo, asking if I would pick her up.

I thought u were taking bus, I typed.

NO! LOL! Change in plans. Problem came up. Come 2 front office.

I found her sitting on the floor outside the main office, scrolling through her phone. She jumped, startled, when she saw me coming down the hall.

"Oh good, you're here. Quick. Go into the office and sign me out, okay?"

"Sign you out? But school's over, isn't it? I thought you were going to be waiting out—"

"Just please. Do it. Okay? Say I have a doctor's appointment or something, and you have to take me."

"But why are you even still here?"

"Nina! Could you please just do this? I'll explain to you later." She looked like the cops were going to jump out of the bank of lockers in front of us. She kept peering into her backpack.

"All right." The office was empty, but there was a sheet of paper on the counter, so I started writing *I am taking Indi Kayla Sanborn to her doctor's appointment—signed, Nina Popkin*—when a woman's voice cut through my thoughts.

"Excuse me. What are you doing?" She was obviously the office magistrate of the highest order, with her short white hair and little Peter Pan collar and tweed jacket.

Parenting without a license, I wanted to tell her.

"I'm, uh, signing Kayla Sanborn out."

"For what reason?"

"For what? For a doctor's appointment. But isn't school out anyway?"

"Kayla Sanborn is supposed to be in the detention room."

"Oh," I said. "I didn't know."

"You didn't get the *note*? We send home notes when students have detention. Parents are supposed to keep track of this, and Kayla is supposed to talk to her guidance counselor. What did you say your name was? You're not her mother, are you?"

"No. I'm . . . I'm . . . a family friend."

"A family friend, huh?" She looked me up and down. She even took off her glasses so she could study me further. "And what is your name? Are you authorized to sign things on her parents' behalf?"

Well, was I?

I took a stab and said, "Yes. I'm a dear friend of her father's." I drew myself up farther. I turned and looked through the glass window into the hallway, but Indigo wasn't anywhere to be seen.

"All right," said the magistrate at last, with a sigh that meant I had caused her untold distress. "There's only ten more minutes of detention, so you can go and get her, I suppose. Next time, though, you have to call ahead. We're getting too lax with the detention rules, letting kids walk in and out as they please. No one takes it seriously anymore."

"I take it very seriously," I said.

"I'm sure you do. Then you can have her bring a doctor's note in tomorrow."

"A doctor's note?"

"Yes. You did say you were taking her to the doctor, didn't you?"

She gave me a self-satisfied smirk, just to let me know that a school magistrate is at the very pinnacle of the high school justice system, and even though I was an adult, I was no better than the wormy tenth graders she dealt with every day, and one is never too old to be truly innocent in the eyes of a school administrator.

◆ ◆ ◆

"*Kayla Sanborn!*" I said, when I got outside the office. She jumped up and we headed down the hallway. "I am seriously calling you Kayla for the rest of the day for what you did to me in there."

She laughed. "Was it super awful? Isn't old Mrs. Meaney, like, the best-named person in the known world? She's the assistant principal."

"So why were you supposed to be in detention? And why didn't you show your dad the note? And what the hell is going on?"

"Oh, it's all a misunderstanding. Don't worry about it." She peered into her backpack again.

"A misunderstanding between whom exactly?"

"Between me and my science teacher."

"Ah! Interesting. What is his version of the facts, and what is your version?"

We had reached the car. As we got in, she put on her seat belt and said very nonchalantly, "Well, *his* version is that I stole a guinea pig from the biology classroom and then lost her and my version is that I still have the guinea pig in question and that I am liberating her because I am an activist."

"A guinea pig. You liberated a school guinea pig?" I started the car and backed up, then turned into traffic.

"*Am* liberating." She reached into her backpack and scooped out a little furry thing and held it to my face. The guinea pig, being an opportunist, of course leapt into the air, bonking itself on the dashboard and then falling to the ground and rushing around the floor of the car, making piteous squeaking noises. I slammed on the brakes as it came scooting over toward my feet, except that somehow in my excitement I might have forgotten to pull the car over to the side of the road first, and so someone slammed into the back of my car—well, actually Carter's car—so for the next hour, I was filling out reports and talking to cops and Indigo was madly looking for a liberated guinea pig among the workings of the seats.

I couldn't get over how pleased she was with the whole situation.

"This was almost like a public statement of activism," she said. "The police and everything."

"True," I said. "But the police weren't technically there to retrieve the guinea pig—they were there to yell about bad driving."

"Yes, but I noticed it was the other driver who got the ticket, so it wasn't like you had to suffer."

"Well, true. He was cited for following too close—but, Indigo, that was a very, very bad idea, stealing a guinea pig and then shoving her under my nose while I was driving. Without warning. We could have really gotten hurt."

"I'm new at activism," she said. "And sometimes things don't go as planned."

I opened my mouth to say something, but nothing came out. Where does one begin? Besides, she was insisting that before we went home, we go buy a huge, palatial cage for the guinea pig, whose name, she told me, was going to be Beyoncé.

"Don't you think you should return this animal? Really? Beyoncé *is* school property."

She looked at me like I was insane. "No, no, no. Her life is a living hell in that school. She's trapped in a cage no bigger than a shoebox. Boys stick their fingers in her cage and poke her. She is humiliated and laughed at. No, she's much better off here. And besides, I served half a detention period for taking her. So that means she's mine."

She gave me a fierce look. "By the way, when are we going back to your parents' high school?"

"I've been busy at work, and I want Lindy to come along, too."

"Have you told her that?"

"Your honor, if it please the court, I haven't had the time to reach her because I've been staging houses. And also I have to think of the right words to suggest it to her."

"I think the right words might be, 'Hey, Lindy, let's you and me and Indigo go see our birthplace.' How would that be? And she could also dye my hair then. Did you ask her about that?"

"Not yet. But I will."

"Jeez. I feel like I have to organize *everything*," she said.

Boat season was now in full swing, and Carter was scarcely at home anymore. He was so apologetic, though, and sometimes out of guilt he'd zoom home for dinner and then have to go back to wrestle with deliveries and unhappy boat owners. It was all complicated and he was exhausted, I could tell. He kept saying it was only temporary, life would smooth out, he was so grateful to me for picking up the slack, he couldn't do it without me.

We still weren't doing absolutely fantastic, I have to admit. I hadn't taken any more clothes back to Josephine's condo lately, now that it had occurred to me how much it would hurt the children if I left, but the post-graffiti fight still lingered between us, a discussion that we were someday going to have to revisit. Sometimes as I drove around staging houses, I argued my point of view with him in my head, and surprisingly, he thought I had some good points.

I did try to catch him up on things one night in bed.

I told him our little motley family had grown by one, since we were now in possession of a stolen guinea pig named Beyoncé, that furry rodent he might have noticed in the dining room, in a cage the approximate size one would buy for a palomino pony.

"Stolen?" he said sleepily. "Who would steal a guinea pig?"

"Funny you should ask. It seems we might have an animal activist on our hands." I tried to match his nonchalant tone. It was difficult since he was nearly asleep, and I was trying to get a rise out of him. But I couldn't, of course.

"Huh," was all he said, his voice seeming to come from the depths of sleep. "What do you know? That's good, right? Good family values."

"Carter, did you hear the word *stolen*?"

He was out cold.

NINETEEN
NINA

Opening night for the play, and Indigo told me that we had to go early because she had a special errand to do at school after the play officially started but before the intermission. She didn't want me to worry; she promised she wouldn't miss Tyler onstage. She'd do it before that.

"But Nicely Nicely is in the opener," I told her. "Where are you going?"

She looked sly and mysterious. "We're going to the biology class, all right?"

"Indigo."

"Maybe I'm going to apologize to Mr. Hamre for taking Beyoncé. He'll be at the play."

"*Are* you going to apologize to Mr. Hamre? Why don't you take Beyoncé back if you're sorry?"

"But I'm not sorry. And Mr. Hamre has some, um, extra credit he wants me to do to make up for what I did. So stop worrying about it. Okay? I know what I'm doing, and I need to get to the school before the play. *Okay?*"

"What's really going on?"

"Listen, just take me to the school early. Then I'll come and sit beside you during the opening, and when I need to, I'll get up and leave. That's all. If my dad asks why I'm doing it, say you have no idea. Say I have to go to the bathroom or something."

"Fine. But what *will* you be doing?"

"Taking a stand."

"Jesus, Indigo. What are you talking about?"

"I'll tell you after. I promise."

"Will you be coming back in to enjoy the rest of the play?"

"Sure! Of course! Why wouldn't I?"

So I forgot all about it and worked all day staging two houses and then showing another condo to a nice elderly couple who were tired of shoveling snow and raking leaves, and then I sped over to pick up Indigo to take her to school. Tyler, the man of the hour, was already at the school for one last, mad dress rehearsal.

Carter texted that he was über busy at work, dealing with some crazy clients. Turns out that boat people, who look so laid-back in their white pants and their open-throated blue shirts and their sunburned hands holding their cocktails aloft, are actually as uptight and furious as anyone else when their shipments of doodads don't arrive on time. So he was harried and apologetic, and was going to try to be on time for the play, but if he wasn't, at least he'd be seeing every other performance of the play through the two weekends it was running. He was so grateful to me for being there on opening night. He owed me, big-time, was the way he put it.

High school auditoriums are all the same, and they are places of deep anxiety for me, the scenes of many humiliations in my misguided youth singing in the chorus, so after I dropped off Indigo, I did a little meditation in the car. Inside the auditorium, all the parents were hovering around, and some of them talked to me—I was Tyler's person, after all—and we wrung our hands and said we knew this was going to be wonderful, and then the opening overture started to play, and Carter still wasn't there, so I took my seat. Indigo came flying in, her eyes bright like two glowing coals. "Everything is all set," she said. "This is going to be epic."

"*Guys and Dolls* is very epic," I said. "You can hardly find a better love story with the wrong person."

"Not that," she whispered. "What I'm doing. My project."

I gave her a worried look, and she squeezed my hand. "You're going to be very proud of me."

Then the lights went down, and the audience settled itself, and soon the stage was filled with gamblers and gangsters—and there was our own personal Nicely Nicely being all funny and singing his heart out, and I was swept up in the play, and then Indigo touched me on the shoulder and said, "Here goes," and she ran down the aisle.

After a few minutes, Carter came pushing his way through the row of seats, with his "Excuse me, excuse me," and he sat next to me and kissed me on the cheek. "He's been great," I said.

"Where's Indigo?"

"Some project she's doing. She'll be back." A little prickle of something moved down my spine, but I ignored it for his sake.

Carter took my hand and whispered, "Your hands are ice-cold. Are you nervous for my little actor son up there on the big stage?" He kissed me on the cheek. "That is so sweet."

"No, I know he's fine. I'm just—"

And then someone screamed onstage.

Adelaide and her dance troupe scattered across the stage, looking like life-size dolls being tossed about, then shrieking and jumping up and down, on one foot and then the other. The audience laughed at first—sort of a nervous laugh that built to a crescendo, and then stopped when we realized.

The stage was full of frogs.

Frogs everywhere. Green, slimy hopping frogs. The girls started running backstage, and people were yelling and screaming, and then grown-ups appeared and the curtain went down.

"Oh shit," I said to Carter.

"An interesting production, to be sure. Funny that Tyler didn't mention the frogs."

We looked up to see Indigo run out on the stage, her hair blooming blue in the overhead stage lights. She was yelling something, and the crowd finally hushed enough to hear her.

"THESE HELPLESS, INNOCENT LAB ANIMALS WERE GOING TO BE KILLED IN YOUR CHILD'S BIOLOGY CLASS! BUT NOW THEY ARE FREE! ENJOY THE REST OF THE SHOW KNOWING THAT YOUR TAX DOLLARS DID NOT GO TO MURDERING ANIMALS!"

And then someone came onstage and led her away.

There was a silence, as though all the air had left the row where Carter and I were sitting, and then he turned to me and said, "That really just happened, didn't it?"

So she was suspended for the rest of the year—which was only six weeks, but still. It amounted to expulsion. No more school. There was a hearing, and there were meetings, and Carter said I didn't have to attend with him, but I knew he wanted me there, so I went. "Did you know this was going to happen?" he asked me about a hundred times, and each time I said no, but deep down inside, I thought maybe that was the wrong answer.

I had known *something*.

I just hadn't known that as a newly minted animal activist she would *right that evening* feel the need to let all the lab animals go. She had to, she explained to her father and to me, and to Jane on Skype.

"They were going to kill those frogs," she said. "We were going to have to *pith* those frogs in biology class. Do you know what pithing is?"

"But what in the *hell* did this have to do with *Guys and Dolls*?" her father wanted to know. "They didn't pith any frogs in *Guys and Dolls*, did they? So why did you have to ruin your brother's play?"

I had never seen him so stunned, not even the night he explained to me that he was a good, competent father who didn't deserve to be questioned about his parenting philosophy.

"I just thought all the parents should know about it," she said calmly. "You can't make me sorry about this. I took a stand. I studied it; I researched the conditions; I acted on my beliefs; and I'm not sorry."

In the weeks that followed, Carter rubbed his head a lot and talked to the school authorities with the right amount of shock and deference. He had conversations with Jane on the phone, talks that often ended in furious whispering. I noticed he had bags under his eyes and that his hair was slightly grayer. He grimly wrote checks, put Indigo back in therapy, hired a private tutor to come to the house, and then one day he said to me, "You know something? I'm kind of changing my mind about this. Unlike painting graffiti all over the hillside, unlike taking drugs or having sex—both of which she has *not* done—this was kind of a wonderful thing she did. She *was* caring for life. It was love."

"*Was* it wonderful?" I said. "Because the frogs didn't look all that happy to me, being let loose on a stage where people were screaming and running all over the place."

"Yes, but at least they weren't killed."

"Well, some of them probably died in the scuffle. I mean, the school system does have a point . . ."

"But her heart was in the right place."

"Shouldn't she be a little bit sorry?" I asked. "Weren't there perhaps other ways of getting her point across?"

"Jesus," he said, walking in circles in the middle of the room. "I just realized I don't know what to think of any of this. What the hell! I don't know anything anymore. I'm a wreck."

"What I think is, you've got to take more control, Carter. You want to be everybody's friend, and that's wonderful, but kids need a much firmer hand. Get in there and make her *know* this isn't appropriate. She's begging for that!"

"She's not begging for that. I know her better than you do. She has a soft heart—"

"This was not the result of having a soft heart," I said. "Look around! Wake up! This is a cry for help! Another cry for help, I might add."

"Nina," he said, and I made a mental note that he hadn't called me Popkin. Silly little detail. But then he said it again, putting his hands on my shoulders: "Nina, I can't listen to what you think right now. I can't."

"Carter, she talks to me all the time. She's sad; she's lonely; she's questioning things. I bought her a dress—a dress! Did you even know that? And she wants to get Lindy to fix up her hair. She's thinking about boys, and she needs somebody to talk to about that. But I'm not her family. I'm not you, and I'm not Jane. Please. Don't turn away from me. You have to hear this."

Sometimes his eyes were so dark that you couldn't see any light in them at all, and this was one of those times. I felt as though I'd gotten on a toboggan, and it was taking me wherever it would, zooming down a hill, without me being in control of it at all.

He took his hands off my shoulders and rubbed his face hard and sighed. "Ah, Nina. I think maybe it's best if we—if you—you know, if we just stop things here," he said. "I don't think I can do this anymore."

I could have pretended he didn't say what he just said, I could have turned and gone to the kitchen, made us cups of tea, baked a blueberry pie, gone for a walk, or done any number of things, and maybe the whole situation would have worked itself out in another hour or two. Instead, I stood there and looked at him. I lifted my chin; I remember that.

"Fine," I said, but there was a sound in my ears like when electrical wires are frying themselves. "Are we talking stop the conversation, or stop the relationship?"

He didn't say anything for a long time. Then he said tiredly, "Whatever you want."

"No. Totally. I get it. Fine. I'll pack up."

"Isn't that what *you* want?" he said.

I went to the closet and pulled out my suitcase. My hands were shaking.

He sighed loudly. "I guess we might have moved too fast, you and I," he said. "Like you always tried to point out to me. Like everybody tried to point out to me."

"Absolutely. No, don't worry. I've known this moment was coming for a long time."

"Will you be okay?" he said.

"Will I be *okay*? Honestly, Carter, I feel like I've just been given a Get Out of Jail Free card."

That sentence would have been magnificent if it was finished with a bitter little laugh, but the sound took a wrong turn somewhere in my throat and came out more like I had choked on a potato chip or something. I turned away quickly before he could see my eyes.

Breaking up over frogs. This was a first. I'd probably laugh about this one day.

Later that week, on a rainy day, I came over when I knew Carter wasn't home, to officially tell the kids good-bye. I stood in their overheated, jam-packed front hall with my coat on, and Tyler gave me a hug and said he hoped he'd see me around. He said I'd been awesome. I told him good luck in college, and he said he'd be fine.

Indigo couldn't look at me at first, and then she gave me a hug so limp it almost needed life support. Her eyes, smeared with mascara, were miserable. "Tyler says this is all my fault," she whispered.

"I did *not* say that," he said. "I said that it's hard for single parents to form a new meaningful relationship when they have teenage kids still at home."

"That would be me," she said.

"It's me, too," he said. "God, Indigo, you make such a huge hairy deal of every single thing! Can you just lighten the fuck up?"

"You lighten the fuck up," she said.

"Okay, okay," I said. "Don't you two go trying to make me miss you so much."

He sighed and rubbed his hands through his hair, a gesture identical to his father's, then left, taking the stairs two at a time, back to his lair. Indigo looked back at me, and the expression on her face broke my already-cracked heart.

"Hey," I said. "This doesn't have to be it for you and me. I miss you."

She folded her arms. "Whatever."

"No, not *whatever*. Why don't I pick you up every week and take you to therapy? You still go on Tuesday? How about that? And maybe after your appointment, we could grab some dinner. How would that be? You and me?"

"Okay," she said.

"Is your dad still really busy at work?"

"Nina," she said sternly. "I am not going to be a spy for you for my dad. I know all about this kind of thing, people using kids to get information."

I burst out laughing. "Oh my God, you are such a piece of work, my darling, lovely Indigo. Just to be clear, I wasn't trying to get *information* about your dad. I only wanted to know if he's too busy to take you places and cook dinner and all that."

"Again," she said. "*So* not appropriate."

"I'm glad to see all your troubles haven't wrecked your integrity." I reached over and hugged her as hard as I could, then held her at arm's length. She looked about as despondent as it's possible for anybody to look and still be standing upright, but then I saw that old glimmer in her eye, the one that said she knew exactly what she was doing.

"You need anything, call me," I said. "And otherwise, I'll see you Tuesday, okay? Okay?"

Her eyes filled up with tears, and she swiped them away.

"Oh, sweet girl. It's okay to cry. Come on, it's going to be fine."

TWENTY
LINDY

Lindy was having a wonderful day. It was just an ordinary Tuesday, and actually a lot of things had gone wrong—it was what Winnie-the-Pooh would have called a "bothersome sort of day"—but the funny thing was, Lindy wasn't bothered by any of it. There had been one hassle after another: an order for shampoos had been misplaced; a stylist hadn't shown up for work, so Lindy had had to do all *her* clients, too; and the music system needed repairing. By three o'clock she'd done two perms, a color, three shampoos and blow-dries, as well as fielded phone calls from the Mothers of Twins about a board meeting change, and from the PTA about a new motion, *and* a call from her mother complaining that Lindy had bought the wrong kind of bread again—the kind with seeds—and the children wanted white bread, so could Lindy bring some home, and could she please not get the wrong kind again? Ever.

She even found herself making a joke with Megan, the receptionist, about how she'd almost gotten hit on by a guy in Brooklyn, and Megan told her a story about her ex-boyfriend, and the two of them had laughed about how weird men were. Not a conversation Lindy would have ever encouraged before.

There was no explaining it, except that she'd noticed (as though she were a sociologist studying her own life) that ever since that ill-fated trip two weeks earlier, she'd simply felt different.

Had it been the trip itself to a new place—or perhaps the hangover? She didn't know. The whole next day she'd had a wicked headache, and she'd been in no mood to do her usual weekend errands . . . so she didn't do them. The list she'd made remained in her purse, and instead of going shoe shopping with Chloe and the twins, she'd sat in the den with Jeff watching endless reruns of *The Twilight Zone*, letting the kids play with their stuffed animals in the living room. Only once did she need to count to twenty-one (odd number, divisible by three).

She could see Jeff giving her funny looks that day. And finally, when it was close to dinnertime and she hadn't made a thing, he said, "You sure you're okay, Lindy?"

They had Chinese food takeout, which they hardly ever did (too much sodium), and after the kids were in bed, when he *didn't* go play racquetball, she was so relieved that she'd started a long, meandering conversation with him that didn't even seem to have any point to it, except it did because then she heard herself saying, "You know, I think I learned something about myself when I went to Brooklyn yesterday."

"That you should always drink water when you drink booze?" he said, smiling.

"Well, that, too. But mostly I realized that I really, really don't want to feel so anxious all the time," she said. "And I'm going to stop."

"Uh-huh," he said. "And how are you going to do that?" He was still smiling at her, like she was an interesting specimen he'd discovered outside while mowing the lawn.

But no matter. She'd ended up telling him the thing she'd wanted to say—that when she was born, her mother had named her Poppet, and also that lately, she'd had such an interesting realization—that it was more than just a name: why, she'd be a whole different person if she'd gone through life as Poppet. Freer maybe, and more whimsical. She might be the type who would welcome the chaos of a messier life, one with less control to it.

She might not feel the need to tap if she were Poppet.

That's what she said to him, and he stared at her.

"It sounds crazy, I know, but sometimes I can feel who I might have been," she said. "Just a little. I feel Lindy and all her anxieties receding, and Poppet showing up the slightest bit."

He started doing the theme from *The Twilight Zone* show. "Doo-doo-*doo*-doo, doo-doo-*doo*-doo. Does this mean that you're not going to turn all the spoons to face the same way in the silverware drawer anymore?" he said.

"Well," she said. "Let's not go too far."

And even though her poor hungover head had been hurting more or less all day, and she hadn't taken a shower and washed her hair, that night after the kids were asleep, they made love downstairs in front of the fireplace—which, it turned out, you could do even without a romantic fire there.

You could just do it because you felt like it.

Afterward, Jeff had joked, "You know, if this is the kind of stuff Poppet likes to do, then I may have to rethink my position on you finding out about your birth mom."

And here was the other thing: the way he'd held on to her, the way he'd gazed into her eyes, she'd known deep down that he really wasn't having an affair. He still loved her; he was a good husband, sweet with the kids. He just wasn't ever going to be able to talk to her the way she wanted to be talked to, that was all. But she could live with that. She could decide to be happy.

Being happy. That's why when she was out buying milk and white bread after work, and she looked up and saw Nina in the grocery store—Nina walking with a teenage girl down the cereal aisle—her immediate reaction *wasn't* to hide or to let out some exasperated sighs, as it would have been earlier, but instead to smile and stride right over.

Nina hadn't called her since the day after the trip, hadn't shown up with a new plan to meet Phoebe, hadn't tried to insert herself into Lindy's life even once. The silence had been weird. And now here she was—the person who'd held Lindy's hair while she threw up, who had seen her at her worst, who'd driven her home and had been funny and generous and non-judgmental. Lindy, much to her own surprise, missed her.

"Nina!" she called. And her sister looked up, surprised, and Lindy hurried over to them and said, "Hi, how are you? And is this . . . Indigo?" and Nina introduced them. Indigo was odd looking, there was no doubt about it, with her bright blue jagged-cut hair and raccoon eyes. But there was something warm and intelligent in those made-up eyes, and when she heard who Lindy was, she actually looked excited.

"You guys are sisters! Omigod, I can totally see that in you. Look at your hair, and your chins and the way you smile—wait, let me get a picture." She whipped a phone out of the pocket of her ratty old jacket, and made them pose next to the oatmeal. "You guys! This is *awesome*! Look! Okay, now a selfie with all three of us. Come on. Cheeeeeese!"

Nina seemed slightly abashed, but there was something else, too, something Lindy couldn't put her finger on. She didn't look right at all.

Her sister was sad.

She touched Nina's arm. "Everything okay? I haven't heard from you."

Nina started to say something, but Indigo interrupted. "She and my dad broke up."

"No!" said Lindy, and she searched Nina's eyes, which now she could tell were puffy and devastated, even though Nina was trying to smile. "Oh, I'm so sorry. When? What? Are you okay?"

Nina tilted her head toward Indigo, and Lindy nodded, understanding. *No sense in trying to talk here.*

"We should get together," Lindy said. "Do you want to come over sometime? Maybe?"

Nina looked startled. "Come over where?"

"Well, to my house, I guess. We could get together, I think. I mean, we need to debrief after our Brooklyn outing, don't we? Figure out our next move."

"Our next move? Excuse me, but aren't you the one in favor of giving this up?"

"I know. I may have lost my mind. But I can't stop thinking about her. I even wrote her a little letter."

Indigo was pretending to be interested in scrolling through her phone, but Lindy could tell she was listening closely to their conversation. She kept peeking at Lindy around the edges of her phone, making faces, smiling.

"You did?" said Nina. "You're kidding."

"I want to know what the story is now. Isn't that what you've been saying? I guess I can't really ignore the whole thing anymore, like I wanted to. I want to see her. I think. I'm pretty sure. Ninety-percent sure."

Nina was staring at her. "Give me the name of the doctor who performed your lobotomy. I need to ask him some questions."

Lindy laughed.

Indigo put her phone away and made the time-out sign with her hands, talking fast now. "See, you guys? This is what I've been *saying*. We need to go to her hometown, and do a fact-finding mission. There's gotta be people who remember her, and we can find out lots of stuff. And then we'll regroup and figure out a plan. It'll be awesome."

Lindy looked at Nina, who smiled. "Yes. I'm afraid we have a teenager on the case."

"I just don't think this is the time to give up," said Indigo. "That's all."

"Call me," said Lindy. "Really. Please."

"I'm glad *you're* saying this to her," Indigo said. "She breaks up with my dad, and she loses her entire mojo. I can't do a thing with her."

TWENTY-ONE

PHOEBE

Now the other one had written to her.

Poppet.

What the hell?

> I'm sure you had your reasons for not showing up the other night, but we sat in the bar, waiting for you, looking into strangers' faces until we knew you weren't coming.
>
> I want to tell you that WE GET IT. We know we're from an awful chapter in your life, and we are so sorry you've had hard times.
>
> I have children myself. I could go into all the reasons I would never have done what you did, but that wouldn't be productive. I wasn't a teenager when they were born. But I think that even if I'd had to give them away, once they were grown and wanted to see me,

nothing—NOTHING—could keep me from flying to their sides.

There is an awful lot of love out here for you, and I hope that someday you will let us show you.

P.S. We had a very nice time at the Cranky Snail bar. Thank you for suggesting it.

She didn't even try to throw this letter away, or put it in the junk drawer. She put it on her bedside table, and she read it thirty-three times that first day alone. And then forty-five times the day after that. At this rate, six months from now, she wouldn't be able to give lessons anymore for needing to sit and reread the letter all the damn time.

Poppet hadn't included a phone number, so it was a perfectly safe letter to keep around. It made her smile, as a matter of fact.

Imagine that.

Smiling when she thought about her children.

TWENTY-TWO
NINA

So if there's anything I know, it's how to survive a breakup. I am the queen of breakups. I never stay mad after the parting. I know that things can go badly even if people did their best, and that's what makes it easy for me to move on. Unless a guy marries me, I am totally over him by Friday.

But this breakup—this one that I'd seen coming for months, that I had been totally prepared for—well, it was different, and it wasn't just because I now was seeing his daughter once a week and being reminded of everything I'd lost.

This time I didn't seem to be able to put it behind me. Oh, sure, I did all my little rituals: removed the photos from my phone (I put them in the cloud so I could see them again, if I ever wanted to remember how bad things had been, so they weren't gone *forever*), and I packed up all Carter's possessions and dropped them off at his house once when I picked up Indigo, along with the presents he'd given me: the gold bracelet that he'd said belonged to his mother and was therefore sacred to him; a quilt he'd bought for me; a lovely brown sweater that I wore nearly every night at his house while I was cooking dinner last winter.

And yet I stayed desolate far beyond the usual five-day limit I allow myself. Weeping in the car. Downloading photos from the cloud just so I could scroll through the pictures again. Playing and singing along to sad songs on the radio. Staring into space. Sniffling when couples strolled through the houses I showed them.

One day a Paul McCartney song came on the radio, and I had to stop myself from texting Carter about Yoko Ono. And another time, I was watching a love scene on TV, and I swear the close-up was of Carter's eyes, gazing down into the woman's face—and well, I cried out in pain and turned off the television.

About a thousand times a day I asked myself what the hell I was thinking with all this grief and woe. There had been so many times I couldn't wait to get out of that house, so many moments when I felt flummoxed and ridiculous and extraneous and completely over my head with exasperation. So many times when all I'd yearned for was a nice two-hour hot bath without somebody knocking on the bathroom door.

And now my mother's condo was like a prison. A place of grief and death, again.

What the hell, indeed.

I missed it all—the fights, the noise, the horrifying combination of chintz and bamboo, the lack of privacy, the alarm clocks. Hell, I missed the carpool moms! I missed cooking dinner and then tidying up the kitchen, and even the silly calendar I'd bought that had all our activities color coded on it. The four different breakfasts I'd prepared every morning just because I wanted to. The goddamned permission slips I was always being asked to sign by sly children bent on doing mischief.

I wondered if now he and Jane might find their way to getting back together. Not that Indigo would ever say.

◆　◆　◆

Life filled up with people and activities, as it always does.

I woke up one morning, and even from the depths of my grief, I knew that Melanie should have a baby shower, and I talked her into letting me give her one. I made a huge fuss over her, baking little pink and blue cupcakes and inviting every friend we ever had. Everyone came, and we played music and unwrapped presents and laughed and talked, and Melanie looked enormous and beautiful and shiny eyed, like a Madonna sitting in my mother's living room, drinking virgin mimosas.

And I did not cry even once.

Lindy called me a few times, and even though I didn't want to, I spilled the whole story to her: about Indigo and the frogs and getting expelled from school, and how Carter had looked at me like *I* was the enemy, and how I just hadn't been able to take it anymore.

She insisted that I come for dinner and meet some other known members of my real family, her darling children—so I did. I sat on her living room floor while her kids climbed on me. Razzie brought me truck after truck after truck, smiling at me shyly, over this automotive offering of the greatest import. And that made Davey decide that *his* gift should be a display of astonishing athletic prowess—leaping from the arm of the couch to the glass coffee table. I managed to stick out one arm and grab him in midair at the last second, then I danced him around the room before he could realize he'd been thwarted.

Meanwhile, Chloe, sitting cross-legged on the rug, chattered on and on about how *interesting* it was that I was her auntie, even though she hadn't known me before, because as anyone could tell you, you *always* know who your aunties are. She explained to the twins with painstaking care and increasing volume the entire story of her mother and me and how we had gone to the same school and *had no idea* we were sisters.

Apparently, though, I passed some sort of secret test, because at last I was taken into the inner sanctum upstairs—a high honor, Lindy whispered—where I was permitted to see Chloe's collection of tiaras and dolls and stuffed animals. There were other tests, too, of course. I was shown some artwork and asked to comment. I had to pick the most beautiful tiara. I was quizzed on my feelings about Olaf and which *Frozen* sister I preferred. (I knew from being coached that I was supposed to say Elsa, and I was met with beams of approval as a result.) I had to tell my age, where I lived, answer why I didn't have any children, and why I didn't have a husband. Had I lost him, like their grandmother had?

"I did," I said. "I lost him."

"Is he in the ground?" Chloe wanted to know. "Because if he's in the ground, then he's not really lost. He's with Jesus. So is yours in the ground?"

"No, he's not in the ground. He's walking around somewhere in the world."

"Well, you should go get him back," she said.

"You," I said, "are adorable. The slightest bit delusional, perhaps, but filled with hope and optimism. I like your spirit, and in twenty years, perhaps we'll have some fascinating conversations about your own love life. I look forward to it."

By the time the children had gone to bed, I was exhausted. As the auntie and guest of honor, not only had I saved Davey's life, but I somehow had been permitted—some might say required—to read bedtime stories and sing two songs of my choosing, turn on the night-lights, tuck in the covers, and lead a discussion on what had been the best and worst moments of Chloe's day. By the time I limped downstairs, I wasn't fit for much—but there were Lindy and Jeff, real adults, smiling at me.

"The woman of the hour," said Jeff. "You seem to have had a crash course in managing three children!"

I staggered to the couch, and Lindy poured me a glass of wine.

"Is it the middle of the night yet?"

"It's, um, seven forty," she said. "We didn't even have dinner yet."

I followed her and Jeff to the kitchen. "How do you *do* this? You do this every single *day*?" I said. "Like, they *live* here with you and everything? Day after day?"

"We should have helped you upstairs," Lindy said. "But we were down here discussing our mother situation, and I was telling him Indigo's idea. Jeff thinks you and I should definitely go to her high school and find out all we can."

She dished up something tomato-ish with noodles and long strands of mozzarella into blue pottery bowls. There was a green salad already glistening on the table, and goblets filled with ice water. We sat at a round oak table, the kind with a pedestal like I've always coveted, and I sneaked a peek over at Jeff, studying him. He was actually a bit of a hunk. Must be all that racquetball she'd told me about.

"I'm intrigued by this secret," he said now. "I bet someone there will know what happened, and all you gotta do is ask the right questions and you'll find out your real story." He poured me some more wine, and we all started to eat.

Lindy laughed. "Yeah, that's what Indigo said."

"I know, right? She actually can't put the idea aside," I told them. "She's fixated on me finding my mother. I'm glad you got to meet her and see her in action. She's kind of . . . indescribable. Wonderful and indescribable."

"Oh, you described her pretty accurately. The hair, the way she dresses, how bold she is. Jeff, you should see this girl. I couldn't take my eyes off her. She's—magnetic. With bright blue hair."

"She asked me one day if I thought you'd be willing to do her hair. With real dye. Right now she colors it with markers and cuts it with pinking shears."

"I'm flattered she'd want me," said Lindy. "Wow."

"Yes. Not many people meet her exacting standards."

After that we went back into the living room and drank more wine and talked about a whole bunch of things—whether it was possible to watch *Frozen* so many times that your brain would turn to mush, for instance, and which was harder, family life with little kids or family life with teenagers.

"I was way over my head," I said. "Parenting-wise. I think I need to start with a little zygote and when I can handle that, proceed to the care and maintenance of a fetus, and then perhaps some months later, move on to a real infant. Work my way up from there. I'm about twenty years away from being able to handle a terrifying teenager."

"Me, too," Jeff said. "I'm about twenty years away from that as well. But it's coming up on me."

Lindy had been staring off into space, but now she spoke. "I just had a great idea. I wonder if Indigo would like to work in the salon. I usually hire a couple of high school girls to help with sweeping up hair and bringing cucumber water to customers. I bet she'd be good with customers. And she probably needs something to do now that she's not allowed to go to school."

"Don't get me wrong, because I think Indigo is one of the world's greatest kids, but I have to say I'm kind of surprised that you'd *want* to hire her," I said. "I did mention the frog caper, didn't I? Although I suppose you don't have that many frogs in the salon."

"And I bet you'd like to keep it that way," Jeff said. I decided I liked him.

She smiled at me dreamily. "I think—well, I think she's a free spirit, that Indigo. And for whatever reason, she's in a tough spot right now. Her mom chose to move away, and then her dad got involved with you—which was a good thing for her obviously—but now that you and he are broken up, she doesn't have much she can count on, much to take pride in."

"Wait. She can count on *me*," I said. Perhaps a trifle defensively.

"I know, I know. But maybe now she can count on me, too. You don't mind that, do you?"

"No," I said. "No, of course not. I'm just surprised is all."

"Well, we'll see if it works. And also, we're taking her with us to Allenbury, right?"

"Seriously? You want to do that?"

"Nina, we've come this far. We might as well find out what we can."

I turned to Jeff. "Did she complain much when you took her for the lobotomy, or did she go quietly?"

TWENTY-THREE
NINA

Indigo and I picked up Lindy the following Monday morning for the trip to Allenbury.

It was about an hour's drive, and we first stopped at the town center and walked around. There was a little town green with a couple of churches and a run-down town hall, a coffee shop, a hardware store. I was a bit reticent, but Indigo had no qualms about approaching random people on the street—older ladies in track suits, for instance—and saying, "Hey, do you know Phoebe Mullen?"

People shook their heads. A bald guy wearing khaki shorts said, "Wasn't she the singer? Had a group?"

"Yeah," Indigo said. "Did you know her when she lived here?"

"Man, I'm not that old," he said.

After an hour of aimless wandering and finding few people wanting to chat, I said we should go over to the high school and seek out somebody who might have worked there forever. Indigo had a notebook and pen out.

"Wait, *are* there really likely to be any teachers who are still teaching there?" she said. "You're what? Thirty-five. So this would have been—yikes, thirty-six years ago. So if, say, one of their teachers was thirty years old back then, they'd be sixty-six now. Retired probably. Half dead."

"No one can afford to retire at sixty-five anymore. I, myself, plan to work until I'm in my eighties, possibly up until ninety-two," I said.

"Okay, then, let's do it," Indigo said. "We're the Bad-Ass, Mother-Seeking Sleuths. The BAMSS."

"Careful, we can't be too badass," I said. "We're dealing with the school system here, you know."

She gave me a look. I guess I'd forgotten I was talking to the champion of school dismantling.

Sure enough, Allenbury High School was intimidating with its old-timey, two-story brick façade and banks of dusty windows; inside, there were the requisite beige tile floors and rows and rows of bent and dented gray metal lockers, and a cloying, unmistakable school smell. Luckily the school didn't have all the security measures that so many had these days, so the three of us managed to walk down the halls without being stopped. To the tired eyes of anybody who saw us, we probably just looked like two teachers walking some kid to wherever.

We'd decided in the car that we would *not* start with the office, because once you get thrown out of there, you're pretty much sunk. We'd take our chances running into old teachers who might gladly give us the lowdown. But as luck would have it, the halls were pretty much empty that day of geriatric teachers—only an occasional straggling kid, lolling about like a derelict. From down the hall, we could hear the sounds of a gym—whistles blowing, balls thumping on hardwood floors, kids running back and forth.

"Do *not*," Lindy whispered, "do anything that is going to get an assistant principal interested. In my experience, assistant principals wield all the authority, and they can be mighty and swift in their meting out of justice in this, their domain."

"Assistant principals are the dogs from hell," said Indigo.

"Wow, let's just think where we are," I said. I stopped walking and held my arms out wide. "Can we take a moment to breathe all this in? This is where Phoebe and our father roamed the halls, lusting after each other. Smell the vibe! You can almost feel the palpitations, the sex hormones."

"Please," said Indigo. "You're gagging me."

"I think we should go to the auditorium, which apparently was their *milieu*. And maybe there's an old drama teacher hanging around who might remember the production of *Kiss Me Kate* from 1977 or so," I said.

We pushed open the door to the auditorium, but it was vast and empty with a darkened stage. Still, we made our way down the aisle, then trotted through the backstage area.

"God, it's like it's never been renovated," said Indigo. "Look at these stupid lights. And the sound system! Look, even the curtain is all torn. What's wrong with this school?"

"Broke, probably," Lindy said.

We opened a random door and found ourselves back in the hallway. A man with a crew cut stopped us and asked who we were looking for, and we said something about finding someone who worked there thirty-five years ago.

"Nobody like that here," he said. "You might go to the office and check."

"Of course! Thank you!" we said.

The doors to the classrooms were closed, but I could hear teachers talking, or students buzzing as we passed. Sometimes people glanced up and stared blankly at us through the little glass windows in the doors, then looked back down. It felt like such a run-down, sad school. The school time forgot.

Suddenly a bell rang, and the doors opened, and the hall was instantly flooded with humans. We were in a sea of teenagers, all moving and talking and yelling to one another. Lockers banged, books were tossed, people were working their way around us, sweeping us along in their wake, arms and legs everywhere—and then, just as suddenly as it had begun, the tide subsided, and it was quiet again.

"Good God, I'd forgotten that part," I said. The three of us were flattened against a bank of lockers.

"See what we go through? I do *not* miss school," said Indigo.

"I feel like I was hit by a tidal wave," Lindy said. "Is there anything left of me? Do I still have my shoes?"

"Maybe we should go to the office now," I said, but Indigo said that was the worst idea ever. "They'd throw us right out of there. We have no authorization, remember."

"Yeah, but at least they'll know who their oldest living teacher is," I said.

"Excuse me," said a male voice. "You seem to be lost. Could I perhaps usher you to the exit?"

It was not what you'd think of as a friendly voice. I looked up to see a tall guy with a shock of thinning white hair. Big nose and eyes that seemed ready to be amused—but weren't so amused right now. He had a name tag that read BARNES.

"Do you have a pass from the office?" he said. "Any authorization?"

Shit, I thought. *We've been caught by the assistant principal.* But then I noticed he was carrying a toolbox. Even in the most financially strapped school systems, the assistant principal doesn't have to change the lightbulbs. So this had to be the janitor! And who doesn't love a school janitor? We'd hit the jackpot.

"Just kidding," he said. "I overheard you talking. About the authorization. But seriously—what are you ladies looking for?"

I said, "We're looking for someone who might have known some former students. From, like, 1977 or so."

"Try me," he said. "Who are you looking for?"

"Um, Phoebe Louise Mullen?" I said.

And then I watched him go pale.

"Sure. I knew her," he said. "She and I were students here together. We were friends. Why? Has something happened to her?"

"No, no," I started to say, but Indigo pushed herself forward. "We need to talk to you. Privately."

"Well, I don't know that I have a lot that can help you," he said. "I haven't talked to her in years."

He looked like somebody who got frightened easily, who moved through life like a rabbit moving across a field. Those waiting-to-be-amused blue eyes probably didn't get a lot of laughs.

"Listen, anything you can tell us about her would help," Lindy said.

"First, it would kind of help if I knew who you are. I'm not much in the habit of talking about my friends without knowing—"

"These are her *daughters*," said Indigo in her I-know-how-to-work-the-system-and-I-*will*-come-for-your-laboratory-frogs voice, and I put my hand on her arm to silence her.

He swallowed so hard his Adam's apple looked like it might pop out of his neck, then he looked around and ushered us into a little room where he said we could talk—but only for a moment. He kept mopping his glistening forehead with a handkerchief he dug out of his pocket.

"So you're the daughters," he said. "Oh my goodness. Oh. My. Goodness. You're Kate?"

"Yes, I'm the one she named Kate," I said, "and this is Poppet."

"Kate," he said. "Kate, oh my heavens. I can't believe I'm seeing you, honey. All these years! Have you talked to your mom? How the heck is she?"

"Aha. So you knew Kate-slash-Nina back then," said Indigo. She had a little notebook and was writing in it: *Janitor knew the mother and possibly Kate, too.*

"Yes," he said. "Oh my gosh. Kate, yes. Yes, I knew you. Before . . . Sure. How *is* your mother?"

We were in what might as well have been a closet, standing among stacks of lights and wires and boom boxes and speakers. He said he was going to change a lightbulb while we talked. He started fiddling with the equipment with nervous, shaking hands, and every now and then he'd allow himself to look at us through filmy blue eyes. He looked like somebody who was expecting the next horrible thing to happen at any moment. I felt sorry for him.

"We don't—well, we don't know her, really," I said.

"Yeah," said Indigo. "So did *you* know she put them up for adoption? Or was it some big secret back then?"

He seemed miserable, and I frowned at Indigo, to shush her. Not that I expected it to help.

"If it was a secret, I feel bad that we're telling it," I said, "but a lot of time has passed, and probably it isn't a very important secret anymore. I mean, who would care if somebody had a baby back in 1978?"

"Secrets are always important," he said. "There's no expiration date on a secret. But, yes, I did know. About the adoptions. Both of them." He put the lightbulb down and wiped his eyes on his sleeve. "I still don't know how I can help you though. Or what you want. Your mother left quite some time ago. I haven't been in touch with her."

"Actually," I said, "we're not Kate and Poppet anymore. I'm called Nina and this is Lindy, and this is a friend of ours, Indigo." I held out my hand and he shook it with a firmer grasp than he looked capable of.

"A. J. Barnes. I'm the maintenance man here, in case you couldn't tell."

"It's a very nice school," Lindy said politely.

"So, Mr. Barnes. We'd like to know what happened," I said. "We want to find out how we got born and who our father was and where he's gone. We know they were teenagers, but that's it. We don't know anything about their families or where they lived. We just want to know the story, who we came from."

"Honey, I think that's your mother's story to tell, not mine. I'm sorry, but I don't really have anything to tell you."

We were quiet for a moment, and I was afraid he was going to usher us out, so I started babbling, really, telling him how we were adopted by different families on the shoreline, but went to the same school, and how we'd recently met as sisters.

"Until a few months ago, we didn't even know our mother's name," I said. "And then we find out she was a rock star. The lead in Lulu and the Starbabies."

He sat down heavily in a wooden chair, mopped his forehead. "I didn't—I didn't know her during the Lulu years," he said. "Just when she was here, at the high school. We were friends then. But like I said, I don't have anything I can tell you."

"We're prepared for this being a sad story," said Indigo. "So you don't have to worry about telling us what happened."

I saw her write: *Subject did not know mother in rock star years.*

"Yes," I said. "Anything would help."

"So were you and she *good* friends?" Indigo wanted to know. Pen poised.

"Yeah, you could say we were good friends. We . . . hung out, as the kids say." He glanced away, traced his finger in the dust on top of a sound console. "But, you know, it was a long time ago."

Lindy poked me in the ribs and mouthed, "Oh my God. This has got to be our *dad.*"

I shook my head at her.

"What was she like in high school?" I said. "Maybe you could tell us that."

"She was—she was beautiful," he said. "Looked a little bit like you girls. And she was funny and . . . dramatic. Everybody loved her."

"I have to ask," Lindy said. "Was she a drug addict?"

His face changed. "No! No, nothing like that. She was . . . smart. A good kid."

Good kid, no drugs. Smart.

I gave Lindy a look. *See? I told you she wasn't a drug addict.*

He suddenly seemed to snap back to reality. Maybe the drug question threw him, because he said, "Well, ladies, I'm pleased to make your acquaintance, but now that I've changed this lightbulb, I really should get back to work. It was a very long time ago, and frankly I don't remember much that can help you. It was a pleasure, though, getting to—"

"But we need your help. We have so many questions. Could you please just talk to us for a moment more?" Lindy said. "Anything you could tell us—anything would help. Do you know where our father is?"

He looked even more rattled, if possible, and shook his head. "You should talk to your mother. You know her name, you can find out where she lives. Because she's the only one who could probably enlighten you as to whatever you want to know."

"Mr. Barnes, I'm going to be honest with you. I wrote her a letter, and she called me. We talked once briefly," I said. "She wouldn't tell me anything. She said there was too much bad stuff. And then she said she'd meet us, but she didn't show up. Do you know what she was talking about—the bad stuff?"

"Oh. Well." He rubbed his hands through his white hair like we were gnats floating around his hairline and he needed to be rid of us. He was so done with this conversation.

It was time for the big guns. I took a deep breath and said very calmly, "Listen. You can't imagine what it's like not to—not to know who you are. Please. You're our only hope. I don't want to make my mother feel bad. I know she was a teenager and probably overwhelmed and scared out of her mind. But we just need to know the start of our own story. I don't know if you can imagine—not knowing anything about your parents."

"I can't—"

"Wait. It's because *you're* our father, right?" Lindy said, and he went totally ashen.

"No! No. I'm not your father. Listen, you have to go now."

"But you *knew* him," I said. "Did he want to give us up? Was he the one?"

"What happened?" Lindy said. "Were they just the most unlucky kids on the planet, or did they not believe in condoms? Or did they want to get married? What happened?"

"And if you're not our father, then what happened to him? Was he around when she was Lulu?" I said. "Why did they break up?"

"They were kids. It was a different time. I'm sorry, but I really have to get back to work." He got up out of the chair like it was a real effort and he'd aged about five years since he sat down. "God damn all this," I heard him say under his breath.

Mother not a drug addict, Indigo wrote. *Janitor not the father. Or so he says.*

"Tell us his name then," I said. I was surprised at how commanding I sounded. Not like me at all. Then Lindy went over and closed the door to the little room. It was kind of an ominous move, if you ask me, but maybe that's why she did it. We both stood there looking at him. She had her arms folded.

"Please," I said. "Just tell us his name. Only that. That's all you have to do."

He closed his eyes and hesitated for such a long time that I figured he was never going to speak again. Then he said, "Your father was Tilton O'Malley. He's dead now, which is a tragedy. A terrible tragedy."

We all fell silent. Indigo gasped.

"Tilton O'Malley." And even though I'd never focused my search on my father, never even really fantasized about him, I felt a pang of loss knowing I would *never* find him.

"I'm sorry," said A. J. Barnes.

I could hear our breath in that stupid little closet.

Tilton O'Malley, Indigo wrote down. *Dead. Tragic terrible death.*

"Maybe he has some relatives in town," Lindy said, clearing her throat. "Ought not to be hard to find some O'Malleys."

"Okay," Mr. Barnes said heavily, "listen to me. His mother still lives in town. I do some work for her sometimes on account of she has nobody else. She's kind of a bitter old woman at this point, frankly. I do her raking and shovel the snow, put up the screens, take 'em down again, that sort of thing." He seemed to be thinking, rambling on until he figured out what he really wanted to say. "I don't know if you should contact her, though. Maybe. But take it slow and easy. Don't hurt her feelings."

"Our grandmother." I looked at Lindy. "We may not have a father, but we have a living grandmother." Indigo clapped her hands.

"Tell us how to find her," Lindy said.

"No, no, maybe you shouldn't bother her. She's very old and she's lonely and—I think we should leave her alone. Let me think if there's any-one else who maybe could tell you about yourselves. You both turned out really pretty," he said shyly. "You look—well, you look like your mom did. But you're a combination, too. I can see some Tilton in you." He wiped something out of his eye and blew his nose on a ratty old handkerchief. "Mrs. O'Malley is not going to be happy about this," he said.

"But then again maybe she'll be happy to see some grandchildren," I said. "I've heard of cases where people like their grandchildren."

"Huh, that'd be good, wouldn't it? I tell you what. What if I let you know where she is, and then you figure out a plan to happen upon her, like maybe your car ran out of gas or something? You don't tell her who you are, and you don't tell her that I sent you there, how would that be? Then you can get a good look at her and feel the way the wind is blowing, and if she's friendly, having a good day, then you can tell her who you are."

"Okay," I said.

"I feel for you. You go opening up the past, and not everybody is delighted to have you remind 'em of stuff they've been trying to forget this whole time. But—well, I get it. It's your life they're trying to forget, and that's not right. It's your story."

"That's right," I said to him, and smiled. We'd won him over, though God knows how.

He mopped his forehead. "I never expected this to happen. I guess I should have. The Internet and all—nothing stays private. Holy heavens. I hope I'm doing the right thing. Listen, be easy with Helen O'Malley," he said. He wrote down her address on a little slip of paper and handed it to me. "Please. Don't give her a big shock. Remember, don't tell her who you are unless it seems like the right thing. Okay?" He smiled and I noticed he had a few back teeth missing. He looked so much older than fifty, especially if you stood him up next to Carter, who was so immaculately groomed and fit. Carter! For a moment I felt a pang, but then I shook Mr. Barnes's hand, and Lindy did, too.

"Thank you," I said. "Thank you so much. I'm sorry if we shocked you. But I appreciate—"

"Yes, you are wonderful. We'll never forget your kindness," said Lindy, and he looked uncomfortable again and said, "Well, I owe it to you probably. It's the least . . . I'm doing this for Tilton, because he can't be here to do it for himself. I think Tilton would want you to know."

"Wait. When did he die?" I asked, but Mr. Barnes was blowing his nose on his handkerchief. He shook his head at the question. "I can't, I can't," he said.

I wrote down our names and phone numbers for him. "In case our mother happens to call you, and she wants to know about her children," I said. "Just think. You'll be the one with the info for her."

"Well," he said. "Hasn't happened yet." His phone buzzed then. "Christ, I'm due in the cafeteria. There's a leak I was supposed to fix an hour ago." He held up his hand and looked at us for a long time, those rheumy eyes seeming like they were memorizing us. "Good to see you. Both of you. Little Kate. My, my. Who would have thought?" He shook his head. "Kate and Poppet."

We walked out into the sunshine in silence, across the sidewalk to the visitors' parking lot.

"You know who he is? I just figured it out." I stopped walking. "I think he's the guy in the picture."

"Wait, what? Do you have the picture?" Lindy said.

I dug it out from my purse. "Look. It is him. The same chin. And eyes. And with all that long dark hair, all white now, what there is of it. God, he looks like he had a hard life, doesn't he?"

"Maybe we should take it back in and show him," Indigo said.

"No," I said. "I don't think he could take any more of us. Now that we're here, let's go see Grandma."

"Our mean old Grandma?" Lindy said.

"She's family. She's who we have." I felt a shiver go through me. Our father was dead. It was going to take some time to truly absorb that; the day seemed suddenly a little dimmer, even though the sun was shining so brightly.

We got in the car but I couldn't bring myself to start the engine. We sat in the warm sunlit silence of the spring afternoon, watching the clouds scuttling across the sky and I said, "I can't believe we ran into him. The one person."

And Lindy said, "I know."

"Our dad's dead. That feels weird, to know that one fact about him, without ever knowing anything else about him when he was alive."

"Let's go," said Indigo. "Come on! Maybe your grandma will tell you everything you need to know."

Helen O'Malley lived on the outskirts of Allenbury, in one of those fake mansions from the sixties—a white stucco house with a portico and a double garage and a long, expansive driveway. And rosebushes. You could tell this had once been an elegant subdivision, but now everything was slightly shabby and run-down. The name O'MALLEY on the mailbox, faded and written in script, almost stopped my heart.

"Well, Poppet O'Malley," I said, parking the car on the street, "are you ready for this?"

"I'm scared. Maybe we should have some lunch first."

"Maybe we can invite Grandma O'Malley out to lunch with us. We'll treat, and she'll take us to her favorite little diner, where they have meatloaf and mashed potatoes and peas, and I'll get a cheeseburger with fries and a Coke, and you'll get the chicken salad on whole wheat with lettuce and tomato . . ."

"Nina," she said. "Come back to us. That isn't how this is going to go."

"But it could! Maybe she'll be so thrilled that she'll want us to meet her bridge club, and she'll say, 'I can't believe these beauties are my own flesh and blood, and isn't it such a shame that they got put up for adoption when I wanted to raise them myself but didn't get a chance to stop the proceedings?' And she'll pinch our cheeks and go in the bedroom where she has a bunch of grandmotherly two-dollar bills that she's been hoarding, just waiting to bestow upon us. One for every year."

"Oh God, you are delusional," said Lindy.

"Come on, you two," said Indigo. "Just chill and let's go see her."

Mrs. O'Malley was clipping her roses, her back to us. She turned as we came up the walk, and we all four nearly scared one another to death. A bad start.

"What do you want?" she said sharply, but I couldn't speak for just needing to look at her and think about how she was my very own grandmother. Tilton's mother. My God. This was a person who would name a baby Tilton, presumably with a sense of pride.

She was standing on the lawn with a white canvas bucket hat on her head, and holding a pair of garden shears that she was wielding like she might stab us with them if the occasion called for it. She had on a navy-blue windbreaker and a tucked-in white polo shirt and faded jeans with a too-high elastic waist. Oh, and red rubber gardening clogs. Was this perfect or what? I loved her. Her white hair was in a ponytail sticking out of the back of the hat. Her weathered face was a net of wrinkles and lines, like her skin had been ridden hard then folded up wet and put away. I thought for a moment I should warn Carter that's what his skin was headed for, and then remembered—again!—that I wasn't with him anymore.

"Mrs. O'Malley?" I said, smiling and stepping toward her. The garden shears rose higher in the air, aimed approximately toward my heart. I stepped back and lowered the wattage of my smile.

"We didn't mean to startle you," said Lindy, jumping in now, which was good because she was the more elegant sister here. She had on a divine sand-colored cardigan, for one thing, and her hair was sleek and turned under just right. *Go, Lindy*, I thought. *I'll just stand here and collect myself.*

"We think we might be related to you, and so we had a few questions," Lindy was saying, and she said a lot of other stuff, too, but the blood started beating so hard in my head that I couldn't hear her, just like that day at the orphanage. I am evidently not good with meeting relatives. I go blurry somehow. Clinically blurry. But I heard the words *granddaughters* and *sorry* and *if you don't mind*.

And then I heard "no."

Grandma O'Malley was striding up the driveway—she was such a strider, tall and thin like Katharine Hepburn, which is who she reminded me of, I now realized—and she made it all the way to her front door before she turned and glared at us.

"First of all," she said, "I don't see how you expect me to believe that you are who you say you are, and *second of all*—"

"A. J. Barnes sent us," said Lindy, although I thought we'd promised not to mention him at all. Too bad. He had to be thrown under the bus in the first two minutes.

"That is no proof whatsoever. A.J. is a very confused young man! Now I must ask you to leave my property immediately. Because even if you are my granddaughters, which I doubt, I have nothing to offer you. No money. Nothing!"

"No, no, we don't *want* anything," I said. I found my hearing and my voice at the same instant, which was miraculous, but Mrs. O'Malley wasn't having any of it. "We just came to *see* you and tell you that we're all right, and that we are very glad we have a grandmother, because we've looked for so long for family, and Mr. Barnes was kind enough to tell us that you're here in this town . . . and so . . . we came here to see if you might want to go to lunch with us, and maybe you could tell us something about our family. Your family, I mean. Who we are, because we really . . ."

She had slammed the door behind her around the time I'd said the part about Mr. Barnes, but I found myself unable to stop the spiel once it was under way. Lindy tapped my arm, and I looked at her.

"Well, that went well," I said.

"That woman is flat-out mean and scared," Indigo said.

"Maybe if we sit on her porch and have a good cry, she'll come out and join us," Lindy said. "Bring us tea and crumpets. She looks like the type who knows what a crumpet is, doesn't she?"

"If she has a crumpet in there, she'll throw it at us."

"I guess this would qualify as a bad day for Mrs. O'Malley. The kind of day we weren't supposed to reveal ourselves in," Lindy said. "But at least we were honest."

"That will earn us a few points in heaven," I said.

"Let's go home," Lindy said.

"I want my mommy," I said. "And by my mommy, I think I mean the one who is dead, not the one who refuses to have anything to do with me."

"Oh, poor Nina Kate," said Lindy. She put her arm around me, and we walked back to the street. Indigo shuffled behind us. She was saying something about not giving up just yet, something about maybe A. J. Barnes warranting another visit.

"We can break him down," she said. "He's a piece of cake."

A police car rounded the corner and slowed near us.

"Don't worry! We're leaving," I called out.

He kept cruising past. Probably wasn't for us after all.

TWENTY-FOUR

PHOEBE

Really, the mothers who brought their children to study piano and voice were some of the nicest people, and if Phoebe could figure out a way to never have to see any of them again, she absolutely would.

The Well-Meaning Moms, she called them. A whole new breed of woman. For one thing, they wore workout clothes—yoga pants and those bright-colored hoodies—at all hours of the day and night. And they all seemed to have long, lanky hair, yet they knotted it up in messy, straggly buns—so artfully artless, really hypocritical, and how did you tie your own hair in a knot anyway, why didn't people use scrunchies anymore—but the main thing was that they were oh so *earnest*. God, they were earnest. Like someone had told them the world was their responsibility. *Has little Joaquin been practicing enough? Has Darcy improved?* Like that was the whole point of things: forward motion, ticking things off the list, getting your children to be better, better, better.

What was *wrong* with the world today anyway? All this striving! These striving mothers with their wide, intense eyes, steering their children around like they were party dogs ready to perform their next amazing trick, and holding their to-go cups of coffee and their smartphones close at all times, like The Most Important Call in the World was about to happen, and the caffeine ensured they'd be ready when it came.

Look, she wanted to say to them. This is music. M-U-S-I-C. It's for fun. It doesn't matter about these drills or these scales. Let your kids play, have fun, why don't you? Can't you all go zone out somewhere with your power caffè mocha caramel latte cappuccinos (oh yeah, she'd heard the words!), and I'll sit here and let them have fun with the piano, bang on the keys if they want, get down on the floor and punch the pedals to see what sounds come out. How long since you've let any of these kids have a free hour when they weren't expected to be improving at something?

But the earnest, no-fun-will-be-had-here attitude wasn't even the very worst part. The worst was that once they'd delivered their little children for the lessons, they didn't know what to do with themselves. Simply did not know how to extricate themselves from the room, despite Phoebe telling them over and over that she preferred to have the children to herself during lessons. So time and again, they stood awkwardly by until she shooed them away, but it was too late, she'd already seen them looking around, she'd seen their eyes taking in her life, how narrow and small and spare it really was, these tragic little blank rooms, this life she'd made that wasn't for public consumption.

They'd look at her as if she were ancient, at least their grandmother's age, when she was not old at all. The loose skin, the wrinkles, the dark spots—she knew they must be thinking it was all the drugs she had done. Rock-star drugs, because didn't all rock stars party into the night, abusing substances and people? That's what the eighties were about, to this striving, earnest generation: wildly inflated stock portfolios and drugs and rock stars and big hair.

She hadn't even been a rock star. That was the part she could never explain. It had all been a big mistake, a joke. These young women thought she'd lived through such glamorous times. It was why they signed up their kids with her. That's what Leila Conway had let slip one day: "We bring the kids for the prestige of piano and voice lessons with Lulu. Do you have a picture of you and the Starbabies? You're our local celebrity!"

"Oh," they said to her sometimes, all too often really, "can we bring you some dinner tonight? Would you like a caffè latte? Something mocha perhaps? I made an extra pot of chicken quinoa soup, and I thought you might need it. Here's a loaf of bread. I noticed your kitchen was . . ."

She squeezed her eyes shut. *No, no, no.*

Their children were so sweet, not one morsel of irritating well-meaningness to them yet. They were curious and aiming to please, and they sat at her piano, their fingers plump and curved just so, and she spoke softly to them. Gently. How she loved it when she had the excuse of taking their hands and moving them across the keys. So carefully, touching those tiny, fresh-from-babyhood hands, being taught to make music.

All of them Kate's little hands.

Kate.

Really, how could she have known how much she would miss? Someone might have stepped in to explain that when she signed the forms. It wasn't just that you were giving up that baby of today, or tomorrow, but you were also giving up her hands on the piano keys later on, the little knuckles with their small etched-in lines, and that soft scent on the top of her head, and the cushy part behind her knees, and the way her ankles were still just little bumps at the bottom of her legs. And oh yes, sorry, but you were also going to miss out on all the big things, too: her birthday parties, the prom, her wedding, and a hundred million daily routines (worth more, in Phoebe's estimation, than any prom or wedding) like cleaning her fingernails and brushing her hair, and the good-nights. All the saying good-nights. They should have typed that on the form: *You've already said the ones you were allotted, the fifteen months' worth, and hope you enjoyed them because now you get no more.*

Kate's eyelashes wet from crying.

"Mama, noooo! Mama! Mama!"

Shit, yes, there had been drugs: that's what she'd like to say to the Well-Meaning Moms. "Yes, I took fucking drugs! I had to! There was something rotting inside of me, a ball of hate that was so lethal it could have taken out the whole State of Connecticut. Just from the losses that were mounting up." Ha! She knew people who hadn't even attended a funeral until they were in their thirties, and yet she'd lost everything by seventeen. Only Mary had been left—Mary and Kevin—after the dust settled, and even Mary left a few years later: *Oh, sweetie, you didn't need me anyway, you were always on the road, and after I divorced Derek and with you gone, we had no home here, not really, but then Shelby's people in Oklahoma wanted us out here, and I thought it would be better for Kevin, the clean start, the horses in the paddock, the down-home values. Why don't you come and join us? Shelby thinks you can get work at the feed store, and he knows some nice men if you're willing to give up some of that New York wild-child stuff you've got going on, ha ha. Now don't take offense, you're always so hair trigger about your so-called rock-and-roll career—did you ever manage to get Keith Richards's autograph because I really wanted that—and if the feed store job doesn't work out, you can always think about a career as a music teacher in the high school here, can't you? Well, don't blame me if you're going to be so negative about everything!*

Now Shea Easton, ten years old, tiny white hands with oval pink nails, was finishing playing a song. Phoebe snapped back to attention.

The phone and the doorbell rang at the same time, and she and Shea both jumped. Shea laughed.

"That's your mom at the door," Phoebe said and went over to the phone. "Quick, grab your coat. I'll see you next time!"

The caller ID said *A. J. Barnes*.

Her hand flew to her throat. Shea was leaving, looking back at her nervously. "Are you okay, Ms. Mullen?" and she waved her off. *Yes, yes, I'm fine. It's just that the present seems to have sprung some kind of leak, and it's being flooded by the past.*

A. J. Barnes? Seriously?

"Go, go, go!" she said to Shea. "Don't let her come up. Quick, here's your music. Run!" She clapped her hands and picked up the phone.

"Are you calling to ruin my life?" she said. It was a joke, of course, but she shouldn't have said it.

"You, as I recall, are the one who ruins people's lives," he said, which was mean of him, so she hung up.

That night, she sat in the dark, smoking and staring out the window.

"Listen," he said when he called back two days later. "Let me just say my bit, and then you can hang up if you want to."

"I don't want to hear *your bit* if it's going to start out like that," she said.

"Like what?"

"You know. We both know what happened. No need to be ugly about it."

"Jesus, Pheebs. It's been thirty-three years, and that's what you say to me? Am I going to ruin your life? What was I supposed to say?"

"Okay." She waited. "So why *has* it been thirty-three years since I've heard from you?"

"You tell *me* why it's been thirty-three years, *Lulu.*"

"I haven't been Lulu for a very long time."

"How was I supposed to know where you were?"

"Well, how the hell do you know now?"

"Look, do you want to hear why I called you or not?"

"First I want to know how you are. If you survived."

"I . . . survived," he said. "Some days go better than others."

"Are you sorry?" she said softly.

"No. I'm never sorry."

"Bullshit."

"I see you haven't changed a bit, Phoebe Louise Mullen. Still feisty. That's good. I got the feistiness beat out of me some time ago."

She put her hand over her mouth, unable to speak. When she found her voice again, she said quietly, "What do you do for work?"

"Janitor. Caretaker, actually, at the old high school. Sort of a courtesy position, I suspect. Joe Granger is the principal now, so he's sympathetic. You'll be interested to know that your ghost roams the place, along with Tilton's. I was talking to him the other day in the room off the basement. The room I believe we used to call the Sex Room, in honor of you guys and your exceptional baby-making abilities."

"Please. Have some decorum and sensitivity." Then she said, "Tilton's ghost shows up here, too, sometimes."

"I kind of like it, don't you?"

"Yeah. I mostly like ghosts better than the regular people I meet."

"So, little Pheebs, has life really been so hard on you?"

"It only hurts when I think," she said sarcastically. "How about you?"

"I guess I let myself forget a lot. I'm working and I have a few good buddies I go drinking with, and we play poker on Saturday nights, and . . . I'm fine." He cleared his throat, and she felt prickles down her arms. There was a reason for this call.

"So you'll probably not believe who came into the school the other day."

"No," she said. Because she knew what he was going to say. She meant *No, don't tell me.*

"They look just like you. A little bit of Tilton in their cheekbones. But your coloring. Your eye shape. Uncanny, really."

"God, how did this *happen*? What is going *on*?"

"The magic of our high-tech world? I don't know. They're nice women. Harmless."

"They're anything but harmless. Did you tell them anything?"

"I told them Tilton's name. They didn't know that."

"Well, that's a surprise. I thought the younger generation had ways of knowing everything."

"They don't know much, these two. They begged me for . . . well, anything. The story."

"We cannot tell them the story, A.J."

"Relax. I didn't tell them the story. I sent them to Mrs. O'Malley."

"You what? You have got to be kidding! How could you have done that?"

"I had to give them something. And they would have found her anyway, once they had Tilton's name. Don't worry. I know Helen, I see her all the time." He was quiet a moment and then he said, "They deserve to see their *grandmother,* Phoebe."

"God, I loved her once."

"I warned you though, didn't I?"

"Oh, you were full of negativity and warnings back then, you jealous old wretch."

"They said you didn't want to see them."

"The girls? Correct."

"And why is that, Pheebs? You don't have all that many people left. Why not take on these two?"

"Because I can't." She was quiet, and she took a drag off her cigarette.

"Well, actually, that brings up the other reason I'm calling you."

She stayed silent.

"An opportunity has come up here, and I thought of you first."

"I say no to all opportunities. I loathe that word."

"Okay, then a gig."

"Second worst word in the English language, after opportunities."

"Okay. A chance to play and help the world, then. You do still want to help the world, don't you?"

After a moment she said, "I'm listening with a jaundiced ear."

"The high school, of which you are a most distinguished alum, is doing a major fund-raising drive to get a new auditorium. With actual state-of-the-art sound equipment that the audience can *hear,* and new lighting that doesn't blink on and off during productions. Somebody asked me the other day if I still knew you, and if maybe you'd come and sing as a benefit. Just an evening of you, singing your songs."

"This sounds like an automatic *no* to me."

"Well," he said. "I want to tell you that it would mean a lot to a bunch of people here. You are loved, Phoebe Mullen. Nobody here really remembers the whole sad story—and no one associates you with what happened to Tilton. So you can sail in here and feel the love, and do something nice for the school at the same time. And, uh, I believe the school was pretty much your savior when the shit hit the fan. It could be a little karmic payback."

"No." She puffed on the cigarette, looked out the window at the Brooklyn skyline. Who was she to be this way?

"So you're in the habit now of pushing everyone away, is that right?"

"Pretty much."

"That's not the Phoebe I knew."

"I'm definitely not that girl anymore."

"But some things might be worth holding on to," he said. "Maybe."

She was silent for a long time, and he let the silence fill up all the empty space in between them. Then she said in a ragged voice, "I'll think about it."

"Really?"

"Yes," she said, and sighed.

"It—it's good to hear your voice. And I gotta say, I want to hear you sing again."

"My voice is actually still good," she said. "I didn't lose it yet. Lost everything else—my tits, my cheekbones, my eyesight, my pride—but I got the voice."

"I'll start working on dates then," he said. "You really will do this?"

"I said I might."

"You might."

There was another long silence, and then she couldn't help herself. "I have one question, and it's stupid, but I really need an honest answer. I've been going around and around in my head with it, and I need somebody to say it, and you're the only one."

"Okayyy," he said. "Shoot."

"No making fun."

"No making fun."

"Think back and tell me the truth, but be kind. Was I a good mother?" she said. "Because I can't remember anything but the bad stuff. Do you remember? Was I a good mother to Kate?"

"You were the best," he said quietly. "You were in love with that child."

"And Tilton knew that, too, right?"

"Yes. Tilton knew it, too. And, Pheebs, you should see her now. She's beautiful. Both of them. They're you, Phoebe."

"I wish I'd raised them. I still wish—"

"Phoebe, don't . . ."

"It was just at the end, that last bad night when I left her with Mary and sneaked out. That goddamned hellhole of a night. I keep reliving it."

"Please," he said, "let's don't."

"And *you*! You didn't tell them what you did?"

"No." He laughed gently. "That's not my story to tell."

"Funny how things don't really go away, you relive them over and over. Does anybody ever get over anything?"

There was so long a silence she thought maybe he'd gone away. Then he said, in his deepest voice, "I did. And you're stronger than you know, Pheebs. We went on to have real lives. We rescued ourselves, didn't we now?" He said good-bye and hung up.

TWENTY-FIVE

NINA

Carter called me out of the blue and asked if I would come to Tyler's graduation. I hadn't heard from him at all—just a terse thank-you e-mail when I sent back his mother's bracelet. But here he was, his voice on the phone saying, "It would mean a lot to him if you came. He misses you." He cleared his throat. "And thank you for arranging that job for Kayla, with your sister. That's been . . . good for her. Sorry I didn't thank you before now."

"Oh. It's nothing really. Glad to help."

"Well, if you'd like to come to the graduation, we're going to dinner afterward. It might be nice to have an evening of celebration for old times' sake."

So that's how it happened that I was at the back of a hot gymnasium, on the hottest June night ever, listening to "Pomp and Circumstance," not being able to sit because I was late and anyway guests needed a ticket, and Carter had neglected to tell me about that. So I was standing on my tiptoes and I saw Tyler crossing the stage and raising his hand in salute to his family, and my eye followed where he was looking, and there was Carter.

He was sitting in between Indigo and Jane—and well, that was a killer.

Their family was all together again, all reconfigured. Maybe. At least it looked like that. Summer was being ushered in, boat season was flourishing, and Indigo had survived the suspension or expulsion or whatever it was; Tyler was going to college, Jane might be back home once again—if she was, I knew Indigo never would have mentioned it to me, that's for sure. I could only see the back of Carter's head, but it was tipped toward Jane. He was saying something in her ear, and I saw her glance down at the program.

This—*this*—is what's hard about breakups: getting used to seeing your ex back living in the world again, without you.

But I closed my eyes and did a little mental gymnastics thing, and then I *was* used to it. Once again my special secret talent of getting over shit was coming to my aid. It had been there all the time. It had taken me a little longer this time, is all. But I was over it. Over him.

And here's the thing, the horrible part. Standing there watching him with his family—being all, you know, familyish—there was a big part of me that said, *Good for you, Nina! You know you couldn't have kept it up for much longer. The driving responsibilities, the figuring out what everyone needs, the meal planning, and then the constant interruptions, the dramas. It wasn't for you, my girl.*

It had been, let's face it, a little bit like being dropped onto another planet: one without quite enough air and light. Or at least not the air and light I was accustomed to.

And I *was* fine now, actually. I'd even decided to start dating again—the Nina Cure-All, as Melanie referred to it. I'd gone out on some dates with guys I'd discovered on Match.com. Nothing of consequence, kind of boring actually, but still okay. And work was good, with the real estate business busier than ever. In the late spring, everybody on the shoreline who has a house for sale wants it *on the market now* and they want to have open houses in which hundreds of people stream through and make bids, and they need to be connected up with all the casual home-buyer tourists who come drifting through town thinking, *Hmm, Margaret, this might be a nice place to settle. Let's look at about fifteen houses in a row! Sound like fun?*

So I was essentially bustling around every weekend, showing houses, meeting new clients, signing contracts. Doing my home-staging appointments in the evenings, because that was the fun part, walking through places, sensing what was needed. A blue throw pillow here, a chest moved over there, and the chandelier replaced with something less elaborate.

And I was hanging out with Melanie, who was now so pregnant she looked like she needed a wheelbarrow to carry her big stomach. She and I were practicing Lamaze breathing like it was our religion, doing the hee-hee-hees and the hoo-ha-hees every available second. It became so second nature that I think we even Lamazed when we answered the phone sometimes.

I was not going to ever get a baby, it appeared, so I was working on auntdom, for which you need no Lamaze whatsoever. I had discovered that aunts are supposed to always have gum, and they are to take the children's side whenever there is a dispute with the parents. But they are also depended upon to explain the parents' point of view in a very diplomatic way.

Aunts are fun and they are healers and soothers and they give out candy, according to popular literature. Which is so much better than what the press says about stepmothers. So I should be thankful.

I was about to leave the graduation ceremony, there being no seats and all, and me not belonging—but then I was spotted.

Indigo saw me first, and then Carter turned and started waving like the maniac that he is. Tyler had managed to graduate, and so he was happy again. He was laughing and pointing to the seat next to him—there had been an extra one for me after all—and then he pointed to Jane and to Indigo and pantomimed something that seemed to involve party hats or circus monkeys or something. The whole family, as one organism, made its way over to me, pushing through the crowd, and there he was. In front of me, crinkly-eyed and smiling.

As soon as I really looked at him—I can't lie—I had to look away. (This, by the way, is rule number eleven of getting over someone: no direct eye contact if you should happen to run into him.)

"Hi, hi!" he said. "Ohhh, Nina, I'm so glad you made it. And this is Jane! Have you two met?"

I have met a lot of exes in my time, and always there's this little frisson of tension, an understanding on everyone's part that this is a bit awkward, but of course Carter doesn't do awkward. Everybody is his friend, everybody is just as equal as everybody else in the Carter pantheon, and so Jane and I were forced to stand there, smiling frozenly, and we shook hands. I knew her completely from living in her house for so long and seeing her photographs and her Skype image and her eclectic decorating taste, and I had already formed deep opinions about her career options, her couches, and her haunted armoire, but I was unprepared for the way she suddenly switched on a warm smile and grasped my hand.

"Nina. I was so hoping I'd get to meet you."

"Well," I said. "Same here."

And then Carter said we were all going out to Lenny's for a seafood dinner and celebration—for once in his life, he'd actually made a reservation, and I *had* to come with them, he wouldn't hear of it any other way, and he threw one arm around me and one arm around Jane, and Indigo trailed behind us. Tyler joined up with us, bringing along about four friends who kept hitting him in the arm and saying, "Yo,

Ty," which sounded like *bowtie* to my ears and made me laugh. *Bowtie. Hey, Bowtie. Whassup, Bowtie?* That *is* what they were saying.

"You did it, Tyler," I said to him. I eased myself out from under Carter's arm, and walked alongside Tyler. "Congratulations. Here's a card from me with just a little something in it for you."

"Thanks, Neens," he said. "Glad you're here. How you doin'?"

"Okay. Life's busy. Good but busy."

Isn't that what grown-ups always say? And here I was saying it, too. Then he told me about his prom disaster—he took this girl he liked from his English class, not his old girlfriend he'd broken up with, just some girl he felt sorry for, and she got so drunk that she passed out in his car on the way home, and he'd ended up having to take her to the emergency room. Carter turned and said how proud he'd been of his son, staying with her until her parents got there.

Jane said, "We've raised our kids right, Cartie. Remember the time—?" And they were off remembering when there was an under-tow at the beach, and a little girl was running right into the water and headed for trouble, and both kids—both Kayla and Tyler—had spotted the problem before anyone else and had gone to the lifeguard for help.

And oh yes, the time that . . . the dishwasher spewed water all over the kitchen. And oh yes, remember the day that Kayla had been crawl-ing around on the floor and had somehow found a pork chop bone and had put it in her diaper? *Oh my God.* And when the draperies fell down at the same time the iguana got loose and he was under the couch cushions but everybody thought he had been responsible for the drapes. They laughed so hard they had to throw back their heads to release all that laughter, bottled-up like soda pop inside them.

You had to be there, they said to me.

I smiled and smiled until my face hurt, as you do when you're the audience for people's favorite, incomprehensible family stories. And then we were at the restaurant.

The place was packed because Lenny's always is, but Jane made sure we got their favorite table, because the owner turned out to be an old friend of hers. It was a rectangular table, which meant that we had to sit in two lines facing each other, and wouldn't you know, I was directly across from Jane. We were not at the fun end of the table with Tyler and his friends, and Indigo was miserable, stuck between her parents and looking balefully at me, the lamplight shining on her hair, which was now no longer indigo blue but was a subtle ombre brown to orange.

"Great hair," I told her. I gave her a thumbs-up, and she smiled.

"Lindy did it for me yesterday afternoon. She thought it would be nice for the summer."

"Excellent," I said. "And what will you do this summer?"

She shrugged. "I've got some summer school classes to make up. You know. Because of the . . . incident." She glanced at her parents, then at Tyler's friends, and slid down farther into her seat.

"Because of your stand," said Carter and put his arm around her.

Jane was eyeing me curiously, and then she said, "Could we talk for a moment, my dear?" And I followed her outside, where a light breeze was coming off the marsh and the sun was beginning to set. She was one of those women who looked like she was in full control, always aware of which pocket of her eight-pocket L.L. Bean vest she last placed her self-confidence in. She walked with perfect posture, for one thing— our mothers were right, good posture goes a long way toward helping you take over the world—and her hair, which was chestnut brown but starting to turn gray, was the proper color for a distinguished person. It made a judgment about other people's silly hair, because it was so sure of itself, this hair. She smiled at me through her gray eyes.

"Let's get a drink while we're out here," she said. "The food won't be coming for a long time, and I've really wanted to talk to you."

We ordered two Coronas from a passing waitress, and I thought, *Here it comes*. I steeled myself. She's moved back in with Carter, having come to her glorious senses. She now sees her real mission in life is to raise these children she gave birth to, and to love their father again, and I should not care, I do not care, but I also don't want to hear about it.

"First," she said, "I want to thank you for all you did for my family. It was . . . it was extraordinary, really, that you took on all those responsibilities when I left. And Carter clearly thinks the world of you."

"Oh, wow, I've never been thanked by an ex before," I said, hoping that would maybe make her stop. I felt like I was the hired help, who had really done an *extraordinary* job ferrying the children around and doing all those meals. And the sex with the husband—*really, he couldn't have been more pleased with your performance! There'll be a little something extra in your pay envelope* . . .

She didn't smile. "Well, perhaps you should have been thanked."

I shrugged and looked out at the marsh, waiting for her to drop the bomb. Instead she started a minor wrestling match to squash the slice of lime into her bottle of beer, and when she'd won that fight, she said, "Families are so fucking hard. Aren't they?"

I gave her a cool look. "They are. I mean, they're made of people, so how could it be any different?"

"Yes, well, I'm sure that to certain people I look like *the* worst mother in the world, taking this job and not taking my kids with me, leaving them with their father—who, let's face it, believes that children don't need any management whatsoever—and you, his new, much younger girlfriend, had to take up the slack."

I started to say something, but she held her hand up to shush me.

"Now I know things didn't go splendidly, how could they, but I think it's a really good sign that when my kid got into the worst trouble of her life, she did it by being an *activist*. So I must have done something right, huh? She's changing the world, in her mind, following in my footsteps, letting those poor animals go."

"Yeah," I said. This old argument again. I couldn't seem to stop myself from saying, "Of course, the frogs may not have seen it quite that way. They probably would have preferred that she take them to a swamp or something."

"But she didn't *have* a swamp handy," said Jane. "And anyway, the point is that I see her becoming an amazing radical feminist activist. I have to say, I'm so proud of her. Suspension and all, she followed her heart. And she acted alone, from what I've heard."

I became interested in my fingernails.

"And what do you do for a living, my dear? I don't think anybody's ever said."

I was about to do my little number about how I take people's homes for sale and take out all the interesting personality quirks of a place and strip it bare until it becomes a generic, boring place that any random person would find attractive, but I realized suddenly that I didn't believe that speech anymore. It was honestly like one of those lightning-bolt realizations. That wasn't what I was doing at all.

"I'm a home stager," I heard myself say, "which means that I design interiors to make people feel like they belong where they live. I'm adopted, so I have this thing about belonging."

"How nice," she said. "One more thing. I understand that things haven't really worked out in a permanent way between you and my ex-husband, and I wanted to say I hope you don't blame yourself. He's an interesting man, but he's an acquired taste. I just wanted you to know I understand what you were up against."

I can't possibly express how much I wanted to be able at that moment to say to her smug little self that, ha ha ha, as a matter of fact, Carter was *not* an acquired taste, and that, yes, Carter might have been a little exasperating and unorthodox, but it was clear he knew how to love, and that he loved those children and was passionate in caring for them, while she—well, she was the emotional equivalent of a big pile of dust packets standing there with her pure-cotton, sustainable, fiber farm clothing and Birkenstocks and her superior attitude, calling me dear and being proud of Indigo for her large, expansive, public expression of lostness. Acting like it was a brilliant referendum on her mothering abilities, when it was anything but. I would have loved to tell her what I really thought of her mothering—how her children sat slumped over after her chirpy little false Skype sessions with them, that they practically needed resuscitating after all the stuff she put them through just on the *phone,* but what was the point? How Carter and I had had to work overtime to cheer them up after even the mention of her—and that her precious little feminist girl had a list of ill-advised behaviors she had worked through, all to get attention, culminating in suspension. It had all been deliberate.

I would have liked to present her with the Fuck-It List and say, *Take a look at* this, *why don't you, and reflect for a moment on the fact that your daughter is fifteen years old and she told me as recently as last week that she still plans to find someone to have loveless sex with ASAP so she can get it out of the way before she cares about anyone.*

Try *that* as a referendum on your mothering!

And no, it hadn't worked out with Carter and me, despite the fact that I'd had more fun there than I'd probably ever had in my life, and yes, I did blame myself. But I blamed him, too, and while I was at it, I mostly blamed the whole human race for coming up with its emphasis on family systems when half the time they didn't work worth shit. And yet I *still* wanted a family so much, and I couldn't stand that I wanted it, that the wanting was this big, jagged, gaping hole right in the center of me.

Okay, so maybe I was a little angry. This was just another example of how family trumps everything else, how ultimately nothing else really matters.

What made me the maddest was how unfair it was that *she* had all the good memories with Carter—having babies and nurturing little kids together. She'd scooped up all the good times, the things anyone would care to remember. When, in the next few years, he thought back about us, it would only be the bad stuff that was memorable: that time my car got stuck in the ice, and the time Indigo got picked up by the police, and the night with the frogs. Compared to raising kids and having a full family life, all he'd remember about us is that we'd had some good sex when we had time for it, and two nights of dancing at the boat club. Maybe some blueberry pies and some jokes about the Beatles.

But so what? They were likely getting back together again anyway, and good for them, because maybe my function had been to remind her of what she was missing now that some other woman was interested in him. That was what she'd called me out to thank me for.

I didn't know how much longer I was going to be able to stand out there and not throw my Corona, lime and all, on her Birkenstocks.

Luckily, by some divine intervention, my phone rang, and it was Melanie, and she was yelling, "It's time, it's time! Will you come? I need you there. John Paul doesn't know anything about, hee-hee-hee, anything. He forgot it all!

"Meet me there," she said. "Oh my God, you're the only person I want with me during this. Can you stand it? How does the breathing go again? Hee-hoo-hee, hee-hoo-hee? John Paul is running around looking for tennis balls because of that list they gave us. We don't need—hee-hoo-hee—tennis balls, do we?"

"Melanie, this is early labor. Don't do the hee-hoo-hee yet. Save it. I'm coming. Don't give birth until I get there."

"Gotta go," I said to Jane, and then I blew good-bye kisses to Tyler and Carter and Indigo and the whole graduating class and ran to my car.

Twelve hours later, after about a million ice chips, four hundred back rubs, three thousand "you've-got-this-Melanies," four hours of hee-hoo-hee Lamaze breathing and another two of hee-ha-hee-hoo breathing, twenty-seven minutes of pushing, and not one tennis ball, there came one exquisite, crystallizing moment.

A baby, an honest-to-god living human being, squeezed out of Melanie and into this world, looking like a cross between a giant piece of wet origami and a refrigerated turkey roaster, all folded up and drawn into himself, and then like magic he unfolded and opened his eyes, and batted his fists in the air and announced his presence with a startled cry. The midwife was holding him, and tears streamed down my face as she handed him over to Melanie, who was smiling and sobbing at the same time, reaching out to take her baby.

I was blubbering like an infant myself. Why do we cry at graduations, weddings, and births? What the heck is it about these happy events that get us every time? I knew I had to get a grip.

John Paul and I smiled at each other across the delivery bed, and I wiped my tears on my sweatshirt. We were all sweaty and exhausted and in awe—that's the only way to describe it, in awe that there were four of us now, instead of three, all smiling and crying and spent.

"This is Noah," Melanie said, and I helped guide him to her breast. And he looked up into her face and then suckled like it had been the thing he'd been training for all these months.

TWENTY-SIX
LINDY

"The children told me they have a new aunt," said Lindy's mother one day after work.

"She's not exactly new," Lindy said. She made her voice nice and even. "I told you about her. Nina."

"Ah, yes. I know who she is. The one you're mad I didn't adopt."

"I'm *not* mad at you for that. All I was asking was *if* they had offered her to you when you adopted me. That's all, so could we please not have this conversation again?"

"I'd be delighted not to have this conversation again. I'd love it if we hadn't had it in the first place." Her mother sniffed. "You know, you can't just go replacing family members with other ones. Just because you and your sister don't get along so well, it's not right to trundle in another sister."

Lindy put her head on the counter, even though it would leave an oily makeup mark on the black, gleaming countertop, which she would have to clean later. "I am not in any way replacing Ellen," she said into the faux-marble surface. "I love and adore Ellen. I am so proud of the way she's saving health care in this country, and—"

"Nursing homes. She was saving health care ten years ago, but she gave up on that. Now she's saving nursing homes. Much more lucrative, I think." Her mother laughed as though she'd told a joke. She was always laughing at her own jokes, then complaining her children hadn't inherited her fine sense of humor. Lindy had often wanted to point out that there was no way she or Ellen *could* have inherited their mother's sense of humor because they didn't *share any genetic material with her*, but that would have been rude. It was rude to mention the adoptions, or other families, or the ways in which people might be different. Differences were rude. That's why it was safer to stay with their own kind: devout Catholics who had a lot of kids and thought materialism was immoral. That was her mother's position.

Which reminded Lindy—she hadn't heard back from Phoebe. Or A. J. Barnes, for that matter. She started putting away the lunch dishes that her mother had stacked in the dish drainer. Out in the backyard, she could see Chloe marching around the perimeter of the yard, next to the fence, holding a tall stick like it was her scepter, and the twins were galloping along behind her, laughing. Soon it would be time to open the pool, and they'd eat dinners on the patio, and Jeff would barbecue.

". . . Albuquerque . . . so you'll need . . . ," her mother was saying. Wait. What?

". . . sure you can find someone for the summer, so let me know," said her mother. "I was thinking of leaving in two weeks."

"You're going to Albuquerque?" said Lindy. This conversation had surely had a beginning and a middle, but they seemed to be at the end of it now, and many threads were lost.

"That's what I said."

"And why, again?"

"To spend some time with Ellen. I've been neglecting her. And she broke her foot, which I told you last week, and she's hobbling around on crutches. Don't you remember?"

Lindy did not remember anything about crutches. Maybe something about a foot, but definitely not crutches.

"Oh, well. You were getting ready for some meeting," said her mother. "You only had half a mind on what I was saying. Kind of like now, actually."

"And how long will you be gone?"

"All summer. I told you."

"You're summering in *Albuquerque*? Don't you know it's going to be hot as blue blazes?"

"And yet people manage to live there somehow. Must be that new-fangled air-conditioning I hear so much about."

"You hate air-conditioning. You say it aggravates your sinuses."

"Lindy, I'm surprised at you. Are you jealous?"

"No! I just don't think you're going to be able to tolerate a summer living in the hottest place in America."

"It's a dry heat. I'll be fine. But will *you* be fine, is the question."

"Well, if I can find child care, I will . . ." She couldn't figure out why she felt so injured. But she did. This was a catastrophe.

"Maybe you could close the shop for the summer. Get to know your kids."

"Close the shop for the summer? Are you out of your mind?" Then she saw her mother's face. Laughing at her. This was a style of joke known as "pulling your leg."

Her mother kissed her on both cheeks. "Ah, my girl, I do love you so. I know I don't tell you enough, but you are the cat's pajamas in my eye."

"The cat's pajamas, huh? Is that pretty high praise in your world?"

"Okay, so you're also the apple of my eye and the grape in my fruit cup."

Her mother was smiling her frowny kind of smile, but Lindy wanted nothing more than for her mother to wrap her arms around her in a hug, but that wasn't in Peggy Walsh's stable of tricks. So she had to be content with the two quick cheek kisses and being the grape in the fruit cup.

"Also," her mother said, gathering her keys and her purse to leave. Lindy knew from experience that this was the moment when she often delivered her killer exit lines. "Also, even if people are related by blood, that doesn't make them family, you know. Your family is us, right here. We're the ones who love you. This new sister of yours that you're so gaga over—and I'm not saying I'm not glad you have her or anything like that, nothing bad on her—but she hasn't been there for you when you needed somebody."

"Would you like to meet her, Ma?"

Her mother got flustered. "No, no, that's not what I'm saying. She's *your* sister. Just don't forget where you came from, that's all I'm saying." She went out to the car then came back, ducking her head slightly, looking almost shy. "But yes. Someday. She's important to you, so I would like to meet her."

Her mother left two weeks later, and after searching for a genuine, certified babysitter and not finding one available on such short notice for the *whole summer,* Lindy debated for a while and then hired Indigo to watch the kids. Indigo was sweet with children, and she promised to follow all Lindy's eleven rules, the typical stuff: healthy foods, naptimes, no boys, no swimming when parents aren't home, no cell phone calls, et cetera, et cetera.

Even with all that, Lindy ended up taking most afternoons off, and all day Thursday and Friday off, and she did her paperwork from home, where she could hear Indigo playing with the kids. Indigo didn't seem bothered by the endless, mindless games of Candy Land and Connect Four, and she liked bouncing the twins on her lap and chasing them in the backyard. But where she excelled was in playing little dress-up games with Chloe. Of course. She didn't mind putting crinolines on her head and being a bride, or wearing a witch mask and offering an apple to Snow White, and one day she fixed lunch in a turban and told Lindy she was the genie from *Aladdin*.

Nina often stopped by for no real reason at all, and Lindy never could tell whether she was pleased or not to see Indigo getting so involved in Lindy's family life. It was strange. Sometimes she'd stand in Lindy's office and look wistfully out the window without saying much of anything. Nearly every time she came, she wanted to know if Indigo was really working out okay, and Lindy always said she was great.

"Are *you* doing okay, is the question," Lindy said one day. She was sitting at her desk doing paperwork for the salon and drinking iced tea.

Nina squared her shoulders and looked at first as if she were going to give her usual line about everything being fine, but instead her face turned suddenly tragic. "I don't know what's wrong with me," she said. "I don't seem to be able to get over this guy."

"Well, you really loved him," said Lindy.

"I know. I thought it was just the idea of being in a family, but I think I really did love him. I think about him all the time."

"Maybe you should tell him."

"Spoken like somebody who married her high school boyfriend and never looked back."

"What? Me? All I'm saying is that maybe if you're straightforward instead of playing games, this could work out. How many guys did you say you've dated? Maybe you could stop dating forever if you said what you really feel."

"Oh, Lindy!" Nina burst into tears, and Lindy got up and hugged her. It always scared her when adults cried, so she started tapping. She got up to fifty-five before Nina finally broke away and blew her nose.

"I'm really okay, don't worry about me." She explained that she'd been running the real estate office single-handedly while Melanie was on maternity leave, and then she'd go over in the evenings and help take care of the baby because Melanie and John Paul were sleep deprived and scared out of their minds.

"And this is the worst part," she said, and Lindy's heart clutched in fear of what was coming next. "Last Monday I closed the office and I took the train to Brooklyn and I went to Phoebe's apartment building. I stood there looking at the trees and sidewalk and the windows. People rushed by with strollers and cups of coffee and briefcases and shopping bags, and I thought maybe I'd see her. But I didn't. It's over. I didn't have the courage to call her or ring the bell, and now I know I never will."

"Oh, Nina. We are just going to have to learn to accept the fact that this is the way it's always going to be. No changes. I'm sorry, but that's just the way it is."

◆　◆　◆

But then something did change. One day in July, Lindy was busy upstairs, working out the salon schedule. Two of the stylists wanted to take time off during the summer, and Lindy had to juggle things around to cover the time. And it was slow in the salon, slower than she ever remembered it being. She was sitting there considering whether she should close Mondays and Tuesdays when she heard Nina's voice, talking to Indigo, and then Nina came clumping up the stairs, saying, "Yoo-hoo! This is your favorite sister!"

Lindy noticed there was something different about her right away. She was wearing a pale yellow sundress and carrying two iced teas and was all out of breath from climbing the stairs.

"You'll never believe!" she said.

"What? You're getting back with Carter?"

"No. God, no."

"You're pregnant!"

"Stop, stop it right now. I'll just tell you before this gets any worse:
I heard from A. J. Barnes that our mother—our rock-star mother—is
giving a benefit concert for that high school! She's going to be performing there in the middle of July. He thinks we should go."

"Get out!"

"No, it's true."

"It can't be true. She would never do that."

"I know. But she *is* doing it. He said he called her and talked her
into it. They hadn't spoken in something like thirty-three years, and he
said it was a struggle to get her to agree, but then she did."

"Did he tell her he met us?"

"I'm pretty sure he did, but you know how he is. He doesn't tell
much. I started to talk to him about our time with our sweet Grandma
O'Malley, and he interrupted, said he had to go fix a pipe or something.
But anyway, Phoebe's performing publicly, so we can see her."

"Oh my God. This is kind of big, isn't it?"

"I think."

"What if she humiliates us in public by refusing to have anything
to do with us?"

"Well, we'll get a strategy together. We'll figure it out."

Nina stared off into space for a long time, and then she went over
to the window and watched the children playing with Indigo. She shook
her head. "Look at this, would you? Did you ever in a million years
think this could have happened—Carter's daughter and my niece and
nephews? This proves that anything can happen. Phoebe Mullen could
turn around and decide she wants to be our mom after all."

"Oh, my poor lamb," said Lindy.

"Now don't you be telling me not to get my hopes up. If I want to have high hopes, I'm going to have them, you hear?"

"Oh, my poor, *poor* lamb," said Lindy, and Nina picked up a wad of paper and tossed it at her head.

"That's exactly what Ellen would have done," Lindy told her. "This means it's getting real, sister-wise."

"Really?" said Nina. "This is what sisters do?" And she ran over to Lindy and started a playful slap fight, then threw about five more wadded-up pieces of paper at her, until Lindy was forced to join in.

TWENTY-SEVEN
NINA

Match.com was not delivering any good men, so I quit them and joined OkCupid.com. But still nothing good. Not one decent guy on the whole site. I had to start carrying my Getting Over a Guy rock in my pocket and doing my little chant as I ran my fingers over it a hundred times a day: *I am fine without this presence in my life. I am already better and stronger. I am over him; I am over him; I am over him.*

Maybe I needed two other rocks, though—one for Indigo and Tyler, too.

Melanie's baby had colic and heat rashes and something called croup, and Melanie said it hurt to breastfeed because he was apparently ferocious in clamping down, and I feared that Melanie was going to declare that he was unsatisfactory and that she'd made a horrible mistake in having him. She didn't go quite that far, but she did turn out to be the kind of mother who didn't believe in slings or cuddling when it was hot, so she carried him at arm's length all over the place, pacing back and forth and staring into his unsmiling navy-blue eyes and grim little mouth, and their apartment didn't have air-conditioning and it got up to ninety degrees on the day he had his two-month vaccinations, and he cried and howled all night. So I went over at two thirty in the morning when John Paul called me, and I rocked both the baby and Melanie. Melanie was the inconsolable one.

"What if I'm as bad a mother as I think I'm going to be?" she wailed. Then she whispered, "I don't have any *feelings* for him, Nina."

"You're just tired," I said. "We need to get you some sleep."

I led her to her bedroom, and took off her bedroom slippers and fluffed up her pillow and made her get in bed, even though she was weeping and saying, "I can't, I can't." And I said, "Yes, yes, you can," and I turned on the fan to block out noise, and I tucked her in bed and kissed her cheek. She was still in midsentence about how I probably needed to be at work, when I quietly closed the door behind me. No need to remind her it was the middle of the night.

Noah was whimpering in his bassinet, drawing up his legs, then kicking them straight out, and balling up his fists next to his ears. I scooped him up, and carried him around and around the room crooning some nonsense verse. His huge blue eyes were fixed on me, and I smiled and rocked him softly back and forth, back and forth. "You have eyelashes now," I told him, "and that is going to improve your life so much because now the dust particles won't be able to just land right on your eyeballs. And you have the plumpest, most delectable cheeks, and really, really fine baby hair. So many of the babies these days come out looking like William Frawley—he was an actor on *I Love Lucy,* a show you may never see, come to think of it, unless you get one of the old-time TV channels like I did—but I think you made a really good choice in asking for some nice brown hair right out of the gate."

He pushed his hands around, like he wanted to touch me, but of course he didn't know how to work all his parts just yet. So I told him that he'd get the hang of things pretty soon, that right now he must feel like a prisoner in a shell of a body that simply did random things. "But it gets better, little man," I said.

He seemed to like that news. He settled down in the crook of my arm and his eyes searched my face, so I told him everything I knew about the uses of arms and legs and elbows and knees, and how fun it was to run and sing, but for now it was probably enough for him to drink a lot of milk and sleep as much as possible—oh, and to notice things.

"You want to be a noticer," I said. "I'm not going to go into all the man-woman stuff yet because that can be overwhelming, but let me just say that it's good when guys are noticers. Women really like it."

He went to sleep.

And I was besotted.

◆　◆　◆

John Paul told me that the guy from work they'd wanted to set me up with—before I met Carter—had recently broken up with his girlfriend, and did I maybe want to go out with him?

"No," I said. Then, "Yes." Then, "Well, maybe. I don't know. Should I? Yes."

John Paul laughed.

"Maybe I should wait until the whole committee of voices in my head comes to a decision and get back to you," I said.

He looked confused. I was beginning to appreciate him a bit more now that we were in the trenches together. It turned out he had a good sense of humor and he obviously loved Melanie, and he was appreciative of me, being all in baby love with his cute little son. I was always bringing little rattles and outfits and offering to babysit and sending everybody off to their afternoon naps so I could rock Noah to sleep by myself.

One night, after we'd all played with the baby and downed a beer and Melanie had gone to bed, I said to him, "This is what I want." I almost couldn't believe I had spoken the words aloud.

"This?" he said. "A baby and a condo?"

"Yes. I want two babies and a condo, or a house. It could be a house. I wouldn't mind that."

"Well," said John Paul, then added something so wise I almost couldn't believe he'd come up with it. "If this is what you want, then you need to take steps to get it, don't you? You can't just keep living like you're living now and expect that it will fall in your lap from out of nowhere. You have to seek it out."

"Huh," I said.

"I'll call my friend if you want. I think he wants marriage and kids."

So, yes, on that basis alone, now there was a new guy.

What the hell, right? Why not? His name was Matthew Smith. He was no Carter Sanborn, but maybe that would be a good thing. A nice, simple Matthew Smith.

He took me to an Italian place, and we sat outside and drank red wine and ate lasagna. He told me about his mother and sister and how they fought all the time, and how it was hard on the men in the family. I didn't tell him I was adopted, because I was sick of that story and watching people react to it. Instead, I found myself talking about the way Noah's head felt like peaches that had been warmed in the sun when I tucked it underneath my chin to carry him around.

And Matthew cleared his throat and said, "I love babies, too."

I studied him like he was a specimen I needed to learn about. He had neatly trimmed brown hair and a tidy little modernish beard, and blue smiling eyes. His nose was long and pointy, but that was okay, and he had bushy eyebrows, and long, slender fingers. He was tall and skinny; I'd noticed that when he stood up as I strode over to the bar to meet him, my hand out for a handshake so he wouldn't automatically assume I wanted him to kiss me.

A person could do worse than to date and ultimately marry a man like Matthew Smith, even if it did mean Christmases with the fighting mom and sister. I could work with that. It might even be a silver lining: I could watch them and think, *Hmm, I am sooo lucky that my mom didn't want to have anything to do with me! Saved me years of fights.*

Nina Smith. If I wanted to change my name when we married, that was a decent one. So anonymous. So Anyone Else But Me.

And he had a job. One like John Paul's, where he'd wear a uniform (he was probably very traditional, and so I'd no doubt be in charge of keeping those cleaned and well-stocked in the closet, but that was also okay; I don't mind laundry), and we'd buy a cute little house and decorate it to our own taste, not someone else's, and we'd have babies and maybe get a sweet golden retriever, so we'd better get a fenced-in yard, one big enough for a swing set and a doghouse, not that the dog would ever be put in it. But it would be a place for him to hide from the baby when getting his ears pulled would be too much for him. And Noah would probably want to come over and play, and that would be great. Noah and my two little girls. John Paul and Matthew out by the barbecue, flipping burgers, while Melanie and I made salad and freshened our drinks and talked about whether the kids were in the right preschool, or did we think they needed more stimulation.

He asked me to walk around the green with him after dinner, and we stopped under a decorative lamppost and he kissed me. It was a routine, standard-issue first kiss: no tongue, not much slobber, a slight pressure of his hand against the small of my back as he pulled me to him. All nice. No explosions. No bolt of lightning making us run back to somebody's car so we could hurry home and rip each other's clothes off.

"I'd like to see you again," he said.

"That would be lovely," I told him. "I'd like that very much."

You see? I said to myself as I drove home alone. *This is the way it's done. Calm, steady, slow, calculated. It's what the rest of the world has always known.*

So my adult authentic life was beginning. I almost felt as if I were standing back watching myself being all grown up and everything. I had lots of weekend showings to do, and I was running by Melanie's to promote motherhood and then running to visit Indigo, Chloe, Razzie, and Davey whenever I possibly could. Razzie in particular seemed to be taking a shine to me, and Chloe was always wanting to try on my sandals and silver bracelets. She would unpack my purse and install games on my cell phone, and put some of my lip gloss on while peering at herself in my compact mirror. She always noticed if I had on new shoes and commented on how my hair looked. In short, she was my fashion guru.

One day I showed up with my bathing suit for a quick dip in Lindy's pool—I was officially a member of the family and could use the pool whenever I wanted, they said—and Indigo swam over to me and said shyly, "Could I go with you to the concert?"

"The benefit?" I eased myself into the water. "Well, yes. I guess so. I was going to ask you if you wanted to go."

"Will you ask my dad?"

"How is your dad, by the way?"

She gave me her sly laugh. "I already told you. Not spying for you!"

I laughed, too, and splashed her with water. "Look, you little minx, if you want me to ask your dad for you, then I think the least you can do is tell me how he's doing. You could say, 'He's fine,' or 'Ever since the house fire followed by the plane crash, we've had to tiptoe around him.' Just make up something. Say anything."

She splashed me back, and then we were in a wonderful, fun pool fight, and I had to go underwater for a while to get her to stop. When I came up, I said, "So. You and Maya still hanging out?"

"Sometimes, I guess. I hafta go to summer school in the mornings because *you know*, and sometimes her brother gives me a ride."

"Her adult brother?"

"*Nina*. He's twenty, and anyway he seems much younger."

"Stunted emotional growth?" I said. "What's his name again?"

"*Marco.*"

"Like Marco Polo? Is he your boyfriend?"

"I told you. I don't want a boyfriend. I don't believe in all that stuff."

"Well, why are you so down? You seem really low."

"I don't know." She looked away. "Maya's off with some new friends, and anyway, she's turning goth, and I don't want to be goth so she doesn't really talk to me anymore. And I'm on Instagram but nobody ever likes my stuff. And I can't think of any more activist stuff I should be doing. Life is boring."

"Um, how's the Fuck-It List?"

She gave a little surprised laugh. "Wait. You know about that?"

"I found it one day, yes. I was watching as you checked items off. So have you given it up? The list?"

"I might have an item or two left."

"What's left? No, really."

She gave me a long look. "Well, I never did get to have sex like I wanted. You know, with somebody I didn't love."

"Oh, right. I remember that insane plan. I thought I talked you out of it. Didn't I deliver a fantastic speech about sex between people being special and meaningful and kind of awful if they don't care about each other?"

She laughed. "You tried."

"Is seeing Lulu in concert on the list?"

"Hardly," she said. "That's just because I have to see your mom."

But then, of all unbelievable things, when the time got close, Carter said no, she couldn't go to the concert. Then she begged me to get on the phone with him, and so I did, reluctantly, and he said no again.

"Why not? She'll be with Lindy and me. We'll take good care of her. It's a high school concert, not a rave in New York or anything."

He laughed uncomfortably. "No, I know, I just don't want her entrenched in all this."

"By all this, you mean my life?"

"No, by all this, I mean this whole—this whole adoption dream fantasy world you've got going on. I think it's not good for her, is all."

"Adoption dream *fantasy* world?" I said, perhaps a little louder than I meant to. "I beg your pardon, but I think it's perfectly appropriate for me to want to find my mother and to find out my story!"

"I'm sure it is. I'm just not sure that dragging it out for this long is doing anybody any good. Least of all my daughter. I have to tell you that I was somewhat disturbed that you took her to confront an old friend of your mother's at some high school. And you didn't even ask me."

"That was part of her work day with Lindy," I said.

"I sort of thought you'd be beyond this by now. I mean, you found your sister, and that's been good, but why take on this old lady who obviously wants to be left alone? When do you give up? I've thought it over, and I just don't think it's a good role model for her, this relentless pursuit of somebody who doesn't care. She's a sensitive kid with her own mother issues."

I disconnected the call before I even realized what I was doing. If you ask me, one of the great losses of modern life is that a person can't slam the phone down anymore. Someone needs to invent an app that would approximate the sound of a slammed-down receiver so the person on the other end could *know* they've really pissed you off. Then I was so mad I almost called him back to yell some more things at him—seriously, who was *he* to be making judgments—and the worst part was he had been sympathetic about everything having to do with my mother before, so happy happy happy for me while we were together, and now it turned out that he was *judging* it all? That he thought I was behaving inappropriately?

I almost called him back just to say, "AND she's *not* old! She's *your age,* in case you forgot!"

Instead, I looked at Indigo. "I'm sorry, honey. He's made up his mind."

"Fine, it's fine," she said. And she walked off.

"It's going to be okay," I called after her. "Fifteen is the worst of it, and then it gets better. You'll see!"

She turned and looked at me, and I could pretty much tell she was thinking I wasn't a good poster child for It Gets Better. Looking at my life could make a young person have second thoughts about growing up at all.

So Lindy and I went by ourselves, and by the time we got to Allenbury, I had pretty much stopped fuming about Carter, mostly because Lindy finally said she didn't want to hear another word about a man I wasn't even seeing anymore. "If you were still dating him, then, fine, I'd know we had to work it out in our heads and hearts," she said. "But we're free of him!"

"You're not. You still employ his daughter."

"Really? You want me to fire her because her father thinks you should be over finding your mother by now?" She laughed.

It was dusk when we got to the high school, and when we found A.J., he said the concert had been moved to the football stadium because so many people wanted to come. The auditorium wouldn't hold all the people.

"What? She's that big?" I said. People were streaming past us, old people, young people, parents pushing kids in strollers. Music was playing over the loudspeakers, and there was a makeshift booth set up on the field for people walking in. Most of the tickets had already been sold by mail, he told me. Then there were so many that the auditorium couldn't hold them all—one of the reasons it needed renovating—and then too many for the gym, as well.

"She's loved here. She and your dad were like the all-stars of their class. Hard to believe now, because they weren't jocks or anything, but they were just cool. That's it, just cool."

"I've never been cool," I said. "I can't imagine that I came from cool. It would have changed my life so much . . ."

He laughed a little bit. "Yeah, well, I wasn't cool either, but I got to hang around with them. We'd go out late at night, and roam the streets and drink and smoke. Be badass, you know. Tilton was always trying to get his mother's BMW . . ."

Then he abruptly stopped talking, like somebody had pulled the plug on his animatronics or something. His eyes went dark. "Sorry, I've got to help with the tickets. You guys have VIP seats, right up in front. And after the concert, wait around, okay? Stay in your seats until you see me."

"Is she *here*?" I said. I peered into the stadium. The makeshift stage under the goalposts was still dark. It was decorated with two Greek-looking pillars and had a stool and a microphone and a bank of lights on it. Lindy took my arm and we sat in our seats, right on the aisle.

I hardly knew what to think. My whole self was on vibrate, like all my nerve endings were in a circus.

And then a high school girl came onstage and talked about the theater program and the auditorium that needed renovating, and about the high school's most famous student, Phoebe Louise Mullen, who'd made a name for herself as Lulu back in the eighties.

"I was too young to remember her," she said, "but my parents always listened to her music, and my dad said she was *hot!*" The audience laughed, and the girl did a little curtsy. "She was so hot, in fact, that my mother didn't even mind when he said that. In fact, she agreed with him. It was a given."

"So, she's been gone from here for a long, long time—but here she is again tonight! PHOEEEEBE MULLEN. LULU OF THE STARBABIES."

And the audience roared its approval, and the spotlights shone on the stage, going in crazy colored circles—and then, nothing happened.

"LUUUULUUUU!"

Still nothing.

"Can you believe this?" I leaned over and whispered to Lindy. "She must have figured out we're here."

The audience started chanting, "LU. LU! LU. LU!!!"

Lindy put her head in her hands. I noticed she was tapping on her leg.

"What's that tapping thing you do?" I said, and she said, "Shut up, please. I'm concentrating to bring her onstage."

A man yelled, "LULU, GET OUT HERE, HONEY!" And everyone laughed.

It worked. A red-haired woman in leggings and a red sparkly dress came walking onto the stage, sauntering, really, and shaded her eyes with her hand so she could see the audience.

"Wow, there are a lot of you," she said. She cleared her throat and adjusted the microphone.

The music system started playing her anthem hit, "Is This the Way You Treat Your Baby?" but she waved it off, and pretty soon the music stopped, and she said, "I haven't been back here in a long, long time, not because I didn't want to but because I didn't know I *could* come back. When you were as bad as I was, I thought there were a lot of things that were off-limits."

The crowd was in a roaring mood, so it roared. I had to put my head in my hands. My heart was beating way too fast.

"Oh my," said Lindy.

"I thought that once you make some pretty big mistakes and you have to leave a place in disgrace, that was it, you know? There's no going home again. But, Allenbury, here I am, home again! Thank you! I promise to leave right after you get your new auditorium money! Promise!"

The song began to play again, and she started tentatively at first. I worried for her voice, and I worried for her nerve, and then I worried for her mental state—but you could see she was cranking up, getting into it. By the time she was singing "Will You Still Love Me Tomorrow?" she was really into it, swaying and closing her eyes while she sang. Then there were some eighties disco numbers, and her voice soared as she danced around the stage, flinging her hand out as she had in the videos. She introduced some members of her old band—she said they were happy to come and play this concert with her.

Lindy and I turned to each other in amazement. "Do you think we're going to talk to her?" I said. "No, no, she's too amazing," said Lindy. "She'll never talk to us. We're way too ordinary."

The audience was on its feet, and Phoebe's face was flushed after an hour of singing. She took the microphone and came to the edge of the stage and said she had a little number she wanted to send out to two special people in her life. She stood in a simple white spotlight, and she started singing a Bob Dylan song, "It's All Over Now, Baby Blue."

"That's for us," Lindy said, grabbing my hand. "She knows we're here. We're the baby blues."

There wasn't a noise anywhere in the stadium. Just her rough, emotional voice singing about leaving and taking what you need because there's no future.

"It's a kiss-off song," Lindy said.

"It's not. It's a regret song. She's sorry. Oh my God, she's *sorry*. That's even worse."

When that song ended, she started in on what she said was the saddest song ever, and one that she hardly ever had the nerve to sing. It was "Love Has No Pride." She sat on the edge of the stage, and the spotlight turned smoky and blue.

And then she said, "Well, I started out happy and I ended sad, and I can't sing anymore without bursting into tears. But I want to thank you all for coming, and for supporting the theater program because that's where I got to play the best roles of my whole life, except one role I can't talk about. You are wonderful and amazing, and thank you for welcoming me back! Now go away and don't come and try to talk to me, because I want to remember this moment just as it is!"

And she ran off stage, where I saw A.J. holding out his arms to her. From where we were sitting, we could see her being enveloped by him, then they broke apart, and he said something in her ear. The audience was screaming for an encore, and stamping their feet on the bleachers, and soon she came out and sang a new song she'd recently discovered and loved: "Emmylou" by a group called First Aid Kit.

It was all about losing love and bravely starting again, and I dabbed at my eyes. And when she was done, even though the audience pleaded for more, the stadium lights came on, and the stage stayed dark, and people at last gave up and filed out. Lindy and I sat in our seats. We checked our phones. We waited to see what was going to happen, and then finally, finally, when everyone was gone, A.J. came out and said, "Okay. She wants to see you."

There should be some fanfare for a moment like this, when you are walking toward a woman in a red dress, and she's the mom you've never seen before, and she's just entertained an audience of foot-stomping suburbanites and had them all swaying in their seats and dabbing their eyes—but the thing is, it feels as though she belongs way more to them than to you. Nevertheless, you move toward her like in the dreams you've had so many times before, and when you get to her, she holds up her hands, as if she wants to stop you from getting closer.

"I want to look at you," she says, and she does. Walks around you like you're a car she might buy, and smiling because you'll do. *It's all going to be okay*, you think, even without the fanfare. It's only a moment in life, one of a gazillion, though the edges of your vision are maybe trembling a little, and then she hugs you and you wonder if anything about this hug could be familiar. Like from when you were fifteen months old and she said good-bye.

She said we had to sit backstage inside the school. No restaurants, no bars. It was fitting, she told us, because some of the happiest hours of her life took place there. She was smaller than I expected, and she looked older than fifty. It was her eyes, really. They had a filmy depth of sadness in them. I almost couldn't bear to look into them, but I also couldn't resist. Her eyebrows had been plucked out of existence and then drawn on in a hard, dark line. In fact, there was nothing soft about her; her mouth with its red lipstick, twisted sideways when she talked, as though everything she was going to say would be ironic and tough. I was shocked at the sadness of her, the way she seemed to guard herself against whatever we might offer her, holding herself apart from any criticism we might give, but also any love. Yet I was part of her—that's what I felt when I looked at her, that she answered some question in me, explained something I'd always felt. She had a slash of a scar on her left cheek and lots of makeup, which she immediately wanted to take off. "I look like a freak," she said. "But oh my God, wasn't that something? That audience. That reception. I never—I just can't."

The band had gone by then, and A.J. led us all to the dressing room backstage, the kind with little makeup stations and rows of lightbulbs around the mirrors. We stood around her while she took off her powder and then she combed out her hair, which was all sprayed and dolled up, faded red with streaks of gray in it. Lindy took an interest in that, I could tell, but I was silent, aware of the way my heart was beating, how my breath kept catching in my throat, and how I kept twisting my fingers behind me.

A.J. brought in some folding chairs and they got to talking about old times, while Lindy and I sat there hardly daring to move, as though any rustling, any breathing from us, would remind them of our presence, and they would stop. It was like being a kid again, up too late listening to the adult conversations, afraid they'll remember you're there and send you away.

Every now and then A.J. caught my eye and gave me a sly smile as he kept reminding her of stories, distracting her with fun, easy bits from the past. Their hilarious wickedness. Oh, and they'd been bad, it seemed. Running the streets like hellions. Both of them from the bad side of town, their apartments one step up from the projects.

"How did you end up living there?" he said. "I don't think I ever really knew."

She was wiping off her makeup and she stopped for a moment and looked at us in the mirror. "Oh, well. When my parents died, I moved there with my sister," she said, then stopped herself. "Are you sure you want to hear all this?" When we nodded, she said, "Okay, the short version. Christ, I told myself I was never going to tell anybody this story. If you're smart, you'll get up right now and leave. Run out of here!"

"No," we said. "Tell us."

"Okay, here goes." She started talking fast, like she didn't want to dwell on any of it, like if she hurried, each word wouldn't hurt so much. "We lived in New York when I was a kid—mother, father, sister, me— and we had a house, nice furniture, all very middle-class. My sister and I went to a Catholic school and everything was fine until Mama got sick with lung cancer. I was thirteen when she died. And then—well, Daddy couldn't take it, so he killed himself." She said that last part all in a rush.

"Oh no," someone said. Might have been me. But she only glanced my way, shrugged, as though this detail had been no more alarming than a recitation of a grocery list.

"Yeah. He stepped in front of a train because he said he couldn't live without her." She closed her eyes for a second. "And the truth of it was, he couldn't. He was a weak man. So Mary—that was my sister, and she was eighteen—she took charge. Then we lost the house, because Daddy, bless him, he was a lovely man, a real salt-of-the-earth singing firefighter of a guy, but he was no businessman, and maybe he'd lost everything in hospital bills, but whatever. Anyway, the bank took the house back, and then Mary met a guy and married him even though she didn't really love him—people did that all the time back in those days, you had to sometimes—and he said he'd take care of us, only we had to move to Connecticut with him, so that's when we moved into that shitty little apartment building, a place for poor people.

"So I was poor for the first time, although it wasn't all bad, living there. That new life. You get over stuff when you have to. You move on. And the good part was that I could sew my own clothes and I got to come to this school, a public high school, where the nuns weren't hitting people, and I got into drama and art and found out I could sing and act and dance, and—well, that's how I managed to get into so much trouble. Because I was poor and I was smart and I didn't have anything to lose. I guess you could say I was a survivor."

She looked at Lindy and me. Her face was bare now, and the scar on her face was obvious.

"What happened?" I said. I touched my own face in the place where the scar was.

Her eyes met A.J.'s in the mirror. He nodded. "I have some whiskey in the back," he said.

"Get it," she told him.

When he left, she swung around to face us. It was like being some-body's drink of water, the way she took us in. Her eyes kept filling up, then she'd blink a lot. "These lights. Hard on old eyes."

"You must be tired after your performance," I said, and she said a night like that, every twenty years or so, was invigorating, was what it was. "I'll never have anything like this again," she said. Then she stretched her arms up overhead and yawned. "I'm already tired of telling this story. Why don't you tell me about you for a while?"

I told her about my real estate career and that I'd broken up with the man her age, and she laughed and said that must mean I was over my father issues. And I said, "But I miss him, even though he has a million problems," and she said, "They all do, honey; that's why I'm loving being alone now. I teach my little piano and voice lessons and I cook my little vegan meals and smoke my little cigarettes, and I don't have to please or put up with anybody."

Then she looked at Lindy, and I explained that Lindy was the busiest, most competent person in the world, with a wonderful hair salon and spa that everybody wanted to go to, and she had such a talent with hair—why, look at mine!—and Lindy reddened slightly and said, "As long as I have control over every single thing, I do okay. But I count things. Like did you know there are nineteen bulbs around that mirror and twenty-seven tiles, and there are five chairs with wheels and seven folding chairs?"

"Oh, sweetie," I said.

"It's interesting, what we have to do to cope," said Phoebe. "We don't even know why most of the time."

I heard A.J. coming back down the hall and I said, "He's the guy in the photo, isn't he?"

"Or is the guy in the photo our dad? That's what I think," said Lindy.

Phoebe looked at us and shook her head. "Listen to the two of you, going on like this. Oh my heavens. Yes, that's A.J. in the picture, and that's his car we're standing in front of, and no, he's not your father. Your father was somebody really amazing. Really, really amazing. And he died."

"When?" we said in unison. I said, "How? Please tell us."

A.J. opened the door just then and brought in the whiskey and four little plastic cups he said he'd gone all the way to the cafeteria to find. She said, "A.J., I think I'm going to tell them."

He said, "It's your choice. It's always been your story."

"Well," she said, "it's not a good story."

"But it's the one you've got," he said.

TWENTY-EIGHT
PHOEBE

It was a mistake, telling. She could feel it.

Oh, at first it seemed like it might be all right—fun and dramatic, even—the way they were so eager, sitting forward in their chairs, tilting their heads, drinking up stories and begging for more and more information, and Phoebe saw how beautiful they were. Felt their gentleness, the tenderness of her daughters. And she knew she was going to break their hearts by the end.

She saw Tilton in every move they made—Helen O'Malley must have had to run into her house and slam the door when she saw two female versions of her beloved son in her garden; she probably thought she was hallucinating. It almost made Phoebe laugh, thinking of what that moment must have been like. Helen rushing away—*Help, the past, the past! It's come leaking into the future, and I can't get away!*

Oh, but they wanted to know everything. There was such—how could she put this?—there was such misguided, misappropriated love in their eyes. At least it looked like love, but she knew it was only curiosity, and that they could turn on her in an instant. And probably would. She inched her way into the story, not knowing at what moment she would shut it down and run back to safety before they hated her.

But what the fuck? That's what she said to herself. She would never see them again after this night, and so what the fuck. Tilton's hand was on her shoulder the whole time, she could feel it, and he said she was right. *What the fuck*, Tilton said. *None of this matters a bit.*

"So I loved Tilton," she began in her once-upon-a-time voice. "He was handsome and funny and the best baseball player in the school, and he was also smart but in that way that smarts isn't everything to him. Kind of a joker, class-cutup type. This is your *father* I'm talking about," she said.

"And after I'd loved him for a while and he loved me back, I started loving his mother and his father, too. I'd go over to their house all the time, and they were so kind and so welcoming. Polite, religious, upstanding people. 'Tilton's friends are always welcome here,' they'd say, but it seemed like I was even more special to them, more welcome. When he and I were the stars in the play, they gave the cast party, and his mother took me aside and told me that I was the best thing that ever happened to their son.

"A.J.," she said, interrupting herself. "Do not roll your eyes while I tell my story."

"I'm not," he said.

"Tilton's mother liked me because I was smart, she said, and level-headed, and I'd keep him on track. They wanted him to go to a good college like his father had. It was really, really important, the most important thing ever, apparently. So we studied together at his house, Tilty and me, and I mean we *really* studied. At the dining room table, because Mrs. O'Malley was pretty strict about PDAs. There was to be no kissing or hand holding, even though I always thought she knew we *were* doing that sort of the thing all the time. Tilty would be grabbing for me as soon as she left the room, and sometimes she'd come back in, and I know she realized what we'd been doing. But she never said anything, just kept saying what a levelheaded girl I was and how it was so nice to have me around.

"He was a year ahead of me in school, and college was looming for him; they talked about it *all the time*, and she'd tell me, 'Yes, Tilty's not going to be here your senior year, and that's going to be so sad for you, but you'll both have outgrown each other by then anyway, sorry to say. Teenage love doesn't usually last. I wish it did,' she said, 'because you are perfect for him.'

"Then I got this magnificent idea: I'd have a baby! And then we could always stay together.

"I don't know when the idea first occurred to me. Maybe when my sister had a baby. I saw how she looked at that little baby, and how her mother-in-law would come over and coo over it, and how having little Kevin around made everything cute and special, how he healed us from our grief, and I thought, *This is how I can be sure I belong always and forever to the O'Malleys. I will do them the favor of giving them the best gift of all: a little grandchild! A surprise!*"

"She *was* fifteen, remember," said A.J.

"I made it happen. I'll spare you the details. Just a couple of things: little closet off the boiler room where no one ever went, me with a soft blanket, and Tilty not believing his good fortune in getting to have actual sex after months of fooling around.

"We went down there during school hours twice a week at least. And then there were the nights when we'd sneak out with A.J. and roam the streets like hoodlums, go down to the ball field, walk behind the shopping center, and we had all these hiding places. After A.J. would leave . . . the woods, in his mother's car, under the bleachers, out behind the drugstore that's now a CVS. Once—only once!—he asked what we were doing for birth control, and I said, 'Oh, sweetie, I've taken care of that.'

"And I got pregnant. That was the happiest day of my life, the day I found out. And Tilty was scared out of his mind. I knew he'd be scared, which is why I hadn't let him in on the plan in the first place. It was a crazy plan, I know, but it seemed like *such* a good idea. Really, the only way I was going to get out of that spare room at my sister's and be part of his life. By then my brother-in-law was tired of me being there, and who could blame him? He wanted his wife and his kid, without a teenage sister hanging around all the time. Tilty said his parents were never going to forgive me *or* him, and that this was the worst thing that could have happened, and that I should maybe *take care of it*. By which he meant his mom would probably take me to have an abortion someplace where nobody knew us, but I cried and said I could never do that, *kill an unborn baby, OUR unborn baby, was he kidding?*

"It wasn't at all like I planned. Long story short, Mrs. O'Malley was furious and said I'd betrayed her trust, and that Tilton and I couldn't see each other anymore, and the school kicked me out and I got sent to a school for pregnant girls, and I had to go there for the rest of the year, but I didn't care, because I was still sure that once this baby was born, the O'Malleys would be thrilled. That once they saw this little baby that belonged to them, through me, they would remember they adored me. Who could resist a baby? I walked around rubbing my stomach, happy because I still knew I'd done the right thing.

"Fast-forward to Kate's birth, which was pretty traumatic because I was fifteen and didn't know much except what they'd taught me at the pregnant girls' school, but I was happy because Tilton and A.J. visited me in the hospital. I sneaked them in, and we had some weed in the basement. Tilty and I stood at the nursery window looking at our baby, and he said, 'This is the coolest thing that has ever happened in the whole history of the world.'

"So you see? I thought I'd done a really good thing after all, and I just had to wait for the rest of the world to catch up to my thinking. And I took you home, Kate, and we lived in Mary's back room with two-year-old Kevin, and it was crowded with Christmas ornaments and decorations, but I was in heaven with those two babies in there, making little noises in their sleep. I'd put you in my bed to cuddle you sometimes. I just loved the smell of your little head. And Tilty would come over once in a while when my sister and her husband had gone to bed, and I'd let him in through the window, and he'd crawl in bed with you and me, and we would all cuddle together, our little family."

"I came with him a few times, too," said A.J., and Phoebe had to tell them that yes, A.J. came, too—they all cuddled in the bed—even though he did not approve of what she had done. *Trickery* was the word he had used.

"*Trickery* was a nice word for what it was," he said, smiling, and Phoebe put her mouth into a straight line and said, "Point taken, A.J."

She shifted in her chair, took a drink, and wondered for a moment if she should end the story here. Then she went on. This, now, was coming up to the hard parts. She closed her eyes for a moment, then took another drink. "But the O'Malleys still didn't accept me as family, not even when Tilton took the baby to show her off to his mom," she said. "I remember that day. He brought her right back and said his mom had started screaming and crying, and wouldn't even let Kate in the house—imagine being scared of a little baby in a pink blanket, just looking around with her big blue eyes. And then Mrs. O'Malley did the worst thing she could have done—she told him that Kate probably wasn't even his child; what proof did he have anyway? So that's when I knew that I needed to *really show her* that Tilty and I were serious, and that we were not going to break up, and that she might as well accept us.

"I decided to have another baby."

"Me," said Poppet.

"You. The world needed you," Phoebe told her. "But this time I didn't tell anybody my plan."

"Correction. You told me. I said that you were out of your mind," said A.J.

"Well, maybe you did. That sounds like you, now that I think of it. But I knew what I had to do, and once again Tilty thought I had birth control and there wouldn't be a baby, and once again, I was praying for a child. Because *this time* my plan was going to work! Mrs. O'Malley would see that I was a brilliant mother and a determined, capable person, and she would remember how much she loved me and wanted me for a daughter-in-law, and when Tilty went to college, I would go with him, and we'd live in married-student housing and raise the babies together, and it would be a beautiful start to a long marriage.

"And then they picked a college for him, and he got accepted, and they told him he had to go. I was seven months pregnant, and he was going to leave. For good."

A.J. shifted in his chair. "Are you sure you want to tell the rest?" he said, and Phoebe said, "Don't be ridiculous. They want to know. Only thing is, my glass is nearly empty and I think I might need me some more of that whiskey."

He got up and poured us all another glass. "My skills as a host are rather rusty," he said. "Shall we talk more about how fantastic that concert was?"

"Don't start now with being a coward, A.J. I've got to get through this.

"So it was summer—August nineteenth, in fact—and the O'Malleys still were not having anything to do with me, and they were throwing Tilton a massive good-bye party because he was leaving the next morning for college, and he just went along with everything they said, didn't fight them. Not at all. That was the most shocking thing to me, that he let himself be pushed around by them. They wouldn't even let me come to his good-bye party, and that was okay with him, too. And he loved me—he really, really loved me, and he didn't want to go to college at all, that was the thing of it—but he just kept telling me he'd flunk out and be home by Christmas and then he'd tell them we were getting married and they couldn't push him around anymore.

"So we had this last night. I snuck out of my sister's house, climbed out the window to meet Tilton and A.J., and we were all sad and wasted, and it was a hot night, and I was so big, so huge with pregnancy—"

"Not *that* big; you could still run," A.J. said. "And you climbed out of the window."

"I did, and I could still run, you're right. We ran from the cops, didn't we? After you guys busted the lights at the ball field."

"You pitched the ball, as I recall."

"I did. Right smack on that bat. Like always. And then we ran, pretending that the cops were going to come and arrest us, and then somebody got the bright idea of going to the beach. Was that you? Or Tilton?"

"I don't remember."

"Anyway, we all agreed. I remember I was mad. And I was worried about leaving Kate with my sister. What if she woke up? Also, I was furious with Tilton. I still thought he was a coward. I hated him right then, hated everything. And we went to his house, I remember that, and we were going to get his mom's BMW, sneak it out of the garage . . . and I had to drive, for some reason. Why did I need to drive?"

"I drove," said A.J. quietly. "You're forgetting the facts. I drove the car."

"You didn't."

"I did," he said in a hard voice. "Try to remember it right. I DROVE THE GODDAMNED CAR."

Phoebe got up then, out of her chair, and went over to him, put her hand on his arm and whispered, even though everyone could hear her. Sometimes when you whisper, it makes more of an impact. She'd learned that in acting school in California. She whispered, "A.J., tonight we are telling the truth. It's okay. We can tell the truth here, because it's the first and last time we're going to have to do this."

He put his head in his hands, and she went back to her chair. Her sequins sparkled in the light when she looked down at them. She loved that about sequins, the way they made you unworldly, like you were in the sky, one of the stars. The girls were round-eyed, unmoving, like statues. These girls, these once-upon-a-time babies, hearing their story, and it wasn't going to end well, but they already knew that part. Phoebe wouldn't stop now; she'd gone past the point where she might have stopped, and now she couldn't. She took another swig of the whiskey.

"The truth," Phoebe said slowly. "The boys pushed the car out of the garage, and I sat in the driver's seat, and I popped the clutch, and they jumped in, and we went out onto the road, only I was . . . impaired, you see, and mad. And I had this moment—kind of like a dream, like I'd figured everything out for us forever and ever, and then I turned to tell Tilty what I'd seen, and—well, there was the loudest noise I'd ever heard, so loud it came from the inside of my head, my brains exploding or something, and . . . the world turned upside down and went black."

Poppet might have made a little sound then, but Phoebe squinted at the sequins, tried to get them to come into focus. Then she said, "A car had hit us. I don't know what happened next. I guess I blacked out. And the next thing I remember is that A.J. here—A.J., this brave man right now hiding his head in his hands—this man, this *hero,* was being taken away by the cops, in *handcuffs.* He had told them he was driving, and that he didn't see the car that hit us, and he didn't know what he was doing. And I was being put on a stretcher because I couldn't walk or move after A.J. somehow put me in the backseat."

"I dragged you out of the car," he said. "And relocated you."

"For my own protection, he did this," Phoebe told them. "He took the blame."

"And Tilton?" said Kate.

Phoebe and A.J. were quiet. Phoebe looked down into her whiskey and swirled the glass, drank up the rest.

"So he . . . died?" Poppet said. "That's when he died?"

Phoebe nodded. Now *this* part.

"And you were born the next morning because things had gotten jostled around inside me, and I guess you decided you might as well get born as stay in *that* crazy uterus, and somehow I came to and everything was explained to me. Mary was there and she was trying to get me to sign away my parental rights. But I threw this fit, a royal fit. They didn't even want me to *see* you because they knew they were going to take you away. I was so mad! And so when they brought in the birth certificate, that's when I named you Poppet. I hadn't figured out a name yet, you were so early, and that seemed perfect. Poppet. A whimsical, secret name to see you off into the world."

She looked over at her daughter. "Oh, baby. Stop crying. Stop it. You wanted to hear this and there's more." She took a deep, ragged breath. Poppet dried her eyes, sat up straighter.

"So," Phoebe said, "I pulled myself together, and I refused to sign the paper, and once you were the right birth weight, I took you home. I loved you so much, both of you. Two babies. But then . . . well, I couldn't stop crying. I couldn't eat or sleep; it was like I was stuck in a kind of gray death. I couldn't take care of you, either of you. I only wanted to lie in that bed. I'd hear you crying, and I couldn't move. Mary was distraught. She said we couldn't go on like this. She'd always been on my side, been my champion, but now I could hear her husband in the other room saying this had to stop, what was going to become of all of us, so after two weeks when they brought me the paper to sign, I just signed it. I didn't even care at that point."

"I came over," said A.J. "Mary thought it would make you feel better. We went outside, and she took that picture before they took you away."

Phoebe looked over at Poppet, whose face had turned ashen. She saw Kate reach over and take her hand.

"I could barely stand up," Phoebe said. "That was the day I thought, *Well, I can't keep the baby, but I can take care of Kate.* And I tried, I really tried. Mary said, *Take it day by day and you can get through.* But there were ghosts all around me: Tilty and Daddy and Mama, and they were more real than you were, little Kate. I stayed in the bed; I went under the bed; I started eating soap chips in the shower. I rocked myself on the floor. It was like each of my arms weighed two hundred pounds and I couldn't lift them up.

"Postpartum depression, they call it now. Then they called it the baby blues. A cute name, huh? For something that makes you feel like you want to be dead, and worse, you want never to have lived. My life felt like it was over. I'd made a mess of everything, and I'd lost Tilton and the whole dream for the future."

She poured more whiskey for all of them and took a deep breath.

"Don't you want to stop now?" said A.J., but she waved him off.

"Then two months later, a lady from the Catholic diocese came and she said they'd found a nice family, a couple who had prayed for a child. Kate would have a good, loving, Christian home. Two schoolteachers for parents so they'd love how smart she was. How smart *you* were. And I said, 'They may have prayed for a child, but they didn't pray for *mine!*' But 'Oh yes,' she said, 'they did.' My little cherubic Kate, with the rosy cheeks, was the one they wanted. Needed, even."

They were silent in the dressing room. Kate started toward Phoebe, but Phoebe said, "No. Let me finish this.

"So it was my sister who made all this happen. Out of love, she told me later. Ha! Be careful when people love you—that's what I've learned. She'd called the Catholic agency and said I was out of control and that I couldn't raise these babies, not while I was grieving so many other losses: my youth, my boyfriend, my parents, my life, my freedom. I'd be better off, she said. She crawled into bed with me and rubbed my head and said, 'Phoebe, I wouldn't do this if I didn't love you more than anything. But, sweetie, even though this hurts now, it's going to be better for you. I promise it will be better.'"

"I thought you'd be better off, too," said A.J.

"I know you did. The whole world did, but sometimes, with all due respect, the whole world can make a big fucking mistake, and I was sure this was one of those times. And then my aunt said I should come to California now that I didn't have any babies, and I could go to high school there and nobody would know what had happened or who I was, and I could start over. So I did. I left just after the trial."

"The trial?" said Kate.

"The trial." She took another drink of the whiskey. "A.J. was convicted of manslaughter and driving while intoxicated and with possession of narcotics, and he went to prison. It was supposed to be my punishment, but he took it instead. He was in jail for five years. Hard time."

She saw the girls look at him.

"Because you were a mom," he said. "I'd do it again, too."

"I wouldn't let you do it again. But whatever. It's too late to fix it, that's the thing. I can't pay you back. You took on this horrible thing for me, and I can't make it right. I just have it hanging over me for my whole life. Can't get around *that*, can we?"

"You made a life," he said. "That paid me back. Get over yourself."

"Legally I'm sure there are ramifications. You know what I should have said at that concert tonight? 'Lulu was only made possible because of *your janitor*, ladies and gentlemen. Take a look at A. J. Barnes, because while he's cleaning up the hallways and changing the lightbulbs, he's a superhero. Without him, Lulu would have been in the slammer instead of writing and performing songs in LA.'"

"Shut up, Phoebe. Put a lid on it, will you?"

"Well. That's the story of your beginnings," she said to the girls. They hadn't said a word. Kate was dabbing at her eyes, and Poppet was staring straight ahead. "A.J. went to prison, I went to California and lived with my aunt after promising not to get pregnant anymore, and I eventually graduated from high school with honors and joined a singing group that became Lulu and the Starbabies, and I did about a million drugs and passed out at concerts, and got married a few times, and cried myself to sleep a hundred million times, and everywhere I went, I thought I saw you. I thought I saw A.J. about four hundred different times, too, but it was never actually any of you. I was out there, a little cork in the ocean, making good for myself, and everybody else was taking the brunt of it. How are you supposed to live with that?

"And I also made a promise to myself, that I have now officially broken, and that was that I would never look for you or tell you this story. Never, ever burden you with this horrible birth tale because everybody deserves a nice story of where they came from. So that, today, is what I'm most sorry for, in a long list of sorries. It deadens you, having to be this sorry all the time." She put her hands in her lap. "And that's why I decided I wasn't going to live that way anymore. That's why, selfish as it sounds, I live day to day just for me."

They didn't move, so she said, "That's it. The finale."

They unfolded themselves then like they'd come back to life or something, in their beautiful skirts, with their sleek copper-colored hair burnished in the lamplight, and their creamy skin and Tilton's eyes and mouth, and they tried to hug her and grab at her arms and kiss her on the cheek, and they said, "Oh, but we are so glad you told us," and "I'm so sorry you went through all that"—all the things you say when you've heard that the person in front of you is in fact a horrifying fraud and a liar and a cheat and you just want to get away from her, but first you have to say something nice—and so Phoebe put her hand up to stop them. She stood up and said, "You are beautiful women, and you have your lives. I gave you your start, but you got raised by other people, not me. So let's let this be the end of it," she said. She smiled at them.

They looked uncertain, so she said, "Listen to me. I am not your mother, and we are not going to have some big family reunion and pretend that the last thirty-three years haven't happened. This is it, and I ask you not to contact me anymore, okay?"

"But we love you, we love you!" they said. "Why can't we see you?" They looked at A.J. for help, but he was looking just as stunned as they were.

"Because I don't have any love left in me," Phoebe said simply. And when that wasn't doing the trick, she let them have the killer line:

"And because I don't want to."

TWENTY-NINE
NINA

We walked back onto the football field—staggered, really—now dark except for the streetlights. It was a stifling-hot August night, full of crickets, full-on summer in Connecticut. Air like the inside of a dog's mouth. Lindy said, "This was like the night that—well, it all happened."

Phoebe and A.J. were walking somewhere behind us, but I couldn't hear them anymore, and though I wanted to run back and say one more thing to her, I couldn't think of what it would be. I just wanted to look at her, and then to shake her for her stubbornness, and kiss her, and tell her everything was going to be all right, that I *understood*. But there was also a kind of hollowness inside me; I was exhausted. I could feel tears backed up inside me. It would have been good to sit down on the curb and simply cry for a little while. I wondered briefly if Lindy would mind if we had a good cry.

"I did not think that was the way this story was going to go," I said.

"Well, my God, she killed him. Our mother killed our father. I guess that was the legal stuff she meant, that she let A.J. take the blame."

"Jesus," I said. "And he's still protecting her."

"I can't get over that part of things," I said. "And he didn't even want her to tell that part of the story, did you notice that? He made that sacrifice, and now he's still protecting her."

"He loves her. She doesn't even know that's why he did it, but it's so clear. I wonder if he always loved her, but he couldn't do anything about it because his friend was her boyfriend."

"They ruined their lives. Can you believe that? That one night ruined their lives. Ours, too."

"No, not ours. That's the main thing of this. We had other parents. We grew up okay."

"I wish there was something we could do for her," I said. "Besides what she wants us to do, which is leave her alone."

"Imagine what our lives would have been like if she'd kept us," Lindy said. "That might have been the real tragedy."

"But she wanted us. We would never have worried that we hadn't been wanted."

"Yeah, but . . ."

We'd reached the parking lot by then, and I looked up, startled, to see Carter leaning against my car, arms folded, watching us walk toward him.

My heart fell into my shoes. For one crazy moment, I thought he had come to rescue me, that he was thinking it might have been hard for me, seeing my mother, who had so far refused to have anything to do with me. My foolish little hummingbird heart started beating so much faster at the sight of him.

"Where's Kayla?" he called as we came near. He unfolded his arms and started toward me with a funny expression on his face. His voice was not friendly.

"I don't know," I told him. "You said she couldn't come, so we didn't bring her."

"Oh, come on," he said. "You mean to tell me she didn't talk you into it? That doesn't sound like my daughter."

"She didn't. Plus, I wouldn't have brought her if you didn't want her here. Also, the concert's been over for hours."

"Oh shit," he said, and looked around. He ran his fingers through his hair, that old familiar gesture. "I am so sick of this crap. So where could she be?"

"More shenanigans?" I said.

"Every time I think we're at the end of shenanigans, something like this happens," he said. He glanced over at Lindy. "Hi, Lindy. How are you?" I realized with a start that of course they'd met before, without me.

"I'm fine, Carter. But I'm sorry you can't find your daughter. Is there anything we can do to help?"

"Oh, she'll turn up, I'm sure," he said, and started to get back in his car. "She's flirting with the edge lately, that's all. Walking the line to see how close she can get before she falls over."

"If it's any consolation, she's brilliant at work with me," Lindy said. "She's so loving and sweet with the children."

"Thank you. That actually does make me feel a bit better. If I can just keep her alive to adulthood, she'll be a fine human being. Oh well, sorry to bother you. How was the concert, by the way?"

"It was the perfect ending to a lovely adoption dream fantasy," I said and was glad to see him wince a little bit.

"Well," he said, and put his key in the ignition. The engine turned over. "I tried to call you a few times. You might see some hysterical messages on your phone when you turn it back on."

And then I knew something I didn't know I knew. Indigo was having sex somewhere. The last item on the Fuck-It List. I wondered only for a moment if this was any of my business, and then I said, "Wait. Carter, I don't know how to say this . . ."

"Yes?" he said irritably. "Just say it, will you?"

"Wait a minute! Are you really Carter Sanborn? Because you do not sound like the same man I used to be so crazy for. What's happened to you?"

"What do you *think* happened to me?" he said. "I've been driving all over looking for my kid, and wondering which dangerous activity she's trying now, and why her whole life has to be one big dramatic risk-taking maneuver designed to make me crazy."

"But you like kids who take risks," I said. "You always said that."

"Nina, if you are any kind of a nice person, you will not remind me of things I used to say about parenting before I had four months alone with them."

"I was going to say, if you check the Fuck-It List, you might notice that the very last item is to have sex with somebody she's not in love with. So maybe that's where she is tonight."

"She is too young to be having sex."

"Yes. That is a fact," I said. "And I think you should go and put a stop to it this minute. Unless part of your parenting philosophy still includes what you once told me, that everyone owns their own sexuality and that it's none of your business what your children do."

He put his head down on the steering wheel. "Jesus, I was a horse's ass."

"Well, yes, that's true. And actually I don't know for sure that's where she is. It was just a thought."

"Well," said Carter, "she's not with Tyler, she's not at the movies, she's not at school, she's not at Starbucks or at the park or at the mall. She's not even with those juvenile delinquents who hang out behind the CVS with their skateboards. And she's not picking up her phone."

"Then I think she might be with Maya's brother." I suddenly felt really scared. "He seems the likely candidate to me."

"I'm afraid I don't know the gentleman," he said.

"He's, um, twenty. Lives at home with his parents. Name is Marco."

His eyes bugged out. "Great. That's great."

"You should go with him," Lindy said to me. "I'll drive your car back to your house and Jeff can pick me up."

"We're always doing that with cars. Just take my car to your house, and I'll figure out how to get it tomorrow."

"I haven't asked you to come with me," said Carter. "You really don't have to."

"Don't be daft. You don't even know where Maya lives, do you? Also, I don't see you barging in and putting a stop to this without backup. I'm coming with you."

"Okay," he said quietly. "Thank you."

I threw Lindy my keys and got into his passenger seat.

"Will my children ever grow up?" he said.

"I expect so." I looked out the window and saw A.J. and Phoebe walking to the far end of the parking lot, where there was one other car left there. Maybe they came together. Or maybe she was going home with him. I wanted to wave to them, but I realized that I didn't *really* want to. It was enough—seeing my mother still in her sparkly dress, with her hair tumbling around her shoulders, walking with the guy in the photo. Almost but not quite leaning on him.

All these years, and you are right now in the same location as your mother. Look at her! Would you have ever passed her on the street and known you belonged with her?

It was a moment, that's all.

"Carter," I said. "Look over there. That's her. That's my mother."

He bent down so he could see her through the passenger window. "Who's the guy? Is that your father?"

"No. My father is dead. Car accident right before Lindy was born. That's A. J. Barnes, who took the blame for it. It's such a long story. I don't even know if I can tell it right now. I have to sort it all out."

"But you got your mom back in your life. That was what you wanted, right?"

"It's not what I thought. She doesn't want to see me anymore. This was the only time."

He pulled out onto the road. "I'm so sorry," he said. "That must feel awful for you."

"I don't really know yet what I feel. Awful is just the start of it, probably."

After that, Carter and I didn't talk much during the hour-long drive back to Oyster Cove. I stared at his hands on the steering wheel, noticed the graceful curve of his fingers and tried not to think of how finished we really were, how those hands wouldn't be cradling my head or moving along my body anymore. This is what I've always done when falling out of love with somebody. I make myself remember what I loved the best about them over and over again until I get desensitized to it. It's the way you kill your feelings. *These hands are simply hands on a steering wheel, nothing more,* I kept saying to myself, *and I am a woman sitting in the car with him, not mysterious, not even sexy to him really, just a past fling.* It was so late and so foggy outside, and I was still so overwhelmed by Phoebe's horrible story and her hard-ass look when she said she didn't want to ever see me again. The night pressing against the windows, the streetlights whipping past, Carter's breathing, the dread of the errand we were on: all of it suddenly seemed awful.

I sighed, and Carter said, "I know. It's nice of you to do this."

"Nice schmice," I said, looking out the window. "I don't want to see her ruin her life. I care about her."

I gave him the directions to Maya's house, where the brother still lived. He had a bedroom on the first floor—with a live boa constrictor in it, Indigo had told me once. She didn't like to go in there because the boa constrictor had figured out how to get the top of his cage off and at any given time *might* be loose in the house.

"I don't think I will be able, myself, to stage a rampage and rescue," I told him. "But I'll be waiting in the getaway car."

"What exactly are we planning to do?" he said. "I've never staged a rescue mission, especially on somebody who doesn't want to be rescued."

"You're the father, and if she's in there with him, having sex, then this is statutory rape. You'll know what to do."

He turned down Maya's street, a sad little residential street with small, squat houses, and he cruised to a stop at the curb. I had to tell him which house was hers, the little blue one with aluminum siding and a forlorn little striped awning. "You do know this guy gives her rides everywhere, right?" I said.

"What? I thought Tyler was giving her rides."

"Carter, Carter, Carter. I don't know what we're going to do with you."

"This is horrible," he said. "I'm don't know what I'm doing."

I got out of the car. "Fine, I'll come with you. I should warn you, though, there may be snakes involved, in which case I'll be running for my life."

We walked up the cracked sidewalk to the front door. The whole house was dark. He said, "Actual snakes, or metaphorical snakes?"

"Actual. Metaphorical ones don't count. What time is it?" I whispered.

"Eleven oh five," he said. "Are you sure this is the house? There's no light on."

"It seems like four in the morning. But I think you should ring the doorbell."

He reached out and pressed the doorbell. Nothing happened, no noise from within the house at all.

"Ring it again," I said.

"Oh God," he said, but he did. We could hear thumping inside, and the porch light came on just as the door opened. A young guy with shoulder-length brown hair squinted at us. Marco.

"Yeah?" he said.

He was wearing cutoffs and a Megadeth T-shirt, and he was holding a beer bottle in his hand.

"I am looking for Kayla Sanborn," said Carter in the firmest voice I'd ever heard from him. "Tell her to get down here immediately."

The guy looked confused.

"Indigo," I said to him. "He's looking for Indigo."

"Oh. She's not here," he said.

"Where is she then?" Carter asked. He banged his fist on the house. "Tell me right this minute where she is, or I'm calling the cops."

Marco raised his eyebrows. "Listen, I don't know where she is. She was here earlier, but she left. I thought she was going home."

"Going home? How was she going to get there? Was she *walking* home?"

"I don't know. Like I said, she just left. I offered to drive her, but she didn't want me to. She stomped out of here like she knew what she was doing. I thought maybe she had a ride."

Carter looked behind the guy, as if he expected to see his daughter there. But I knew Marco was telling the truth.

"Hi," I said. "You're Maya's brother, right? I'm Nina."

"Oh, yeah, hi."

"So what time was Indigo here?" I said.

"I don't know. About an hour ago?"

"And . . . it sounds like . . . well, was she angry?" I said.

"Huh?"

"You said she stomped out of here. So I thought maybe that meant she was angry about something."

He let out a long breath. "Look, I didn't do nothing to her, you know? She came over, and she had these . . . ideas . . . and I told her that wasn't gonna happen. I don't mind driving her places when she needs a ride and all, and I know she's good people, but she . . . well, she wants more from me than that." He glanced sideways at Carter, who was pacing the porch, back and forth, making little growling noises. "I'm sorry, man. But you gotta know that nothing happened here tonight, and she got mad."

Carter glared at Marco, then said to me, "Let's go." He had his phone out and he was punching in Indigo's number. It went to voice mail, and he exhaled loudly.

We walked back to the car in silence, listening to the distant sounds of sirens and engine noises. Saturday night noises. Our footsteps on the sidewalk made my head hurt.

He got in the car and stared straight ahead, his hands on the steering wheel. "I don't know what to do next. For the first time, I can't imagine what to do next. She was trying to get that guy to go to bed with her, wasn't she? What the *hell*?" He looked over at me, helpless. "What am I going to do?"

"It looks like it. It was the last item on the Fuck-It List."

"I know kids start young these days, but she's fifteen years old, and this guy is twenty! She's out of her mind! Where the hell *is* she? I'm going to have to go to the police, aren't I? I am!"

"Wait," I said. "The important thing right now is to find her. Right? Marco may not be the perpetrator here, you know. It sounds like he—"

"Who can believe him? He's a lowlife, and he's been driving my kid places and God only knows what else he's been doing with her!"

"Let's try to be calm," I said. "I know you're upset, but we don't know that anything bad has happened. She's flamboyant, it's true, but she's basically a smart, resourceful kid who knows how to take care of herself. I think this is all going to end up fine. Let's just keep looking for her."

He punched her number into his phone once again. Voice mail. I could hear, "This is Innn-diggggoooo. You know what to do!" and then he disconnected the call and rubbed his hands through his hair.

"I am sorry. I'm losing it, and I don't know what I'd do without you here."

"Well," I said. I took a deep breath. "What I think we should do is drive toward your house and look for her. Maybe she's walking."

"Oh God. Walking alone at this hour? Jesus! Listen. Here's a thought. Why don't you call her from your cell phone? Maybe she'll pick up for you."

I put in her number, but nothing. I looked over at him. "Wait a second. Do you have Maya's phone number? No, of course you don't. Maybe I do." I scrolled through my phone, and sure enough I found it. Indigo had put it there once when she couldn't find her own phone.

To my surprise, Maya answered. "Yes? What?" In the background, loud, thumping music was almost drowning out our connection.

I put my hand around the phone. "Maya! Maya, is that you?"

Drumbeats.

"Stop it, you guys! I SAID STOP IT RIGHT NOW! Noooo!" And then she was laughing and maybe crying at the same time, I couldn't tell. There was a crash, and her voice again over the drumbeats, which were fainter now. "What?" she said, her voice right against the speaker. "Who is this?"

"It's Nina. I'm looking for Indigo."

"WHAT? I CAN'T HEAR YOU! YOU GUYYYYYYS!"

Carter put his head down on the steering wheel.

"Maya! Maya, please take the phone and go someplace quiet. This is important!"

"What?" said Maya in my ear.

"Maya, this is Nina, and I AM LOOKING FOR INDIGO. IS SHE WITH YOU?"

There was muffled talk and she came back to the phone. "She's here."

I reached over and touched Carter's shoulder. "She's there," I whispered. Then to Maya, "Would you put her on the phone, please? Her dad is very worried about her."

More muffled voices, then Maya said, "She doesn't want to talk to him."

"Then have her talk to me!"

"She doesn't want to talk to you either." She put her mouth up to the phone, so close I could barely make out the words. "She's had kind of a tough night, and she's really, really upset about some shit."

"Where are you guys?"

"We're . . . we're at a party. Some friends are, uh, giving a party at this guy's house."

"How did you get there? Your brother said she was at your house before." I mouthed to Carter, "She's at a party." He closed his eyes like he was in pain.

There was a long silence, more muffled voices, and then Indigo came on the phone. I handed it over to Carter. "Talk to her," I said to him.

He took the phone and told her that he was coming to get her. He managed to get the address, and said she'd better be outside when he got there. Then he handed the phone back to me and started the car.

"Wow," I said. "You have a dad voice. Good for you!"

"Nina," he said. "This is not the time for this, all right? Could you just maybe be quiet?"

She wasn't waiting outside when we got there, so I stayed in the car while he went in to get her. For some reason, I liked picturing Carter among a sea of teenagers, all of them drinking and smoking and doing unspeakable things—things that a few months ago he would have said weren't any of his business. I dreaded the ride home with the three of us, dreaded hearing him mishandling the whole thing, which I was sure he would do. Why did I even need to go through this anyway?

Then Lindy called me on my cell phone, wanting to know what had happened. I told her, and when she asked if I wanted her to come get me, I jumped at the chance.

"I'm tired and I don't want to be here for this next part," I said. "This is it."

"Did she have sex with that guy?"

"I don't think so," I said.

"Well, that's something at least. Are *you* all right? You've had quite a night."

"Just please come," I said.

I wrote a quick note to Carter and left it on the driver's seat. *Good-bye. Got a ride with Lindy!*

THIRTY
PHOEBE

A week went by before the first phone call came.

The caller ID said: *Nina Popkin*. Phoebe had been playing the piano in the front room. After glancing at the name on the screen, she didn't even get up to answer it.

Of course it would be Nina who would call first, and not Lindy. Nina *remembered* her. At some cellular level—not consciously perhaps—the essence of Nina remembered her mother. Phoebe believed in essences. She had the essence of Tilton around her all the time, stronger at some times than others. And now Nina—Kate's—essence was right alongside the two of them.

Sitting across from Kate the other night, telling her the story of her birth and all the stuff that happened later, she felt the way she'd felt years ago, looking into those babyish blue eyes. All that trust and love.

It had been hard—beastly hard—to meet all that emotion and then get up and leave, to stand there and say that nothing had changed. But it had to be that way. There wasn't enough left of Phoebe to keep try-ing. She'd said what she came to say, and she wanted to go back to the way it was.

So she didn't pick up the phone that time—or the three other times.

"Hi," said Nina in voice mail after the fourth attempt. She cleared her throat. "Um, I just wanted, you know, to talk to you, see how you are. Well, I guess that's all." There was a hesitation, then she said, "Love you," very fast and clicked off.

◆　◆　◆

Mary.

"I don't see why you don't simply talk to her. You told her the whole horrible story, didn't you? So what do you have to lose? It's done."

"You don't understand a thing about it."

"I understand your stubbornness, you crazy old thing. You've got these daughters, they want to know you, and one of them particularly wants to love you. And you turn them away. Who among us can afford to turn love away?"

"It's not love. It's—"

"Then what is it, Phoebe Louise? Tell me that."

"I'm a . . . curiosity. I can't stand the way they looked at me, like I was from another planet."

"That—that is so not true. I can tell that's a lie all the way over here in Oklahoma. You know what's going on? You're a coward when it comes to letting people love you."

"I—"

"Coward."

"But—"

"Coward."

"Listen, *you* made me give them up. You are the one who said it would be best. And now you dare to call *me* a coward, when you wouldn't help me keep them? How dare you?"

"I still think it could work out for the best."

"That's what you said when you made me give them up."

"Phoebe."

"What?"

"I'm sorry about that. But we'll never know if it was for the best, will we?"

"For the best, not for the best. How can you judge something like that? I've been made to remember those days again, and it's awful."

"Don't shut everybody out, okay? We all did what we thought was right. You, too."

One day late in August, the doorbell rang, and since she was expecting Botany Hastings-Jones for a lesson, she simply hit the buzzer. (And yes, there was a neighborhood girl named Botany. Soon kids would be called things like Sociology and English Lit.)

Then there was Nina standing in her kitchen. Like an apparition. Only real.

"What? What are you doing here?"

It was hard to believe how startled she could still get. She, who was fearless in Brooklyn, walking through the streets with confidence, giving money to homeless people, talking to panhandlers on the subway, smiling at the old people and the people dressed in rags, the guys whose faces were frozen into scowls, the distracted young moms with too many children climbing all over them. She, who had told herself she'd lived through the worst that life had to offer, was startled out of her mind by the sight of a woman—her daughter—standing in her kitchen.

"Hi," Nina said. She looked so non-threatening, so . . . ordinary. She was wearing a blue T-shirt and white jeans and little sandals. Her hair was up in a scrunchie, and she was smiling. "I was in the neighborhood, and I thought I'd stop by to see if you'd like to grab lunch. No biggie, just lunch."

"I thought you—that we—weren't going to do this," said Phoebe. "I *said*."

"Yeah, but this is just lunch. Not a relationship. Just something to eat."

It was ridiculous, how crazily her heart was beating. She liked it that Nina wasn't surveying the apartment, judging the sparseness of the place. Nina looked only at her, and her face was open and friendly.

And it *was* time for lunch. She'd been thinking that after Botany left, if her mom paid in cash, maybe she'd treat herself. Go down the block and have a spring roll at the Thai place.

But what *about* Botany? Where was she, anyway? She was now fifteen minutes late, so Phoebe was technically within her right to leave a note on the door, saying she had to go out. That they could reschedule.

"Okay," she said, and Nina smiled a little half smile. Nothing triumphant or too self-congratulatory. Nothing mean or overzealous. Just a little half smile. And they walked downstairs and down the street, and over to the Thai place together.

There wasn't any bad talk.

No more questions.

Nina said she was seeing someone new. "But it's no big deal. Just a guy. Likes kids and marriage, so who knows?"

Phoebe respected that, Nina not needing to spill the whole story. And when they said good-bye, there wasn't any angst. Just a light, friendly hug. They smiled, and Nina walked to the subway and Phoebe walked back to her apartment.

THIRTY-ONE
NINA

One day the phone rang, and it was Carter. Not the furious, defeated Carter . . . and not the madcap, hey-gang-let's-get-some-lobsters-and-ice-cream Carter either. Not even the Carter of the Dad Voice.

This was a new, mysterious Carter.

I am tired of all the Carter incarnations, I told myself. Still, my heart was beating too fast.

"I'm sorry I didn't call to thank you for the other night," he said. "No excuse for that, after what you did for me." He cleared his throat. "For us."

"No, it's fine," I said. "I'm sorry I didn't check back in. Lindy told me what happened. Indigo's grounded for a while, I take it?"

"Yeah. Well, we're taking it one day at a time over here. Some good days, some bad days. You know. How are you?"

"Good. Busy. You know how it is."

"Yeah." He was silent, and I could picture him running his fingers through his hair, looking up at the ceiling, readying himself for what came next. Then it came: "Um, I hate to ask you this, but I kind of need a huge favor," he said.

"Okayyyy," I said.

He had broken his foot. He couldn't drive places. It was time to take the children to their various locations. Tyler to Vanderbilt University in Nashville. Indigo to her mom's in Virginia. Would I—?

"Would I *take* them? No. Sorry, but I can't possibly."

"Not just *you* taking them," he said. "I mean *us*. Would you go with us, and drive me back home?"

There was a long silence while we both waited for my answer. I massaged my temples while I looked out the window. I tried to imagine what it would be like, getting in a car with these children, with this impossible man, and pretending we were an ordinary family going off to deliver a boy to college and a girl to her mom's sustainable farm somewhere in Virginia. *What would we talk about? How weird would it be? How long would it take? Why would I want to be in the car for endless hours with these people, and then say good-bye again? Horrible. Terrible. Painful.*

But he needed me.

But he could find someone else, couldn't he?

But he needed me. And he didn't ask for help much.

Ha! The last time he needed help—that did not go well.

Still, he was nice. And I cared for him. And the children.

But think of *me*, said my heart. Have we not seen enough action? Do we have to get over this guy all over again? Because that is not our usual way. One breakup per person, that's how we do it.

We already are over him, said my brain. Remember when he said he didn't want to hear anything you had to say? And when he said you were wasting your time looking for your mother and badgering some old lady who didn't want to see you?

Shut up, I said to my brain.

Carter cleared his throat. "Maybe think about it. Call me when you know."

"No, I'll do it," I heard myself say.

"Really, you should think about it."

"How long do you think we'll be gone?"

"I think . . . blah blah . . . blah . . . driving schedules . . . all depends . . . checking in at college . . . then the farm . . . God knows . . . weather . . . hotel rooms . . ." I couldn't pay attention no matter how hard I tried. I was just listening to the timbre of his voice. Listening for a lilt of the old Carter, which was missing.

"How did you break your foot?" I asked.

"Oh. Jumping off a boat onto the dock. Came down on it and twisted it at the same time. Have to wear a huge boot now."

"And when do you want to leave?" I said.

"Would tomorrow be okay with you?"

Tomorrow? I closed my eyes. Ah yes. This was Carter we were dealing with. I laughed, and he did an approximation of a laugh, more like air rattling around in his nose and throat.

"I'll call Melanie," I told him. "And see if she can handle things without me for a week. It won't be more than a week, will it?"

"Oh God. If it's more than a week, I think we all will have killed each other."

That was probably true. "Are you sad to give them up?" I said, but he had already put the phone down.

I'll be honest with you. Fifteen minutes into the trip, and I couldn't imagine why I'd ever agreed to go. They picked me up at my mother's condo, and the van they arrived in looked like something the Beverly Hillbillies might have rejected as being too old and horrifying. It had everything but Granny's rocking chair on the top. It turned out to be an old van they'd borrowed from one of Tyler's friend's parents, and its main attribute was that it came with a roof rack, so all of Indigo's and Tyler's suitcases could go up there. Tyler's music equipment was shoved into the back of the van, as were boxes and boxes of Indigo's paraphernalia and books. Including a cage with Beyoncé, who was maniacally running on the wheel, like she alone was responsible for powering the car on its trip to Nashville.

I got in the driver's seat. Carter was propped up in the passenger seat, his right foot resting on the dashboard, encased in a black foam rubber boot that he called The Abomination. He was wearing running shorts and a blue T-shirt with a picture of a sailboat on it. Tyler and Indigo were in the middle seat with pillows propped between them as a barrier. Indigo had a new nose piercing and she'd cut off all her hair again and re-dyed it purple—a statement, no doubt, about having to move away. Tyler, hunched forward like he was spring-loaded, kept cracking his knuckles, and each time he did, she'd yell at him to stop because it was disgusting. He finally answered that cracking his knuckles was the only thing keeping him from liberating Beyoncé from the squeaking wheel, and *where was an oil can when you needed one.*

"Hi," I said to them. "Long time no see. You guys ready to go?"

"Hi," they said at the same time, and then Indigo hit Tyler for some unfathomable reason, and he laughed instead of hitting her back. "You do that one more time, and I'm letting that rodent go."

Carter closed his eyes. "Please," he said to them. "Nina is doing this out of the kindness of her heart, so don't make her hate us." He looked over at me. "Thank you, thank you, a million times thank you."

"Are you in pain?" I asked him.

"I'm afraid you'll have to be more specific," he told me. "What kind of pain are you referring to?"

"Oh. Okay then."

He closed his eyes again, and I started the engine. "Does anybody know exactly where we're going?"

"Nashville, Tennessee, via I-95," said Tyler, and he handed me the GPS he'd been programming, which I stuck on to the windshield. Indigo said, "For what, we do not know."

He hit her in the arm and she said, "Stop it, Tyler, you idiot, or I'm telling."

There was a scuffle in the backseat, and Carter said, "Both of you, put on your headphones and leave each other alone."

"I am telling," I heard Indigo hiss. "It's not fair. Tyler gets to go and start his regular life, and I have to go live on a fucking farm in the middle of Pig Fart, Virginia, and I have to leave every single one of my friends that I've had since I was a *baby*!"

I looked at her in the rearview mirror, remembering back to the time when all she'd wanted was to join her mom. Now, with the speed of a teenage mind, all that had changed.

"Usually you say you don't have any friends," Tyler pointed out.

Thwack! She hit him. I glanced over at Carter and steered the car onto I-95.

"Could you please tone down your language the slightest bit?" asked Carter. "There's no reason to insult the digestive systems of pigs." He winked at me.

The engine was making a horrible rattling noise so I couldn't hear if Indigo laughed or not, but I slammed the van into fourth with a screeching sound, and for a moment everyone sat in reverential silence at the startling fact that we had lived through the first gear-shifting of the trip.

There was a rumble from the backseat and Carter said, tiredly, "Headphones."

Then he turned and smiled at me, and I felt the same exhilaration I used to feel when I was making a beef stew for the three of them and thinking I was doing them some actual good. I could hear the music leaking out of their headphones, and I turned on the radio to some jazz station.

Carter was watching me. "Really, Nina. I want to thank you yet again for coming on this trip."

"It's fine. I care about the kids."

"And. Well, I want to say I'm sorry about the night with Indigo and the party. I was really freaking out, and I think I was rude to you."

"Possibly rude," I said.

We rode for a long time. After about an hour of silence, he leaned over and whispered, "You know what went wrong?"

"Excuse me?" I could barely hear him over the noise of the engine.

"What went wrong. Do you know?"

"In what sense?"

"In the sense of you and me."

"You and me? You mean our breakup? I guess I have some ideas."

"Yeah, well, good. Because I really can't figure out why it all unraveled so fast. Enlighten me."

"Are you doing an update for your list of romantic crimes for when you meet the next woman?" I said.

He gave me a smoldering stare. "There won't be a next woman, I'm thinking."

"Ha," I told him. "But since you asked, here's the list. The first problem was that you were still half in love with your ex-wife, and another was that we jumped into things too fast, and another was that we never had a chance to make any memories for ourselves—"

"Hold on. The first one is definitely not true—and what the hell? You think we didn't make any memories for ourselves?"

"No. All your memories were with Jane."

"I have memories. What about the time we danced at the club and then the police called? And riding around looking for a place to live for me. And what about the first time we—you know—?"

I glanced into the backseat, but both kids were plugged into their devices and not paying any attention. Indigo had tears running down her cheeks as she typed furiously on her phone.

"Memories involving the police station are not the kind I'm thinking about. And, the fourth and most fatal thing, which I have only recently figured out, was that I want babies and a life with a family of my own, and I think you sensed that and kept me at arm's length."

"Huh," he said after a long time. "I don't believe there was ever a mention of babies."

"There couldn't be. We were too taken up with the freak-outs of daily life. And I didn't feel appreciated. I was doing so much—so much, Carter!—and you were just skating along in your own life, and telling me to take it easy."

"You felt I wasn't tough enough. You were the sole voice of reason in a household of misfits."

"That part is definitely true."

About four hours later, the van ran out of gas because it turned out the gauge didn't work. Of course we'd have a van with no gas gauge! Perfect. Tyler and I were preparing to walk back along the highway to the last gas station we'd seen, when Carter put his hand on my arm and said, in a low voice in my ear, "By the way, just for the record, not in love with the ex-wife."

I said, "Half. You were half in."

"Not even one millionth in."

"Well, numbers two, three, and four still stand."

"Whatever," he said, turning away. "It doesn't matter."

It was while Tyler and I were taking turns carrying the gas can back that I remembered something dire. I had a date with Matthew that night, and I hadn't called to cancel. I gave a momentary thought to the lavender silk sheets I had put on the bed in anticipation of what I'd thought might be our first night sleeping together, and of the special underwear I'd bought. Little black bikini things still in my top drawer with the tags on them. I thought how right about now he would be getting ready to pick me up, expecting we'd go to some fine air-conditioned establishment and sip wine—he liked cabernet better than beer, the first guy I'd ever met like that—and that we'd move our relationship along the continuum toward wherever we were headed. Instead I was out walking along a trash-lined highway, hoping not to be killed by speeding trucks and wondering if I was always going to have the smell of gasoline stuck in my nostrils. My T-shirt was plastered to my back, and the wind was whipping my hair around.

"Tyler," I said. "I have to stop and make a call."

"All right." We moved over into the weeds, and he put the gas can down and sat on the ground. He had a pinched look on his face, the expression of somebody who's always accommodating everyone else and things still aren't going right. I felt sorry for him.

"Soon," I told him while I waited for Matthew to pick up the phone, "all this will be just a memory and you'll be at college. You'll be away from your crazy family and you'll have fun! Your whole life is about to change."

"Is it?" he said. He was fidgeting again, cracking his knuckles, and looking all around. "I just want to get there and get it all started."

"Well, sure. I get that."

Matthew answered in his silky, comforting voice, but I suddenly couldn't think of a single thing to say that would make any sense to him. *Hi, Matthew. I really did intend to go on a date with you tonight, but then my ex-boyfriend asked me to drive him and his kids to Tennessee, so I'm on a stretch of highway with eighteen-wheelers roaring past me, and I'm out of gas, and whoops, I just forgot to let you know.*

"Matthew! Hey, I am so very sorry, but I can't make it tonight."

Whoosh. A giganto truck nearly blew me off the side of the road.

"What was that?"

"A truck. I'm kind of on the side of a highway just now. In Pennsylvania of all places, ha ha."

"Ha ha ha," he said. "*No*, really, where are you? I bought you a present."

I closed my eyes. *You want to know where I am, Matthew? I'm in hell. My life went back to being nuts. Sweetie, I'm sorry, but I can't go out with you tonight.*

"Do you want to know what the present is?"

"I guess so. Sure. Tell me." Bugs were swarming around my sweaty face.

"Are you *sure* you want to know? Because maybe you like surprises more."

"No, no. It's fine. Tell me if you want to."

"Sunscreen!" he said. "I noticed when we went to the beach last week that yours was nearly out, and also you were using a kind that still has PABA in it. Which means that it's also probably pretty old."

"Oh. Wow. Well, thank you."

"So where did you say you are?"

"Never mind," I said. "Listen, I gotta go. But I'll call you in a week or so when I'm back."

"I'm almost at your house. You sure you're not there? Did you say a week?"

"I'm fairly certain I'm not there."

"It's okay. Shall I leave the sunscreen on your porch? It's a good brand. Do you think someone will steal it?"

"Those old people in the condos are ruthless bastards," I said. "I wouldn't risk something that valuable around them."

Another truck had drowned out my words, and he said, "What? WHAT DID YOU SAY?"

I said, "It's over, Matthew. There's no point. I don't want to see you anymore."

"What?" he said again. "What? What? Wait. Where are you, again?"

Tyler and I walked back. The sun was going down, and a breeze had kicked up, and life suddenly felt so wonderful and frazzled and full of possibility again. I gave him a glorious smile, and he gave me a doubtful one back.

"I wasn't eavesdropping," Tyler said, "but . . . were you . . . like, did you just break up with somebody? On the phone?"

"I did," I told him.

"For reals? Like it's over?"

"It's over."

"I broke up with Lolly in June, and we went back and forth for, like, another two months. She still texts me all the time whenever she can't sleep or something. I sorta like talking to her."

"I'm kind of an expert on breaking up," I said.

"Why do you want to be an expert on that?"

"I don't. Not really. I mean, I'd like to find the right person, but I keep screwing it up. I think I'm destined to be alone, which is, you know, perfectly fine once you give up on the idea of there being someone meant for you. You know? When you think of life as a search for a soul mate, then you get really weirded out if you're not finding the right person. But when you give up, it's all lovely. Like right now, for instance? I feel great."

"Ninety percent of people aren't with their soul mates," he said. "That's what makes the jukebox play. I read that somewhere."

I smiled at him.

"So, like, it's none of my business and all, but why wasn't my dad the right one? He told me he loved you and that you guys were going to get married. Of course my dad's view of things and the rest of the world's view aren't always the same." He laughed a little.

"Yeah. Your dad's a great person. Unique."

"Did you love him?" He was looking at me seriously, so earnestly that I had to look away. I owed him something.

"I did. I mean, I do still, kind of. But sometimes love isn't enough. There were too many other things going on. It's hard to explain it. We had a lot of factors working against us."

"Was it Indigo? And me? I guess we're a lot of hassle. But we're going to be gone now, so maybe you and my dad . . ."

"No, no," I said. "Really, Tyler! Some of the best times, some of the happiest days I've ever had were spent with you and your family in that little house. It's just that—I don't know—it wasn't *mine* somehow. It wasn't my place. My opinion didn't count. And I felt—well, I was always just a substitute for your mom, kind of a stand-in. I can't explain it really. But it wasn't you. Honest."

"Okay. Well, it was nice of you to drive us here. We're kind of weirded out right now, I guess. Good-byes and all. It sucks." After a minute he said, "What do you think that guy is doing right now? The one you broke up with? Is he, like, going to be writing love songs to you and telling all his friends how unhappy he is?"

"I think he's just fine. I don't think I meant all that much to him frankly."

But really, I realized with some surprise, I had no idea. When I got home, probably Melanie would roll her eyes and say, *Oh, Nina,* the way she did whenever I broke up with a guy. John Paul probably wouldn't get it, and he'd be a bit cool toward me for a while because Matthew was his friend. Nobody would get it, because I didn't get it myself.

It's me, it's all me. I'm to blame.

I thought I said that out loud, but maybe not, because Tyler didn't answer. He kept walking, frowning and scuffing up the dirt alongside the road with his cowboy boots. *Those boots are going to do just fine in Nashville,* I thought. He was going to be just fine. I wished I could get him to see that his life was really beginning and it was going to turn out wonderful.

But he wouldn't believe it coming from me.

We stayed in a cheap little motel the first night—all four of us in one room, Indigo and me in one of the double beds and Tyler and Carter in the other, and Beyoncé in the bathroom running on her wheel. It was a small, ugly room with brown carpeting and brown paneled walls, and a window that wouldn't open and a bathroom door that didn't close right.

When the lights were out, you could still read a book in there because of the streetlight just outside the window.

I tossed and turned and listened to Carter's snoring, and thought, quite against my will, about Matthew. At 2:00 a.m. a text came in with its little gong sound and I tiptoed over to my purse, and sure enough it was from Matthew, as if I'd conjured him up by thinking about him.

Did I do something wrong? he wrote. *Tell me what it was and I will fix it.*

I stood staring at the phone for a long time, then took it into the bathroom and looked at Beyoncé for a while more before I typed: *No. You were so nice. I don't deserve you. I don't know what is wrong with me. You are perfect and I am so fucked up and you are lucky to be away from me. But all I know is that it is over and I'm sorry if I hurt you.* (I typed that last part after thinking of what Tyler said on the side of the road.)

Then I pressed "Send" and went back to sleep to the gentle snores of the guys and the sad, soft sniffles of Indigo, whose life was ruined by having to move to a farm.

"If we drive fast and don't stop for lunch," said Carter the next morning, "we could make it to Vanderbilt today, but I kind of think I'd like to take it easy. My foot and all. I say we have pancakes first thing because there's a wonderful place around here that serves the kind of pancakes that are thin and buttery and have an edge to them that's just incredible. In fact, I want a whole order of pancake edges!"

"They don't let you order pancake *edges*," said Indigo, who was still half in tears this morning. She'd been sitting on the floor, texting madly on her phone and blowing her nose while the rest of us packed.

Carter looked around at all of us. "Anybody else in for this?"

"I am," I said. He smiled at me, one beleaguered adult to another.

"Also," he said, "we are going to have to watch that odometer so that we can calculate when we next need gas. Otherwise, we're going to run out of gas about twice a day."

"Now, before we leave," he said, "who needs anything?"

"I need a break from having to sit next to Tyler," said Indigo.

"You two can't possibly get along?"

"He reads my texts over my shoulder. I can feel him doing it."

"I do *not* read your texts! Do you honestly think I have nothing better to do than to read what you write to your stupid friends?" Tyler said.

Carter rolled his eyes in my direction and hobbled into the bathroom, where he proceeded to have a minutes-long fight to close the bathroom door that he eventually won by slamming it as hard as he possibly could. I wondered if we were going to have to hoist him through the window when he wanted to come out.

The children didn't seem to be worrying about that. Indigo was still staring down Tyler, who was sitting on the bed looking at his own phone.

"First of all," said Indigo to Tyler, "you are reading my texts, or you wouldn't know I was writing to my friends—and second of all, it's rude the way you roll your eyes whenever you think something I've written is stupid. That's how I know you're doing it, because you let out these humongous sighs whenever I say anything that you think is weird."

I was standing in front of the mirror, combing my hair. "Also," I heard her say in a low, stage-whispery voice, "I can't stand it anymore and I am going to tell Dad *today*. I am *going* to tell him, Tyler."

"Fine, fine. I won't look in your direction for the rest of the trip."

"No! I want you to drive the car and talk to Dad, and Nina to sit back in the backseat with me!"

"What?" I said. "Me?"

"Yes. We can do our nails. I have some black nail polish and some silver sparkle stuff with one of those microbrushes so we can paint decorations. Little stars and things."

"In a moving car?" I said. (For the record, I have never once in my life wanted black, decorated nails.)

"We can do them at rest stops," she said. "And also when we stop for pancakes."

"Okay. I'll sit back there with you, but I may not get my nails done. I don't want black nail polish."

She looked at Tyler and burst into tears, so I went over and put my arm around her like she was a frail invalid in need of special chairs and lifts and blankets, and I walked her out to the car very gently and kissed the top of her crazy purple head, and she kept sniffling and weeping the whole time, which was pretty admirable when you think about it—crying for so long and so steadily yet being mad at the same time.

"Kayla, it would help me immensely if you would stop crying," Carter said to her. He'd somehow freed himself from the motel bathroom, and he and The Abomination cruised over to the car, easing themselves down the curb. Tyler and I loaded the suitcases into the back, and I gathered all the paper cups and fast-food wrappers from yesterday and plumped up the pillows and stacked the magazines they'd brought and untangled the headphones. Then I brought out Beyoncé and her cage and refilled her water dish and we were off, Tyler grinding the gears and lurching the van in and out of traffic while Indigo sniffled and tried to paint her nails.

Melanie was texting me, asking what the hell had I done to Matthew, the nicest guy in the world. Was I crazy? Was I going to trash men's hearts all over the planet for the whole rest of time? Did she need to protect *Noah* from me?

Good God, Melanie, I texted back. *It just wasn't right. No big deal. He's the nicest man in the world, but I can't be in love with him the way you have to be to get through the next fifty years.*

But he really, really liked you. Are you sure you gave him a chance?

I'm sorry. It just wasn't right.

After a while she wrote, *You're ridiculous. And I mean that in the best possible way.* And I wrote, *You're ridiculouser.*

So that meant that she and I were fine again. We texted about Noah, who might be getting a tooth, and John Paul who might be getting a raise. *How's it going on the trip?* she said, and I wrote, *Hard to say. No one has killed anyone yet, but still could happen. Stand by.*

I might have sighed because then Carter said, "Are you all right, Nina?"

"I'm fine."

"She broke up with a guy yesterday," Tyler said. "Over the phone." Carter turned to me. "Seriously! Over the phone! Are you okay?"

"I'm fine."

"Really?"

"Yes. Totally fine. I promise."

Next to me, Indigo had given up on her nails and was typing and crying once again. Loudly.

"Jesus," said Carter. "This car may qualify as a mobile emergency room soon. Tyler, is there anything you want to get off your chest while we're at it?"

To my shock, Tyler slammed his hand against the steering wheel and yelled, "INDIGO! YOU FUCKING TOLD HIM, DIDN'T YOU?"

"I didn't tell him anything," she said calmly.

"Tell me what?" said Carter.

I had stopped breathing some time before, so I hardly noticed the lack of oxygen in the car when Tyler suddenly swerved the van over to the side of the road, and turned off the motor. Traffic kept flying past us, but we sat there in that heated tin can, the engine making ominous ticking noises. I looked over at Carter, whose mouth was open, like a fish.

"Okay, *here* we go," said Indigo under her breath. "Tell him, Tyler! TELL HIM."

The silence grew heavier, and then Tyler said, "Dad, I'm not going to college."

"You're not—*what?*" said Carter. "Of course you are. You're going to Vanderbilt—that's why we're in the car." I watched a whole cascade of emotions play across his face. He stared at Tyler, who was looking down at his hands. "You're not . . . you're not going to college? Then where the hell are we going?"

Tyler was white-faced and nodding. He fiddled with the keys dangling from the ignition. In the suddenly airless interior of our prison, the sound of the keys clanking was intolerable, and Carter finally reached over and batted his hand away. Beyoncé got on the wheel to try to make things right noise-wise, but Carter said in a low voice that if someone— *anyone*—did not get that goddamn guinea pig to stop that noise that instant, the whole cage was going to be dismantled and thrown in the weeds. Indigo flung her body over the back of the seat and took Beyoncé out and put her on her lap. Which was concerning, I'm not going to lie.

"What the *hell* is going on here?" Carter bellowed, but he didn't have much of a bellow, not really. He was more mystified than anything else. Our eyes met. I wanted to tell him that the guinea pig was free-range, but that seemed the least of anything.

"I *paid* for that college. You are going. I know you're going," Carter said. "Is this just last-minute nerves? Because if that's all it is, we can talk this through."

Indigo leaned forward, poking her head into the front seat. "Tyler took the tuition money you and Mom put in his account, and he never paid the school."

"You did WHAT?" Carter roared.

"*And* he's going to be a musician in Nashville, and he's already lined up some meetings. And he and his friend Jamesie are going to get an apartment. Isn't that right, Ty?"

"Kayla, would you please shut up and let Tyler tell me what's going on?"

"He's too ashamed to talk about it," she said. "He's not owning his actions, like my therapist said to do. He was never going to tell you, and then, whatever, in four years or so you'd go to graduation, and he'd have to think of something. But maybe by then he'd have a recording contract or something and he'd be famous so you wouldn't care."

"Are you two *insane*?" Carter said. "Is all this true, Tyler?"

Tyler flung open the door of the van and I had this horrible moment of thinking he was going to run into traffic, but he didn't. Instead he ran up the embankment next to the road. We were parked near a field of scrubbed-out weeds and rocks in the tan-colored dirt, and he ran up the hill and down the other side as fast and hard as he could, and Carter exhaled this huge explosion of breath, watching his son vanish over the rise of the hill once he'd reached the bottom and headed up again, and then he looked at me and said, "Please tell me you didn't know anything about this."

"I didn't," I said.

"Thank God."

The engine was ticking so loud it sounded like a bomb, and I rolled down the window and said I should probably make sure he was okay.

"He's okay. Let's just wait for him," said Carter. He leaned against the window of the van. "I need to think of what's next for him." Then after a moment he said, "He took all that money for school. He basically *stole* the tuition money."

"But wait. Didn't you pay the school yourself? I know my parents did," I said.

"No. I'm an idiot. Jane and I were splitting it, so rather than have us send in two checks, Tyler said he'd open a checking account and we could both deposit to that. Then he would pay the tuition. It sounded so responsible."

"He never wanted to go to college, you know," said Indigo. "You were the one who said he had to go. You didn't even ask him."

"That's because college is important," said Carter. "Oh, never mind. Why am I even talking about this? It's useless."

"I'm going to find him," I said. I got out of the car and stretched a little, surprised at how hard my heart was hammering in my chest, and I went over to the passenger window and touched Carter's arm. "It's going to be all right. You'll see. This is all going to work out."

His eyes had that intense, bing cherry look to them again, and his mouth was set. "Is it? I've impressed upon this kid every single day of his life that going to a good school is the one thing you can do for your future! He wants to be a musician? Fine, be a musician on the side. But get a good education! Let me out of this car. I think I'm going to go kill him."

"Also," said Indigo. "Another thing you need to know. I've decided that I really, really can't go live with Mom. I have friends now at school and I can't leave. I belong with you."

"Your mother is—what the fuck is happening?" said Carter, and he looked at me and rubbed his hands through his hair so hard I thought he might go bald right then. Then he threw back his head and laughed. "Oh, Nina, Nina, thank God for you, witnessing all this. Otherwise, I'd be pretty damn sure I was in the middle of a nightmare. When did I lose control over my life?"

"I don't know," I said. "Maybe you never had it."

"He *didn't* ever have it," said Indigo. "And anyway, I saw a note that Mom wrote to you, Dad, and she didn't really want me to come! Like, she literally doesn't even want me there while she's getting this farm going and everything, so why should I have to go and just try to keep out of her way? What's that going to be like for me? Really, Dad. It sucks is what. Why can't I just stay with you and be friends with Maya and live my life?"

"Wait, I thought Maya was turning goth and you weren't a fan," I said.

"She changed back. Goth is ridiculous in the summer. You could melt. And anyway, she's so over that now."

"So Tyler isn't going to college, and you're not going to your mom's," Carter said slowly. "And you knew this all along. *And* you let the frogs out of the biology lab and got expelled for the year, *and* you have a list of your personal aspirations that could curl a father's hair. And speaking of hair, you keep cutting yours off in an expression of some sort of countercultural individuality that I frankly can't fathom"—he reached back and touched her hair in such a gentle, fatherly, exasperated way—"*and* you wear the damnedest clothing anybody ever saw, and you cry all the time and you're so cute and so beautiful and I love you so much, but you completely mystify me, Kayla."

"Indigo," she said.

"Kayla," he said. "I don't think I can ever think of you as Indigo, because when I look at you, you're that little baby I named Kayla way back fifteen years ago. That sweet pink little baby who stared up at me. And now I let you wear combat boots and torn skirts and purple hair and I let you paint your freaking nails black and I even supported you as much as I could when you ruined Tyler's play, and when you dangled from a rope painting graffiti in the middle of the night—"

"I didn't really ever dangle. I was going to, but the cops came."

"It still counts," he said. "Intention is nine-tenths of the law."

"Possession is what is nine-tenths," I said. I was still standing at the car window. "Intention is what the way to hell is paved with, I believe."

He looked at me and said, "I don't know what I'm doing anymore."

But he did know. He and The Abomination got out of the van and hobbled themselves up and down the hills and embankments, and he found Tyler, and the two of them sat together for a long time out in the field under a lone tree, and they talked and talked. There was some yelling. There was gesticulating. I straightened the back of the car and repacked it. We were too far away for Lindy to come and collect me this time, but I thought of calling her anyway. No use.

The guinea pig did what they always do when they're out of their cages—she made a run for it, and now she was charging through the car in a rodent rampage, but that was okay because it gave Indigo and me a useful, fun activity of chasing her around the seats, until Indigo trapped her under the accelerator pedal, and I put her back in the cage, and she thanked me by getting on the wheel and trying to save the world one last, long time by running as fast as she could.

Then Indigo and I painted our nails black with little silver stars— because what the hell.

When Carter and Tyler came back, Carter looked like he'd been humbled by life: softer somehow, maybe grayer even. His eyes were like the eyes of a golden retriever who just wants love.

That night, we stayed in a motel with a rec room and a restaurant. It was near Nashville and there was good music all over town, so the four of us ended up at a little country music club. Carter and I had a glass of wine, then we walked back to the motel, and after we were sure the kids were sleeping, we slipped outside—well, I slipped and he hobbled—and we went down to the pool where there were little white plastic lounge chairs. It was dark except for the aqua light shining in the pool. The air felt like it had been formed of racing tires that had been melted down and released into the atmosphere.

He said, "I thought I could do this, but every day is like some new freaking story. I'm out of my mind. Aren't I? Tell me the truth. Am I out of my mind? Am I going to live through this?"

"Carter, I think you're going to be okay. This is the real stuff, now. You've got these kids, and they aren't raised yet, but they love you."

"They do? This is what love is? Immense torture and shenanigans followed by hair-raising shocks?"

"I don't know. Maybe."

"You're not going to try to tell me that this is the best thing that could have happened, are you?" he said, and I said I might be.

"Because that would be like when you told me not to say you were in my thoughts and prayers. Remember that?" he said.

"I definitely remember that."

He said a whole bunch of other stuff. He asked me if Matthew meant anything to me, and I laughed. "No."

And he said he was so sorry about Phoebe not being willing to see me, because no one could live without me once they knew me. So I told him about taking her to lunch, and how it felt fine simply to be in her presence, to know she and I belonged together.

"I always thought that she had me and then she gave me up because she didn't care," I said. "I thought the day I was born must have been the worst day of her whole life, but it turns out it was actually the best day. That's what she told me. 'It was the best day.' She wanted me so much, but she was only fifteen years old—kind of like Indigo having a baby, can you imagine?—and she was an idiotic teenager who thought she could make her life work out and get to be loved just by having babies. It was so crazy, what she did, but it turned out that she actually had a plan. Trying to be free, trying to get her boyfriend's mother to let her marry him. And it didn't work. Not at all, and he got killed in the bargain. Which was terrible. But it wasn't what I thought. It never meant she didn't love me. I know that now."

"Can you move on, do you think?" he said.

I looked at him. "I can. I have her in my life now. Somewhat. If I don't pressure her, I think I can stay."

"And there's Lindy," he said. "You got Lindy. We all somehow got Lindy!"

We sat there for a long time, then he reached over and took my hand. "You know what we need? We need a real moment between us, one that's not driven by the kids or me needing something from you or you being scared of never being wanted. This not being wanted thing is big with you. It's kind of your issue."

I was silent. There were crickets everywhere. Nashville is full of crickets. Beyond the blue marble that was the pool, there was only darkness as far as I could see. I couldn't speak right then, so I just squeezed his hand.

"Jesus, what am I going to do with my children?" he said.

I swiped at my eyes. "I think you're just going to keep raising them and loving them and listening to them."

"I guess so. You were right about a lot of stuff," he said. "These few months of trying to be their friend as well as their mother and father—that was horrible. And after I stopped being their friend, I heard things coming out of my mouth that I never thought I'd hear. Words like, 'Because I said so,' and 'You're going to be grounded for the rest of your life if you do that one more time.'"

"Good. Sounds real at least."

"After that terrible night searching for Kayla—well, I hate to say it, but I grounded her, and she reacted by helping around the house and being a human being. That was an eye-opener."

There was a long silence and he said, "The timing of this is shitty, but I want to tell you that I love you."

"Why is it shitty? Never mind, I know. Because it sounds like you love me only because you're freaking out about being alone with your kids."

"But we both know that's not what is happening. I've missed you like I've never missed anybody in my whole life. You were the spark."

"So why did you break up with me?"

"I don't know. Because I had to get it together. Because I couldn't make you be the bad guy while I tried to figure out how to be a full-time dad. I had to get over myself." He reached over and lightly touched my hair. "Also, if we replayed the tape, I think it might have been you who wanted to break up. I seem to remember something being said about a Get Out of Jail Free card."

"I probably shouldn't have said that. The truth was I couldn't get over you."

"When you told me that list of what went wrong—when was that? It seems like a year ago, but I bet it was just yesterday."

"Yesterday, I think. Before the world blew up."

"That list—it kind of knocked me over. You know? I mean, I know we jumped in too fast. I knew that at the time, but I also knew you were the one I wanted. What I didn't know was that you wanted a baby."

"I want a real life, Carter. I don't want to always be the number-two person who came along and rescued your already-made family and who doesn't really, really belong. When Jane was here and you guys were talking about your years of memories and all that you've shared, I felt like some little kid sitting at the grown-up table. Someone who will never, ever have all that. And it sucks, Carter! I've never had people who are *mine*."

"About that," he said. "I've been meaning to talk to you about that view of yours. People don't *belong* to other people, Nina. We all belong to ourselves. And no one ever feels included. We just muddle through. At least that's how I feel. These kids are only on loan to me. They're going to grow up and move on with their lives, and I'll see them from time to time, but they aren't *mine*. Not really. And Jane wasn't mine. And you aren't *mine*. I think we're together because that's what we choose, what we want. Right?"

"I thought it was something different," I said.

"No. It might be lovely to belong so completely to other people, but it would be god-awful stifling, too."

"Huh. What about if I had a baby? Like Melanie's baby. He belongs to her."

"Nope, not even Melanie's baby. Think about it: when you're there, playing and taking care of him, a bit of him belongs with just you at that moment. We're all like little pinballs in the machine, bumping up against each other and pinging away, coming together again and again, and making a life of our own choosing."

I looked at him. "I hate that!"

"Do you? Because I like it."

"You do? Really?"

"My children love you," he said. His eyes were shining. "They can't articulate it. Won't say the words. But they missed you when you were gone. You were important to them in a huge, fundamental way. They belonged to you. In your corner, you know. On your roster."

I laughed.

He leaned forward and kissed me. "I want you so much right now I can't stand it. Do you remember the time I suggested we do the ol' houghmagandy? The horizontal dance? The princum-prancum?"

"Princum-prancum is a new one. Did you just make that one up?"

"Nope. The magic of the Internet," he said. "Euphemisms for sex over the last four hundred years. So, you see? We do have our memories. But we have to build it, Nina. Maybe that's the piece that's been missing for you. You need to just decide you're going to feel a certain way. And then you trust it to grow and change. And sometimes it dies before you think you're quite ready—but most often, you can keep it alive if you want to. You keep going simply because you don't stop. You don't ask yourself every day if you're still in the relationship. You just are. It's a bit of work. But you can do it."

"I can?"

He took my hand again. "I do love you. I love you so much. You take my breath away, everything you do. My friends love you, my children love you, even my ex-wife thinks you're astonishing. Maybe the assistant principal at the high school doesn't love you, but everyone else does. Even your mom. She loves you the only way she can, so much that it still hurts that she lost you all those years ago."

I stared down at my hands. I didn't trust myself to speak.

"Can we try again?" he said. "Please? We'll figure out where to live, and how many children we're going to let live with us, and when we're going to kick them out, and if there's going to be a new one. Okay? Can you accept that this right here might be the family you're supposed to have? You'll wear black nail polish and we'll do the princum-prancum until we drop."

"You're my family?" I said. "I can't quite believe you're supposed to be my family."

"Well, but I am," he said. "I happen to know it for a fact, and I think you'll come to see it, too. What if we get married, and take it day by day after that? You know, we'll keep going because we just won't stop. Day after day after day, we won't quit."

The next day I snuck away and called my mom.

It seemed like I had to tell her I was getting married to Carter. You're supposed to tell your mom those things. Also I had some questions. "What was it like, belonging to your family?" I said. "You know, before your mom and dad died, before you lived alone with your sister, before you decided to make your own family? Did you ever have that safe feeling of knowing where you were meant to be?"

She had no idea.

But she said one thing that made sense. She said that belonging was just a state of mind. That you had to create it yourself. That you could go your whole life feeling bereft because of this loss or that loss. She said she was sorry about giving me up, but she still felt I'd ended up in the right spot, with Josephine and Douglas Popkin, whose names I had to tell her because nobody had ever told her who adopted me. She liked being Lulu and that wouldn't have happened if she'd kept me.

She said that Nina Popkin was a much zippier name than Kate Mullen—but wasn't it sort of interesting that I had two names when most people only had one? She said I could spin things any way I wanted, being Kate one day and Nina the next if I wanted. That I could take joy in that little switch.

For herself, she said she was sick of telling herself the story in a way that made her feel bad. Maybe, she said, it had all worked out the way it was supposed to. And even if it hadn't, she'd decided to accept the life she had as a good thing. Maybe singing again had helped her get there, she said. She laughed her raspy, dry, cigarette laugh that I was already coming to love, and said, "You might as well marry him. He's got crazy kids and it sounds like he's fairly crazy himself. So it'll be entertaining if nothing else."

And I said, "Will you be there?" but she'd already hung up. The way she did when she was done with a conversation and had to go off and play the piano and recover from feeling.

That was just the way my mom was.

EPILOGUE
NINA

Thanksgiving, three years later

Noah came first, holding a stuffed dog and a toilet brush, running like he was a wind-up toy, with that maniacal gleam in his eye that meant he was liable to do anything. Melanie said the toilet brush was his latest must-have toy, and she had given up fighting over it. I heard her clicking up the walk behind him, hurrying because she said she never knew if he was going to detour into the hedge looking for some stray piece of nature—dog poop, bird carcasses, prickly bushes—that he hadn't truly explored before. She was steering a massive pregnant belly in front of her, larger than when I'd seen her at the hospital two weeks ago. Way larger.

"You've got to hurry up and push that baby out or they won't be in the same grade at school," I said, which made her laugh.

"I think we have until December thirtieth officially," she said.

"See that you make the deadline," I told her.

John Paul was coming up behind her carrying a plate of something wrapped in aluminum foil. He smiled and pecked me on the cheek. "I gotta see her. Where you hiding her?"

"She's asleep," I said. "You're not supposed to wake them up, right? Aren't they like sleeping dogs? You have to let them lie?"

"When they're this age, you can't wake them even if you try," said Melanie, the presiding expert on everything now: marriage and babies and whether toilet brushes were an appropriate toy.

But I am the expert on teenagers—as I so often wanted to say to her. *And* on second marriages and being embarrassingly fecund and pregnant around two kids old enough to know precisely how it had all come about.

That did not bear thinking about. This was Thanksgiving, after all, which everyone knows is the *familiest* of all the family holidays—and somehow I'd gone crazy and invited everybody over. Never mind that I'd just had a baby, never mind that I was a zombie, that I had bags under my eyes so deep that *those* bags had their own bags.

Everyone promised they would help me with the dinner, that I wasn't to lift a finger. Just give them directions, they said, and they would do it all. Lindy was bringing the turkey, already cooked, and then Jeff would arrive later with the children. And Jane—yes, *that* Jane! She and her new husband were in town to visit Tyler and Indigo—and they were bringing a vegan sweet potato dish and a crustless, sugarless pumpkin pie, both of which sounded awful to me, but I wasn't in a position to argue about people's offerings.

Melanie brought vegetables and the kinds of pies that people would actually eat.

Mrs. Walsh didn't have to bring anything because she was one of the Mom Emeritae, as Jeff explained it to me. She and Phoebe were off the hook for cooking; they were the moms to be honored.

And me, of course. A mom to be honored, so new at it, still so tender and vulnerable and protective. Still wanting to spend all my time draped over the bassinet, gazing at my new baby's fat cheeks and her curled-up fists, that little blister on her lip from all the nursing she did. I called Carter in to appreciate every sneeze, every squeak she might make in her sleep. And he came, even though he had seen new babies sneeze and squeak before.

"Did Phoebe actually say she would come?" Lindy had asked when she arrived.

"She did *say* she would, but of course that doesn't mean a thing," I said. "She's batting about fifty-fifty with invitations. And our dear darling grandmother didn't respond. So that's a no."

"Just as well," Lindy said. "Oh, also, my sister Ellen is coming. You'll be relieved to know that my brothers are going to their wives' families for the holiday, so we don't have all that to contend with."

"We could handle it," I said, and she replied, "Yeah, you say that now. But just wait."

It *was* crazy. I was so tired, so post-apocalyptically zombielike, that it was like being on hallucinogens. I was trying to manage things like a regular, efficient person would, stirring pots on the stove, offering people samples of dip and chips and olives, when Lindy steered me back to the living room and said my assignment was to sit on the couch and look at the fire that had taken Carter, Tyler, and Jeff twenty minutes to get going. She swung my legs up on an ottoman.

And from there I watched it all, a kaleidoscope of family scenes. Chloe and Davey playing in the backyard with Tyler, who was throwing a ball to them. Melanie and Jane talking, heads together, washing vegetables at the sink. Ellen walking outside with her three children, showing them the jack-o'-lantern that was still sitting on the outdoor table, grinning. Lindy kissing Jeff on the nose after he made her laugh. Carter handing out beers and chatting with Jane's new husband. Noah running through the kitchen with the toilet brush, and Mrs. Walsh tackling him before he could sprint into the dining room and contaminate, as she said, *the entire dinner with those germs.* Melanie protesting it was a new brush, brand-new, from the store, never used, and Mrs. Walsh not backing down.

"It's a toilet brush, isn't it?" she said. "Anything with the word *toilet* in it is not going *near* the Thanksgiving table."

Melanie looked furious for a moment, then Lindy stepped in, guiding her to sit next to me. "Sit here and think lovely thoughts about the next generation, will you? And try to forgive the older generation who make insensitive remarks."

Indigo came in with a tray of stuffed mushrooms and cheese and crackers and grapes, hobbling because Razzie was giggling and holding on to her leg like a baby chimpanzee.

"Really," I said to Melanie, who was now tucked in beside me, "you should have managed your life as well as I did. You have to have the teenagers first, and then have the babies. You know what happens when the baby can't sleep through the night? We have any number of teenage volunteers who love to walk her around."

Indigo smiled and set to work peeling Razzie off her leg like he was a decal.

"I have got to get me a teenager," said Melanie. "I don't think Noah's going to be much help."

"You saved me last night," I said to Indigo. "And thank God for that. I'd walked about four miles around the dining room table before you took her. When was that, 4:00 a.m.?"

"Four thirty. And I walked another eight miles with her after that," she said. "Even after she fell asleep. The way she snuggles up—who wants to put her back down?"

I smiled at her and she socked me lightly on the arm and fed me a mushroom. "Open wide," she said. "You've got to keep your strength up. Someday she's going to grow up and be a teenager like me."

"Unlikely. Nobody could be as interesting a daughter as you. Also," I whispered, "don't let your mother know that the stuffed mushrooms came from Costco and are probably not organic."

"I think she already knows," Indigo said. "I saw her reading the wrapper."

"Oh, crap," I said.

I reached over and fluffed Indigo's hair. It was blonde, with pink tips. She was a senior now, and might actually be certifiably sane. Even borderline wonderful. Sure, she still dressed in combat boots and short skirts, but she didn't cut her hair with the pinking shears anymore, and she didn't have a Fuck-It List. She was dating a nice guy who was coming over later for dessert, and—oh yes—bringing his parents for us to meet.

"They want to see the baby, too," she'd told me, and I'd said, "Bring 'em on! Let's have a big blowout."

Tyler, home from college, had asked if his friend Jamesie could stop by, and I'd said yes to that, too. We would sit on the floor if necessary. Tyler said he and Jamesie might play music later on. He'd written a song for the baby.

It was all going to be great, except that I had a headache starting up. I felt like I was moving through a dream that I couldn't wake up from: all the noise and chaos and conversations all going at once were getting to me. I caught Carter's eye across the room, and he made his way over to me and sat next to me on the couch, giving Melanie a big grin.

"Are you happy?" he whispered, kissing the top of my head.

"I don't know. Is everybody being nice to everyone else?" I said, and he laughed and whispered, "No. Of course not. Jane is in the kitchen arguing with Lindy about organic food labels, and Jane's husband has now told me three times that he thinks sailboats are stupid. And Mrs. Walsh says that she's not going to sit next to Phoebe because that woman gives her the willies."

"If Phoebe even comes," I said.

"Yeah, Mrs. Walsh may have paid her off to keep her from coming."

The baby started crying just then, and Carter's eyebrows shot up. Indigo said she'd go get her, but Carter said no, he wanted to, but in the end I said *I* needed some quiet time and, as the mother, I pulled rank on both of them.

I went to the back bedroom, and scooped up my red-faced, rooting little baby. It still felt so incredible to hold her, to see her big blue eyes staring into mine, to stroke that tiny face, hear the grunts and coos and smacking noises she made. I sat in the rocking chair to nurse her in the dimness. I was wiped out by love, by how warm she felt in my arms and how wonderful she smelled—like baby cream and milk and something else that was just her. Amazing! Outside the room, I could hear everybody talking. An argument was blooming about something political. Mrs. Walsh had a definite opinion about whatever Lindy was saying. Jane laughed loudly, just once, a laugh like a punctuation. And Indigo said, "Mo-oom!"

I fastened the baby to my breast and winced as she latched on, feeling the familiar tug of her mouth and the sting as the milk let down.

After a while, there was a bit of commotion, possibly the front door opening and closing, people saying, "Hello! Hello!" and then in a few minutes, Carter was in front of me, smiling, with Phoebe behind him, wearing a long purple skirt and a black knit cardigan. He gestured toward me with a flourish and urged Phoebe forward. She had her hair twisted up in a bun, and her eyes were all made up with lots of mascara and eyeliner. My heart did what it always did when I saw her: started beating harder, happy to see her. My mother. The mother I might have never known.

"Hi," I said to her. "I'm so glad to see you! And look—the baby! Your granddaughter!"

I wanted her to hug me. In my fantasy, I wanted her to say, "Ohhh, this is amazing! Oh, how I have longed for this moment! She's beautiful!" Maybe she could mention that the baby looked like me, or like Lindy. Maybe she could look at me and say something kind and wise and beautiful.

But she didn't. She peeked over and fluttered her hands, and then in her cigarette voice, she said, "Sorry I'm late, and I can't stay long. But I just wanted to check in."

"I'm glad you're here. Do you want to hold little Tillie?"

"I still can't believe you named her that," my mother said.

"It's Tilton, really. I wanted to honor my dad," I said. "I thought you'd be pleased."

Her face changed a bit; was that pleasure? I couldn't tell.

I pulled Tillie away from my breast and tipped her toward her grandmother, but Phoebe was already distracted by something in the hallway. She wasn't even looking at me. "There are so many people here," she said to Carter. "What were you two *thinking*?"

He laughed a little.

"Well, I'm going to go get a drink," she said. "Nina, come out when you're done."

And she was gone. She, who had done the best she could, but who wasn't going to be my mom, not for real. Real but not real. I realized that the grandmother who would have known just the right thing to say, the thing I needed to hear, was Josephine. Sweet, loving Josephine Popkin.

I kissed my fingers and held them up to the sky in a kind of silent salute to her.

I heard Phoebe saying hello to everyone; then someone asked her if she wanted a glass of wine, and Lindy announced that dinner would be served in ten minutes, so people should start gathering.

"Let's go meet your public," I said to Tillie.

I took her into the bright, warm living room, where Tyler was strumming his guitar and the fire was blazing. The children were coming in from outside, led by Jeff. There was A.J., smiling and wiping at something in his eye.

"A.J.!" I said. "I'm so glad to see you! I had no idea you could come, too!" and he dipped his head shyly and said he'd given Phoebe a ride, but he didn't need to stay.

"Of course you'll stay," I said. "I'm thrilled to see you."

He leaned over and smiled at the baby as Indigo came over and put her hand on my back. "My sister," she said.

The baby sneezed, and suddenly we were the focus of attention. People floated toward me, and I heard Ellen saying, "Oh, she's here! She's up!" and Melanie said, "Did you hear that sneeze? Was there ever a cuter baby sneeze?"

I held Tillie close to me, and she thrust one of her powerful feminist fists out from underneath the blanket, and waved it around in the air, which someone said meant that she'd be as feisty as her mother, and maybe as flaky, too. And then somehow they were all laughing at me: Melanie telling stories about me writing up histories for all the adopted kids in the school, and Lindy remembering the day I abandoned her to the nuns and ran back to play with my friends in the playground, and Indigo laughing about me driving and crashing the getaway car the day she liberated Beyoncé from the science lab. Finally I said, "Okay, that's enough, you guys. You have to stop because I'm a mother now and I get to decide what my kids know about me."

"*Kids?*" said somebody. "Carter, are you hearing that?"

And then they all laughed and went back to arguing about politics and the best way to cook a turkey, and whether it was necessary to be vegan to be a good person. Everyone was talking at once, smiling, scowling, trying to be heard over everybody else.

It was the strangest thing: I felt for a moment as if I were a movie camera, pulling back from the crowd and seeing them all there, mingling in unlikely groups and splitting apart. Like atoms or something, coming together and repelling over and over again. I switched off their voices in my head—the high-pitched and low, the argumentative and cajoling—and just saw them there, my family. My crazy, impossible, troublesome family, all of them difficult and amazing and hardly able to stand the others around them, but here they were. In my house, in my living room. I was there with my husband and baby and stepchildren, and my husband's ex and her new husband, and friends and my sister and mother, and my *sister's* sister and mother. And the man who'd brought my mother back to me.

It was my family and I had scraped it together myself, practically bullied them into being with me, into knowing who I was. Me. A person who belonged to them.

I caught Carter's eye and he blew me a kiss. My mother and A.J. exchanged a look, then slipped out onto the deck, his arm at the small of her back. *Well, well,* I thought. *Look at that!*

I didn't know why I was suddenly crying, except that I was postpartum, and I was part of a family that wasn't even remotely what I had imagined. And it was wonderful and terrible all at once, scary and messy and crazy and complicated. Perhaps impossible.

Melanie called us to dinner just then, and I wiped my eyes and did as I was told.

ACKNOWLEDGMENTS

I am filled with gratitude for all the people who helped me with this book—to Alice Mattison, who doesn't mind reading early drafts and fighting with me when necessary to make sure the book is honest and real; and to Kim Steffen, who walks with me every morning and helps me hear my characters talking; to Leslie Connor, Holly Robinson, Linda Balestracci, Nancy Hall, Nancy Antle, Michellee Speirs, Marcia Winter, Edie Kufta, Deirdre Morro James, Grace Pauls Ritchie, Sharon Wise, Laurie Ruderfer, Marji Lipshez-Shapiro, and Beth Levine, all of whom gave support, encouragement, and love. Barbara Pine told me about the function of a social worker in adoption proceedings. Nicole Austin Hitchcock not only kept my impossible hair looking good (or as good as possible), but also explained to me what a keratin treatment is. Many, many thanks to the people who come to my Words at Play writing workshop and trust me with their stories. Sending lots of thanks to the adoptees in Connecticut, who told me what it's like to be adopted and to have the records sealed.

A special thanks to Karen and Terry Bergantino, who allowed me to spend a feverish week writing at their beautiful, quiet condo.

I couldn't do this without the help and support of my wonderful agent, Nancy Yost, who gives me encouragement and keeps me going, in the most entertaining way possible. And many thanks and much gratitude to Jodi Warshaw and all the wonderful folks at Lake Union, who have given me a publishing home.

And to my husband, Jim, and my own wonderful children—Ben, Allie, and Steph, and the people they have brought into my life: Amy, Mike, Charlie, Josh, Miles, Emma, and Alex. No thank-you could ever be big enough.

ABOUT THE AUTHOR

Maddie Dawson grew up in the South, born into a family of outrageous storytellers. Her various careers as a substitute English teacher, department-store clerk, medical-records typist, waitress, cat sitter, wedding-invitation-company receptionist, nanny, day-care worker, electrocardiogram technician, and Taco Bell taco maker were made bearable by thinking up stories as she worked. Today she lives in Guilford, Connecticut, with her husband. She's the bestselling author of four previous novels: *The Opposite of Maybe*, *The Stuff That Never Happened*, *Kissing Games of the World*, and *A Piece of Normal*.